NEW DAWN Underground

A Novel

By

Amanda Matti

Proofreader:
Lia Fairchild, Finishing Touch Editing,
www.facebook.com/finishingtouchediting

Beta Readers:
Cheri Roy
Breeanna Allen

Cover designed by Amanda Matti

ISBN: 9781735321349

About the Author

Amanda Matti served six years in the United States Navy as an Intelligence Analyst and is an Iraq War Veteran. Her first book, A Foreign Affair, tells the story of her deployment to Baghdad where she met her husband, an Iraqi national who served as her translator. Her second book, Voicing the Eagle, chronicles her husband's story serving as an interpreter for U.S. forces during the Iraq War. Amanda lives in San Diego with her husband and their two daughters. To learn more about Amanda and her books, visit her website at www.AmandaMatti.com.

Connect with Amanda online at:
facebook.com/AuthorAmandaMatti
instagram.com/Author_Amanda_Matti

Email Amanda at: Amanda@AmandaMatti.com

Other Works by Amanda Matti
Available at ALL major retailers.

A FOREIGN AFFAIR
A true story of love and war.

VOICING THE EAGLE
The incredible true story of an Iraqi interpreter.

Dedication

For my amazing husband, Fadi.
Who never reads my books,
so will likely never see this.

Prologue: The Raid

Northwestern Iraq—March 12, 2012

Two Black Hawk helicopters sliced their way through the pitch darkness of the Iraqi night. They had lifted off minutes before from Balad Air Base just north of Baghdad and were en route to a remote area of northwestern Iraq. U.S. Army Major Brendan Jacobs and his elite Delta Force team readied themselves. Their mission was a top secret Joint Special Operations Command (JSOC) operation to capture or kill Malik Khalid—leader of the New Dawn Underground Islamic militant group. Between his thumb and forefinger, Jacobs clutched a small white gold band. The ring belonged to his fiancée, Elora. She'd pressed it into his palm three days earlier with instructions to keep it with him for good luck. He held the ring to his lips for several seconds before slipping it into a small chest pocket on his uniform.

The Black Hawks flew low, tightly hugging the curvature of the Earth to avoid radar detection as they approached the rural compound. According to intel, the destination served as New Dawn Underground's northern base of operations. The group—known colloquially as NDU—had been steadily growing in Iraq and was recently responsible for a string of coordinated bombings across Baghdad. NDU had detonated massive explosions at the Ministry of Interior, Ministry of Defense, and the unofficial headquarters of an Iranian-backed militia. Dozens of Iraqis and several Americans perished in the attacks, including the U.S.

Ambassador, Richard Casey, and three men in his security detail. U.S. intelligence agencies were conflicted as to whether NDU had specifically targeted Ambassador Casey or if he'd simply been in the wrong place at the wrong time. Either way, the ambassador's death prompted the U.S. to designate NDU a foreign terrorist organization, and Washington, along with the American public, demanded justice for the murder of the ambassador and other Americans. That justice was now on its way.

"ETA two minutes!" The chopper pilot's voice rang out through the comms headset in Major Jacobs' ear.

The soldiers conducted a final lock-and-load check of their HK416 assault rifles and braced for landing. The raid was scheduled to begin at 0300 local time and was to be wrapped up with choppers back in the air by 0345. That gave the team under an hour to locate and capture or kill Malik Khalid, get him on a chopper, and sweep the compound for intel. They had limited details regarding Malik Khalid's identity. They only knew he was thirty to thirty-five years old, between five foot ten and six feet tall, born and raised in Baghdad, and spoke fluent English. It was not a lot to go on, but infrared satellite images of the compound indicated there were only eight to ten individuals currently inside. If worse came to worse, the Delta team would zip tie and haul them all back to Balad and sort out who was who later.

The chopper took a sudden dip and began to descend. The Black Hawks landed on opposite corners of the compound, just outside the perimeter wall. Coming to a bumping halt on the ground, the soldiers poured out of the bellies of the choppers.

Twenty-year-old New Dawn security guard Ahmed Assad was patrolling the perimeter of the NDU compound when he heard a low rumble approaching from the depths of the blackened desert. He stood paralyzed in terror as he watched a Black Hawk touch down a dozen yards from the compound's outer wall. *Fuck, Americans!* Swallowing his fear, the young militant regained control of his legs and dashed inside the compound's three-story building to warn the others, including his uncle, Hakim Assad, who served as NDU's de facto Chief Financial Officer.

"*Amo Hakim! Amo Hakim!*" Ahmed bellowed for his uncle in Arabic as he stormed up the stairs to the second floor of the compound. "The Americans are here!" he shouted as he burst through a door leading into a living area. Inside, half a dozen men were gathered around a large table cluttered with laptop computers, documents, and random dirty dishes from a meal long over. They had already heard the choppers and were taking countermeasures. They'd covered their faces with traditional red-checkered headscarves, and several were destroying the laptops with hammers while others stuffed documents into a cast iron oven to incinerate them.

"Leave the rest!" one of the masked men shouted to the others. "Grab the detonators and get down to the tunnel." Another man swiped two mobile flip phones off the table as the group abandoned the room.

Fearing the gates into the compound might be booby-trapped, each Delta Force team used explosives to breach separate portions of the perimeter wall on opposite sides of the compound. Once inside, they conducted precision sweeps across the yard as they moved toward the main building. A pair of soldiers located the compound's main power supply and cut the electricity, plunging the building and yard into total darkness.

The militants inside scrambled down the stairs to the ground floor and passed through a doorway behind the stairwell leading to a small kitchen. The men filed across the dark kitchen, feeling their way to the door of a small storage closet. The first man to reach the closet yanked the door open, jumped inside, and frantically slid his hands up and down the back wall, searching for a latch. Once his fingers found the latch, he yanked it to the side and a small hinged door popped open in the false wall. The men began squeezing through the tiny door, one-by-one, and scurried down a ladder that dropped into an escape tunnel. Before it was his turn to slide through the escape door, Hakim stopped in his tracks and spun around to push his way back into the kitchen. "The external hard drive," he whispered, wide-eyed, in frantic Arabic to the man behind him.

"Leave it," the masked man replied.

"We can't. It contains the only complete list of account numbers. Without it we are fucked. I have to go back."

"No." The man pushed Hakim back toward the escape door. "You go into the tunnel; I'll get the hard drive."

The masked insurgent doubled-back through the kitchen and poked his head out the doorway beneath the stairwell to scan the area. It appeared the Americans hadn't breached the main building yet. He darted through a doorway across from the stairs, snatched a small black hard drive off a shelf, shoved it into his pocket, and sprinted back to the kitchen. Stepping into the kitchen, he charged forward in the direction of the storage closet but had the wind knocked out of him when he slammed into what felt like a brick wall.

Major Jacobs had entered the kitchen seconds earlier,

cleared it, and was falling back to exit when he collided with the masked insurgent. Significantly larger and heavier than the insurgent, Jacobs was able to maintain his footing following the collision, while the insurgent collapsed flat on the floor.

"*Kef!* Don't move!" Jacobs commanded in Arabic as he shoved the barrel of his rifle down into the man's masked face. "Show me your hands!"

The insurgent froze in surrender with his hands palms up next to either side of his head. Unable to confirm if the masked man was their primary target, Jacobs opted not to put a bullet in his head in case they needed to pump him later for intel. Jacobs was about to radio for backup to assist in securing his detainee, when a loud clatter came from inside the small storage closet. For a split-second, Jacobs took his eyes off the man on the ground to assess the possible new threat. The insurgent seized the opportunity and made his move, performing a lightning-fast leg sweep that threw Jacobs off balance. Springing to his feet, the militant followed it up with a skillful butterfly kick that sent Jacobs flying across the kitchen. Jacobs slammed hard onto his back, and his rifle landed several feet away. The insurgent tried to make a move for Jacobs' rifle, but Jacobs twisted and got a hand on the man's leg, tripping him up before he could get to the weapon. Jacobs pounced on top of the masked man, and the two rolled across the kitchen floor, wrestling for dominance. As they scuffled, the insurgent clawed at Jacobs, tearing off his reverse American flag patch from the right shoulder of his uniform.

When the pair stopped rolling, Jacobs ended up on the bottom. He swung up and landed a solid right hook to the insurgent's face. The blow stunned his attacker long enough for

Jacobs to reach down and unsheathe his field knife from a holster near his thigh. With the knife in his right hand, Jacobs stabbed at the man on top of him. The blade connected with its target, ripping into the flesh on the left side of the insurgent's lower back. The man cried out in agony as the blade flayed his skin, but Jacobs failed to bury the knife deep enough to immobilize his assailant. The blade sliced the man at an angle, resulting in a gnarly gash but didn't hit any vital organs or cause debilitating injury. Jacobs drew back to stab at the man again, when a gunshot rang out, causing a deafening reverberation in the tiny kitchen. While the two had been rolling across the floor, the insurgent had managed to reach down and pull a 9mm pistol from an ankle holster above his right foot.

When Jacobs' arm came down to jab again with the knife, there was little force behind the blow, and his arm sank to the floor. The insurgent scrambled to his feet, revealing a point-blank gut-shot wound to Jacobs' lower left abdomen, just below his body armor. Jacobs pressed a hand to his wound and attempted to reach for his rifle with the other, but the insurgent stomped a booted foot on Jacobs' lower arm. The insurgent's eyes darted back and forth several times between Jacobs and the pantry door behind him. Finally, he dropped to one knee, grabbed Jacobs by the front of his uniform and yanked him to a sitting position. Jacobs cried out in pain and tried to resist, but in one swift move the insurgent was behind him and had him in a choke hold. Jacobs slipped toward blackout as the insurgent tightened his arm around his neck, applying precision pressure to his carotid artery. Seconds from passing out, Jacobs heard the thud of boots approaching the kitchen. The insurgent heard them too. He released his hold on

Jacobs, letting him fall back to the floor. Popping back up to his feet, the masked man looked down at Jacobs, aimed the pistol, and pulled the trigger. He watched as the bullet tore a fatal hole through Jacobs' throat. Convinced Jacobs would remain forever silent, the insurgent spun around and made his getaway through the storage closet in plain view of Jacobs. He slipped out through the false wall and closed the small door behind him before sliding down the ladder and escaping into the tunnel. As he scrambled down the tunnel, he ripped the checkered scarf from around his face, balled it up, and pressed it into his stab wound to squelch the bleeding. Halfway down the tunnel he came across Ahmed and Hakim.

"Are they following you?" Hakim asked, his eyes scanning the tunnel.

"No."

"We thought they got you," Hakim said as Ahmed flicked on a lighter so the men could see each other in the dark tunnel.

"It was close—*too* close." He glanced down at his side where he was pressing the scarf into his wound. It was now soaked in blood.

"You're shot!" Hakim shrieked, noticing the bloodied scarf.

"No, stabbed. I'll live."

"Did you get the hard drive?"

The man reached into his pocket, pulled out the sleek black external hard drive, and gave it a small triumphant shake.

"Thank God," Hakim said with a relieved sigh.

The three men continued down the tunnel to where it dumped into a drainage ditch approximately three hundred yards from the compound. Their fellow escapees were lying in the grass just outside the tunnel opening, waiting for them to catch up. When they saw Hakim and the others emerge from the shaft, they sprang up to continue their getaway.

"Down, back down!" Hakim ordered. "They aren't following us." Hakim looked back in the direction of the compound, but it was still in total blackness. "Who has the detonators?" he asked, looking around at the men. One of the escapees crawled over to Hakim and placed the small flip phones in his waiting open palm. Hakim handed one of the phones to the man with the stab wound; both flipped the phones open and proceeded to punch a series of numbers on the keypads.

Back at the compound, a mortally wounded Jacobs was soon discovered by his fellow Delta Force team members. "Man down, man down," the call went out over the radio. The team did their best to dress Jacobs' wounds there on the kitchen floor before rushing him to one of the waiting Black Hawks. The chopper lifted off into the night with Jacobs and several team members, leaving the rest of the unit behind to finish sweeping the compound and bagging evidence.

The Delta Force Commander radioed the situation room back at Balad Air Base, where the general and other high-ranking officers who'd planned and organized the raid were anxiously awaiting a mission status report. "Primary target *not* yet located. Team is currently sweeping for intel and searching for possible escape tunnel access. One team member injured and medevaced to Balad. Permission to extend mission deadline by twenty mikes to locate the escape point and track targets."

"Damn, this whole thing has gone fucking sideways," the general spat from within the situation room, ensuring he was muted to the team on the ground before he made his comment. "Pull them out of there and send in the drone to light the place up before shit gets even worse."

The officer in charge of comms flipped the switch to connect the general with the Delta Force team. "Negative, extract your teams and prepare for Liz Taylor," the general commanded. Liz Taylor was the code phrase for Plan-B, sending in a Reaper drone to level the compound with Hellfire missiles strong enough to penetrate and destroy any subterranean bunkers or tunnels.

"Roger," the Delta Force unit leader responded.

The Delta Force team evacuated the compound and fell back to the remaining Black Hawk. As the chopper was lifting into the air, the compound exploded into a massive ball of flames reaching hundreds of feet into the desert sky. The explosion was so powerful it rocked the Black Hawk, tossing the men inside around like shoes in a dryer.

"We have *not* cleared the blast zone!" the Black Hawk pilot radioed. "Repeat: We are not yet clear!"

"What the hell is going on out there?" the general in the situation room roared as he banged a fist on the table. "Who cleared the drone for launch?"

"The drone hasn't fired its missiles yet sir," the situation room communications officer replied, shaking his head. "It wasn't us."

"What's your status?" the general barked, addressing the Black Hawk pilot.

"The blast reverb rocked us, but we're okay."

The insurgent escapees watched as the flames from the compound licked up at the night sky, illuminating the surrounding desert. Hakim and the man with the stab wound both stared expressionless into the flames, their thumbs still resting on the green *Send* buttons of the flip phones in their hands.

Jacobs was still semi-conscious as the chopper screamed across the black void racing back to Balad Air Base. From where he was lying, he had a perfect view of the night sky out the Black Hawk's open door. He stared in awe at the millions of stars stretching across the sky in a magnificent arc, wrapping the desert in a sparkling blanket. His thoughts wandered to Elora, and he whispered to the stars that he was sorry he let her down. He thought of his two children, thirteen-year-old Bryce and nine-year-old Brooklyn, and asked God to watch over them. Halfway between the compound and Balad, Major Brendan Jacobs exhaled a final labored breath and slipped away into the night.

Chapter 1

CIA Analyst Elora Monro stood on the tarmac of Dover Air Force Base awaiting the arrival of a C-17 cargo plane bearing the remains of her fiancé. Her friend and colleague, fellow CIA Analyst Nick Hildebrandt, stood next to her. Nick had also been close friends with Brendan, he was even slated to be one of the groomsmen in Elora and Brendan's upcoming wedding. Now, instead of marrying Brendan, Elora was burying him. She and Nick stared silently off into Delaware's gray March sky—watching, listening. They heard a low rumble begin to approach from the east and looked up just in time to see the C-17 break through the cloud cover. As the plane dipped its wings to circle the airfield and line up for landing, Nick placed a supportive hand on Elora's shoulder and gave it a gentle squeeze.

"Are you okay?"

"Nope," Elora replied, feeling her chest tighten as she struggled to maintain her composure.

Nick didn't press further but kept his hand on her shoulder.

Elora was thankful the mission and Brendan's death had remained classified, meaning there were no loitering reporters with cameras to capture the arrival of his body. She looked forward to having at least a few minutes alone in peace with him to say goodbye. She was going over in her head what she wanted to say to Brendan, when a commotion and the sound of footsteps approaching from behind pulled her away from her thoughts. She turned to see who was coming and her heart sank. It was Brendan's ex-wife, Ashley, flanked by their two children and a few others in tow, including an Army colonel and a chaplain. The chaplain and colonel had gone to Ashley's home the day before to inform her of Brendan's death and assist her with telling the children if she wished. Elora didn't think Ashley would bring the kids to the air base to receive his body. She was wrong.

Ashley marched across the tarmac toward Elora with puffy red eyes and tissues in hand, yet her makeup—which she'd slathered on extra thick today—remained perfectly intact. Obviously, she'd had the foresight to wear waterproof mascara. She wore a skin-tight black dress with three-hundred-dollar Jimmy Choo shoes, and not a hair was out of place in her perfectly coiffed shoulder-length blonde bob. She was the picture-perfect grief-stricken military widow. Her Village of the Damned-looking children were the ideal accessories to complete her look, props in her show to garner added attention and sympathy. Ashley had been using those kids as tools and weapons since the day they were born—hell, before they'd even left the womb. She'd trapped Brendan into marrying her when she tricked him with the age-old *I'm on the pill* bit a few months after they started dating. Brendan was in his final year at West Point, and Ashley was a waitress at a local dive bar frequented by the cadets; their entire relationship was basically the plot to *An Officer and a Gentleman*, playing out in real life.

Ashley halted her entourage a couple of feet from Elora and Nick, facing them squarely. "I don't want her here," Ashley declared in a condescending tone, looking down her nose at Elora.

Unaware of the existing family drama, the Army colonel and chaplain exchanged confused looks. "My children are here to say goodbye to their father, and I'm here to grieve the man I was married to for fourteen years. We shouldn't have to do this with his *mistress* looking over our shoulders," she added in a disgusted tone.

Elora was surprised Ashley was making a scene but not shocked; it was par for the course when it came to Ashley. "I'm not his mistress," Elora corrected, crossing her arms. "I'm his fiancée."

"You're a home-wrecking cunt. That's what you are!"

"Are you seriously going to do this right now?" Elora asked, raising her voice over the sound of the incoming C-17, now touching down at the far end of the runway. "You've been divorced for three years."

"I know you were fucking Brendan years ago, when he was still *my* husband," Ashley said through sharply narrowed eyes. "I was his wife for over a decade; you were his side-whore."

Ashley's comments were typical, but the fact she was saying them right in front of the children was out of character. That was low even for Ashley.

"Come on, guys, not here, not now," Nick said, stepping in, trying to diffuse the situation. "Both of you can have your time with Brendan—separately. I'm sure Elora is willing to wait until after the kids have had a chance to say goodbye to their dad," he added looking at Elora, urging her to acquiesce with his eyes.

Elora pursed her lips but gave a curt nod, indicating her willingness to wait but also making it clear she wasn't thrilled. Though Elora had grown accustomed to Ashley's tirades, her words still stung. Elora couldn't deny there was truth in them. Fact was Elora had had an affair with Brendan several years before his divorce. They'd met ten years prior while the two were studying at the Defense Language Institute (DLI) in Monterey, California. Elora had enlisted in the U.S. Air Force right after high school and went to DLI following basic training to study Arabic for eighteen months. Several weeks after arriving at DLI, she fell head over heels for a fellow classmate, a handsome Army officer ten years her senior. Elora and Brendan embarked on a ten-month affair that was not only scandalous due to the fact Brendan was married, but also a violation of the military code of conduct; relationships between officers and enlisted personnel were strictly forbidden.

Elora wasn't proud of the affair and still harbored a great deal of guilt over it. A part of her tried to chalk it up to being "young and dumb," but she wasn't stupid, and she knew the affair was selfish. Brendan talked about divorcing Ashley a few months into the affair, but then Ashley wound up pregnant, again. Elora didn't see it at the time but looking back, she realized it was a manipulative move by Ashley to hang onto Brendan. Ashley knew he was slipping away; she may have even known about the affair. Out of desperation, she used the same trick that helped her rope Brendan into marrying her in the first place, trapping him with a baby. With Ashley expecting a second child and neither Elora nor Brendan wanting to end their military career, they decided to break off their affair. It was one of the most excruciating points in Elora's life. Emotionally devastated, she struggled with mild depression for a year after the breakup.

Fast-forward a few years, Elora separated from the Air Force and landed a position as an analyst at the CIA. A few months into her new job, she stepped off the elevator one morning at work and nearly collided with Brendan. He'd recently become a member of the Army's elite Delta Force unit and served as an Intelligence Liaison Officer between the CIA and Delta Force, meaning he was frequently at Langley. A couple of days later, Brendan and Elora got together for coffee and to catch up. Brendan made it a point to inform her of his recent divorce from Ashley while Elora ensured Brendan knew she'd dated off and on since their affair but was currently single. They quickly rekindled their romance, picking up right where they'd left off several years earlier. A year later, Brendan proposed.

They'd planned an intimate ceremony with just family and a few close friends for later that Spring. Instead of putting the final touches on her wedding preparations, Elora was now standing on the tarmac of Dover Air Base, waiting to receive and bury the body of the man she'd been in love with since she was eighteen; and, once again, she was fighting over him with Ashley.

"Are you fucking kidding me right now, Nick?" Elora screeched into the phone.

"Elora, they're his kids and she's their mother. What do you want the Army to do?"

Nick had just spoken with the director of the funeral home handling the burial and called Elora to fill her in on the funeral arrangements and itinerary. Brendan would be laid to rest the following afternoon with full military honors at Arlington National Cemetery. His son, Bryce, would be accepting the

American flag traditionally folded and handed to the spouse or child of the fallen soldier at the graveside service. Bryce would be seated front and center at the funeral, meaning his mother, Ashley, would be at his side. Elora was content to sit at Bryce's other side, but Ashley torpedoed this idea.

"This is fucking bullshit and you know it. They divorced years ago, and he and I were two months from getting married! You're telling me that because I didn't immediately start popping out babies when Brendan and I first met, I have less rights to him than a woman who manipulated his life from the day she met him?" Elora took a deep breath and tried to quell the rage coursing through her veins. "Look, I am completely on board with Bryce being the one who accepts the flag from his father's coffin," she continued in a calmer tone. "I can even live with having Ashley at my side. What I will not rollover and take is Ashley barring me from my own fiancé's funeral and conjuring this bullshit excuse that my presence will be emotionally traumatic for Bryce and Brooklyn."

"I am so sorry, Elora, I truly am," Nick said. "I know how much Brendan loved you and I know he'd be pissed knowing this was happening. But as far as the Army is concerned, neither you nor Ashley have any more rights here than the other. She's his ex-wife and you weren't his wife yet. The only ones here with any claim acknowledged by the Army are the kids, which..."

"Which, by default, gives Ashley the upper hand because she's their mom," Elora said, finishing his sentence for him. "Yeah, I get it." She decided to change the subject. "What about my ring?" she asked, referring to the small white-gold band she'd given Brendan the day he left for Iraq. He'd promised to keep it on him, so she was confident he'd had it with him when he died. "Is the ring my dead father gave me in middle school going to end up with the kids too? And, by default, Ashley?"

Nick exhaled. "No, at least not any time soon. For the time being, everything that was on Brendan's person when he was killed will remain in evidence lockup until JSOC completes their investigation into the raid."

"What about Brendan's autopsy? When will the report be ready?"

"Supposed to be done this afternoon. It too won't be available to the family until after the investigation but, as a member of the NDU task force, you'll have access to it as soon as you return to work," he added in a hinting tone. "We should have a copy of the autopsy tomorrow morning."

"Well, it's nice to know I have *some* privileges. Can you tell Derek to put a copy of it on my desk as soon as it comes in?" Elora asked. "I'll be in tomorrow after the funeral."

"Elora don't," Nick pleaded. "I got you cleared to take the week off; stay home, mourn Brendan, try not to think about work for at least a few days."

"Are you kidding? The *only* thing I can think about right now is work, specifically wiping NDU off the face of the planet. You and I both know—hell, everyone on the task force knows—that—" Elora stopped short, knowing what she was about to say was not something she should discuss over a non-secure phone line. "Look, we'll talk about it tomorrow when I come in."

Nick wanted to argue but knew it was futile. "Are you going to be okay tonight? You want me to come over?"

"No, but thank you. You've gone far above and beyond for

me already. I know this is hard on you too."

"You don't have to thank me. If there's anything you need don't hesitate to ask. Have a good night."

"You too, Nick."

A few minutes after hanging up with Nick, there was a knock on the front door of Elora's townhouse. *Shit, who is that?* Elora ran her fingers through her long auburn hair, which she hadn't washed in days, and threw it up into a quick ponytail to camouflage the disheveled mess as she went to answer the door. She looked through the peephole and saw a UPS driver standing on the stoop. She relaxed and opened the door. The delivery driver handed her a certified envelope and asked her to sign his clipboard. She glanced at the sender info on the envelope as she closed the door: JSOC PERSONNEL DEPT, FT. BRAGG, NC — Brendan's home base. She ripped open the envelope and slid the paperwork out. LAST WILL & TESTAMENT: MAJ. BRENDAN D. JACOBS, U.S. ARMY. Elora plopped the documents on her kitchen counter and poured herself a glass of wine. There was no way she could go through Brendan's will stone sober. She also had a nagging feeling in the back of her mind that she was going to be even more pissed off after reading it.

She took her wine, curled up on her couch and began flipping through the paperwork. The final page of the packet caught Elora's eye. A penned note in Brendan's handwriting.

Elora My Love,

If you're reading this, I guess I didn't make it back. Please know how sorry I am that I let you down. There was nothing in this world I wanted more than to be your husband and to make you my wife. It kills me to know—ha ha, see what I did there?

Elora rolled her eyes; yup, this was written by Brendan.

Sorry, I couldn't help it. In all seriousness, it kills me to imagine leaving you behind before we've had a chance to live our life together. A life I've been dreaming about since the day I met you. You took my breath away—in every way. Even at just 18 years old, you could more than hold your own in a roomful of military men who outranked you. You captivated me then, and you continue to captivate me each day. You are going to go so far in this life. You've already come so far, but I know you are destined for greatness. I'm just sorry I won't be around to see you change the world. And it is because I know how incredibly strong you are that you'll understand my decision regarding the disbursement of my life insurance benefits. Ensuring Bryce and Brooklyn are taken care of is my number one priority in this world, and I know you agree with this. Again, I am so sorry I never got to marry you. Please don't cry for me, I can't bear to think of tears on your beautiful face. Live your life, love again, and know that I'll always be with you.

Forever in love with you,
Brendan

He'd asked her not to cry but Elora couldn't help it. The full weight of the tragic events of the last seventy-two hours came crashing down on top of her all at once. She was only twenty-nine years old but knew enough about loss and grief to know she would eventually be able to move on, but in that moment, it was as if there was an impenetrable wall between her and the rest of her life. The entire future she'd envisioned, the love of her life, everything was suddenly gone, and she was alone. She shuffled through the paperwork and found the life insurance benefit distribution page. Sure enough, Brendan had allotted her a mere ten percent share of his four-hundred-thousand-dollar life insurance payout. About enough to cover the deposits she'd have to forfeit when cancelling the reservations for their upcoming wedding and honeymoon. Ashley would be getting the remaining three hundred and sixty thousand plus a hundred-thousand-dollar death gratuity. Elora knew this was the right thing to do; the children came first. Brendan was being a responsible father, but she still felt bitter. Then, she felt guilty for feeling bitter. From there it was a vicious cycle until she succumbed to exhaustion and passed out on the sofa into a fitful sleep.

Chapter 2

Elora pulled into the parking lot of the CIA headquarters outside Langley, Virginia. Nick followed behind her in his car; the two were coming from Brendan's funeral at Arlington National Cemetery. Nick had urged Elora to go home after the funeral but she flat-out refused.

"If I go home right now and sit alone in my house, I'll go fucking crazy," she'd told him. "I want to work—I *need* to work. I can't rest until I know the assholes responsible for Brendan's death are in prison or dead, preferably the latter. The NDU Task Force still has a job to finish. You and I both know Malik Khalid wasn't killed in the raid. We don't know for sure if he was even there that night. We still have work to do, and I will not stop until that son of a bitch is brought down."

Nick didn't have the heart to tell Elora there had already been talk of dissolving the CIA's NDU Task Force, of which he was the team leader, and Elora, along with three other analysts, were members. "Okay, let's go to work," he'd simply said with a smile and followed her on the twenty-minute drive from Arlington out to Langley.

Nick and Elora walked into the NDU Task Force suite on the fifth floor of the CIA headquarters building and were greeted by fellow team members Derek, Jason, and Lori, who were all surprised to see Elora, but not shocked.

"Hey Elora, how are you holding up?" Derek asked.

"I've been better," Elora replied with a fake grin.

Everyone on the team knew the drama Ashley had caused regarding the funeral, so none of them dared to ask how the funeral had gone. Elora was eager to dive back into the mission anyway and decided to waste no time.

"Did we get a copy of Major Jacobs' autopsy report yet?" she asked. She kept her references to Brendan professional, to both safeguard herself emotionally and prove to the team she could compartmentalize her work and personal feelings. Elora knew it was a real possibility the agency would remove her from the NDU Task Force because of her personal connection to Brendan. She wanted to avoid that if possible.

Derek briefly looked past Elora to Nick, who subtly shook his head. "No, we haven't received it yet," Derek lied, shifting his focus back to Elora. "But we have received a preliminary report on the post-raid investigation. Iraqi authorities accompanied by an FBI forensics team have been on site sifting through the rubble since yesterday morning."

"Okay, it's four o'clock now," Nick said, glancing at his watch. "Let's all meet in the conference room in ten minutes to go over the FBI report and regroup."

Elora sat at her desk and shoved her purse underneath as Nick approached and squatted beside her chair.

"If at any point you need to leave, get up and go," he told her. "You don't have to say a word. Just go home. Or if you want to talk to someone, go see the counselors downstairs. They are in every day from six a.m. to six p.m. Whatever you need, just do it."

"Thanks, Nick, but honestly I'm okay."

The rest of the team fanned out to their desks to gather

their laptops and files before heading into the conference room.

The CIA had formed the NDU Task Force after New Dawn won a noteworthy number of seats in Iraq's 2010 Parliamentary elections. NDU and its leader, Malik Khalid, had originally popped up on the CIA's radar in 2007 when the organization began making waves as a minor militant group bombing government targets and picking fights with Iranian backed militias in Baghdad and northwestern Iraq. In the beginning, the U.S. intelligence community dubbed NDU a minor grassroots uprising. Considering they had no foreign government backing, it was predicted they'd soon fizzle out from lack of resources and funding. However, Malik Khalid proved himself a gifted businessman and built a small fortune trafficking weapons, narcotics, bootlegged alcohol, and other illegal commodities across the Middle East.

Though Malik Khalid was rapidly expanding his organization, he himself remained a relatively mysterious figure, making him all the more dangerous. There was still no detailed intel on his background, what he looked like, or if "Malik Khalid" was even his real name. The CIA knew he was a Sunni Muslim, well educated, and from Baghdad. There was also rumor that his parents and siblings had died in a U.S. airstrike near the beginning of the Iraq War, fueling his intense hatred of the U.S. and opening the door for his radicalization by pro-Saddam resistance fighters.

Currently, Malik Khalid's arch nemesis was Iranian Revolutionary Guard General Ali Ansari who commanded a Tehran-backed paramilitary force in Iraq. Ansari and Malik Khalid had been engaging in a game of cat and mouse for the last eighteen months. NDU had made at least two attempts to assassinate the

Iranian general but both failed – one being the explosion that killed U.S. Ambassador Casey.

The CIA's NDU Task Force had spent the last two years investigating NDU's international drug and weapons trafficking operations and monitoring the expansion of their political power in Iraq. They also tracked the movements of the NDU militia, trying to predict major attacks and operations. Everyone on the team took it as a personal failure when NDU successfully launched the massive coordinated bombing attack that killed the ambassador and several other Americans. When they had enough intel to convince JSOC to conduct a raid on the NDU compound, everyone on the Task Force was desperate for a win. Elora had even more riding on it—her fiancé. When the raid went sideways and resulted in the death of Major Jacobs, the team plunged even further into depression.

In the conference room, the NDU Task Force members took their seats as Derek walked around, plopping a copy of the FBI's preliminary report on the post-raid investigation in front of each member. Derek, who'd had a chance to flip through the report, gave the team the highlights.

"As you all are aware, the NDU compound was leveled. JSOC had called in a drone airstrike to light the place up, but before the drone launched, the entire compound imploded," Derek explained. "The prevailing theory is that the militants donned explosive vests, slipped into an underground bunker, and then detonated themselves—perhaps even unintentionally. According to the report in front of you, this theory seems to hold water. Investigators did locate a subterranean tunnel running beneath a kitchen in the main building, and the FBI forensics team discovered human remains in the collapsed portion of the tunnel." Everyone at the table perked up when they heard Derek mention the dead bodies in the tunnel.

"Have they identified any of the remains yet? Is one of them Malik?" Jason asked excitedly as he scanned the report.

"Did they say how many bodies they found?" Lori added on the heels of Jason's question.

"The FBI is running DNA analysis on the remains now but, so far, no conclusive IDs have been established," Derek announced. "At this point they've determined there are at least five bodies, but excavation efforts are still underway."

"So, it's possible we got him after all," Lori said.

Elora remained silent, staring at her report.

"If they are able to identify Malik, do you think the president will do a press conference..." Jason began but Elora cut him off.

"He wasn't there," she said, without looking up from her report. "We all know he's still alive." She finally lifted her eyes to meet her colleagues' stares. "Everyone here knows how smart this asshole is. He wouldn't get caught like a rat in a trap, and he sure as hell wouldn't blow himself up. He'd surrender first and bet on being able to talk his way out of it, because that's the type of cocky son of a bitch he is. Even knowing as little as we do about him, we all know *none* of those bodies in that tunnel are Malik Khalid, nor do they belong to any of his top leadership." She shook her head and tossed the report back to the center of the table. "Malik made it out. Or he was never there to begin with. We still have a job to do. And before any of you makes a comment about Brendan, this has nothing to do with what happened to him. If it had been one of the other guys who died or even if everyone had made it home safely, I'd be sitting here saying the same damn thing. We failed and we still have a mission to finish, and you all know it."

"I hear you Elora and I agree with you," Nick said, breaking his silence in the meeting for the first time, "but, as you well know, what we think, or what we even know, doesn't count for shit. I've received word that the National Security Council is considering the raid a success. They too have reviewed this preliminary summary and, pending the final report, they're ready to declare Malik Khalid dead and NDU neutralized."

Elora shook her head and fought back tears of frustration. "You know that's a huge mistake. The suits in Washington just want to wrap this up with a big fake bow so they can stick it in their win column for the next election."

"I have a meeting with the Task Force Oversight Committee tomorrow," Nick added, dodging Elora's comments. "I wanted to tell you all while I have you here, I have a strong feeling they're going to disband our Task Force and reassign us. It's been my incredible privilege and honor to lead this team. You are all amazing analysts." He paused and looked at Elora, "I know how much you have sacrificed for this mission. They'll likely keep us up and running for a few weeks to finalize our mission reports and conduct debriefings, but unless new developments arise between now and then, we all need to prepare ourselves, personally and professionally, to put the NDU mission to bed."

"So, we're just going to let him go?" Elora asked. "Where's the justice? The justice we owe Ambassador Casey, and the justice Brendan deserves?"

"It's over Elora," Nick said, hardening his tone a bit. "I'm sorry—it's time to move on." He was referring to the mission, but Elora knew he also meant move on from Brendan. "Let's go ahead and call it a day," Nick continued. "I want drafts of everyone's End of Mission reports on my desk by next Friday. Again, thank you all for your service and dedication to this mission."

As everyone was gathering their things to leave, Elora again asked Derek to let her know as soon as Brendan's autopsy report came in from the medical examiner. Derek gave her an awkward nod and scurried out of the room.

"Hang back for a minute please, Elora," Nick asked. The rest of the team hurried out, and Elora made a preemptive attempt to defend herself.

"Look, Nick, I'm not trying to be difficult, I just think...."

"We have Brendan's autopsy report," Nick interjected, cutting her off.

Elora shot him a confused look. "Okay. So, Derek lied to me?"

"He did what I asked him to do," Nick replied with a hint of sternness.

"Well, can I have a copy?" Elora asked, wondering why Nick was being so cryptic.

"Elora... it's not something you need to see. It has no bearing on your mission, and it will only upset you."

"Are you fucking serious?"

"Elora, you're a lot more fragile right now then you're letting on—than you're even admitting to yourself. I'm trying to protect you."

"Nick, I'm not a broken little girl. Give me the fucking autopsy."

Shaking his head in resignation, Nick pulled a manila file folder from beneath the stack of papers in front of him and flung it across the table. The folder smacked down and slid a few inches across the tabletop in front of Elora.

"Thank you," she declared with indignation.

Nick did not reply and left the room.

Elora returned to her cubicle near the middle of the office and sat with the folder on the desk in front of her. With her hands folded in front of her mouth, she stared at the closed file for a few moments. Taking a deep breath, she finally opened the folder.

Her fellow NDU Task Force members sat in silence at their respective cubicles as Elora flipped through the report. It was well after five o'clock. They were free to go home, but everyone remained at their desks fiddling and pretending to wrap up their day. They all knew what was in the folder.

Elora skimmed through the report:

- POINT BLANK GUNSHOT WOUND—LOWER LEFT ABDOMEN: NON-FATAL ABRASION LEFT SIDE OF CHIN
- BRUISING & SOFT TISSUE HEMORRHAGES: ANTERIOR REGION OF NECK
- LEFT RIB 9 FRACTURED LATERALLY
- SUPERFICIAL ABRASIONS
- CONTUSION OF LEFT ANKLE
- FRACTURE OF MANDIBLE
- LACERATION VERTEBRAL ARTERY, JUGULAR VEIN AND SUBCLAVIAN ARTERY—RIGHT
- GUNSHOT WOUND TO NECK & CHIN, LOWER

CERVICAL, UPPER THORACIC, SPINAL COLUMN: FATAL

CAUSE OF DEATH WAS THE RESULT OF A GUNSHOT WOUND AT APPROXIMATELY 24-36 INCH DISTANCE TO THE NECK WITH A TOTAL TRANSECTION OF THE LOWER CERVICAL AND UPPER THORACIC SPINAL CORD AND OTHER STRUCTURES OF THE NECK. DIRECTION OF THE WOUND WAS FRONT TO BACK. BULLET TRAVELED THROUGH J.V. AND V.A. TO SPINAL CORD. SEVERING OF THE SPINAL CORD AT THIS LEVEL AND TO THIS EXTENT WOULD HAVE PROVED FATAL SHORTLY AFTER OCCURRENCE.

Realizing she had stopped breathing somewhere in the middle of reading the report, Elora inhaled sharply and the crushing weight of grief and anger immediately landed on her chest. She visualized every injury Brendan suffered with stunning clarity in her mind. Struck with nausea, she slapped her hand over her mouth as she began to heave. In a split second, Lori and Jason were at her side. Lori shoved a trashcan beneath Elora's chin, and Jason placed a steadying hand on her back as she violently vomited into the waste bin. Derek arrived on the scene with a box of tissues, and Elora pulled out a couple, pressing them to her mouth.

"I'll bring you some water," Lori said as she removed the soiled plastic liner from the trash can.

"Thanks guys," Elora said, wiping her mouth with a tissue. "I'm okay now."

Chapter 3

In the weeks following the Delta Force raid on the NDU compound, the National Security Agency continued to send daily reports to the Task Force regarding NDU communications. Chatter about NDU across all channels—social media, radio, cell phone, etc.— had died down since the raid, and NSA labeled NDU "dark and quiet." This supported the theory the U.S. had severed the head of the snake and the organization was dying. However, final DNA analysis on the remains found beneath the NDU compound was inconclusive. Whether any of the bodies belonged to Malik Khalid was still unknown.

As Nick had predicted, the CIA's Task Force Oversight Committee voted to dissolve the NDU Task Force. They gave the team six weeks to wrap up their final mission reports, close out their logs, and seal the case file on the NDU mission. They also issued everyone on the team a pat-on-the-head Certificate of Achievement in recognition of their efforts to neutralize the NDU terrorist organization. Nick shredded the certificates without ever even telling the team they'd existed. He knew his people would consider the award an insulting slap in the face. As the shredder finished gnawing its way through the certificates, Nick's desk phone rang.

"NDU Task Force—Hildebrandt," Nick said, picking up the receiver.

"Good afternoon, Mr. Hildebrandt, this is the west

entrance Security Desk. There is a Mr. Tim Blackwell from the National Security Agency here to see you. Would you like us to escort him up to your office, or do you want to come down and speak with him here?"

Nick had no clue who Tim Blackwell was but was intrigued. "Bring him on up," Nick said.

A few minutes later, the buzzer for the main door into the Task Force office rang out. Nick answered the door and escorted his visitor into his office. The two introduced themselves, and Nick gestured for the man to have a seat. "So, Mr. Blackwell, what can I do for you?" Nick asked as he took his own seat behind his desk.

"First of all, please call me Tim. I'm the team leader of the NSA task force that's been conducting SIGINT operations on the New Dawn Underground organization. In short, I'm the NSA version of you," Tim said with a smirk.

Nick stifled a chuckle. "Two years we've been passing intel back and forth and we're only just now meeting each other? Gotta love the U.S. intel world. We're best at keeping secrets from each other."

Tim smiled as his eyes fell on a tower of storage boxes in the corner of the office and then moved to the stacks of files and documents that had been pulled from the shelves and piled atop the credenza. "I take it you all got the same order we did—pull the plug on the NDU mission?"

"That about sums it up."

"Well, you may want to stop packing. Our 'dark and quiet' organization," Tim said making air quotes with his fingers, "just came back online. NDU-related chatter started picking up a few days ago."

"Malik Khalid?" Nick asked, leaning forward in his chair with renewed interest. "Any indication of whether he's dead or alive?"

"So far, word on the street in Iraq is Malik Khalid was indeed killed in the raid, and even if he wasn't, he's so deep in hiding right now he's been pretty much rendered obsolete. Either way, it seems there was a second in command groomed and ready to take his place. We're expecting an official announcement of a new NDU leader any day now."

Nick waved a dismissive hand at the news of a new NDU leader. "These assholes always try to stick someone in to fill a dead leader's shoes. Nine times out of ten, the organization collapses within a few weeks or months. Guys like Malik Khalid aren't easily replaced. If he is in fact dead or, as you say, been rendered obsolete, NDU is a sinking ship. As soon as whatever funds they have left run out, they'll disappear into the desert."

"We had the same theory, but have you been keeping up with NDU's business activities over the last few weeks?" Tim asked. "Although they've been quiet, imagery and forensic accounting intel indicate the business side of NDU hasn't slowed down; in fact, they just closed a lucrative deal selling arms to one of the Syrian rebel splinter groups. Their social work in northern Iraq hasn't diminished either, and the NDU militia continues to maintain security patrols across the northwestern region of the country. You know full well those assholes don't work for free—someone's still signing their checks. It's been weeks since the raid that supposedly killed Malik and his top management, yet NDU is continuing to run like a well-oiled machine. If it's not Malik himself pulling the strings from some deep yet well-connected cave somewhere, then someone with intimate knowledge of NDU's inner workings has stepped up and transitioned into a leadership role. Which means NDU is not about to fade quietly into the night."

"And you think they're about to announce to the world who this 'someone' is," Nick commented.

"Exactamundo," Tim replied.

"So, what are they waiting for? Why haven't they announced this new leader yet? They've got to be fearing a power vacuum will soon cause panic within the ranks."

"They're playing squirrel," Tim answered with a shrug. "We just got close to ripping out their throat, so they dropped down and played dead for a while hoping we'd get bored and walk away, which is exactly what we're about to do." Tim gestured at the storage boxes around the office. "Also, no one knows for sure if Malik is dead or alive—we sure as hell don't know, that's why there hasn't been a power vacuum yet—a majority of NDU's support base thinks he's still alive. Rumors are rampant right now: Malik is dead. Malik is alive. Malik was captured. Malik's being interrogated in Israel. Malik transformed into a fucking bat and flew away! You name it, it's a theory currently floating around Iraq. In the meantime, everyone on NDU's payroll is still getting paid, and life is proceeding as normal. In a few months, whether Malik Khalid is dead or alive won't even matter to NDU members or supporters. NDU is using this time to prove that Malik was not indispensable, that the organization is self-sustaining and can thrive with or without him at the helm. Malik specifically designed it like this. He knew he wouldn't be around forever and ensured there were contingency plans in place should he suddenly disappear. Personally, I don't think he *wanted* to be in charge forever, which is why he kept such a low profile. You've been in this game long enough to know militant leaders are, by nature, attention whores; they don't remain unknown for long because their ego inevitably betrays them, but Malik is different. He's a mysterious motherfucker who has yet to compromise himself for fame. He's managed to build one of the most dynamic grassroots militant organizations of the last century, and still no one even knows what the fucker looks like."

"I take it the main reason you came all the way down here is to tell me we need to convince our respective bosses not to cut surveillance on NDU," Nick said.

"At least not yet," Tim replied. "NDU is down right now but, mark my words, they are far from out. Do what you can to get the agency to extend your Task Force mandate at least another three months. That's all it'll take to determine if NDU is going to stay down. I've already put in the request for a three-month extension on my end. But if you guys are shut down, they'll inevitably shut us down, and perhaps vice versa. That's why I came here. You and I need to be on the same page and making it clear we want the same things."

"If Malik is alive, do you honestly think we'll be able to track him back down and get to him in just three months?" Nick asked. "It took us two years to find him the first time, and he wasn't buried as deep as he likely is now, if, of course, he's alive at all."

"All I know is we should continue to keep tabs on NDU and try to learn as much as we can about them," Tim suggested. "They're one of the most organized groups in Iraq, and they're gaining power in the political sphere. Fact is, they've done more to provide social services and security in the regions they control than the actual Iraqi government, which is earning them strong support amongst the people. Hell, they may just end up being the Iraqi people's best hope for a decent future," Tim added with a chuckle, but Nick was not amused.

"They're a goddamn Islamic terrorist group," Nick snapped, rolling his eyes.

"Meh..." Tim said with a shrug. "Yes, they are Muslim. Yes, they have used violence to achieve political goals. Technically, all this makes them a terrorist group, but they are less Islamic extremists and more nationalist extremists. They aren't doing this in the name of Jihad, they do it in the name of Iraq. They hate foreigners—all foreigners and anyone not loyal to Iraq. For them, Iraq comes first, religion comes second. Obviously, they don't like us but, above all, they despise the Iranian influence currently rampant in Baghdad. Hence why they've been trying to kill that Iranian Revolutionary Guard general who's been marching around Iraq like he owns the damn place. I don't need to tell you that we ourselves aren't too stoked about how loyal the current Iraqi government is to Iran. NDU is still immature and wet behind the ears, but they've got potential. Iran's power in Iraq is growing stronger by the minute and threatening our interests and assets in the area, NDU may just be able to counterbalance that threat before it destabilizes the entire region."

"I can't believe what I'm hearing right now," Nick sneered. "NDU fucking assassinated our ambassador six months ago, and now you're saying we should back them?"

"That was arguably an accident," Tim said, holding a finger

in the air. "The circumstances surrounding the ambassador's death are very gray."

Nick's face hardened into a stony glare. "One of those NDU assholes shot out the throat of a Delta Force soldier during the JSOC raid last month. That soldier happened to be my friend and the fiancé of one of my Task Force analysts. They left him to die on the floor of that shithole compound choking on his own blood," Nick continued through clenched teeth. "Don't you dare sit here and fucking toy with the idea of letting these assholes get away with this shit; worse yet, giving them a goddamn helping hand. You're fucking insane."

Tim sat back in his chair. "I'm sorry. I had no idea you knew Major Jacobs personally."

"Well that's shocking considering you seem to fucking know everything else."

"Talk to your bosses, get them to extend your team's mission," Tim said, rising from his chair. "If you want to bring NDU to justice, you won't be able to do it if they shut you down. It was a pleasure meeting you. I'll show myself out."

The sun was beginning to set as Elora's taxi pulled into Arlington National Cemetery. It was May 15th, the day she and Brendan were supposed to have been married. The cab driver couldn't disguise his curious look when he'd pulled up to Elora's townhouse to find her waiting in a white wedding gown. She was clutching a half empty bottle of Disaronno liquor and was noticeably tipsy. The driver was even more confused when she told him where to take her.

Elora stepped out of the cab, holding the hem of her gown off the ground, revealing a pair of Nike flip-flops on her feet. Wobbling as she walked, she made her way to Brendan's gravesite. His headstone had just been installed, but the plot was still covered in loose dirt as the grass had not yet filled in. Unconcerned about soiling her dress, Elora dropped to her knees and sprawled out on Brendan's grave with her cheek to the ground, placing her head where she estimated his chest would be positioned six feet below her. The cemetery was quiet and deserted, and Elora lay there for a few minutes, listening to the sound of her own breathing.

"God, I miss you," she finally whispered into the ground. Tears streamed down her cheeks and dripped into the soil. She heard them *plop, plop, plop* into the dirt and imagined the sound of Brendan's heartbeat.

"I don't know how to keep going without you... It's so hard. The only thing that keeps me getting out of bed each morning is my anger. I'm so fucking pissed that we haven't been able to bring you justice. I *will* find Malik Khalid, and I will slit his fucking throat. Then I will crush NDU and track down who did this to you. I will burn that entire god-forsaken shithole of a country to the ground if I have to; I swear to God."

Elora heard footsteps and half rolled over to see who was approaching. It was Nick.

"May I sit, or would you rather be alone?" Nick asked.

"Welcome to the party," Elora replied, laying her head back down on the ground.

"I figured you could use some company today," Nick said

as he took a seat on the ground beside Elora. "I went by your place. When you weren't there, I had a feeling I'd find you here."

"I waited ten years for him," Elora said through tears. "I've been in love with him since I was eighteen." She pushed herself up to a sitting position and brushed the dirt off the front of her dress. "Of course, when we first met, things were...complicated, to say the least." She took a swig from the Disaronno bottle and wiped her mouth with the back of her hand. "He was married... He was an officer... I was enlisted... It was a fucking minefield," she added, shaking her head. "He was preparing to leave Ashley, at least he said he was. Then—big surprise—she ended up pregnant with Brooklyn. We figured it was the universe's way of telling us to let it go."

Nick maintained his silence and just listened. He knew that was what Elora needed most of all in that moment, simply to talk, and for someone to listen.

"We hadn't spoken in years when I bumped into him in the hallway at Langley a few months after I started working at the agency," she continued. "I was no longer in the military and he had divorced Ashley, it was like fate had worked everything out and brought us back together." She took another swig from the Disaronno bottle. "But you know what they say, if you want to make God laugh, just tell him your fucking plans. Twisted motherfucker."

Nick nodded but still did not speak.

"Speaking of motherfuckers," Elora continued with a loud sniffle. "Are we going to track down Malik Khalid or let him get away with this shit? He is still out there—I can fucking feel him." She leaned forward to look Nick in the eye. "You've got to convince them to keep us up and running—don't let them disband our Task Force. We were so close, Nick. I know we can find him again."

Nick hadn't yet told anyone on the team about the visit he'd received from Tim Blackwell at NSA. NDU still hadn't announced a new leader, nor had they even confirmed the death of Malik Khalid, but Tim had been right about NDU's status—they were still active and operating.

"I'm working on a proposal to request a three-month extension of our mandate," Nick informed her. "But you *cannot* let this get personal. If they do extend us, and you want to have any shot at remaining on the team, you've got to keep it together. They wanted me to cut you loose after Brendan's death, but I convinced them you're an irreplaceable asset and a professional. Please don't make me have to eat my words."

Elora perked up at the possibility of Langley keeping the Task Force together. "I can handle it," she said. "I won't let you down, I promise. Three months isn't a lot of time, but we'll make it work." She slowly stood up and scooped her Disaronno bottle off the ground. "I better head home before you have to carry me," she said, placing a hand to her head that was beginning to throb.

"Do you need a ride?" Nick asked and moved to stand.

"No, no stay here with Brendan," Elora said, already walking off. "I'll catch a cab at the bottom of the hill; I need to walk a bit anyway."

Nick sat alone in silence next to Brendan's headstone, but he had so many things he wanted to say to his friend. Nick and Brendan weren't best friends, but the two had known each other for several years and were good buddies. He spent a few minutes collecting his thoughts and then finally spoke.

"I'm so sorry this happened to you. You were a good man, an excellent soldier and a great friend. You didn't deserve this...and Elora doesn't deserve this. She's hurting, man," Nick said, shaking his head. "She's hurting a lot, and I wish more than anything that I could help her. She's so fucking amazing...but I guess you already knew that. God, I was so jealous of you. I thought you were the luckiest motherfucker alive. Ugh, I don't know how to do this. How do you tell your dead friend that you want to date his girl? I feel guilty but I also think I can make her happy. I swear to God, I will never hurt her. And I know I will love her for as long as I breathe, I can promise you that much."

Nick wasn't sure when Elora would be ready to move on. The one thing he did know, though, was that Elora would never be free of Brendan until she was done chasing ghosts. Nick wasn't convinced Malik Khalid was still alive, but he knew Elora would never be free of her grief or free to open her heart to him (or anyone for that matter) until they found Malik and killed him or confirmed he was already dead.

Nick sat with Brendan for another twenty minutes before he finally stood up and faced Major Jacobs' grave. "I hope you find peace, brother." He reached into his pockets pulled out a single dime and placed it atop the smooth granite headstone. "I hope we can all find peace, but we won't rest until we bring you justice."

Nick was abruptly jolted from a deep sleep by the obnoxious ringing of his CIA-issued cell phone which was lying on the nightstand next to his head. He glanced at the clock as he reached to answer his phone and saw that it was just after 3:10 a.m.

"Hildebrandt," Nick answered groggily.

"Nick, it's Derek. I think you better come into the office."

"Give me twenty minutes," Nick said with an exhausted sigh.

Nick rolled out of bed, threw on some clothes, and was out the door in under five minutes. He arrived to the NDU Task Force office and made a beeline for Derek's cubicle. "What have we got?" Nick asked, walking up behind Derek's chair.

"NSA sent a report over forty-five minutes ago." Derek clicked on his screen and opened a digital intel report. "NDU officially confirmed the death of Malik Khalid two hours ago, and they announced a new leader. His name is Samir Al-Bakr," Derek answered, looking up at Nick.

Though this was big news, Nick wasn't sure it was call-him-into-the-office-in-the-middle-of-the-night big.

"Okay..." he began a bit perplexed, "we were expecting this. Not sure why you couldn't wait until I came in at nine to give me this news. Do we even know anything about this Samir Al-Bakr guy?"

"Oh, wait, there's more," Derek answered excitedly and resumed clicking on his computer. "There's a video."

"Video?" Nick was now a bit more intrigued and leaned in closer over Derek's shoulder. "Video of what?"

"Video of Samir Al-Bakr himself giving an acceptance

speech."

"You're shitting me," Nick replied, stunned. "Malik Khalid headed up NDU for a decade and we never got so much as a polaroid of him. This asshole's in charge for an hour, and he's already filming infomercials and syndicating them world-wide?"

"It seems NDU is ready to mainstream," Derek said as he clicked on the file to launch the video.

Nick stared at the screen as the video played. The first thing that jumped out at him was the semi-professional production quality of the video. Following a brief intro featuring the New Dawn Underground logo, the video cut to a well-dressed Iraqi man wearing an expensive-looking Western-style business suit. Samir Al-Bakr appeared to be approximately thirty-five years old, was clean shaven, and stood confidently behind a podium. He spoke Arabic as he addressed the camera, and Nick watched for a couple minutes before turning to Derek.

"Derek," Nick said, interrupting the video, "you know my Arabic is shit. Did NSA happen to send over a transcript of what this asshole is saying?"

"Oh right, yes they did," Derek said, pausing the video.

"Wonderful. Send a copy to my printer and forward me the video so I can review it in my office, please," Nick instructed. "Standing here over your shoulder is killing my back. Also, see that everyone on the team gets a copy of the transcript and video as soon as they arrive. I want everyone ready to give their feedback in the conference room at ten a.m."

"Roger that boss."

Nick holed himself up in his office, where he watched the entire video and read through the transcript several times. It read as follows:

It is with great sadness we announce to all New Dawn Underground members and supporters, as well as the world, that our beloved founder and leader, Malik Khalid, was tragically murdered during an illegal raid on our headquarters outside Mosul several weeks ago. This raid was backed by the corrupt Iraqi administration in Baghdad and carried out by invading American Special Forces soldiers. I stand here today to inform you that I, Samir Al-Bakr, have assumed command of New Dawn Underground and assure you that our organization is still as strong as ever. We continue to grow, and we will fight to the death if need be until we have achieved a free and united Iraq that is loyal to no one but the Iraqi people—serving the needs of the Iraqi people and the Iraqi people alone. The Americans have been invaders in our land for a decade. Now, Iran too invades us like a cancer. The resources of our nation feed children beyond our borders while our own children languish in hunger and poverty. New Dawn Underground will not rest until this injustice is rectified and the people of Iraq once again benefit and prosper from the riches that lie beneath our great country. New Dawn Underground will no longer hide in the shadows. Like any nation defending its sovereignty, we will attack all foreigners we consider invaders on our soil, and we will not apologize for those caught in the crossfire as we defend our sovereignty and the rights of the Iraqi people. We will continue to resist until we've expelled all foreigners from our borders and restore power to those who are loyal to no one but Iraq. We are prepared to bring this fight to the global political arena as well, where we will denounce any and all foreign nations who continue to meddle in the political affairs of our state. This includes the current corrupt Iraqi government, a majority of whom are traitorous puppets of Tehran. Rest assured that our pen and sword are both mighty. This is a warning and promise to the world—a "New Dawn" has indeed arrived. May Allah bless the Iraqi people and our great nation.

At ten o'clock the NDU Task Force members gathered in the conference room to discuss the video and share their analyses.

"All right, people," Nick said, dropping a file containing his notes and a copy of the transcript on the conference table. "This is what we've been waiting for; NDU just poked their head out of their hole, and it doesn't look like they plan to retreat back underground any time soon. I know most of you have only had about an hour or so to review the video and transcript, so I will open the floor to Derek first. He's been here since around three a.m. reviewing the video and called me in shortly after, so please excuse our yawns. Derek, what's your take on the video?"

Derek cleared his throat. "Word is coming in that a copy of this video has gone out to every major news organization from Al Jazeera to CNN, so it's clear they are trying hard to make a global statement. I've started digging to see if I can come up with any background on this Samir Al-Bakr guy and NSA is running through all their old intercepts to see if his name is ever mentioned anywhere. If he truly is the one who's been pulling NDU's strings over the last few weeks, then he's been around for a while. He has to have more than a working knowledge of the group to have been able to keep things as well on track as they have been. So far, though, facial recognition software hasn't pulled up anything, and who knows if 'Samir Al-Bakr' is even his real name. We all know how cryptic Malik Khalid was, so I'm sure this guy knows how to cover his tracks as well. However, he has already established himself as more of a public figure than Malik ever did. We know what he looks like, and he doesn't seem to be using any kind of voice distortion software in this video, so we know what he sounds like too. This is already a lot more than we ever had on Malik."

Derek paused and picked up a TV remote control off the conference table. He pointed the remote at the flat screen TV hanging in the corner of the conference room and hit the *Play* button to roll the NDU video on the screen. He let the video play for a few moments before pausing it halfway through Samir Al-Bakr's speech.

"He speaks Arabic with the common Baghdad accent and dialect, so he was likely born and raised there. He is well-spoken and poised. I'd say it's safe to assume he's well educated—most likely a University of Baghdad graduate. Like Malik, Samir is most likely a Sunni Muslim, though he's not touting the message of Jihad in this video. A majority of the fighters in their militia are devout Sunnis, so NDU often posts Jihadist messages across social media when trying to rouse their base and recruit members. The fact he is clean-shaven and wearing a Western-style business suit indicates he's not trying to appeal to the extremists. This video isn't meant for their people. It was specifically made for us, and the Western world."

Derek played the remaining minutes of the video then stopped it and placed the remote back on the conference table.

"In my opinion, this video speaks volumes to NDU's desire to go mainstream," Derek continued. "They're trying to legitimize their operation and make it clear they no longer want the world to view them as a guerilla terrorist group. They're making power grabs in local and national elections across Iraq, and if they can maintain their current cashflow from their international business dealings, they could soon be a bigger threat in Iraq than Al-Qaeda."

"He already talks as if he's running the country," Jason noted. "He mentions defending the nation's sovereignty and restoring the rights of Iraqi citizens. Pretty high aspirations for a militant group. Something else that sticks out to me is the part where he says, 'We will not apologize for those caught in the crossfire as we defend our sovereignty.' He may be referring to Ambassador Casey's death. Saying they 'will not apologize' and referring to him as getting 'caught in the crossfire' suggests they didn't intend to kill him. It's pretty clear they aren't sorry he's dead either, but it does support the theory that the Ambassador's death was unintentional and not part of a plot."

Nick looked around the table at the rest of the team and saw Elora roll her eyes at Jason's comments. "Does anyone have anything else they'd like to add?"

"Are we actually buying his story that Malik is dead?" Elora asked. "For all we know this asshole *is* Malik himself. He fits the profile."

Derek shrugged. "It's possible. Can't rule it out."

"There's something else too," Elora continued. "He makes a noticeable pause, or... I'm not quite sure how to explain it, but it's almost like a hiccup in his speech when he says 'Khalid' and a few other words."

"Yes! I noticed that too," Derek interjected.

"Well, you two are the only ones here fluent enough in Arabic to pick up on something like that," Nick said. "What are you thinking?"

"At first I was thinking it was simply a fumble in his speech," Derek replied. "Like he was just tripping over his words a bit, but after reviewing the video several more times, it appears to be more of an impediment."

"Like a stutter?" Jason asked.

"Yes, perhaps he suffers from a mild stammer," Derek speculated. "He may have had a severe stutter as a child and learned to overcome it."

"Okay, let's wrap it up," Nick announced. "Anybody have anything else to add?" Everyone shook their heads. "Considering these new developments, it shouldn't be difficult now to persuade the Task Force Oversight Committee to extend our mission end date," Nick continued. "We'll need to keep tabs on NDU while they undergo this regime change, until we know for sure what's going to come out on the other side before we pack it in."

"What about another JSOC raid?" Elora asked impatiently. "If NDU is stepping out into the light to try and mainstream, as Derek suggests, then it shouldn't be too hard to figure out where they are and wipe out their leadership. This Samir asshole is another Malik Khalid in the making, we should take him out before he has a chance to coordinate another bombing attack across Baghdad that kills more Americans. And if Malik Khalid is in fact still alive, he is probably in contact with Samir. We can try to take Samir alive and then force him to lead us to Malik—whether he's dead or alive. We still have no DNA evidence to support Malik's death."

"We're not there yet, Elora," Nick replied, shooting her a look that said dial it back a notch. "I'll work on getting us the extension from the board today, and then we'll continue our designated surveillance and reconnaissance operations for the time being," he announced to the group.

Chapter 4

Nick was successful in getting the Task Force board to extend his team's mandate an additional three months. In the two weeks since NDU had announced Samir Al-Bakr as their new leader, Nick and the team had worked round-the-clock trying to learn as much as they could about NDU's mysterious new front man. Unfortunately, they'd come up nearly empty-handed. For all intents and purposes, the guy was a nobody, but the team considered this good news. If NDU's supporters didn't know anything about Samir either, it would be difficult for their base to rally around him.

The NSA scoured their NDU traffic archives but only found Samir mentioned in a few random phone calls and emails. Nothing indicated he was anything more than an auxiliary player in the NDU organization. There was no evidence to support he was even a member of the NDU leadership, much less Malik Khalid's right-hand man or second in command. The Task Force figured if NDU was starting over with a nobody, it was possible Malik and his entire inner circle had in fact been killed off in the raid, and Samir Al-Bakr was simply an opportunistic con artist taking advantage of the power vacuum. Whomever Samir Al-Bakr was, the CIA was about to get to meet him in person.

Lori walked into Nick's office and closed the door. "I just received some interesting news from one of my sources at *The New York Times*," she said.

The task force had a couple dozen assets within a variety of media outlets such as *CNN* and *The New York Times* who kept their ear to the ground. If any NDU related info or chatter came across the news wires, they'd feed it back to Lori.

"It appears NDU has been reaching out to major Western media outlets," Lori said, handing Nick a single-page memo on the development. "They're offering semi-exclusive interviews with their new leader, our friend Samir Al-Bakr."

"Seriously?" Nick replied, intrigued as he scanned the paper.

"So far, we know they've made contact with editors at *CNN*, the *New York Times*, the *BBC*, and the *Washington Post*," Lori continued. "And I'm certain they've reached out to others. They plan to invite three correspondents to meet with Samir and the rest of the new NDU management in UAE next month during the three-day Economic Investment Summit in Dubai, which Samir will be attending as a special guest of His Highness Sheikh Mohammad Al-Rafid."

"The young crown prince of Dubai who was buddies with Malik Khalid," Nick added with a knowing smile.

"Bingo," Lori piped in. "The chosen correspondents will be granted a private interview with Samir and will also attend the summit's closing event, a black-tie gala held the final evening of the conference. Here's the catch: NDU is requiring written confirmation from the reporters' managing editors that the articles they write about Samir and NDU will run as cover stories in their respective publications. To top it off, they want final editing rights to the articles before they are published."

Nick rolled his eyes at the final editing rights demand.

"We know UAE is a hub for NDU's international weapons trafficking activities," Nick said, thinking out loud. "Which the UAE government claims are all legitimate business dealings. So, it makes sense that Al-Bakr would be heading there as soon as possible. He needs to forge his own relationship with UAE to ensure NDU can continue operating business-as-usual now that Malik is out of the picture."

"Makes sense," Lori said.

Nick had a feeling Al-Bakr was meeting with high-profile Western media outlets to kick off NDU's global PR campaign to build their new image as a legitimate organization. If NDU was able to muster enough positive momentum throughout the global media, they would soon be in a position to send a delegation to the U.S. and EU to request removal from the Foreign Terrorist Organization list.

"Do we know if any of the media outlets have offered to send a correspondent to UAE yet?" Nick asked Lori.

"According to my sources, they're all currently 'mulling it over' and haven't made any commitments yet."

"Think they'll give us an interview?" he quipped with a snort, but his sarcastic comment failed to illicit even a smirk from Lori. "What? It was a joke," he said defensively.

"It's actually not a bad idea," Lori replied thoughtfully. "What if we sent someone in posing as a journalist to interview Al-Bakr and gather intel directly from the source?"

"A CIA operative posing as a journalist to get close to a target," Nick snickered. "That's about the oldest fucking cliché in the book."

"Because it works."

Nick shook his head. "If a mission like that goes sideways, every major media outlet from here to fucking Bombay will be crawling up our asses demanding blood."

"Do you have any better ideas on how to get us alone in a room with Al-Bakr?" Lori replied, crossing her arms.

"Nope. I guess we'll go pitch this idea to the team," Nick said, rising out of his chair. "Then you can start packing for your trip to UAE," he added with a sardonic grin that sent the color draining from Lori's face. "Aw, what's the matter? Does it not sound like such a good idea anymore?" he asked teasingly.

"It's not that… I mean… I would…" Lori stuttered then paused and took a breath. "Nick, normally I'd jump all over this assignment but, well, I was going to tell you this week anyway."

"What Lori? Spit it out."

"I'm pregnant."

"Oh shit. I'm sorry, I didn't mean it like that. That was a good 'oh shit.' Uh, congratulations?"

"Thanks," Lori said with a half-smile. "But you can understand why I can't be traipsing off to the Middle East to meet with the leader of an international terrorist organization right now."

"Understood," Nick said with a sigh. "A female op would be best for this, but there's no way I'm sending Elora. She has zero field experience, and I don't think she's ready to handle something like this, especially with everything that's happened. I'm thinking Derek."

Lori nodded. "I agree. Derek's a good option."

Lori and Nick briefed the rest of the team on the recent developments. When Nick announced his decision to have Derek pose as the undercover journalist, Elora immediately spoke up in protest.

"Nick, send me," Elora said. "You know they'll be less suspicious of a female journalist and more likely to underestimate me."

"No way, Elora. I'm sorry, you're just not ready."

"I can do this, Nick. Please, let me do this," Elora pressed. "The fact that I have no field experience is an advantage—it's a lot less likely anyone at that summit will recognize me."

Nick contemplated Elora's words and recalled the realization he'd come to while sitting at Brendan's grave several weeks ago. Elora will never be free until she's done chasing ghosts. Perhaps sending her to UAE to meet those ghosts head-on would push her out of her current rut of depression. "All right, Elora, you can have this assignment," Nick said, surprising the rest of the team. "But I'm coming with you."

"Fair enough," Elora replied.

"Why don't we just have the UAE authorities nab Al-Bakr for us when he arrives?" Jason asked confused. "Then we can go there to question him and avoid this fake journalist song and dance altogether."

"Detain him on what charges? They can't hold him accountable for the crimes of his predecessor," Nick said. "And I hope you are aware we do not have an extradition treaty with UAE."

"Yes, I know that," Jason said defensively, "but I also know you have a good relationship with the Dubai Police Force Commander. Can't you call in a favor with him? He helped us out a lot last year when we were in Dubai collecting intel on NDU's business dealings in UAE."

"We aren't that tight," Nick said, shaking his head. "And even if he owed me his life, an op like that would be way beyond even his power to execute." Nick shifted his attention back to Lori. "Lori, what do we need to do to make the journalist plan work? You mentioned they're going to select correspondents from three outlets. How do we ensure Elora is one of the reporters they choose?"

"Of course, they're trying to land as big of fish as possible. To even have a shot, she'll need to pose as a senior correspondent with one of the major outlets like *The New York Times* or *Washington Post*," Lori explained. "We'll need to build an identity for her, get her fully credentialed and on the official payroll at the company, the whole nine yards. She'll need a completely developed backstory."

"We'll need a media outlet willing to play ball with all this," Nick interjected. "Which one do you have the most pull with, Lori?"

"The *Washington Post* will likely be the easiest to work with since they're local. I have fairly tight relationships with several of the managing editors over there."

"Okay, let's go with them. Derek, have the nerds downstairs start working up an alias and backstory for Elora."

The nerds were the several dozen computer hackers and SEO geniuses—most recruited directly out of MIT—who sat in the basement at Langley surrounded by massive mainframes. They could completely erase the identity and digital footprint of a person, or create an entirely new identity from scratch. They had the power to turn anyone into a viral sensation overnight, or make every online post, photo and video of Kylie Jenner disappear in a matter of hours.

"Be sure they put her in the system at one of the major Universities as a journalism graduate," Nick continued. "Lori, once they get Elora's alias identity established, we need the WaPo to start planting articles with her byline, including a few cover stories to give her more clout, we have less than six weeks to make a name for her. Also have them publish a string of post-dated online stories across their website dating back at least five to seven years. Most importantly, make sure we get copies of all the articles they publish under her name so she can study them. NDU will do their research—the last thing we need is Samir asking her about a story she wrote and her having no clue what the hell he's talking about."

"Lori, I want to help you, I do, but you know this kind of thing puts us in a shitty position." Lori was on a secure phone call with Grant Feinberg, deputy foreign editor at the *Washington Post*. Needless to say, Feinberg was less than enthusiastic about helping the CIA pose as one of their reporters. "Our correspondents are often accused of being spies and we bend over backwards trying to build trust and prove to the world that we don't have CIA agents hidden amongst our rosters. If your girl gets caught, it'll put all our journalists on foreign soil at risk. Shit like that takes months, sometimes years, for the heat to die down," Grant explained.

"I completely understand, Grant, but as you said, your

writers already deal with accusations of being spies every day anyway. Sometimes they are even captured and held prisoner by militant groups under these false charges. Do you know how many legitimate journalists, just in the last eighteen months, we in partnership with JSOC coordinated rescue missions for?"

Grant remained silent on the other end.

"Sixteen, Grant," Lori continued, answering her own question.

"Only one of those correspondents was ours," Grant countered.

"Well the next time one of your reporters ends up chained to a drainpipe outside a Taliban cave, I hope the CIA and JSOC will have the proper motivation to assist when you call begging us to mount a rescue op."

Grant audibly exhaled as he mulled it over.

"Look, I'm not going to say we require a quid pro quo every time we have to save the ass of a journalist. All we're asking for here is a simple favor between friends."

"You really know how to make it difficult to say no to you," Grant grumbled.

"Thank you, Grant, we appreciate it. Once you get the green light from the big boss, please get in touch with the contact from New Dawn Underground who reached out to you. Let them know one of your top Middle East correspondents, Elora Reid, will be happy to come to UAE and interview their new leader. Also, have your HR guys start work on her credentials and assign a couple of writers to pound out a couple dozen fabricated stories under the byline Elora Reid. I'll email you some headlines and story ideas; we need the articles slanted in a way that will appeal to

NDU. When they look through Elora's previous articles, we need them to get the impression she's someone who'll have a sympathetic view of their cause. As an overall theme, have them stick with content critical of the current Iraqi administration."

"Wait, so her alias is Elora Reid?" Grant asked confused. "Isn't her real name Elora?"

"Nick doesn't want to give her a full alias. This is her first field op so we're only changing her surname to mitigate blunders."

"I'm sorry, come again? Did you just say this is this chick's *first* field assignment?" Grant asked, dazed.

Lori hadn't even realized her flub. "Yeah, let's not mention that part to your boss," she suggested.

"Ya think?"

Chapter 5

Nick and Elora landed in UAE and headed for the Armani Hotel, which was conveniently located next-door to the venue hosting the economic summit. NDU had taken the bait the CIA had sprinkled across the web and printed pages of the *Washington Post* over the last few weeks and invited Elora to be one of three Western media correspondents to join them in Dubai and interview their new leader.

Elora had spent the last two weeks, including most of the thirteen-hour plane ride from D.C. to Dubai, studying her backstory and the articles she'd supposedly written for the *Washington Post*. Nick had spent the plane ride monitoring Elora, keeping an eye out for any sign that she wasn't prepared to handle the assignment ahead of her. She looked nervous but otherwise composed, and Nick knew she hadn't cut any corners in studying her backstory.

"You sure you're ready for this?" Nick asked her as they made their final descent into Dubai. "We can still back out. Call it off and hop the next flight back to D.C."

"No, I'm ready. The hardest part of this week is going to be restraining myself from stabbing Samir Al-Bakr in his fucking throat with my pen. Everything else will be a cakewalk."

Elora and Nick checked into separate rooms at the Armani Hotel under the names Elora Reid and Nathan Briggs. According to their cover story, Nathan was one of the WaPo's foreign desk editors. While checking in, the reservations agent handed Elora an envelope. Inside was an invitation for Elora and Nate to attend a meet-and-greet upstairs in the hotel's Sky Lounge on the 122nd floor at 8:00 p.m. for a formal introduction to Samir Al-Bakr. Elora and Nick settled into their rooms and freshened up.

Elora stared at her reflection in the hotel room's bathroom mirror. She'd changed into a professional pencil-skirt business suit with black heels, touched-up her makeup, and ran a brush through her hair. Reaching into her purse, she pulled out a white gold necklace with a heart-shaped charm outlined in alternating diamonds and emeralds. The necklace had been a Valentine's Day gift from Brendan—the last gift he'd given her. She put the necklace on and gave herself one final look-over in the mirror, then took a deep breath. "I'm going to nail these assholes to the wall for you, Brendan," she said to her reflection. "Let's do this."

Elora and Nick stepped into the hotel's Sky Lounge, scanned the room for the NDU group, and were soon approached by the lounge hostess.

"Miss Elora Reid?" the hostess asked in Arabic-accented English.

"Uh, yes, that's me," Elora replied.

"Your party is waiting out on the private terrace. Please follow me."

Elora and Nick exchanged glances, then fell in step behind the hostess, who led them toward a bank of glass doors on the far side of the lounge. The trio stepped out into the warm evening air, and Elora was instantly captivated by the spectacular view the open-air terrace offered of Dubai's glittering nighttime skyline. The hostess led them to the far corner of the terrace where eight men were seated around a large, semi-cordoned off table overlooking the incredible view. Elora and Nick immediately recognized Samir Al-Bakr from his video, which they'd each watched more than a hundred times, and Elora's pulse began to race. *Showtime.*

Samir and the two men seated on either side of him stood up from the table when they saw the hostess approaching with Nick and Elora in tow. All three men wore expensive Western-style business suits, similar to the suit Samir had been wearing in the video. The other men at the table were dressed less formally, wearing matching black, collarless blazers and dark gray slacks—the NDU security detail. Elora halted a few feet from the table and forced a smile, her gaze rigidly fixed on Samir Al-Bakr.

"Welcome! You must be Ms. Reid and Mr. Briggs," the man to Samir's right said in English coated with a thick Arabic accent. "My name is Nawar. I am Mr. Al-Bakr's personal translator. Allow me to introduce Mr. Samir Al-Bakr, leader of the New Dawn Underground organization and political party in Iraq and CEO of the organization's corporate sector."

Don't forget militant terrorist group leader, Elora added bitterly in her head.

"It's an honor, sir," Elora said in her best schmoozing tone. Though she was nearly fluent in Arabic, she was not about to offer that information to NDU and spoke through the translator.

Aware of the Islamic custom of men not shaking hands with women, Elora did not offer her hand and waited for Samir to take the lead. To her surprise, Samir did not hesitate in offering his hand for her to shake.

"Nathan Briggs, foreign editor, *Washington Post*," Nick said, extending his hand to Samir once he'd released Elora's. The two shook and then Nawar shifted his attention to the man on Samir's left.

"And this is Mr. Al-Bakr's chief of staff and head of security, Zaidan Al-Sadiq."

Elora pivoted to greet Samir's chief of staff and was instantly struck by Zaidan's electric green eyes, which were boring into her. This man wasn't looking at her, he was looking *into* her, and Elora was immediately nervous and uncomfortable. "Very nice to meet you," she said, but again, waited for Zaidan to extend his hand out first. He greeted her with a simple *Salam Alaikam* and offered a handshake without hesitation. Zaidan looked to be in his early thirties and stood a couple of inches taller than Samir, which put him right at about six feet tall. Body analysis conducted on Samir's video had estimated him to be five foot nine to five foot ten, which Elora, now seeing Samir in person, could confirm as accurate. Zaidan had a slender but athletic build and was a tad bulkier than Samir. His angular face, cat-like jade eyes, and light scruff of beard reminded Elora of the brooding French male models in cologne ads.

"Please, have a seat," Nawar said, gesturing for Nick and Elora to sit across the table from Samir and Zaidan.

"I wanted to start off by thanking you for inviting us out and offering this exclusive interview," Elora said to Samir as she took her seat. "I know you had a long list of reporters to choose from. I'm honored I made the shortlist."

Nawar translated Elora's statement into Arabic for Samir and Zaidan.

"Of course, it is our pleasure," Samir replied in Arabic.

"But your work is what earned you this opportunity. We were especially impressed by a feature you wrote back in 2008 bringing attention to the Iranian support of many high-ranking Iraqi government officials. Your analysis regarding the negative ramifications of this influence was spot on. What was the title of that article again?"

"Tehran's Master of Puppets pulling the strings in Baghdad," she rattled off without hesitation as soon as Nawar translated the question. The question was a test and she knew it. Luckily, she'd studied the fake article for several hours and vividly recalled the title (a play on a popular song by the heavy metal band Metallica) as she thought it was clever.

"Ah, yes - that was it. Shame that piece didn't garner more attention than it did," Samir added.

Well, that article was written three weeks ago and planted for you to find, so.... But Elora kept this thought to herself and responded with a simple, "Thank you, I'm honored you appreciate my work."

A cocktail waitress delivered two trays of traditional Arab appetizer to the table and asked if anyone would like to order drinks. Wanting to follow their hosts' lead, Nick gestured for Samir to order first. Samir ordered *Arak*, a popular Mid-Eastern alcoholic drink made from fermented dates, while Zaidan asked for a scotch on the rocks. The translator, Nawar, simply requested some water. So much for the Islamic law forbidding the consumption of alcohol. Nick followed suit and ordered a rum & coke, and Elora ordered an Amaretto Sour.

After the waitress departed, Samir addressed Elora and Nick again in Arabic. Although Samir was heading up the meeting, Elora couldn't help but keep half her attention on his chief of staff. Zaidan never broke his stony gaze on Elora and Nick, studying the pair with an intensity that even made Nick shift back and forth in his seat. Elora sensed her every move and expression were being analyzed.

"Our purpose for this mass media outreach is to get word across the Western world that New Dawn Underground is no longer merely a rogue militant group," Samir said through Nawar. "We are growing, we are organized, we are not funded by or reliant on any foreign power and, above all, we are passionate about making a truly positive difference in the lives of our fellow Iraqis."

The waitress returned with the group's drinks and placed them around the table. Elora waited for the waitress to leave before she spoke.

"And part of your plan includes murdering U.S. Ambassadors? In addition to other Americans?" Elora asked in a combative tone.

"The death of Ambassador Casey was…unfortunate," Samir replied with a hint of remorse. "But, as you well know, the U.S installed and continues to support an incompetent Iraqi government that is a puppet of Tehran. We cannot promise the safety of U.S. troops or officials caught between the corrupt Iraqi regime and our quest for liberty."

"Just so we're clear, I will not be swayed to slant any of my opinions or conclusions in the article I write," Elora explained. "I won't compromise my journalistic integrity to paint you or New Dawn Underground in any sort of positive light if that's not what I believe. I intend to write the truth about you and NDU as I see it."

"We fully support you in this," Samir replied after Nawar translated Elora's comments. "And we look forward to showing you this truth. Now, if you'll please excuse me, I have another engagement I must attend to. I leave my chief of staff here to go over the weekend itinerary and answer any questions you may have. Please enjoy your choice of anything from the menu with our compliments. Likewise, for the duration of your stay here at the hotel, feel free to charge anything you desire to your rooms, and we will take care of it. It was a pleasure to meet you, Ms. Reid."

Samir and the five members of his security detail departed, leaving Elora and Nick alone with Zaidan and the translator.

The foursome sat for a moment in awkward silence as Zaidan stared at Elora and sipped his Johnnie Walker. Elora returned his glare, refusing to break eye contact; she got the sense she was in a psychological game of chicken. Nick and Nawar bounced their glances back and forth between Elora and Zaidan as if they were watching a tennis match, waiting for someone to break point.

Finally, Zaidan spoke, bursting the tension in the air like a giant balloon. "Your necklace is very beautiful," he commented casually in Arabic and took a sip of his scotch.

Without thinking, Elora instinctively reached up and brushed her fingertips across her necklace—*well before* Nawar had translated Zaidan's comment.

Elora realized her mistake, but it was too late. *Fuck.*

Nick caught the flub too.

"Ugh, thank you," Elora replied in English, trying to roll past her blunder.

"*Alafu*," Zaidan replied with a sly smile.

"He says, 'You're welcome,'" Nawar translated.

Elora rolled her eyes. "May we go over the itinerary now, please?" she asked, trying to move things along. "It's been a long day."

"Yes of course," Zaidan replied and opened a zippered portfolio case sitting in front of him on the table. He pulled out two printed sheets of paper and handed one each to Elora and Nick. He summarized the itinerary as Nick and Elora studied the sheets. "You have the day free tomorrow to attend the various summit activities or explore the city, if you like. The following day, please report to Mr. Al-Bakr's penthouse presidential suite here in the hotel at eleven a.m. to conduct your interview. The suite number is noted there at the bottom of your sheet, along with a special code you will need for the hotel elevator to access the penthouse floor. For security reasons, that code will not be active until fifteen minutes before your interview time and will expire one hour later. On the final day of the summit, we invite you and the other journalists to attend the end-of-summit black-tie gala in the ballroom at eight p.m. as guests at our VIP table. A badge granting you access to the VIP section at the gala will be delivered to your room prior to the event."

Zaidan pulled two more printed sheets of paper from his case and again passed them to Elora and Nick. He began explaining in Arabic while Nawar translated. "You will have thirty minutes to speak exclusively with Mr. Al-Bakr. On the front of this sheet is a list of approved questions you may ask him. On the back are instructions on how to submit your article to us for review prior to publication. You will need you to sign this sheet, and I will provide you with copies."

Elora nearly fell off her chair. "You're fucking kidding, right?"

Nawar's face went blank as he contemplated how to translate Elora's colorful question. While Nawar hesitated, Elora continued ahead of him.

"Perhaps before you set your sights on delivering the Iraqi people from their current tyrannical regime, you should Google the phrase '*a free and fair press*,'" she said narrowing her eyes at Zaidan. "You don't hand a journalist a list of *approved questions*, in addition to all these other ridiculous stipulations; you're insane. Did the other journalists you flew out here agree to this bullshit?"

Nick didn't even try to counter Elora's outburst. The situation had already digressed beyond anything he'd be able to save, so he began prepping mentally for an early departure from UAE.

"You either agree to these terms or there will be no interview," Zaidan replied flatly once Nawar had figured out a way to sugarcoat Elora's last statement.

"Then there's no interview, and I'll gladly catch the next flight back to the U.S.," she bluffed.

Zaidan leaned back in his chair and studied Elora's expression as he weighed his options. "How about a compromise?" Zaidan offered after several tense seconds. "You may ask any questions you like during the interview, but we still get final review of the article before it goes to print. If we aren't happy with it, it doesn't get published."

"Still bullshit," Elora declared. Nick gave her a swift jab to the leg beneath the table with his toe. "But okay," she added quickly, muffling a grunt elicited by Nick's kick. Zaidan tipped his head and lifted his glass in salute to their agreement. "I'm still not signing this, though," Elora clarified, waving the question list in the air.

"No need," he said with a smirk. "I fully trust your *journalistic integrity* will not allow you to go back on our agreement."

Nick and Elora strolled along the pedestrian walkway that circles around the giant Dubai Fountain across from the hotel. They didn't trust speaking anywhere inside the hotel and decided it would be at least a bit more secure to talk outside.

"Did you pick up on anything the translator didn't convey last night?" Nick asked Elora.

She shook her head. "He pretty much gave us what was said word-for-word. Of course, after I made that serious fuck-up when Zaidan complimented my necklace, they knew better than to say anything compromising," she said, rolling her eyes.

"Don't be so hard on yourself—you did well last night."

"It was an amateur mistake that I shouldn't have made," Elora said, brushing off Nick's attempt to console her. "It was fucking stupid."

"The translator didn't even notice."

"Zaidan noticed," Elora said.

"Yeah, well, I don't think much gets past that guy," Nick

admitted with a sigh. “He’s pretty fucking intense, but being chief of staff and head of security for an international terrorist organization takes a unique level of intensity. Derek is already working on pulling up anything he can on Zaidan. My gut tells me this guy isn’t a new NDU hire.”

“I agree. I have a feeling Zaidan and Samir both know the truth about what became of Malik. If he is still alive, I’d bet a lot of money those two know where he is,” Elora speculated. “Hell, I’m still not convinced Samir isn’t Malik himself.”

“Well, in less than 24 hours you get to sit down one-on-one with Samir and ask him *anything* you want,” Nick said with a wink. “Stick to the interview questions the Task Force came up with, and make sure he lets you record the meeting. We should be able to infer a lot by analyzing his responses and tone when he answers those questions.”

“You think Zaidan will be there with Samir during the interview?” Elora asked.

“Zaidan’s probably with Samir every time he takes a shit – I’d plan on him being there if I were you.”

“Do you buy Samir’s bullshit about wanting to better Iraq?”

“I think it’s possible he believes it. Even Saddam had himself convinced he was doing what was best for the Iraqi people too. I guess it all depends on your perspective.”

Elora and Nick took a seat on a bench overlooking the water and sat in silence for several moments, taking in the view. Across the waters of the massive fountain, they gazed at the modern mirrored skyscrapers that defined Dubai’s skyline. A city that only in the last two decades seemed to rise from the desert floor and burst into incredible life. A city still very much under construction and growing by magnificent leaps and bounds. A city in one of the few Mid-Eastern countries that had managed to get their shit together.

"Do you want to head back to the hotel and do some more role-playing, or do you think you're ready for the interview tomorrow?" Nick asked, breaking the silence.

"I think I'm ready. Then again, I felt pretty confident going into last night's meeting, and I fucked that up, so who knows."

"Oh, come on, cut yourself some slack, You didn't fuck it up. You did great."

"Thanks Nick."

"Do you want me to be there with you tomorrow?"

"No, I'm hoping if I'm there alone, they'll think of me as more vulnerable, and it will encourage them to relax their guard, perhaps be a bit looser-lipped."

"God, I don't like the idea of sending you alone in there with them, but you're right."

"Thanks for offering anyway," she added, "and thank you for being such an amazing support and friend throughout...well, everything. I don't know how I'd make it through all this without you."

"Brendan was my friend. Looking after you is the least I can do," Nick said, leaning closer to Elora. "But I don't do it solely out of a sense of duty to him, I do it because you're my friend too and someone I care about."

Elora lifted her eyes and met Nick's gaze. His blue eyes sparkled in the desert sun and, though Elora knew what was coming next, she was still caught off guard. Nick leaned in and pressed his lips to hers. She quickly jerked back, breaking their brief kiss. "Nick, I can't," she whispered, looking down, afraid to meet his eyes again. "I'm sorry. I'm just...not ready. Please, don't hate me."

"No, no I'm the one who should apologize," Nick said, backpedaling. "I completely understand, it's too soon. I shouldn't have pushed you."

"You've been so wonderful these last few months," Elora said, trying to smooth things over. "I don't know where I'd be right now without you. I don't want to do anything to ruin what we have. I don't think I'd survive without your friendship right now, so doing something that could jeopardize that scares me to death. Just, give me a little time?"

"Of course, I'm not going anywhere."

Nick had been her rock since she lost Brendan, but Elora knew that her feelings for him would likely never progress beyond friendship. She felt guilty for giving him hope and berated herself for being such a coward.

Chapter 6

Elora looked at her watch; it was 10:48 a.m. The special elevator code Zaidan had given her to access the penthouse floor should now be active. She boarded the elevator and punched the code into the small keypad next to the main floor button panel. The elevator made a unique *ding!* and climbed to the penthouse level. The doors opened and Elora emerged out into a hallway, thankful the elevator did not open directly into the suite like many hotel penthouses. She followed the hallway around a corner to a pair of massive double doors with two men posted outside. Elora immediately recognized them as two of the NDU security guards who'd been present at her first meeting with Samir and Zaidan at the Sky Lounge.

The security guards tipped their heads at Elora and opened the door to the suite for her to enter. Elora walked into the suite's foyer and continued to a large living area where two white sofas faced each other with a glass coffee table between. Samir sat on one of the sofas, while Zaidan and the translator sat in armchairs on either side of the sofas. The couch across from Samir's was empty, and the coffee table between the two held several bottles of water and four drinking glasses.

Samir, Zaidan, and Nawar all rose from their seats to greet Elora as she entered the room.

"Ah, *marhaba*," Samir greeted Elora.

"Welcome, Ms. Reid, please make yourself comfortable,"

Nawar translated, gesturing for Elora to have a seat on the sofa across from Samir. "The staff has taken the liberty in providing us with some water. Is there anything else you would like or prefer to drink?"

"No thank you, water will be fine," Elora replied as casually as possible. She glanced over at Zaidan, who did not utter a word. After Elora took her seat on the couch, Zaidan resumed his seat in the armchair, crossing one leg over his knee and propping his right elbow on the arm of the chair with his hand under his chin. He stared expressionless at Elora, his piercing eyes slightly narrowed, as if she were a painting hanging in the Louvre.

Elora reached into her bag and pulled out a notebook, pen, and her smartphone. "Does anyone mind if I record this interview?" she asked.

"No, of course not," Samir replied.

Elora engaged her phone's audio recording app and set the phone on the coffee table between her and Samir.

"So, let's dive right in, shall we?" Elora proclaimed, trying to break the ice. *Mr. Al-Bakr, why did one of NDU's maggot fighters shoot my fiancé in the throat?* Suppressing her fantasy question, Elora decided to open with a more diplomatic one. "Mr. Al-Bakr, in a nutshell, what is it you want the world to know about New Dawn Underground?"

Samir smiled. Zaidan did not. "Your question is rather…broad," Samir replied.

Elora made no offer to withdraw or reword her opening question and waited for Samir to respond.

Realizing he was going to have to tackle the question as it was asked, Samir wrinkled his forehead and contemplated his response. “What we want the world to know is quite simple. We desire peace and prosperity for Iraq and the Iraqi people. Our country sits on trillions of dollars’ worth of oil and other natural resources, but the Iraqi people haven’t seen a single significant improvement in the nation’s infrastructure, social services, or economy. Yet many of the politicians at the head of the government, like our prime minister, have become millionaires over the last decade. A revolution is long overdue, and we plan to light the fires of that revolution in Iraq.”

As Nawar finished translating Samir’s response, Elora scribbled some quick notes on her notepad, then asked her next question.

“You’ve specifically asked for your message to be disseminated across the Western world. Why? What is it you’re hoping to gain from this international publicity?”

“New Dawn Underground remains listed as a designated terrorist organization by the U.S. as well as several nations of the European Union. This negatively impacts our ability to carry out a legitimate and peaceful revolution in Iraq. Malik Khalid is dead, and we buried his radical ideals and violent methods with him. We want the Western world to understand that we do not consider them our enemy, so long as they stay out of Iraq and do not meddle in our affairs. The same goes for our neighbor to the east. An overwhelming majority of the high-ranking politicians at the head of the Iraqi government right now are Iranian loyalists; Tehran has influence in nearly every aspect of our government. They use this influence to siphon our resources and enrich themselves while impoverishing the Iraqi people, and their tyranny does not stop there. As we speak, Tehran’s Republican Guard troops, commanded by Iranian General Ali Ansari, are patrolling Baghdad under the guise of maintaining security when, in fact, they are an invading force with the sole purpose of protecting Iranian assets and interests in Iraq to maintain the flow of money to Tehran. They bolster their forces and disguise their presence by absorbing local Iraqi militias, who they support and fund, into their ranks. With a decimated economy leaving young men few options to feed themselves and their families, they are all but forced to join the militias General Ansari commands in exchange for a steady paycheck. Our wishes are simple: we want foreign occupiers, including U.S. troops as well as General Ali Ansari and his Iranian goons, expelled from our country."

"Though all of this sounds quite noble, New Dawn Underground has been designated a terrorist organization for good reason," Elora challenged. "You say you've changed your violent ways, but what about the illegal international 'business' dealings you continue to engage in? The weapons trafficking, money laundering, dark web transactions, drug trafficking, there are even accusations of human trafficking... The list goes on."

"As you say in America, innocent until proven guilty," Samir replied through his translator. "What court of law has convicted us of any of these alleged crimes?"

"Okay, fine," Elora replied through semi-clenched teeth. "Let's talk about the crimes NDU has *openly* admitted to. Do you condone the string of coordinated bombings Malik Khalid orchestrated across Baghdad last year that claimed the lives of several Americans, including our Ambassador, Richard Casey?"

Samir's face shifted to a solemn expression as Nawar translated Elora's question. "New Dawn Underground has never acted offensively, only defensively. We only use violence against those who attack us or exploit our land and people. The bombings across Baghdad last year were in response to General Ali Ansari's unprovoked attacks on our militia and supporters in northern Iraq. NDU operates security checkpoints along the Syrian border that help quell the flow of foreign Jihadists entering Iraq. Our militia has been the only force successful in reducing the inflow of these extremists—far more effective than the Iraqi Army or any other official government force. Yet the Iraqi Central Government labeled our militia members terrorists and demanded Malik and his men pledge fealty to General Ansari or face harsh consequences. Malik told General Ansari, pardon my language, ma'am, to go fuck himself. In response, General Ansari attacked our checkpoints, killing dozens of our militia members. He then proceeded to march his goons through several villages in our territory and burned schools and hospitals to the ground in an attempt to persuade civilians to abandon support for NDU by terrorizing them. So, Malik retaliated in the form of the Baghdad bombings."

"And how is it you came to take Malik's place after his death?" Elora asked. "What exactly is your history with Malik Khalid?"

"Malik and I were schoolmates in Baghdad. We met when we were fourteen. I'd recently moved to the area and was being pushed around by some bullies in the schoolyard one morning when Malik stepped in and stood up for me," Samir recalled with a fond smile. "I suffered from a stutter when I was younger, so several of the other boys were making fun of me because of the way I talked. Malik beat the shit out of them, four boys all larger than himself, and never broke a sweat—it was incredible. I stuck by his side from that day forward and we became like brothers."

"Until the end?" Elora asked, narrowing her eyes in suspicion. "Were you at the NDU compound with Malik the night of the U.S. Special Forces raid this past March?"

Samir shifted on his sofa. "No, I was not there the night of the American attack. I was in Mosul attending to some NDU business. Under Malik, my main responsibility in the NDU organization was to oversee our foreign and domestic business dealings. I graduated from the University of Baghdad with a master's degree in economics. I focused on the business side of things, while Malik focused on the militant and political side. He was always a fighter, he grew up without a father so, like me, he was a target for bullies too. He was simply much better than me at developing street fighting skills," he added with a chuckle. "His father was killed in a U.S. airstrike during the first Gulf War when Malik was only ten years old. This made him responsible for taking care of his mom and baby sister. Sadly, the tragedies in Malik's life did not stop there. In 2003 his mother and sister were killed by U.S. Marines in Mosul. So, you can understand why Malik harbored vengeful thoughts toward the U.S.—his heart was twisted by tragedy. After he died, I wanted to continue Malik's work in a more legitimate and peaceful manner. But Malik was my friend and, at his core, he was a good person, albeit misguided in some respects."

"So, Malik was, in fact, killed in the compound explosion?" Elora asked.

"Yes, of course," Samir replied with a befuddled look. "His body was found among those in the tunnel bunker beneath the compound."

"Well, several bodies were found," Elora clarified, "but there is no conclusive DNA or other evidence to confirm any of those bodies were Malik Khalid. It is still speculated by many that Malik Khalid faked his death."

Samir smiled at Elora as if she were a naïve child. "Ms. Reid, I find it hard to believe that a distinguished journalist of your stature would be led down a rabbit hole of rumor and speculation," he said in a chiding tone.

"I have several *very* reliable sources who stand by this theory," Elora countered, staring him down.

"It is no doubt you are an excellent journalist," Samir replied, resuming his sugar-coated tone. "After all, this is why we asked you here to Dubai." Samir clapped his hands together and stood up from the couch. "Unfortunately, our time together is now up," he said cordially. "I have a meeting downtown I must now depart for. Again, I'd like to express my appreciation for you traveling all the way here from Washington D.C. I look forward to seeing you tomorrow evening at the gala, and I very much look forward to reading your article. I have every confidence it will be nothing short of groundbreaking."

Elora flashed a broad smile and raised her eyebrows. "Oh, you bet," she replied, trying desperately to disguise the cynicism in her voice.

Departing the penthouse following her interview with Samir, Elora rode the elevator down to the lobby and exited the hotel. She and Nick had planned to meet in front of the Dubai Opera House, not far from the hotel, to discuss how the interview went. When she reached the Opera House, she found Nick already there waiting for her.

"Hey, you," Nick said, bringing her in for a hug. "So, how did it go?"

"Ugh, I feel like I need a shower," Elora replied, scrunching her face up in disgust. "That guy is a fucking slime ball."

"Samir? What did he do? He better not have fucking touched you."

"No, nothing like that," Elora said, shaking her head. "He was polite and professional, but…I don't know. I can't explain it, Nick. Deep down I know something is off," she said with frustration. "He's fucking lying about something…or, everything."

"Did he answer all the interview questions? Do you think you got some valuable info the team can run with?"

"He did, plus he gave up some personal info about Malik, and his and Malik's history."

"That's great!"

"He swears Malik died in the raid, but my gut still tells me Malik is alive and that Samir knows where he is. When we get back to Langley and go over the recording with a fine-toothed comb, hopefully we'll be able to connect some dots and put together a few leads."

"Was Zaidan there?"

"Yes," Elora replied with an eye roll. "Zaidan and his silent judging stare."

"Did he comment or answer any questions?"

"He didn't say a single word. He's like a big black cloud. All he does is hover and keep you wondering when a massive bolt of lightning is going to strike you down. That dude gives me the fucking creeps."

"Well, after the gala tomorrow night, hopefully you won't have to deal with either him or Samir ever again."

"We've got what we need. I wish we could go home right now."

"Me too, but that'll be a surefire way to burn any bridges we may need in the future, or even blow our cover completely."

"Yeah, I know," Elora said dejectedly.

"But I guess we have the rest of today and tomorrow up until the gala free," Nick said, slipping into a more cheerful tone. "This is your first time in Dubai, isn't it? You want to go exploring? You haven't lived until you've Lawrence-of-Arabia'd it on a camel across some real sand dunes," he said with a cheesy grin.

Elora laughed in spite of herself. "As much as I'd love to ride camels across the desert with you, I think I'm going to hole up in my room and get a jump-start on writing this NDU article. The WaPo Editor needs it at least forty-eight hours before we want it published. Plus, of course, it has to get a stamp of approval from *Mr. Creepy* first."

"Don't waste your time on that article. When we get back to Langley send a copy of the interview recording down to the nerds, and they'll pound it out in a lunch break."

"No, I have to be the one to write this one. If it's not written by me, they'll know. *He* will know," she added, referring to Zaidan. "Like you said, we don't want to burn any bridges in case we need to employ this ruse with them again."

Chapter 7

Elora sat at the small desk in her hotel room reviewing Samir's interview recording for what felt like the hundredth time, when she was interrupted by a knock on the door. She looked over her shoulder just in time to see an envelope slide in beneath her door. She padded over and scooped it off the floor. The envelope was from the hotel's stationary and had *Ms. Elora Reid* written on the front. Inside she found her VIP badge for that evening's gala with a short, handwritten note:

Dearest Ms. Reid,

The honour of your presence is requested at the Presidential Suite this evening at 6:30 p.m. for a pre-gala reception with drinks and hors d'oeuvres.

Sincerely,
Zaidan Al-Sadiq
Chief of Staff, New Dawn Underground
Elevator Code: 84639

Elora stuffed the note back in the envelope and immediately headed down the hall to knock on Nick's door. His face lit up when he answered and found Elora. "Hey! Everything okay?" he asked, stepping aside so Elora could enter.

"Yeah, everything's fine. I was just curious if you'd received your VIP gala badge yet?"

"It was dropped off a few minutes ago. Why?"

"Did it happen to come with an invitation to attend a reception NDU is hosting in their suite before the gala?" Elora asked as she pulled the folded paper from her envelope and passed it to Nick. "My badge came with this note."

"Nope, I didn't get any secret notes. How rude," he said, feigning offense as he scanned the note. "I think Mr. Creepy has a crush on you. You must have really made an impression at that interview."

Elora curled her lip in disgust and snatched the note back from Nick.

"If you're not comfortable going, just politely decline," Nick suggested. "Or, if you want, I can go with you; but, again, going on your own may get you further. Though it appears you may have already gotten further than you realize," he added with a sly wink.

"You can shut up now."

"Oh, come on, I'm just messing with you. Bottom line, don't do anything you're not comfortable with, and you know I'm here to support you one hundred percent—whatever you decide to do."

Elora bit her lip and stared at Nick for a moment as she mulled over her options. "Well, I guess I better go start getting ready."

"You sure?"

"I'll be fine," Elora said and slipped back down the hall to her room.

At 6:45 p.m. Elora inspected herself in the full-length mirror hanging beside her hotel room closet. She was wearing a long, one-shouldered, dark green evening gown that hugged her figure. The shade of the dress matched the emerald stones in her necklace from Brendan. Her hair was pinned up in a French twist with a few loose strands dangling around her face. She reached up and touched her necklace, giving it a few soft strokes for luck as she closed her eyes and thought of Brendan.

Spinning around, Elora grabbed her small clutch purse from off the bed and slid a pack of Marlboro menthol cigarettes and a lighter inside. She wasn't an addicted smoker but used smoke breaks as an excuse to escape awkward social settings. She wasn't a people person and despised large crowds.

Elora punched the new code from the invitation into the elevator keypad and once again rode up to the Penthouse floor. As she approached the suite, the two NDU security guards posted outside again nodded to her and opened the door.

As she stepped into the Presidential Suite foyer, she was expecting a lively scene with sounds of conversation, clanking dishes, and perhaps some music, but the suite was dead silent. She halted in her tracks, her forehead wrinkling in confusion. She popped open her clutch and fished out Zaidan's invitation, checking to ensure she had the time and location correct—she did. She shoved the note back into her purse and crept to the end of the foyer, peeking around the corner to see into the suite's large living room area. It was empty. Elora cleared her throat as loudly as possible. "Hello?" she called out in an unsure tone. "Excuse me, anyone here?"

Within seconds, Zaidan emerged from the small study off the living room. "Ah, Ms. Reid, welcome. Please come in and have a seat," Zaidan announced, in nearly perfect English with a hint of a British accent. His sudden command of the English language took Elora by surprise, but she quickly recovered and took a seat on the same white sofa she'd sat on the day before while interviewing Samir. The coffee table in front of her held several platters with traditional Arab appetizers. *This must be the hors d'oeuvres promised in the invitation.*

"Would you care for a drink?" Zaidan asked as he strolled over to the room's stocked wet bar. "Amaretto Sour, correct?"

"Uh, yes...please," she replied. He remembered what she'd ordered in the Sky Lounge the night they met.

Zaidan mixed Elora's drink and then poured a scotch on the rocks for himself while Elora watched. Since she'd mainly focused her attention on Samir the other times she'd been in Zaidan's presence, this was the first time she'd had a chance to observe him without distraction. He was wearing black suit pants and a white dress shirt with the sleeves rolled up to the elbows. The top couple buttons of his shirt were open, revealing a smooth, defined chest below. She had to admit, Mr. Creepy was attractive.

"Where is everyone else?" Elora asked, glancing around the room to force herself to stop staring at Zaidan.

"Everyone else?"

"I was under the impression this was a get-together for all the journalists you'd invited to Dubai?"

"No, I only asked you here tonight," he replied plainly.

"Oh, okay," Elora said with a twinge of uneasiness in her voice. "Will Mr. Al-Bakr be joining us?"

"No, he is out." Period, end of sentence.

Zaidan finished preparing the drinks and approached Elora with one in each hand.

"Your drink, madam," he said, handing Elora her Amaretto Sour. "You look lovely, by the way."

"Thank you," she replied curtly as she lifted her eyes to meet his. Zaidan's hypnotic eyes instantly pulled her in and Elora's breath caught in her throat. *Okay, so he's* more *than attractive.*

Zaidan flashed her a seductive sideways smile, and Elora's cheeks flamed. *Aw, fuck.*

"Your English is very good," Elora said, raising her eyebrows, trying to move past the moment she and Zaidan just had.

"And your Arabic is, at least, decent," Zaidan replied, slipping into Arabic as he took a seat on the sofa across from Elora.

"Excuse me?" Elora wrinkled her forehead in feigned confusion.

Zaidan took a sip of his scotch as he leaned back in his seat, keeping his eyes fixed on Elora. "You gave that little secret away when I complimented your necklace the night we met," he said, switching back to English. "But you're already well aware of your slip-up and the fact that I caught it, so let's just fast-forward past all this, shall we?" Elora looked down at her hands and blushed. "I see you're wearing the same necklace again tonight," Zaidan commented. "Someone special gave it to you." It was a half question, half statement.

"Yes," she replied, but did not elaborate beyond her one-word answer.

"Your editor, Mr. Briggs perhaps?" Zaidan pressed.

"No," she declared firmly.

"My misunderstanding. I was under the impression you two were…involved."

"No, we're colleagues...and friends," Elora clarified, looking Zaidan in the eyes. "He's with me on this trip strictly for professional support."

Zaidan flicked his eyebrows up in an unconvinced expression.

Elora racked her brain, trying to recall if she'd made any gestures or said anything about Nick in her few encounters with Zaidan to give him his false impression. Then she remembered Nick's attempt to kiss her on the bench out by the fountain, and it dawned on her. "I'm sorry, have you been following me!"

"I'm sure you understand how diligent we have to be when it comes to security," he replied coolly.

Elora rolled her eyes. His NDU watchdogs had been keeping an eye on her. "Okay, my turn to ask some questions," she said, narrowing her gaze. "Where did you learn English?"

"American movies mostly, lots of bootlegged cinematic treasures."

"Ah, I see. What were some of your favorites?"

"I watched Mel Gibson's *Braveheart* at least a hundred times." He paused to take a sip of his scotch. "It was my favorite until *Gladiator* with Russell Crowe came out."

"Quite similar characters, those two," Elora said, recalling her memories of the two movies. "Both warriors fighting against oppressive, tyrannical regimes," she said, cocking her head to the side. "Is that what you see yourself as, Mr. Al-Sadiq? The Iraqi William Wallace?" she asked with a touch of sarcasm.

"If a woman says she likes the movie *Pretty Woman,* do you immediately assume she aspires to be a prostitute?" he replied straight-faced.

"Touché," Elora conceded. "But your level of fluency didn't come from just watching movies."

"I also studied English in college. I majored in Political Science, and many of the courses are taught in English. Those who couldn't keep up took supplemental English language classes. Which is where I met Samir—we were both in the same night class. Many of his economics courses were in English, so he and I were, as you say, in the same boat."

"Wait, Samir speaks English too?"

"Of course," Zaidan replied with a smirk. "We are not all ignorant sand-heathens in Iraq."

"No, of course not."

"So, I was wrong about you and Mr. Briggs. I wonder what else I may be wrong about regarding you," Zaidan commented, arching an eyebrow.

"Well, I'm not here to talk about myself," she replied, shutting down further probing into her personal details and background.

"You're right, let's talk business then. Have you started writing our article?" he asked, slipping into a commanding professional tone.

"I've broken ground on it, yes."

"I very much look forward to reading it."

"Oh, I'm sure. I can't wait to see your suggestions."

"I assure you, our needing to review it before it's published is merely a formality," he said. "I'm confident there will be little, if any, changes needed."

"Right, whatever."

"The reason I invited you here tonight was to let you in on

an idea Mr. Al-Bakr is exploring," Zaidan said, shifting the subject. "Should this initial venture into Western PR prove beneficial to NDU's cause, the next step is to invite a correspondent to join us in Iraq. We want to bring someone in to see firsthand what we're doing on the ground and write about it," Zaidan explained. "We want the Western world to see the positive impacts NDU is having in the daily lives of the average Iraqi citizen in the areas we currently control."

"So, this is a job interview? Are you trying to put together your own little Western PR team?"

"We simply want to make it clear to the West that we're prepared to be completely transparent regarding our activities and operations," Zaidan said.

"Cut the bullshit. You don't care what the western world thinks. You're just desperate to get off the FTO list," Elora said, cutting her eyes at Zaidan.

"You definitely have no inhibitions when it comes to being direct, do you?" he commented with a slight chuckle. "But you are correct; being on the U.S.'s list of Foreign Terrorist Organizations has adverse effects on our international business operations," he admitted. "We hope to begin lobbying efforts soon to be removed from both the U.S. and UN Foreign Terrorist lists."

"So, this all comes down to money."

"Doesn't almost everything in this world?"

"And you're considering inviting me to come review your operation in Iraq?" Elora asked.

"You're on our shortlist, yes."

Elora tried to stifle a snort but failed. "I find it hard to believe there is anyone else on your shortlist that's been as openly defiant and critical of your organization as I have been. How is it you're even considering me for this embed?"

"I would never trust this assignment to a journalist with no backbone who doesn't ask the hard-hitting questions," Zaidan declared. "Those who feed us the bullshit they think we want to hear are the first ones I eliminate. We consider our perfect candidate to be, shall we say, a healthy skeptic."

Elora nodded knowingly.

"We should be going now," Zaidan said, glancing at his watch. "The gala will be kicking off soon, and I need to speak with my security team beforehand."

"Of course," Elora said as she stood up and grabbed her purse. "Guess I'll see you later this evening."

"I'm going to the ballroom now; my team is already there. Why don't you walk with me?" Zaidan said as he shrugged on his tuxedo jacket.

Elora hesitated, straining her brain to come up with an excuse not to accompany him.

"The private bar in our VIP section should be open already," Zaidan added with a wink.

"Sure, what the hell," Elora caved, "you had me at open bar."

Elora, Zaidan, and two NDU security guards rode the elevator down to the hotel lobby. When the doors opened, Zaidan offered his arm to escort Elora to the ballroom.

"Shall we, Ms. Reid?"

Elora froze, feeling like a rat trapped in a cage. The thought of walking across the crowded lobby on the arm of the NDU leader's chief of staff made her nauseous. Elora tried to think of a polite way to decline but came up empty and surrendered. She looped her right arm into the crook of Zaidan's left, and they emerged from the elevator, shadowed by the NDU security guards. Elora kept her head down, trying not to make eye contact with anyone as the foursome strode across the lobby toward the ballroom.

Nick, who was sitting in the lobby bar, nearly choked on his rum and coke when Zaidan waltzed by—with Elora on his arm. *What the fuck?* Nick jumped out of his seat, flung some money at the bartender, and ran out to follow Elora and Zaidan.

As the group approached the main doors to the ballroom, Elora remembered her VIP badge in her purse. "Oh, let me get my badge from my purse," she said and tried to remove her arm from around Zaidan's.

"No need," Zaidan said and squeezed down on Elora's arm to prevent her from breaking their link.

"Right," Elora muttered.

The hotel security staff was checking the badges of all guests entering the ballroom, but with a simple tip of the head from Zaidan, the NDU entourage walked right in. He escorted Elora to a roped-off corner of the ballroom that contained four round tables of eight with a small private bar behind the tables. The two NDU security guys halted at the entrance to the VIP section and posted themselves at parade rest on either side of the velvet roped opening.

"Please, make yourself comfortable," Zaidan said, dropping Elora off at one of the VIP tables marked *Reserved*. "Relax, order a drink. I'll be back shortly."

A few minutes later, Nick arrived at the VIP section but the NDU security guards blocked him from entering. Elora rushed over to intervene before the situation escalated. "Ugh, yeah, he's with me," she said, flashing the burly guards an awkward smile. Their expressions remained icy, but they stepped aside for Nick to enter.

"You want to explain to me what the fuck I just witnessed?" Nick said as he followed Elora to their table.

"They didn't remember you, that's all," Elora said, trying to brush off the incident.

"I was referring to you parading through the hotel on Zaidan's arm?" he added in a loud whisper.

"We rode the elevator down together. Before we got out, he offered me his arm. What was I going to do? Shove it away and tell him to fuck off?"

"Yeah!" Nick said, pulling back with a sarcastic nod. "That's *exactly* what you could have done."

Elora shot him an *are-you-serious-right-now* look. "Oh, and that would have helped us accomplish a lot."

Nick opened his mouth to respond, but a commotion near the VIP entrance distracted everyone's attention. Nick and Elora turned to see Samir and Zaidan entering the roped-off VIP section, surrounded by a handful of NDU security guards. A few yards behind them trailed a man wearing traditional Emirati clothing: a long white robe and white head covering secured with a black cord around the crown. Nick and Elora immediately recognized the man as the thirty-four-year-old crown prince of Dubai—Sheikh Mohammad Al-Rafid.

"Smile, *Nathan*," Elora commanded through the clenched teeth of her own fake grin.

"Fuck, are they coming to sit at our table?"

"I think so."

As Samir and Zaidan approached the table, Elora and Nick rose to greet them. "Ah, Mr. Briggs. So *nice* to see you again," Zaidan said, though his tone seemed to mean quite the opposite. Zaidan's tone, however, was the last thing Nick noticed; like Elora had been earlier, he was floored by Zaidan's sudden perfect English.

Samir exchanged pleasantries with Elora and Nick and took a seat at the table a couple of chairs down from Elora. The half dozen NDU guards who'd arrived with Samir scattered and posted themselves at intervals around the VIP area.

Elora watched Zaidan step away to whisper into one of the guard's ears. While Zaidan was out of earshot, Nick leaned in close to her.

"So why the fucking song and dance with the translator at our first meeting if Zaidan and Samir both speak perfect English?"

Elora shrugged. "Welcome to the party."

Just as Zaidan returned, the prince arrived at the table with his own entourage of security personnel. Prince Al-Rafid zeroed right in on Zaidan, and the two greeted each other in a manner that made Elora realize they were more than acquaintances. The prince flashed a wide grin and laughed as he took Zaidan's hand. "Long time no see, brother!" he said in English. "We have catching up to do."

"Great to see you again, your highness," Zaidan replied, returning the prince's smile and then shifting his attention to Elora. "Please, allow me to introduce Ms. Elora Reid, foreign correspondent with the *Washington Post*."

"Charmed, Ms. Reid," the prince said as he extended his hand.

"It's an honor to meet you, sir, uh...your highness," Elora stumbled as she shook hands with the prince. *Shit, real smooth, Elora.*

Prince Al-Rafid smiled at Elora's fumble as he took a seat across from her at the table. His bodyguards fanned out and strategically positioned themselves near the prince but remained inconspicuous. Zaidan slipped into the empty seat between Elora and Samir. As soon as he sat down, Elora noticed Samir place his hand on Zaidan's forearm for a few seconds and give it a slight squeeze. She wondered if it was a signal of some sort. The gesture seemed deliberate, although Zaidan did not appear to acknowledge it.

Elora was desperate to break away from the crowd for a cigarette, but she knew it was still too soon to slip out, so instead, she headed over to the private bar to order another drink. As the bartender mixed her drink, Elora scanned the ballroom, now filled with more than eight hundred guests: hundreds of the most successful leaders from throughout the global financial industry. *Jesus, this would be a prime opportunity for a terrorist attack.* Elora shook her head at her own morbid thought and berated herself for always being the ultimate pessimist.

She was relieved to return to the table and find the dinner had been served while she was at the bar. She settled in and enjoyed the meal while engaging in idle chit-chat with her fellow table mates, which included the other Western journalists NDU had invited to Dubai to interview Samir—correspondents from CNN and the BBC. Out of respect for the Western guests, conversation at the table was carried out in English. The prince regaled the group with tales of his latest adventures on a recent African safari, then discussion switched to the current political situation in Iraq. It seemed the prince saw eye-to-eye with NDU and made no attempt to hide his support for their cause. It was rumored the prince and Malik Khalid shared a friendship and that the Prince helped clear the way for many *legally gray* business dealings NDU conducted in UAE. Much to Elora's relief, though, Malik was never mentioned throughout the course of the conversation.

Once she finished her meal, Elora's social anxiety reached its limit, and she decided to cut out for a smoke break. She grabbed her purse and whispered in Nick's ear that she was going to step out for a few minutes.

"I'll go with you," Nick offered.

"No, please stay," Elora said, gesturing for him to remain in his seat, "finish your meal."

As Elora worked her way through the ballroom to the exit, Zaidan made eye contact with the security guard whose ear he'd been whispering in earlier and gave him a subtle nod. A few seconds later, the bodyguard slipped out of the VIP section and followed in Elora's path.

Elora exited the ballroom and made her way back to the lobby elevators. She rode up to the floor that housed the Sky Lounge and made a beeline for the outdoor terrace. With most of the hotel guests attending the gala downstairs in the ballroom, the Sky Lounge was nearly empty, and Elora had the terrace to herself. Standing at a section of the terrace railing that offered a prime view of Dubai's glittering nighttime skyline, she fished her cigarettes out of her purse and lit one up. Her anxiety levels instantly dipped as she exhaled the smoke into the desert air above the city while gazing out at the incredible view. Finished with her cigarette, she knew she should return to the gala, but she had no desire to leave the quiet terrace. *Fuck it.* She pulled out another cigarette and lit up.

Her sights settled on the colorful skyscrapers aglow with neon spotlights, but her thoughts were far from UAE. She was thinking about Brendan—picturing his face and wondering if she'd ever forget what he looked like or the sound of his voice when he said her name. She'd read articles about military widows who said that after several years, they had trouble even remembering the sound of their spouse's voice. Elora prayed that would never happen.

"Amazing view, isn't it?" Zaidan's husky voice startled Elora from her daydream, and she spun around with a hand clutched to her chest.

"Jesus Christ, dude, what the fuck?" she blurted.

Zaidan was standing so close they would have been nose-to-nose, but even in her four-inch heels, he was still a couple of inches taller than Elora.

"Apologies. I didn't mean to scare you."

"How the hell did you even find me?" she asked, taking a drag from her cigarette, still trying to bring her heart rate back to a normal speed.

"Were you trying to hide?"

"No. I just needed some air and a cigarette." She caught sight of an NDU security guard lingering in the doorway between the terrace and indoor lounge. She twisted her head sharply back toward Zaidan and narrowed her eyes. "Having your goons follow me still I see."

"Merely to lookout for your well-being," Zaidan countered.

"It's Dubai, not Fallujah."

"It's the Middle East."

"I sense you have some serious trust issues. Do you have your men following your other journalist guests?"

"As a matter of fact, yes. Should something happen to a Western journalist, be it tripping over a loose step and twisting their ankle or getting kidnapped by Jihadists, it would not be good for New Dawn's image. So, yes, we take measures to ensure the safety of our guests."

"I take it the blonde BBC woman and gentleman from CNN at our table downstairs are who I'm competing against for the Baghdad embed gig?"

"Yes. Though I suspect it won't be much of a competition," Zaidan replied with a cryptic smile that made his eyes glow.

Butterflies rush into her stomach, and she squeezed her cigarette between her lips in an attempt to tamp them down.

Zaidan stepped up next to Elora and leaned over the terrace railing to take in the panoramic view. "It is a beautiful city, isn't it?" he asked rhetorically. "Not long ago, this was just a Bedouin town of mud and clay huts. Now look at it. The tribes finally put their differences aside and united to develop one of the fastest growing, most technologically advanced nations in the Arab world. Hell, in the *entire* world."

Elora nodded at Zaidan's remarks but remained silent.

"Iraq has the same potential," Zaidan continued. "If we could figure out how to leverage our strengths instead of squabbling like toddlers over our differences, we could be just as prosperous as UAE. Iraq once held the most advanced cities in the world. I dream of one day seeing the major cities of Iraq transformed into cosmopolitan metropolises, once again on the cutting edge of technology and commerce. Cities where people come from around the world to study, conduct business, seek excitement...fall in love," he added shooting Elora a quick glance.

"And you think New Dawn is a vehicle that can help move Iraq in this direction?" Elora asked, her voice heavy with doubt.

"No," Zaidan replied. "I *know* it is."

"When did you link up with New Dawn? You mentioned you met Samir when you were both in college. Did you also meet Malik Khalid around that time too?" Elora tried her best not to jump right into asking questions about Malik, but she couldn't help it.

"I met Malik about a year after I met Samir. He was like Samir's protective big brother. When Malik launched his New Dawn organization—well, it was more of a club back then—Samir tried to recruit me, but I wasn't interested. It wasn't until a couple of years later, when I saw for myself the legitimate accomplishments New Dawn was achieving, that I reconsidered. They established a basic level of security in regions the central government had deemed 'lost causes.' They brought the utilities back online—electricity and water. They were providing basic social services, renovating and building schools and hospitals. All basic needs we'd been begging the government to provide for years but, for some reason, still couldn't figure out how to bring to fruition. Malik finally said, 'Screw it, we'll do it ourselves,' and they did. Yet, instead of the government being thankful or even taking note, they tried to shut NDU down and soon began attacking them. That's when I decided I no longer wanted to be on the sidelines. It was time to make a stand, and NDU already stood for the change I wanted to be a part of."

"NDU may have started out with benevolent deeds and aspirations, but they eventually stooped to the level of their enemies. How do you justify their violent methods?" Elora asked, crossing her arms. "Their brutal militia? The bombings across Baghdad that killed and injured innocent people—that killed Americans, including our Ambassador? Not to mention their criminal activities, the weapons smuggling, the drug trafficking, the human trafficking…"

"First of all," Zaidan interjected. "New Dawn does not engage in human trafficking in any way, shape or form."

"That *you're* aware of," Elora challenged.

"Not at all. Period," he declared, looking her dead in the eye.

"Okay, fine. I noticed you didn't deny any of the other activities I rattled off—including the murder of innocents. Do you just close your eyes to all that *other* stuff?"

Zaidan took a deep breath and responded in a calm tone. "Revolution is never black and white, and it is always bloody. The main thing is to ensure the ends justify the means, and the positives outweigh the negatives. I do not condone unprovoked violence, and I'll be the first to admit that Malik was a bit of a loose cannon who sometimes crossed the line. But when Malik was killed and Samir assumed control of the organization, I convinced him this was our chance to legitimize the movement and transform it into something Malik never could have achieved. I was honored when Samir genuinely liked my ideas and appointed me his chief of staff. Samir has my complete confidence. I have total faith in his ability to bring about true change in a more peaceful manner that is still efficient and effective."

"So how did you also end up as the head of security?"

"After high school I spent eighteen months at the Iraqi Military Academy—Iraq's equivalent to your West Point," Zaidan explained. "While there I gained weapons and combat training, studied military strategy and doctrine, learned about intelligence collection and information security, and acquired various other useful *skills*. However, I washed-out before the end of my second year—I wasn't cut out to be a military man. I'm not good with blindly following orders," he added with a twisted smile.

"But you obey Samir."

"More like, Samir and I see eye-to-eye," Zaidan clarified. "And if we don't, he is responsive and open to me questioning him. I don't have to shut my eyes and force myself to follow commands I don't agree with."

"Have you ever challenged him?"

"Yes, just this evening as a matter-of-fact."

"Oh, really?" Elora asked with renewed interest.

"The shoes he originally put on tonight were fucking hideous, and I told him so."

Elora rolled her eyes. "Ah yes, I'm sure defying Samir's fashion blunders is a crucial component in ensuring he doesn't turn into a maniacal tyrant like his predecessor."

"We should probably be getting back downstairs," Zaidan said, stepping back from the balcony railing. "I'm sure Mr. Briggs is positively squirming in his seat right now wondering where you and I disappeared off to," he added with a wink. Once again, he offered his arm to escort Elora. "Shall we?"

This time, however, Elora thought of an out. "Thank you, but you go on ahead. I'm going to duck into the ladies' room before I head back."

"Of course," Zaidan replied, seeing right through her lie.

Chapter 8

As their flight touched down on the tarmac of Dulles International Airport, Nick swiveled in his seat to face Elora and presented his hand for a formal shake. Elora looked at him, confused, but slipped her hand into his. "Congratulations on completing your first field operation," he said, giving her hand a gentle shake. "Welcome to an elite association of men and women dedicated to safeguarding our nation's security, with absolutely *zero* chance of public honor or recognition," he added sarcastically.

"Thanks. I guess?"

"You did well. I'm proud of you," Nick continued, slipping into a more serious tone.

Elora smiled. She hadn't yet told Nick about Zaidan's hints of offering her an invitation to do an embed assignment with NDU in Iraq. She knew Nick would be vehemently opposed to the idea, so she figured she'd cross that bridge if and when they came to it. One thing she *never* planned to tell Nick about was the note Zaidan had sent to her room before she left for the airport.

Elora,

Mr. Al-Bakr sends along his best wishes for a safe journey home and hopes you enjoyed your time here in Dubai. We sincerely appreciate you traveling all this way to meet us and learn about the new direction we plan to take the New Dawn Underground. We both anxiously anticipate the completion of your exposé and very much look forward to reading it. It was a pleasure getting to know you this week. You are a most interesting young woman and I very much enjoyed our private chats. I do hope we get a chance to meet again one day—perhaps it will be soon.

With warmest regards,
Zaidan (The Iraqi William Wallace)
Chief of Staff, New Dawn Underground

Elora had spent much of the flight back from UAE replaying the one-on-one chats she'd had with Zaidan. Over the week, he'd transformed from intensely mysterious and creepy to intriguingly intelligent and passionate. Plus, she could no longer deny it—he was gorgeous. Though she wasn't ready to admit it to herself, Elora hoped to see Zaidan again. She understood why Samir had chosen him as his chief of staff. What she didn't understand was why Zaidan was tangled up with NDU. And she still wasn't convinced Malik Khalid was truly dead.

"Did you want a lift home?" Nick asked as their plane came to a stop at the gate.

"No thanks, I'll just grab a cab." Elora decided it was time to make a conscious effort to no longer blur the lines of their relationship.

"Feel free to take tomorrow off," Nick offered. "Get some rest, recover from the jet lag."

"Thanks, but I'll be there in the morning. I'm anxious to complete the debriefing and share everything with the team. I also need to get that article written, and I'll be a lot more productive at the office than at home."

Nick didn't argue. "As you wish."

Once she got through customs, Elora headed to the airport ground transportation exit and hailed a cab. She began to rattle off her home address to the driver but halted midway through. "No, scratch that," she told the driver. "Arlington National Cemetery, please."

Once they arrived at Arlington Cemetery, Elora guided the driver to the area where Brendan's gravesite was located. "Do you mind waiting?" Elora asked the driver. "I'll only be a few minutes."

"Not a problem. Are you visiting a friend?"

"My fiancé. Feel free to keep the meter running," she added.

"Take your time," the driver said as he reached over and paused the fare meter.

"Thank you," Elora replied, meeting the driver's eyes in the rearview mirror.

"It's my pleasure, ma'am. Please convey my respects to your fiancé."

"Of course," Elora squeaked, swallowing back tears.

Elora stepped out of the cab and weaved her way through several rows of white headstones until she stood in front of Brendan's grave.

"Hey, baby, I'm back," Elora said, kneeling and placing her hand on Brendan's headstone. "I missed you. I think it was a productive trip, though. We gained a lot of intel on the new leadership at NDU. Hopefully, the team will be able to leverage this info to track down Malik. I know he's still out there somewhere, and I plan to find him, even if I have to go to Iraq myself and dig him out of a bunker, which I just may get an opportunity to do. I'll give you the details once I learn more. In the meantime, rest in peace, my love." Elora leaned forward and placed a soft kiss on the top of the white granite marker. "Oh, my cab driver sends his respects," she added as she stood up and brushed the dirt from the knees of her pants. "He's a good guy, stopped the meter while I was here," she added with a wink.

The next morning at work, Nick gathered the NDU Task Force together for a meeting to go over the Dubai mission. As the team filtered into the conference room, they each congratulated Elora on the successful completion of her first field op.

"Thank you all for holding the fort down while we were in UAE," Nick said, kicking off the meeting. "Elora has a little over thirty minutes of audio recorded interview with Samir Al-Bakr. I want everyone to review it and have a preliminary analysis on it ready to present at tomorrow's meeting. Elora also had a couple of one-on-ones with Al-Bakr's chief of staff, Zaidan Al-Sadiq. She'll have a written report by end-of-day detailing any pertinent info she gleaned from her encounters with him. While we're on the subject—Derek, were you able to dig up any info on Al-Sadiq?"

Derek shuffled his documents and flipped open a manila folder. "Unfortunately, not a whole lot. I did manage to get a copy of his university records from Iraq's ministry of higher education." Derek cleared his throat and read from the open file. "Zaidan Al-

Sadiq: Age thirty-two, Sunni Muslim, born and raised in Baghdad. He graduated with a degree in Political Science from the University of Baghdad in 2002." Derek held up a photocopy of an Iraqi National I.D. dated 1999 with Zaidan's photo and information for the group to see, then continued reading from the file. "He spent almost two years at the elite Iraqi Military Academy before transferring to the University of Baghdad to study Political Science. His university records don't indicate *why* he left the Military Academy. I tried to have one of our guys in Baghdad locate his military record but no luck. It was likely lost when the old Ministry of Defense was destroyed during the war. As to why he left the Military Academy, my educated guess would be an injury—nine times out of ten that's...."

"He washed out," Elora interrupted. Derek fell silent and the entire team turned their attention to Elora. "Or, more accurately I guess, he simply quit," she added. "At least that's what he told me."

The team continued to stare at Elora, waiting for her to elaborate further.

"I'll include a full account of the conversation in my written report," she said and gestured for Derek to continue.

"That was about all I had anyway," he said, closing the manila folder and looking to Nick.

"Quick question," Lori interjected. "The managing editor at the *Washington Post* is breathing down my neck. We asked them to reserve us a cover position in next Sunday's WaPo for our 'article,' so he wants to know when he should expect a draft of the story. I wasn't sure where we stood with this. Will there even be an article? I need to let him know ASAP whether he needs to continue holding that space for us or not. I don't want to burn any bridges with them."

"Yes, there will be an article," Nick confirmed. "Elora is writing it herself. If the article never gets published, it'll burn Elora's cover," Nick explained. "Although I don't expect we'll need to use this cover again, it's always good to maintain it as an option should a need arise in the future."

"Actually, Nick," Elora jumped in. "There may be an opportunity to take this to the next level."

Nick raised his eyebrows and waited for Elora to elaborate.

"The night of the gala, Zaidan indicated that NDU is toying with the idea of inviting a journalist to come to Iraq to report on their operation from there, like an embed assignment. Considering we still haven't gotten any solid info on Malik Khalid's whereabouts, going to the source may give us our best chance at finding him."

"And you're considering doing this yourself?" Nick asked, sounding skeptical.

"Well…yes?" She didn't understand why Nick sounded so doubtful. "We barely scratched the surface in UAE; landing an invite like this would be an opportunity to infiltrate NDU's inner circle."

"No," Nick declared. "There's a *big* difference between an op to Dubai to attend a glorified prom versus a field op to a combat zone. I'm proud of what you accomplished in UAE, but you're not ready for an undercover embed."

Elora respected Nick as a supervisor and adored him as a friend, but it pissed her off when he spoke to her like she was a child. She knew his words were coming from a place of love—

perhaps *too* much love—but she knew it was time to put her foot down, and she did not have any hesitations about doing it in front of the entire team.

"First of all," Elora announced, raising her voice, "I don't appreciate you speaking to me like I'm a thirteen-year-old girl asking to go on her first date."

"Elora, I didn't mean it…."

"Please, do not interrupt me." Elora demanded. "Second of all, I served six years on active duty in the military—including two combat deployments to Iraq. This would not be my first rodeo. I'm not a wide-eyed, naïve dingbat asking to go pet the fucking camels. I'm well aware of the dangers and how to conduct and safeguard myself within a combat zone. I understand your concerns and *why* you may be hesitant to send me on such a mission," she continued with a razor-sharp glare. She hoped he'd catch that she was referencing the unwanted kiss he'd tried to give her in Dubai. "But we need to prioritize the needs of the mission above any *personal* feelings we may harbor."

Elora hated having to pull this card on Nick, but she'd made a promise to Brendan and she intended to keep it. She would not rest until she found Malik Khalid—dead or alive. Getting Zaidan and Samir to invite her to Iraq to continue writing about NDU was the next step. And she was ready to do whatever it took to ensure she got that invitation.

The rest of the team didn't move, speak, or even breathe once Elora had finished her tongue lashing of Nick. The two stared each other down in silence for several long seconds while the team bounced their gazes back and forth to see who would flinch first. Nick was the first to cave.

"You're right," he sighed. "I'm sorry."

Elora unclenched her jaw and relaxed back in her chair, but otherwise made no response to Nick's apology.

"I'm only trying to look out for you," Nick added.

"By patronizing me?" she snapped.

"Fine, let's say your plan works and NDU asks you to come be their personal Western media correspondent in Iraq. What then? What's your plan? Track down Malik Khalid and kill him with your bare hands?" Nick asked, trying his best not to sound condescending.

"If he is in fact dead, I plan to find out where he's buried so we can send in a team to exhume the remains and get a DNA sample. Then we can close this fucking case for good. You know we can't seal it without DNA confirmation. If my trip to Iraq uncovers evidence that Malik is alive, I'll follow his trail as far as I can, gather as much intel as possible and pump it back here to the team. Then we can all come up with a plan to track him down and go after his ass again."

Nick looked around the room at the rest of the team to gauge their reactions to Elora's plan. Lori and Jason continued to stare at the table, so Nick turned to Derek, demanding an opinion with his expression.

Derek shrugged. "Honestly, I think it's a decent plan. If Elora can get NDU to invite her to Iraq, it'll at least give us something tangible to present to the Task Force board to convince them to extend our mandate another few months," Derek said.

"Okay fine," Nick relented. "So, let's make sure NDU picks Elora for this embed. Lori—you're up. What do we need to do?"

"Well, NDU's primary goal is achieving prolific Western

media exposure—*positive* exposure," Lori clarified. "Getting Elora's article on the cover of the Post likely isn't going to be enough to seal the deal. I assume BBC and CNN have plans to publish their reporters' NDU articles prominently as well. Elora's article needs to go viral—across the web, social media, even television coverage, which the nerds downstairs should be able to pull off. We need her article to make as loud of a splash as possible and then hope it's enough to catch NDU's attention and outshine her competition. The content of the article itself is going to be vital as well. I don't think this is something we leave up to the nerds to bang out on a night-shift—we need a seasoned journalist to write this one."

"I'm writing it myself," Elora reiterated.

"I'm not sure that's the wisest decision," Lori countered.

"I know what they're looking for. If the article kisses NDU's ass, they'll kick it and me to the curb. Zaidan will see right through that shit. The article is going to have to engage a delicate balance that puts a positive spin on NDU yet remains genuine. It's hard to explain," Elora said shaking her head. "Just trust me on this."

"Going back to the main hurdle here, if you do end up going to Iraq, they are going to watch you like a hawk," Nick said. "You're not going to be able to move around at will and flip through their file cabinets looking for clues. Do you have a strategy?"

Elora swallowed hard. She did have something in mind that she'd been contemplating but she wasn't sure if it was time to share it with the team yet. Nick mistook Elora's silence for a complete lack of preparedness and chastised her again. "Yeah, that's what I thought," he huffed. "I don't think you've thought this through at all."

"I think I can flip him," Elora blurted.

"Flip who?" Nick asked.

Elora bit her lip and as her pulse increased. She knew that once she answered, at best Nick would laugh, at worst he'd recommend she be evaluated for insanity, but she'd already opened Pandora's box, so she had to follow through.

"I think I can flip Zaidan."

"Mr. Creepy?" Nick asked with a surprised snort.

"He's not an ignorant militant," she explained. "Samir is a shady motherfucker who is playing us to get what he needs to gain more power. If he gets what he wants, he'll make Saddam look like the fucking Dali Llama. Zaidan is loyal to Samir, but I think Zaidan is more loyal to his morals and has a level of integrity he won't compromise—not even for Samir. A time will come when Samir's masterplan will require Zaidan to cross a line he won't be willing to cross. If we play our cards right, we may be able to flip Zaidan in that moment."

"Elora, you just completed your first field op—a simple one at that," Nick pointed out. "Do you honestly think you're ready to go charging into a designated combat zone and start flipping assets?"

"No," Elora agreed. "But I can do this."

Nick silently stared at Elora for several long seconds, then gave a slight nod. "We'll need a full character profile on Zaidan to support this theory before we can even consider it," Nick said. "Derek, I want you and Jason to work together on that. Once we have the profile complete and analyzed, if there are any red flags or evidence to counter Elora's theory, we scuttle this plan. Are we all in agreement?"

Everyone in the room nodded.

"All right, people," Nick announced. "Let's get to it. Elora, you've got an article to write. Lori, you've got an article you need to make go viral. Derek and Jason, you've got a character profile to draw up. And I'll work on getting us another extension from the Task Force board."

The next few weeks were a whirlwind for Elora. Her exposé on Iraq's "dangerous yet alluring" New Dawn Underground militant group and their new leader Samir Al-Bakr, had hit the cover of the *Washington Post* and promptly went viral. The article, entitled *Iraq's New Dawn Underground: A New Hope or a New Hype?* was syndicated by more than seventy global media organizations and translated into several languages. It was one of WaPo's most emailed articles of the year and racked up thousands of social media shares. It was amazing the kind of publicity a couple hundred thousand dollars' worth of internet advertising and a team of eight CIA digital content nerds with advanced expertise in search engine optimization and web algorithm manipulation can generate.

Of course, making the article go viral was the easy part. The attention her article garnered blew her CNN and BBC competition out of the water. But would the actual content of the article be enough to impress and lure NDU into offering Elora the Iraq embed gig? So far, there'd been no word from NDU. The only consolation was Lori had managed to find out that NDU hadn't reached out to the BBC or CNN correspondents yet either. Elora feared NDU may have changed their mind about bringing a reporter into Iraq altogether. This fear fell hard on top of her existing worry that her article had not packed the proper ingredients to land her the invite. *Maybe I missed the mark and offended them?*

When she sent the rough draft of her article to NDU, she hoped to get some sort of feedback or even requests for edits to give her an idea of whether or not she was on the right path. Unfortunately, she'd gotten back only a simple three-word reply—*Approved for publication*. That was it. She had no clue who'd reviewed the article or who even emailed back the approval as the email address was an ambiguous alphanumeric Gmail account, and the reply contained no name or signature. She'd included a cell number linked to a burner phone at the bottom of her original email. If NDU did decide to reach out, she wanted to make it easy for them to get in touch with her directly.

Elora was curled up on her couch with a bowl of ramen noodles, watching the latest episode of *The Walking Dead* when her burner phone rang. Her heart instantly started racing. "Oh fuck!" She sprang up from the loveseat, sloshing ramen noodles across her living room, and ran to her dining room table. Her work bag was lying on top of the table with the burner phone buried somewhere inside. Elora grabbed the bag and flipped it upside down, dumping the contents out across the tabletop. She plucked the burner phone from the disheveled pile and flipped it open. "Elora Reid—Washington Post," she blurted breathlessly into the phone.

"Good evening, Ms. Reid," the unmistakable voice of Zaidan Al-Sadiq replied on the other end. "Did I catch you at a bad time?"

"Uh, no—not at all. I was…um…jogging, yeah, working out," Elora said and then silently flinched at her idiotic excuse. She didn't run unless someone was chasing her. "What can I do for you Mr. Al-Sadiq?"

"Please, just Zaidan."

"Right, sorry. What can I do for you, *Zaidan*?"

"I wanted to call you and congratulate you on the massive success of your article," he said in a formal tone.

Elora waited for a follow-up to the congratulations, but Zaidan remained silent on the other end. "Well, thank you," she finally responded. She didn't want to come right out and ask him if he personally liked the article and hoped he'd say more on his own. "I appreciate you taking the time to reach out. I'm honored you gave me the opportunity to come out and learn more about the organization."

"It was our honor to host you."

"You know, I think there is a lot more the people, and even heads of state, here in the Western world could benefit from by learning more about New Dawn," Elora goaded, trying hard not to make it sound like she was kissing his ass yet knowing she was failing miserably.

"As a matter of fact, that's the other reason I'm calling you this evening."

Yes! Elora mouthed as she pumped her fist in the air.

"Samir is still interested in bringing a journalist here to Iraq for a few weeks to write a series of articles on various New

Dawn activities. Would you be interested in taking on this assignment?"

Hell Yes! Elora wanted to scream but maintained her composure. "I am definitely interested," she replied as calmly as possible.

"Wonderful—I will have my staff email over a proposed itinerary tomorrow morning. We'll need an answer by the end of the week."

"You got it." As soon as Elora hung up with Zaidan, she immediately called Nick.

"I'm in!" Elora shrieked when Nick answered. "Call a Task Force meeting tomorrow morning."

Chapter 9

"Keep your eyes and ears open. You got it?" Nick lectured Elora as they stood in the international terminal of Dulles airport. Her flight to Baghdad was scheduled to depart in an hour. "I know you're hell-bent on finding Malik Khalid, but remember, this is a *secondary* objective," Nick continued. "Our main concern is what the current New Dawn leadership is up to and what direction they plan to take this whole thing."

The consensus in Washington was that New Dawn's power and influence remained at a level that Langley needed to keep a finger on their pulse, at least until they had an idea of what direction NDU would swing—either legitimate political party or continue down the bloody militant group path. The embed gig was going to put Elora in a unique position to gather intel that could help determine New Dawn's mindset and future plans. The bigwigs in D.C. wanted more info before deciding whether the U.S. would stand down regarding NDU or mount another attack against them.

"We all want justice for Brendan and Ambassador Casey, but you *cannot* lose sight of the bigger picture," Nick said. "We do what best serves the interests of the United States—current *and* future interests."

Elora nodded. The character profile Derek and Jason had put together on Zaidan proved inconclusive on whether he was a good candidate for Elora to try to flip as an asset. So, it was decided she would not actively pursue this objective. If she managed to learn or collect additional evidence that provided more insight into Zaidan's background, they'd reevaluate at that point.

"If for one split second I sense you're allowing vengeance to guide your actions over there, I will pull your ass out of that country so fast your fucking head will spin."

"I know," Elora assured him.

"Likewise, if at any minute you feel like you're in personal danger or at risk of having your cover compromised, you immediately request extraction. We will try by all means possible to get you out quietly, but if need be, we will come in guns blazing. The main thing is that you do *not* hesitate to make that call. You follow your gut. Always use *this*," he said, touching a finger to Elora's forehead, "but make sure you also listen to *this*," he added placing the palm of her own hand on her stomach. "Together they will keep you alive."

According to the itinerary NDU had sent over, Elora would be in country for about a month. She'd split her time between Baghdad and the region of northwestern Iraq that New Dawn controlled. New Dawn's Baghdad headquarters was where the political arm of the organization was based. They were responsible for managing and organizing election campaigns for New Dawn party candidates, producing and disseminating propaganda across multiple mediums, spearheading government lobby efforts, etc. Elora was set to get an intimate look into all these activities and write articles on New Dawn's current issues and events in regard to their political activities and aspirations. Afterward, she'd tour the New Dawn controlled regions of northwestern Iraq to view their infrastructure projects and humanitarian work.

Elora glanced at her watch. "I better go ahead and get through security."

"Good luck over there." Nick leaned in and gave her a goodbye peck on the cheek. "Take care of yourself."

"I will. Visit Brendan for me?"

"You bet."

Elora fidgeted with her emerald necklace as her flight touched down at Baghdad International Airport. When the plane came to its final stop, she tucked her necklace inside her shirt and grabbed her bags. Wanting to move around the country easily, Elora had packed light—a wheeled duffle bag and a backpack. She hoped there would be an opportunity to do laundry at some point along the way, or she'd be wearing her underwear inside-out by week two.

She cleared customs and proceeded to the main terminal where crowds of people waited to greet arriving passengers. The itinerary packet from Zaidan's staff indicated a driver would be there, holding a sign with her name on it. Elora skimmed the crowd as she moved with the flow of traffic coming out of customs. Finally, she saw a group of suited men at the far end of the terminal holding signs. She approached the group and scanned their signs. Her eyes lit up when she spotted it—*Ms. Elora Reid,* written in black Sharpie on a simple white poster. The man holding the sign had a serious-looking face and appeared to be in his late twenties. He wore the familiar NDU security uniform of dark gray slacks with a black, collarless blazer.

"*Marhaba, ismi Elora Reid,*" Elora said to the man holding the sign with her name. His eyes perked up when she introduced herself in Arabic.

"Welcome to Baghdad, Ms. Reid," the man replied in Arabic. "I'm Fareed. My men and I will be escorting you to the New Dawn headquarters."

Elora followed Fareed out of the airport and into the parking lot. He led her to a white Nissan Armada SUV and opened the rear lift-door so she could put her duffle bag in the back. Fareed then held the driver-side rear passenger door open for Elora to climb into the backseat. Inside the vehicle were two fully armed NDU security personnel. One sat in the front passenger seat, while another sat in the backseat with Elora.

Fareed maneuvered the SUV out of the parking lot and onto the main thoroughfare that connected the airport to central Baghdad. Elora immediately recognized the road they were traveling along—the infamous Route Irish. During the height of U.S. military operations in Iraq it was the deadliest twelve kilometer stretch of roadway in the entire world. When Elora deployed to Baghdad in 2006, hundreds of Americans had already been injured or killed along Route Irish. Countless attacks from IEDs to ambushes claimed casualties on nearly a daily basis as coalition forces traveled between the airport and Baghdad's Green Zone. The route still wasn't *safe* by any stretch of the term, but it was a lot quieter than it once was. A small victory, but when it comes to Iraq, you take what you can get.

Reaching the city, Fareed exited the highway and headed

northeast into Baghdad's Mansour District, an upscale neighborhood home to many foreign consulates—the Baghdad equivalent of Embassy Row. They turned onto a semi-residential street lined with large homes surrounded by walled courtyards. Fareed pulled the SUV into a driveway and stopped in front of a massive white iron gate manned by a pair of NDU security guards. Beyond the gate loomed a large three-story concrete building. It was built in the typical Iraqi architectural style with large arched windows and doorways. Fareed rolled down his window, and one of the gate guards approached the vehicle. He greeted Fareed and then peered inside to examine the interior and scrutinized the faces of each passenger. The second guard walked around the SUV, rolling a mirror beneath the car to ensure no explosives had been planted on the undercarriage. Familiar with military security protocols, Elora was impressed with the NDU security team's procedures.

The guard searching the outside of the vehicle gave his partner a thumbs up. The lead guard pulled a walkie-talkie from his utility belt and rattled off a phrase that made no sense to Elora. She realized it must have been a code to instruct the guards inside the compound that it was safe to open the main gate. The gates slowly swung open with a loud screech, and Fareed rolled the SUV into the compound yard. In addition to the main three-story building at the center of the property, there were two other structures in the compound. A large two-story outbuilding that looked like a garage and a smaller single-story structure that resembled a guest house.

Fareed pulled the Nissan around a circular driveway and stopped beneath the drive-thru carport in front of the main building. He shut off the car and hopped out to open Elora's door. "Follow me, please, Ms. Reid. Mr. Al-Sadiq is awaiting your arrival in his study. The staff will take your luggage up to your room."

They entered the main building's dramatic two-story foyer, which had a large parlor off to the left and a conference room with a massive table off the right. Elora trailed Fareed straight through the foyer, past a wide staircase and down a hallway that led to the rear of the building. They turned right at the end of the hallway and entered an office. Sitting behind a large executive-style desk was Zaidan.

"Ms. Reid, what a pleasure to see you," Zaidan announced in English as he stepped out from behind the desk to greet Elora with a warm smile. His emerald eyes burned like jade beacons from behind his black eyelashes, hooking Elora in an instant. *God damnit.* She made a mental note to avoid eye contact with Zaidan when at all possible.

"Welcome to Baghdad. I trust you had a comfortable journey from America?"

"Yes, thank you," Elora replied, quickly shifting her gaze from his face.

"Please, have a seat. I'm sure you're exhausted." Zaidan gestured for Elora to take a seat in one of the guest chairs across from his desk. He then turned to Fareed and switched into Arabic. "Thank you, Fareed, that will be all."

The office walls were lined with floor-to-ceiling shelves overflowing with books, and there was a window looking out over a small back patio and yard area. The office also contained a small leather sofa and a credenza against the wall behind Zaidan's desk. Atop the credenza was a collection of liquor bottles and upside-down drinking glasses on a silver tray. Among the liquor Elora spotted a brand-new bottle of Disaronno and did her best to suppress a smile.

"I apologize Samir isn't here to greet you himself," Zaidan said, leaning back in his chair. "He's at a lunch meeting with potential campaign donors interested in supporting our NDU candidates. It turns out democracy is quite expensive," he quipped with a sly smile. "He'll be here tonight to welcome you himself over dinner. In the meantime, did you have any questions or concerns for me?"

Elora shook her head. "I think I'm good for now."

"I assume, you have brought a camera along with you?" Elora nodded. "Feel free to photograph anything you like; I simply ask for the opportunity to review all pictures prior to you submitting any to your editor for publication. Is that satisfactory with you?"

"Of course."

"Great, then I shall show you around and drop you off at your room upstairs. You'll have some time to relax and settle in before dinner this evening."

"Perfect."

Zaidan led Elora on a brief tour of the compound and informed her of the basic security protocols—namely, never leave the premises without an armed escort—then showed her to her room on the third floor of the main house. It was a large room with a king bed, upon which Elora's duffle bag was already resting, and private en suite bath. "You have satellite TV, and there is high-speed Wi-Fi throughout the entire main building here. There are extra linens and fresh towels in the closet, and the bathroom is fully stocked with toiletries." Zaidan paused and glanced around to make sure he'd covered everything. "And, on that note, I will leave you to relax. Please join us downstairs for dinner tonight at eight. Is there anything else you need before I go?"

Elora looked around and then shook her head. "I'd say you pretty much covered it."

Zaidan smiled and left the room, closing the door behind him.

Elora let out a massive sigh that was a combination of exhaustion, relief, and anxiety. Jet lag was now setting in full force. She glanced at her watch and saw she had five hours until dinner—plenty of time for a solid nap. Aside from an hour or two of dozing on the flight, she'd been awake for almost thirty-six hours. First order of business, though, was to call Nick and let him know she'd arrived safely. She pulled the satellite phone out of her backpack and dialed Nick's burner phone.

"Elora?" Nick answered after a single ring. "Is everything okay? Did you make it to Baghdad?"

"Hey, Nathan," she said in a relaxed tone, using his alias in case her room was bugged. "Yes, I'm here; all is well."

Nick breathed a sigh of relief. "Okay, great. Keep me posted. We're all missing you here back home."

"Thanks, Nate. Tell everyone I said hi."

"Good luck," he added, hoping she heard the multitude of sentiment he camouflaged in those two words.

She slid the phone back into her backpack and fought the urge to collapse onto the bed and nap. Instead, she opened her duffle bag and dug out a fresh change of clothes. She wanted to shower and brush her teeth before passing out.

Chapter 10

The next morning, a line of four white Nissan Armada SUVs idled on the street in front of the New Dawn compound. The NDU entourage was heading out that day to conduct a campaign stop at a popular Baghdad street market with one of their Parliamentary candidates, Walid Hassan. Zaidan led Elora to the last vehicle in the line and gestured for her to get in the front passenger seat as he slid into the driver's seat. From behind the wheel, Zaidan watched Elora closely as she climbed in next to him. She met his gaze and her cheeks grow hot. The morning sunlight transformed his smoldering eyes into an impossible sea green color that took her breath, and, once again, stirred the butterflies in her stomach. A hint of a smile passed across Zaidan's face before he shifted his focus to the rearview mirror.

"Are you locked and loaded back there?" Zaidan asked Fareed, who was sitting in the backseat clutching an AK-47 tightly to his chest. Their eyes met in the rearview mirror and Fareed gave Zaidan a simple nod.

Zaidan slipped off his blazer and draped it across the center console. Elora saw he was wearing a double shoulder pistol holster with two Browning 9mm handguns tucked into each side. She tried to look away, but her attention caught on his fitted dark gray button-down shirt, which clung to his chest and abs in all the right places. Her eyes trailed down his torso to where his shirt was tucked into a pair of snug black chino pants—clinging to *another* part of his body. Elora finally forced her eyes front and willed her mind to crush the lewd thoughts it was seconds from conjuring.

In addition to the AK rifle Fareed was holding in the backseat, there was a second AK wedged between the front seat floorboard and the SUV's center console. Yes, this was Baghdad and Zaidan had promised a high level of security during Elora's visit, but she still sensed they were *expecting* trouble. There was a level of tension in the air that Elora was familiar with, recalling the same atmosphere several times during her past deployments to Iraq.

"Simply precaution," Zaidan commented, noticing Elora cataloging all the firepower in the vehicle.

The rest of the entourage finally emerged from the compound and began loading up into the other SUVs. The first vehicle held a reporter and cameraman from a local Baghdad news channel, along with two private photographers NDU had hired to snap pictures of the day's events. Samir and his security detail went into the second vehicle. The third vehicle was for the election candidate, Walid, and his family. The convoy would swing by and pick them up from their home on the way to the market.

When everyone was loaded up in the SUVs, Zaidan plucked a two-way radio from the cup-holder beside him and radioed for the lead vehicle to pull out. The caravan snaked its way west through the Mansour neighborhood and crossed a set of railroad tracks. Several minutes later, they pulled up in front of a large upper-middle class home. Elora watched as Walid Hassan, his wife, Sura and their three children, ranging in age from eight to fourteen, climbed into the SUV in front of her.

The convoy continued into a busy area of downtown Baghdad bustling with pedestrians. The line of white Armadas turned off onto a side street and parallel parked along the curb. The New Dawn entourage poured out of the vehicles and gathered on the narrow sidewalk along the wall of a building that ran the length of the alley. Walid and his family members wore homemade campaign T-shirts and clutched stacks of flyers they planned to pass out to potential voters as the group meandered through the bazaar and socialized with the public. Though their tactics were rudimentary, in a country still taking its first steps toward democracy, Elora found their efforts inspiring.

Zaidan asked Walid and his family to pose with Samir so the photographers could get a few group photos before everyone spread out to mingle. Everyone smiled wide for the camera, and a couple of the kids flashed peace signs as the photographers snapped away. Zaidan whistled and the NDU security team jogged over to gather around him. He proceeded to give his men some last-minute instructions before the team broke from their huddle and fanned out to their assigned positions.

Zaidan had one of the security guards remain with the vehicles and told the rest of the group to move out. The entourage turned the corner and headed down busy Mutanabi Street, famous for its booksellers and other merchants. Elora kept toward the rear of the procession and remained on full alert, recalling that Mutanabi Street had been the site of a gruesome suicide bombing several years earlier that killed dozens of civilians.

Walid and his family greeted vendors, shook hands with shoppers and chit-chatted with the locals as the group moseyed through the marketplace. The children giggled with excitement as they proudly distributed the flyers displaying their father's photo to passersby. Walid stopped every so often to pose for photos with willing participants and waved to curious onlookers gazing down on the scene from windows and balconies above the marketplace.

Zaidan maintained a serious expression as he scanned the crowds and rotated throughout the New Dawn group. He walked near Samir at some points and fell back closer to Elora at others. He stopped every so often to whisper in the ear of one of his security men and several times yelled out a general order for the entire group to tighten up. The market was shoulder-to-shoulder in some areas, and Zaidan's anxiety was palpable. Elora could clearly see the apprehension flash across his face when he'd momentarily lose sight of a member of the group.

Once the New Dawn entourage had made it a quarter of a mile down Mutanabi Street, Zaidan gave the signal for them to reverse course and head back in the direction of the vehicles. They crossed the street and worked their way back up the other side of the road to greet and mingle with a new set of merchants and shoppers on the return trip. It took twenty minutes for the group to make it back to the side street where the caravan was parked. They crossed back over Mutanabi Street and approached the line of familiar white Nissan Armadas. As everyone began to cluster again beside the row of SUVs, Elora backed off to the far side of the street to take some photos of the group. Just as she began clicking away on her camera, the sound of gunfire erupted in the small alley. She instinctively ducked behind one of the parked cars across from the convoy, and dropped down into a crouched position. Peeking around the rear bumper of the vehicle she was hiding behind, she saw half a dozen men dressed in black tactical gear with facemasks firing AK-47 rifles as they closed in on the New Dawn convoy. Those in the New Dawn group not yet in the vehicles charged the rest of the way toward the SUVs and dove inside for cover. The four security guards around Samir, including Fareed, shielded him with their bodies as they shoved him inside the lead vehicle and then peeled away from the scene. Elora heard the unmistakable screams of victims being struck by the attackers' bullets, and knew she needed to find better cover. For a split second, she thought of trying to make a run for the convoy, but she was pinned down by the incessant gunfire and decided to take cover closer to her position. She dropped to her stomach and scooted her body beneath the car she was crouched behind. Once concealed beneath the vehicle, she turned her head just in time to see a second Armada evacuate the street, tires screeching and leaving trails of smoking rubber behind. The rear doors flapped open as the vehicle tore around the corner to race away from the ambush.

A contingent of the New Dawn security team remained behind and was engaging the attackers. Elora prayed they could hold them off; she desperately wished she had a weapon of her own to defend herself. At present, she was a sitting duck beneath the car with nowhere to go. Her hopes dwindled as she watched one of the New Dawn security men across the road take a round to the upper thigh and collapse. Just as he hit the ground, Elora saw someone climb on top of the hood of the front NDU vehicle. Focusing her eyes, she recognized the unmistakable facial features of Zaidan. He held an AK-47 up to his shoulder and fired it in controlled bursts, picking off three of the attackers with precision marksmanship. The masked men collapsed in the road almost directly between Elora and the New Dawn vehicles across from her. The gunfire suddenly halted and Zaidan slid off the hood of the SUV. He jogged back to check on the downed New Dawn man who'd taken the hit to the thigh. He was bleeding profusely.

"Get him to the hospital," Zaidan barked at two other New Dawn security guards who'd been returning fire from behind the remaining NDU vehicles.

The men ran from behind the Nissans, scooped up their comrade, and lifted him into the backseat of the lead SUV. Zaidan disappeared around the other side of the vehicles, and Elora heard the doors slam shut. She watched the third Armada speed away down the small side street and disappear around the corner onto the main road. *Oh, fuck! Did they all just take off without me?* One NDU vehicle was left in the alley, but she wasn't sure if anyone from her group was still there. She thought Zaidan had seen her under the car from across the street, but she wasn't positive. She realized he might not have noticed her after all and may have thought she'd already evacuated in one of the other cars that left. She considered crawling out from under the car and making a run for the main street. As she was calculating how long it would take her to make it from the car out to Mutanabi street, one of the three masked men lying in the street made a loud groaning sound. Elora spun her head back around to look at the gunmen Zaidan had taken down and saw one was moving. He rolled over, moaning and writhing in pain as blood pooled around his lower abdomen.

Elora was about to make her escape when she heard footsteps on the ground and froze. *Fuck, fuck, fuck!* She was beyond relieved when she saw the footsteps were Zaidan's. He slung the AK-47 he was carrying across his back and pulled the two

Browning pistols from the holsters beneath his blazer. He walked up to the injured, moaning gunman and squatted next to his head. Elora watched as Zaidan bent close to the wounded man and appeared to whisper something in his ear. Zaidan then stood back up, pointed one of the pistols several inches from the man's forehead, and pulled the trigger. Elora jumped when the shot rang out. The masked man slumped to the street with half his skull blown out the back of his head. *Holy shit.*

Zaidan stepped over the man he'd just executed and checked the other two bodies for pulses. Confirming they were dead, he popped back up and scanned the area. He then began approaching her position. Elora relaxed. *He does know I'm here.*

Zaidan was halfway to Elora when he caught movement out the corner of his eye. He stopped dead in his tracks and saw the top of a masked head crouched behind the passenger side fender of the car parked behind the one Elora was hiding under. Unaware of the gunman behind her, Elora began to wriggle herself out from under the car to meet up with Zaidan. As she moved, her shoes scratched against the loose gravel on the road and the resulting noise alerted the attacker to her presence. Zaidan raised both arms, leveling the pair of pistols in the direction of the crouched gunman, but he didn't have a clear shot past the vehicles. The gunman dropped down to look under the car in front of him, and Zaidan began sprinting the remainder of the distance to Elora.

"Elora! Move toward me, now!" he yelled out in English as he approached.

Hearing the panic in Zaidan's voice, Elora abandoned her delicate technique. She engaged all her strength and pulled with her arms while simultaneously pushing with her legs to launch herself out from under the car. As the masked man aimed his weapon beneath the vehicle to take a shot at Elora, Zaidan dropped to one knee from his sprint and slid like a runner stealing second base. As he slid, he fired both pistols beneath the vehicles in the direction of the gunman. None of the shots hit the gunman, but it caused him to retreat long enough to give Zaidan time to get a hand on Elora. He ripped her the rest of the way out from beneath the car, wrapped an arm around her waist, and spun her like a rag doll away from the gunman. Shielding her with his body, he used the pistol in his free hand to pop off a couple more shots at the assailant. This time, one of the shots connected with the gunman's shoulder. The masked man howled in pain and dropped his AK-47 to press the wound on his injured shoulder.

Zaidan turned his attention to Elora, spinning her around to face him. He scanned her from head to toe, noticing her ripped and bloodied pants. "Are you injured?" he half screamed in her face.

Elora shook her head. "No, no, just scratches," she yelled back.

"Go to the truck," he commanded and shoved the keys in her hand. "Get inside and lock the doors."

Elora hauled ass to the SUV, tore open the door, and dove into the driver's seat. She locked the doors, slid the key into the ignition, and started the engine in case she needed to make a quick getaway. She had a perfect view of Zaidan and the injured gunman through the windshield of the SUV. She squeezed her eyes shut, figuring Zaidan was about to put a bullet in this guy's head like he'd done the last one. But Zaidan had other plans for this one. He holstered one of his pistols and grabbed the injure man by the collar with his now free hand. He pushed the gunman flat on the concrete and pressed the muzzle of the pistol into the man's cheek while straddling his body. He said something to the man as he rolled him over on his stomach, repositioning the pistol to the back of the man's head. The gunman pleaded for his life as Zaidan yanked him to his knees and then up the rest of the way to his feet. Zaidan turned him to face Elora's direction and gave him a shove to initiate the pair's half walk, half shuffle toward the SUV.

When Zaidan and his captive had almost reached the SUV, Elora hit the unlock button and hopped out to open the rear passenger door behind the driver's side. "I take it he's coming with us," she quipped.

"Yes," Zaidan replied gruffly. "You'll need to drive."

"Yeah, I kind of figured that."

Zaidan shoved the injured man into the back seat and climbed in after him. He half sat on top of the man and pressed one of his Browning pistols into the side of the man's skull.

Elora climbed back into the driver's seat, pressed the door lock button again, and shifted the SUV into gear. "You're going to have to tell me where to go," she said, making eye contact with Zaidan in the SUV's rear-view mirror.

"Go out to the main road and turn right."

For the next fifteen minutes, Zaidan guided Elora through the streets of Baghdad, until she saw the familiar New Dawn headquarters compound come into sight. She slowed the SUV and turned into the main entrance. Already aware of the attack, the two armed guards on duty at the gate were on high alert and leveled their AKs at Elora as soon as she pulled into the driveway. Elora slammed on the breaks and threw her hands up in surrender.

Zaidan opened the back door and climbed out of the SUV, pulling his prisoner out after him. As soon as they saw Zaidan, the gate guards sprang into action and assisted him in moving the wounded prisoner. Elora lowered her hands but remained in the vehicle.

"Put him in the holding room and have someone keep an eye on him," Zaidan instructed the head gate guard. "Have Nazar patch up his shoulder. I'll be up later to *talk* to him."

"Yes, sir," the guard replied and led the captive away to the two-story outbuilding.

"Where is Samir?" Zaidan asked the remaining gate guard as he pulled his cell phone from his jacket pocket and quickly dialed a number. "Have you heard from Fareed?"

"Fareed radioed and said they were taking Samir to the safehouse," the guard answered. "I assume they are all fine, otherwise they'd have headed to the hospital."

"Let's hope," Zaidan replied, his cell phone now pressed to his ear with the number he'd dialed ringing on the other end. "Samir!" he blurted into the phone. "How are you brother? Are you hurt at all? *Hamdulillah*—thank God." Once he learned Samir was safe and uninjured, his tone shifted from panic to relief. He then told Samir and Fareed about the assailant he'd brought back to the compound. "Wait a few hours for things to cool off, then come back here. We need to *talk* to this asshole tonight to figure out what the fuck he knows."

Zaidan hung up the phone and turned back to the gate guard. "Is everyone else accounted for?"

Elora overheard the guard tell Zaidan that the NDU security member wounded in the firefight had made it to the hospital. He was undergoing surgery, but the doctors expected him to survive. She also learned that one of the photographers had been shot in the hand. Walid and his family were shaken up but unharmed.

Once Zaidan ensured everyone was accounted for, he shifted his attention back to Elora, who was still sitting behind the wheel of the SUV.

"Pull on through the gate and park it in the carport," he instructed her.

Elora parked the car and edged out of the driver's seat. Her adrenaline had subsided, so she was now feeling the pain of the many cuts, scrapes, and bruises covering her arms and legs.

Zaidan walked up behind the SUV and watched as Elora winced in pain while getting out. He jogged up to her and offered a supporting arm. "Let's head upstairs and have a look at those gashes," he said as he helped her hobble into the main house.

Zaidan led Elora upstairs into an expansive suite at the end of the second-floor hall, she recalled Zaidan telling her during her tour that it was the room Samir stayed in. She tried to conceal her open-mouthed gape as they walked through the massive, regal bedroom and into a large bathroom covered in floor-to-ceiling marble. During her first Iraq deployment, Elora had gotten a chance to see inside one of Saddam's former palaces—this suite reminded her of the rooms in that palace.

Zaidan gestured for Elora to have a seat on the edge of a two-person jacuzzi tub and then rummaged through a cabinet for first-aid supplies: bandages, rubbing alcohol, and a pair of medical scissors. He set the items on the floor next to Elora and kneeled in front of her.

"All right, let's see what the damage is," he said, picking up the medical scissors. "These pants are goners—do you mind if I cut them off here above the knees? I want to make sure you don't need stitches for any of your gashes."

"I don't think any of them are serious," she said. "Some soap and water with a few bandaids should suffice." She thought it was sweet that he was personally tending to her scrapes but also wished he'd just give her the supplies and let her clean and bandage herself up in privacy. The fact that she hadn't shaved her legs since leaving the U.S. fueled this desire, but she surrendered to Zaidan's first-aid treatment.

He cut her tattered pants' legs off at the knees and tossed the filthy scraps against the wall. Taking Elora's left leg in his hands, he extended it to examine her injuries. Satisfied the wounds on her left leg didn't need anything beyond standard first aid, he moved on to her other leg. He surveyed the splotchy patchwork of scratches and dried blood mixed with sandy dirt, his eyes lingering on one particularly gnarly gash above her right knee. He cleaned the scrape with some soap and water but determined it too did not require professional attention. Zaidan conducted his examination without a word, and the silence was beginning to make Elora feel awkward.

"Well, you've got some nasty road rash, and it looks like you'll see a few bruises," he finally said as he gently lowered her right leg. "But you'll live to write another article," he added with a sly smirk that Elora found incredibly sexy.

"Thanks, *Doctor* Zaidan," Elora jested, flashing a flirtatious look of her own. Zaidan smiled, but there was something hidden behind his smile, though she wasn't sure what.

"You did well today," he said, eyeing her from beneath his brows. "Most American girls would have had—as the Americans say—a *total meltdown* out there and would be begging for the next flight home right now."

"Well, it wasn't my first rodeo. I've done several combat reporting embeds with U.S. military units in Iraq and Afghanistan," Elora lied. "I did about shit my pants, though, when I thought you all had left me behind under that car. That was a bit terrifying." She tried to sound nonchalant about the incident, but Zaidan could hear the fear in her voice.

"I'd never leave you behind," he countered almost defensively. "I'm sorry you had to go through that."

"And I'm sorry one of your men got hurt, the photographer too, but I guess we're lucky no one was killed."

"We were *extremely* lucky," Zaidan countered. "They got there late. Most of our people were loaded into the vehicles by the time they showed up and opened fire. Had we come back two minutes later, I fear today would have been a much bloodier outcome for us."

"I guess it's a good thing you turned the group around in the marketplace to head back when you did."

"I had a bad feeling from the minute we stepped onto Mutanabi Street," Zaidan said in a solemn tone. "I was so sure something was going to happen in the marketplace that it really took me by surprise when we were ambushed there in the alley, but my gut was right after all."

Elora recalled what Nick had told her about always listening to her gut before she'd boarded the plane to Baghdad. She wanted to ask Zaidan why he'd essentially executed the wounded assailant in the street but wasn't sure how to broach the question. She decided to go with her gut. "I saw you shoot that guy," she blurted, trying not to sound judgmental. "The wounded one," she clarified.

Zaidan inhaled slowly before responding, then lifted his piercing eyes to look directly into hers as he answered. "It was a mercy kill," he said. "He was fatally gut-shot and in a lot of pain. He'd have never made it off that street alive."

Elora narrowed her eyes and considered his answer for a few long seconds. She searched his face to analyze the validity of his statement, but he didn't flinch.

"You said something to him before you pulled the trigger," she added. "What did you whisper in his ear?"

"I told him I forgive him, and that Allah will too."

Elora maintained her laser-locked stare as she mulled this over, but Zaidan gave no indication of insincerity. She relaxed and broke eye contact, accepting Zaidan's explanation.

"I do apologize that it wasn't a relaxing day at the mall," he added, trying to lighten the mood.

Elora shrugged. "I've had worse shopping trips. Today was nothing compared to Black Friday at Best Buy."

"I'm not sure what half of what you just said means, but perhaps one day you'll explain it to me," he said, returning to his feet.

Sensing he was about to leave her to finish cleaning up on her own, Elora realized she hadn't thanked him yet and stood up to stop him. "Thank you, by the way," she blurted. "You know, for saving my life, and all," she added, glancing down at her newly-minted Bermuda shorts.

"You're welcome," he replied. "The last thing we need is our *famous* American correspondent being assassinated while here as our guest—that's not good for business."

"Ah, so you saved me simply to safeguard New Dawn's reputation?"

"Mostly," he answered matter-of-factly.

"And partly?"

"And partly because you intrigue me. I'm curious to learn more about you," he said, raising one brow. "And it's difficult to do that if you're dead."

"Oh, well that's…comforting. I guess?"

"There are few people in this world I've found interesting enough to bother getting to know," he said.

Elora's cheeks flushed, and she dropped her head to escape Zaidan's intense gaze. Taking her by surprise, he leaned in close to her, reaching out with his left arm. Elora froze and held her breath, thinking he was going to put his arm around her. Zaidan's cheek slid past hers and their chests were within an inch of each other. The intoxicating scent of his cologne washed over her and her knees went weak. She was anticipating his embrace when he retreated, clutching a white bath-towel in his hand. Elora rolled her eyes at her overreaction when she realized he'd simply reached passed her to retrieve a towel from the shelf behind her.

"You should go ahead and get all those cuts washed out," he said, dangling the towel in front of her. "I'll leave the alcohol and bandages on the counter here for you to disinfect and patch up the deeper ones."

Elora released the breath she'd been holding. "Right," she said with an embarrassed smile. *You did that on purpose, asshole.*

Zaidan smirked; he knew exactly what he'd done.

"I'll have one of the cleaning staff leave a robe for you on the bed out in the room," he said, breaking the tense silence. "Please take the remainder of the afternoon to rest and recuperate. We have a dinner meeting scheduled tonight for eight o'clock at the Al-Rasheed Hotel, so let's meet downstairs at seven thirty. I'd like to discuss your first article. Obviously, the campaign stop is going to have an interesting twist to it now, but we can spin it in a manner that will work to our advantage. I apologize for shifting right into business mode so soon after today's unpleasant event, but if we canceled our plans every time someone shot at us here in Iraq, we'd never get anything done."

"It's all right. I'm okay," Elora said. "Thanks again for the first aid."

"You're welcome. Now, if you'll excuse me; I have some pressing matters to attend to downstairs."

Elora figured his *pressing matters* were related to the injured prisoner he had locked up in the compound garage. She closed her eyes and tried to shake the thoughts from her head. She finished undressing and stepped into the large walk-in shower next to the tub. As the soothing warm water washed over her face, images from the attack flashed into her mind. She tried to shove them down, knowing that rehashing such thoughts over and over in your head is what makes you go crazy. However, she kept flashing back to the moment Zaidan had executed the wounded man in the street. She'd believed him when he'd said it was a mercy kill. Elora could see with her own eyes the man was in bad shape. What concerned her was the ruthless look in Zaidan's eyes, and the emotionless expression on his face when he'd pulled the trigger.

She'd seen men show more compassion when putting animals out of their misery. Then again, the animals hadn't been shooting at them first.

She also couldn't shake her curiosity regarding the manner in which Zaidan had spoken to Samir on the phone. Granted, Samir was more than Zaidan's boss; he was also a friend and they had just endured a traumatic experience, but still, there was a unique level of tenderness and compassion in Zaidan's voice that seemed out of character for his personality.

Although Zaidan and Samir's mysterious relationship was a big question in Elora's mind, there was an even bigger one plaguing her at the moment. What was going to happen to the injured attacker Zaidan had brought back? Was he going to turn him over to the authorities? What was he going to do to him *before* turning him over? Her stomach churned at the thought of Zaidan and his men brutally interrogating and torturing him, but another part of her was not so bothered by the man's current situation. He had, after all, tried to shoot her while she was hiding under the car. He was part of a militant group that tried to murder the entire NDU entourage, of which she was a part. She reconciled that he was going to get what he deserved.

As for Zaidan, he was polished and professional on the outside, but when she looked into his eyes—his very enchanting eyes—she saw a dark hole. Her concerns ebbed as she recalled the gentleness of his touch when he'd examined her injuries, and she blushed again at the obvious flirtatious manner in which he'd grabbed that towel from behind her. She couldn't deny the rush of excitement she felt when she was close to him. It was something she'd never experienced before and wasn't even sure how to describe. It was like a fiery electric current coursed through her veins when she was near him, and the closer he got, the stronger the current. It amazed her how her feelings for Zaidan had changed since they first met. She'd felt so uncomfortable in his presence; he'd made her skin crawl. But the more she thought about it, the more she realized it was the same sensation—the same electricity. She'd been so resistant to him in the beginning that instead of the electricity giving her butterflies as it did now, it made her flustered and anxious. Zaidan had many layers, and all Elora knew for sure was that what she'd encountered so far only scratched the surface.

Chapter 11

The sun was setting as Zaidan, flanked by Samir and Fareed, marched across the NDU compound yard toward the two-story garage. They climbed a small wooden staircase to the second level of the garage and headed down a narrow hall. At the end of the hall, Zaidan gave a silent nod to an NDU security guard armed with an AK-47 standing watch outside a locked metal door. The guard unlocked and opened the door for Zaidan and the others to enter.

The wounded attacker sat in a white, plastic chair, his hands chained to a metal table, his feet bound together with plastic zip-ties. He was shirtless and his injured shoulder was wrapped in a large bandage taped around his chest, the white gauze already showing signs of seeping blood. He was half slumped over, sweat dripping from his pale face and pooling on the smooth surface of the table.

Zaidan took a seat in the empty chair across the table from the prisoner. He stared in silence at the wounded man, studying him for several long minutes. The young militant kept his head down, his eyes fixed on his chained hands folded atop the table.

"What is your name?" Zaidan finally asked in a calm, level tone.

The detainee did not answer.

"Look, we can do this the easy way or the hard way," Zaidan continued. "Answer my questions and we drop you off at a hospital. Be a dick and I'll make you wish I'd shot you in the fucking face and left you dead in the street with your buddies. So, let's try again. What. Is. Your Name?"

"Abbas," the captive mumbled through clenched teeth.

"Good," Zaidan said with a satisfied nod. He leaned forward, resting his arms on the table. "How old are you, Abbas?"

"Twenty-two."

"What militia do you fight for?"

Abbas pursed his lips and did not answer. He squeezed his eyes shut and winced at the burning pain in his shoulder.

"Abbas, what militia are you with?" Zaidan pressed.

Abbas kept his eyes clenched and shook his head.

"Did doc give him any antibiotics?" Zaidan asked, turning to Fareed. "This asshole may be here a few days; the last thing we need is him dying on us from a fucking infection."

Fareed nodded. "Doc shot him up with penicillin and said his wound was a clean in-and-out."

"You hear that, Abbas?" Zaidan said, shifting his attention back to the young militant. "I know it hurts, but it sounds like you're going to be just fine. This is great news, if of course, you tell me what I want to know. In which case, you get to go home to your family and live a long happy life. However, if you don't answer my questions, the fact that you're *not* dying is going to be *bad* news. It means you and I will stay in this room for as long as it takes for me to get what I need. You will be alert as I cut your fingers and toes off one by one until you answer my simple questions. Once we've finished removing all your digits, things will get even more creative from there. I can assure you of one thing, though. You will remain alive for a very, very long time."

Zaidan paused to let Abbas process his statement. "What militia are you with?" he asked again.

A flicker of fear flashed across Abbas's face. He swallowed hard but still did not speak.

"You're a brave kid, Abbas, but whoever you're protecting, trust me, they're not worth it." Zaidan leaned back in his chair and gave Abbas a few more seconds to reconsider, but he remained silent.

"Take his shoes off," Zaidan said to Fareed as he popped up from his chair and slipped out of the room.

Fareed and the NDU guard swooped in and grabbed Abbas. He yelped in pain as they ripped him out of the chair and slammed him face down on top of the metal table. Fareed pinned him down while the young NDU guard yanked his boots off.

The guard was pulling off Abbas's last sock when Zaidan came back in, holding a large pair of bolt cutters. He walked around the table and squatted in front of Abbas's head, brandishing the bolt cutters so Abbas got a good look at them.

"I'm going to ask you once more," Zaidan said, looking Abbas directly in the eye. "What militia are you with?"

Abbas was shaking in terror but still refused to answer. Zaidan stood back up and walked around to the end of the table. Abbas squealed and squirmed beneath Fareed and the NDU guard, but Zaidan held his left foot and was able to get the bolt cutter around the big toe.

A split-second before Zaidan snapped the handles shut to sever the toe, Abbas screamed out. "*Badr Brigade*! I serve with the Badr Brigade!"

Zaidan pulled the bolt cutters away from Abbas's foot.

"See, that wasn't so difficult now, was it?" Zaidan sat back down in his chair, but Fareed and the NDU guard kept Abbas pinned on top of the table. "Where are you from, Abbas?"

"Kar…Karbala," Abbas said, panting.

"You seem like a decent kid, Abbas. What's a good kid from a proud Iraqi city doing fighting alongside Iranian thugs? Why risk your life to attack your own people at the command of an Iranian Republican Guard General?"

Abbas dropped his head down on the table, his forehead pressed against the cold metal. "My family in Karbala is starving," he said in little more than a whisper. "My father died in the war, and now my mother and little brother have nothing. Badr Brigade gave me a job—I get paid and I can feed my family."

"So, you're only doing this for a paycheck?" Zaidan asked.

"No." He cocked his head to look at Zaidan. "You Sunni scum have been shitting on the Shiites for generations," he spat with venom. "I pledge loyalty to Supreme Leader of the Islamic Revolution, Ayatollah Khamenei, who will bring peace and prosperity to our nation!"

Zaidan shook his head. "You brainwashed little shit. You have no clue what you're a part of. *No one* in Tehran is trying to bring peace and prosperity to Iraq, you stupid fuck! You're a tool. *They're* the reason your family is starving in the first place. They're bleeding our country dry. You're taking their fifty dollars a week in exchange for fighting their proxy war that's impoverishing your own country."

"You're a lying Sunni dog," Abbas replied with acid in his tone. "You're all nothing but terrorists and fucking torturous butchers!"

"We fight for a united Iraq, where no Iraqi is above another—Sunni, Shiite, Christian, Yazidi…whatever. At the end of the day, we are *all* Iraqi, and our first loyalty should be to our nation. You've been duped, Abbas." Zaidan stood back up from his chair. "Open your fucking eyes. These assholes have been pulling all the strings within the Iraqi government for ten years, yet they still haven't figured out how to turn the fucking lights back on. It's bullshit. They're keeping us in the dark on purpose, so they can rape us of our resources and future." Zaidan dropped the bolt cutters and let them clatter to the floor.

"Have a couple of the guys dump him in front of the hospital," Zaidan instructed Fareed in a defeated tone. He then spun around, stomped back down the stairs, and stormed out the side door of the garage. Stepping out into the dusk air, he halted and took a deep breath to calm his nerves. He stared out across the compound yard with his hands on his hips, an apprehensive expression etched across his face. A few seconds later, Zaidan heard the door open behind him. He knew it was Samir, but he did nothing to acknowledge his presence.

Samir could practically feel the tension radiating off Zaidan's body, so he remained back and patiently waited for his chief of staff to cool down. Finally, Samir stepped up behind Zaidan and placed a reassuring hand on Zaidan's shoulder. Zaidan closed his eyes and dropped his head, exhaling through pursed lips. Samir moved closer and placed a second hand on Zaidan's other shoulder.

"It's not your fault," Samir said in a comforting tone no louder than a whisper.

"We almost lost people today," Zaidan countered. "*You*

could have been killed today."

"But we didn't," Samir replied, giving Zaidan's shoulders a soft squeeze. "Everyone is alive because of *you*." Samir bowed his head and lightly rested his forehead on Zaidan's upper back. He inhaled and closed his eyes.

"Samir...don't," Zaidan said softly.

"I know, I'm sorry." Samir lifted his head, but his hands remained on Zaidan's shoulders.

Seconds later they heard footsteps coming down the wooden stairs inside the garage. Zaidan took a swift step forward out from under Samir's grip. He spun around to face the side door of the garage, just as Fareed and the NDU guard emerged with the wounded militant in tow.

"Come right back here after dropping him at the hospital," Zaidan instructed Fareed. "We have a dinner meeting tonight at the Al-Rasheed Hotel. We'll need to double the security detail, so I need both of you back in time to join us."

As Fareed and the other guard scurried away with Abbas between them, Zaidan's two-way radio crackled to life, and he heard his callsign come across the waves.

"Z-Chief? Come in, Z-Chief. This is Doc."

Zaidan reached beneath his blazer and pulled the handheld radio off his waistband. "Z-Chief here. Go ahead Doc."

"Z-Chief, Sherlock is back from London. He's waiting for you in your office."

Sherlock was the radio callsign for NDU's intelligence director, Bashir Mustafa. *London* was the codename for the NDU intel collection office, which operated out of the back of an internet café on the outskirts of western Baghdad.

"Roger. Be there in two." Zaidan clipped the radio back on his belt and turned to Samir. "Head up and get ready for dinner. We leave in half an hour."

Zaidan stepped into his office and greeted Bashir with a handshake. He then made a beeline for his stash of whiskey perched on the credenza behind his desk.

"Can I get you a drink?" Zaidan offered.

"Bourbon neat, please."

Zaidan made Bashir's drink, then poured a whiskey for himself.

"How's the interrogation going?" Bashir asked, settling into the guest chair in front of Zaidan's desk.

"He's a fucking foot soldier," Zaidan replied in an irritated tone. "He barely knows more than we know; actually, we may know more. Fareed is dumping him at the hospital now." Zaidan handed Bashir his drink and took his seat behind his desk. "How about your team? Any new info yet on this morning's attack?"

"We know it was Badr Brigade, operating under direct orders from General Ansari."

Zaidan rolled his eyes. "I'm changing your callsign to *No Shit Sherlock*."

Bashir flashed a tight smile. "Yeah, I figured you knew as much."

"So, did you come all the way over here to tell me what I already fucking know?"

"No. I came to tell you something else that isn't going to make you happy."

"That's just fucking fantastic," Zaidan said with a sardonic chuckle as he rubbed his forehead in annoyance. "Please, enlighten me."

"Your *Washington Post* reporter…"

Zaidan swallowed his mouthful of Johnnie Walker. "Elora?"

Bashir nodded slowly. "Her name isn't Elora Reid."

Zaidan's eyebrows lifted in interest as he waited for Bashir to elaborate.

"Her real name is Elora Monro," Bashir continued. "Zaidan…she's CIA."

Zaidan sat back in his chair and steepled his hands in silence as he processed Bashir's news.

"Is this information reliable?" Zaidan finally asked.

"Yes. It comes from our source inside the U.S. Defense Intelligence Agency."

"Fuck," Zaidan muttered half to himself. "What else do we know about her?"

"My men are digging into her full background now. I should have more info for you in a day or two."

Zaidan's expression looked tense but not as angry as Bashir feared.

"In the meantime," Bashir continued, "how do you want to handle the situation?"

Zaidan tapped his fingers on his desk in thought for several seconds before answering. "Who else knows the truth about her?" he asked.

"Just you, me, and our mole inside the DIA."

"Keep it that way. Don't even tell Samir," Zaidan instructed. "I'll handle this myself. How is our project coming along in the south?" Zaidan asked, moving on to a different subject.

"Slow but steady," Bashir answered with a sigh. "Karim is gaining some supporters and the militia is now a couple hundred strong."

The *project* Zaidan was referring to, was a Shiite militia NDU was building from the ground up in a Shia neighborhood on the outskirts of southern Baghdad. They'd groomed a charismatic young Shiite named Karim Sadat to lead the organization. Samir and Zaidan both knew Karim from college. Like them, Karim was a secular nationalist, resentful of the power Tehran was wielding in Baghdad. NDU had been pumping a significant amount of money into the group, hoping to grow their militia numbers by offering a handsome salary to fighters who joined. The long-term plan was to establish the militia as a prominent anti-Sunni organization with flashy rhetoric that would make waves and capture attention. The attention they specifically wanted to attract was General Ali Ansari's. If rumors were true that Ansari was working to unite the prominent Shiite militias and bring them under his leadership, they hoped to bait him into extending Karim an invitation to merge his militia with the others under the General's umbrella. This would open the door for NDU to infiltrate General Ansari's faction, gather intel, and, hopefully, create an opportunity for them to take him down. The process, however, was painfully slow and even more painfully expensive, but Zaidan had confidence the plan would pay off in the end.

"We need them to start moving against some targets," Zaidan instructed Bashir. "The time for idle threats is over. They need to back up their rhetoric with some action in order to move to the next level."

Bashir nodded and Zaidan glanced down at his watch. "I have to head out," he said, rising from his chair. "Get me that additional info on Elora as soon as you can," he said, reaching out to shake Bashir's hand, "and good work."

Elora sat on one of the parlor sofas waiting to leave for dinner, when she heard footsteps approaching from down the hall. Within seconds, Zaidan appeared in the doorway.

"Good evening, Ms. Reid." His tone was curiously formal. *So, we're back to 'Ms. Reid'?* Elora returned his greeting and waited for him to come in and have a seat, but he remained standing in the doorway, his stone-cold gaze zeroed in on her.

After several seconds of awkward silence, Samir came down the stairs and stood beside Zaidan. He too sensed a strange tension in the air. "Are we ready to go?" Samir asked, his eyes darting back and forth between Zaidan and Elora.

"Yes," Zaidan replied coldly. "*Yalla*—let's go," he added, spinning on his heels and swiftly moving to the front door.

"Are you sure we shouldn't have dinner here in the compound tonight?" Elora asked, halting Zaidan mid-stride. She understood Zaidan's point of not allowing the attack to derail plans, but she was still leery of taking such a risk for something as frivolous as going out to dinner. It seemed like an unnecessary hazard.

"I told you," Zaidan replied, turning his head to glare at Elora. "We will not hide. We've remained in the shadows too long as it is."

"Zaidan is right," Samir said, stepping up in support of his chief of staff. "As you say in America, we must get right back on the horse. We will not be intimidated or suppressed by these terrorists."

Elora couldn't help but laugh at the irony of Samir's statement in her head, but she didn't allow her face to reveal her sentiments.

"We will have extra security with us tonight," Zaidan added, his ice-cold tone coming off as less than reassuring.

"Okay," Elora relented and threw her hands in the air, "*yalla.*"

Two of NDU's white Nissan SUVs were idling in the carport. Samir climbed into the back seat of the second vehicle joining five NDU security guards, including Fareed, who was driving. Zaidan instructed Elora to get into the backseat of the lead vehicle while he himself slid into the driver's seat. Elora entered to find four armed NDU security guards waiting inside.

"You weren't kidding about the extra security," Elora quipped as she buckled her seatbelt.

Zaidan ignored her comment. He threw the vehicle into gear and gunned it out of the carport and down the driveway. He made a hard-left turn onto the street that forcefully tossed Elora against her door, but she did not utter a sound. There was no doubt in Elora's mind now, Zaidan was pissed off about something. She thought perhaps he was still upset about the ambush, but he'd been so gentle and attentive when helping her clean up her wounds. Something must have happened between then and now that caused a major shift in his mood. She speculated it had something to do with the wounded man they'd taken back with them from the marketplace. She'd thought about broaching the subject over dinner, but considering Zaidan's current demeanor, she decided to shelf that idea for the time being.

Ten minutes into their drive, Zaidan guided the SUV over to the curb and parked along the street a block down from the Al-Rasheed hotel. The second SUV carrying Samir parked behind them, and everyone unloaded onto the sidewalk. The security team left their AK rifles inside the vehicles but all carried pistols concealed in holsters beneath their blazers. Zaidan had two men remain behind to stand watch over the vehicles while the rest of the group made their way down the street toward the hotel.

Along the way, the entourage passed a line of vendor carts manned by street merchants beckoning them to stop and browse the various trinkets they were selling. Elora and the others ignored the calls of the retailers as they continued along their path toward the hotel. The group had almost reached the end of the mini bazaar when Elora sensed she was being watched. She casually glanced to her right and met the eyes of a young boy who looked about eleven years old. She gave the boy a small smile, and he cheerfully returned it with a wide grin. The boy was standing proudly beside a wooden cart with tiered shelves displaying a dozen oil paintings of various sizes. Elora stepped out of the NDU procession and approached the boy, halting in front of his cart to peruse the artwork. The boy jumped up in excitement and dashed to Elora's side as soon as she arrived.

Zaidan, who'd been walking behind Elora, let out an annoyed sigh when he saw her step out to browse one of the carts.

He hollered out for the rest of the group to stop and followed her to the cart. He stood a few feet behind her, arms crossed over his chest and an impatient look on his face as Elora greeted the boy.

"*Marhaba, shismak?* What's your name?" Elora kindly asked the boy in Arabic.

"Malik," the boy replied with a wide grin.

Elora's stomach tightened. Although quite a common name, it still struck her as a strange coincidence. She shook it off and turned her attention to the artwork.

"Who made all these?" Elora asked, figuring the artist was likely his father or another relative.

The boy puffed up with pride. "I painted them all myself," he announced.

"Wow," Elora said, genuinely impressed. "They are all beautiful. You're incredibly talented."

Elora's eyes were drawn to a painting sitting on the top shelf, half hidden behind another piece of art. "May I?" she asked the boy as she lifted her arm to reach out for the painting.

"Yes, of course," the boy encouraged.

Elora pulled the canvas down off the shelf and turned it to catch the light coming from a nearby streetlamp. The painting depicted a vast night sky filled with stars and the Milky Way. Beneath the sky, a lone Bedouin girl of five or six years old sat cross legged in the sand, her head tilted back to gaze up at the sky with the empty desert stretching out all around her. Elora was instantly enchanted by the painting.

"How much for this one?" she asked the boy.

"Uh…twenty-five dollars, American?" the boy blurted, sounding unsure of his own answer.

Several of the NDU security guards let out snorts of laughter when the boy quoted his price. Zaidan shot them an icy glare that brought their cackles to an abrupt halt.

"How about ten dollars?" Elora countered.

The boy bit his lip and furled his brow as he contemplated Elora's counteroffer.

"Fifteen?" the boy replied, again in the form of a question.

"Done," she said with a smile.

The boy's face lit up with delight, and he practically wiggled out of his skin in excitement as Elora reached into her backpack to retrieve his money. She pulled out fifteen dollars and handed it to him. She then passed the painting back to the boy, who looked at her in confusion.

"I noticed you don't have your name anywhere on it," Elora said as she reached back into her backpack and pulled out another ten-dollar bill. "I'll pay you ten dollars to sign the painting for me."

The boy's eyes bulged in surprise.

"Well, go ahead," Elora encouraged.

The boy hopped around behind his cart and amended the painting as Elora requested. A minute later he returned, gently blowing on the bottom right hand side of the painting before handing it back to her with a plastic bag to carry it in. She held it up again to look at it, seeing it now had his name written in fancy English scroll fonts in the bottom corner. "Now, it's perfect," Elora said, and handed the boy his extra ten dollars. "Who is the little girl in the painting?" Elora asked as she slid the canvas inside the plastic bag.

"My little sister," the boy replied, his smile fading. "She

lives in the stars now."

Elora knew what that meant. Her expression changed, softened and saddened by the subtle ache in the boy's voice. "I will treasure it forever," she said, pulling the bag to her chest.

The boy's ear-to-ear grin returned and remained as he watched Elora and the rest of the group disappear down the street and into the hotel.

Throughout dinner, Elora endured a barrage of penetrating stares from Zaidan that she could not decipher. The entire meal was beyond awkward, and at certain points she was sure she'd suffocate beneath his incessant glares. Her mind raced as the uncomfortable evening wore on. *Do I have food on my face? Is something stuck in my teeth?*

Samir and Fareed chit chatted with each other while Zaidan brooded in silence, and Elora did her best to cope. In an effort to thwart Zaidan's razor-sharp glares, Elora made several unsuccessful attempts to engage him in conversation.

"Did you find out who was behind this morning's attack?"

"Yes," Zaidan replied but did not elaborate.

Feeling her patience reach its breaking point, Elora stabbed at her food with her fork and tried one last time. She figured this would get his attention.

"How did the interrogation go?" she asked, mirroring his icy glare.

Samir and Fareed halted their chatter mid-sentence and turned their attention to Zaidan and Elora.

"Exactly as I knew it would," Zaidan responded after a few tense seconds. "I asked questions I already knew the answers to, and he responded right on cue. Anything else?"

Elora gave up and remained silent for the rest of the dinner. So much for discussing her first article.

She was beyond relieved when Zaidan finally gave the signal that it was time to wrap up dinner and leave. The group made their way back to the vehicles and loaded up to return to the compound. A few minutes into the drive home, Zaidan picked up his two-way radio and called to Fareed in the other vehicle.

"I have to make a stop," Zaidan told Fareed over the radio. "Take Samir back to the compound. We'll be along later."

"You sure we shouldn't stick together?" Fareed asked. "We can follow you wherever you're going."

"No, it's fine," Zaidan replied. "Go on back."

At the next roundabout, Elora watched the other SUV continue straight through, while Zaidan took the first right turn and headed toward the Tigris River.

Zaidan guided the Nissan into an open area that looked like an old park and stopped the SUV in a gravel lot. He instructed the security guys to remain in the vehicle, then he exited the car and went around to open Elora's door.

"Come with me," Zaidan said to Elora. "Let's take a walk."

Elora shot him an apprehensive look. "Are you sure?" she asked, surveying the dim lot.

"It's fine," Zaidan said, but his tone was less than reassuring. "Leave your bags here with the guys. You won't need them."

Elora took a deep breath and slipped out of the backseat. She stuck close to Zaidan's side as the two crossed the gravel lot and headed toward an open area blanketed with patchy dying grass. The moonlight was just strong enough for Elora to make out the skeletal remains of dilapidated playground equipment—a decaying metal slide, rusty monkey bars, and something else that was in such a sad state of disrepair she was unable to identify it. They continued past the playground equipment to the far side of the park overlooking the river. There they picked up a stone path, now cracked and half overgrown with weeds, and followed it down to a concrete boardwalk that ran along the bank of the river. The river-walk was lined with crumbling brick buildings and shops with shattered or boarded-up windows. Furniture that once adorned the outdoor patios of boutique cafés and ice-cream parlors was now piled into a mound of twisted wicker and rusted metal. Zaidan led Elora over to the railing that ran along the river side of the walkway and protected pedestrians from tumbling down the steep embankment into the Tigris below. Elora propped her arms up on the battered railing and gazed out across the river. Reflections from the few lights lining the riverbank danced across the surface of the water, creating an ethereal glow that was almost pretty.

"I wouldn't lean too hard on that fence," Zaidan warned. "It's not exactly in great shape."

"Ah, good point," Elora muttered, pulling her arms off the railing and taking a step back.

They stood in silence for a few minutes as Elora continued to take in the view, though she could feel Zaidan's intense stare drilling into her, and the hairs on the back of her neck prickled to attention. In her peripheral, she saw him slip his right hand beneath his blazer, and she snapped her head around to glare at him. He pulled his hand back out from beneath his jacket, and Elora saw he was clutching a pack of cigarettes and a lighter.

"I didn't know you smoked," she said as Zaidan flipped open the top of a Zippo lighter and lit a cigarette.

He slowly exhaled a lungful of smoke into the night air and watched for a few seconds as a soft breeze began to carry it out over the river. "There's a lot you don't know about me," he replied cryptically, eyeing her with another piercing gaze.

I could say the same, Elora thought. Zaidan stubbed the butt of his cigarette out on the railing, then flicked it over and down into the river. Elora scrunched her nose disapprovingly at Zaidan's flagrant littering but didn't comment.

"You never told me who gave you that necklace," Zaidan said, ignoring the chiding expression on Elora's face.

Elora briefly glanced down and realized she'd been unknowingly twiddling the charm of her necklace between her fingers. "My fiancé gave it to me," she said flatly, dropping the charm and folding her arms across her chest.

"You're engaged?" Zaidan asked, a hint of surprise in his voice.

"*Was* engaged," Elora clarified. "It uh…didn't work out."

"I'm sorry."

"It's not your fault," she replied automatically with a shrug, then reconsidered. *Well, actually…*

Zaidan was intrigued but decided it wasn't the right time and changed the subject. "My parents used to bring me here as a kid," he said, looking down the boardwalk. "I'd play at that park up on the ridge, and then we'd all come down here for ice cream cones by the river."

For the first time that evening, Elora saw half a smile brush across Zaidan's lips as he recalled the memories. "Sounds like a lovely childhood. Do your parents still live here in Baghdad?"

"They're both dead," Zaidan replied with little emotion.

Elora dropped her eyes to her feet. *Shit*. "Oh… I'm sorry."

"It's not your fault," he replied, slyly mocking Elora's own response from a few minutes earlier, and ironically following it up with the same internal comment. *Well, actually…* "That was a nice thing you did earlier tonight—buying that boy's painting," Zaidan continued, again shifting the subject. "Though I hope you know you got ripped off," he added with a smirk. "Twenty-five dollars is more than he makes in a month."

"It was worth every penny," Elora countered defensively. "And I wasn't just being nice. I honestly like the painting."

Zaidan's brows narrowed as he studied Elora's expression, his eyes practically glowing in the moonlight. Elora held his gaze for several intense seconds until she breathed an internal sigh of relief when a crooked smile began to play across his lips. His features relaxed and the smile flowed into faint dimples in his cheeks. The butterflies awoke again deep in Elora's core. She forced her eyes away from the dimples and turned to look back out at the river.

"You should smile more often," she said, breaking the silence.

"Sadly, there's not a whole lot to smile about in Iraq these days, but we're working on that," he added in a more optimistic tone. "Do you remember the night of the Gala in Dubai, when we were up on the terrace?" Elora nodded. "I imagine an incredible skyline like that being right here, lining the banks of the Tigris," Zaidan said, sweeping an arm out over the river. "I want to live to see that one day. Most of all, I want to be a part of making it a reality. I like to come here every now and then to remind myself why we can never give up. Why we must stop at nothing to reclaim and rebuild our country." Against his own advice, Zaidan leaned down on the walkway railing, bringing his head level with Elora's. "Seeing the memories of my childhood crumbling around me is an incredible motivator." He took a deep breath and turned to meet her eyes, their faces mere inches apart. A soft breeze blew down the river, and Elora shuddered as Zaidan's intoxicating scent enveloped her. A shiver ran down her spine and her heart rate doubled. Before she was even conscious of her own movements, she leaned in and pressed her lips to Zaidan's.

Caught completely off-guard by Elora's kiss, Zaidan instinctively jerked his head back and pushed away from her.

Elora slapped her hand over her mouth, embarrassed by her brazen kiss and, even more so, Zaidan's reaction. "I'm... I'm sorry," she stuttered, her eyes wide. "I shouldn't have..." Her apology trailed off as she spun around and began speed-walking back toward the path leading up to the parking lot, but she didn't get far before Zaidan dashed after her. Cutting her off, he took her face in his hands and completed the kiss she'd started. Waves of electricity pulsated throughout Elora's body. She sighed when Zaidan finally severed the kiss, but her eyes remained closed as she recovered from the rush.

"What are we doing?" she asked in a breathless whisper.

He continued to hold her face in his hands and searched her eyes. "Come on, we should head back," he said, dodging her question. "The guys are probably getting restless."

Back at the NDU compound, Zaidan invited Elora to his office for a nightcap. She sat across from his desk while he made their drinks, her eyes lingering on the patch of bare skin exposed beneath the two open buttons at the top of his shirt.

Zaidan handed Elora her drink, then sat behind his desk and raised his glass in a toast. "To Iraq, may her people enjoy peace and prosperity in the not-too-distant future."

Elora lifted her glass to meet Zaidan's and tipped her head. The alcohol warmed her inside as she drank, but a fire was already burning in her core that had been lit earlier by the river. She fantasized of crawling across his desk, grabbing Zaidan by the shirt, and having her way with him, but the rational side of her brain struggled to rein in her overactive imagination. *What the hell are you thinking, Elora? This is not part of the plan; you shouldn't have kissed him.* She tried to reconcile her lust by convincing herself she may be able to use an affair with Zaidan as leverage to get more information. Plus, she had no intention of falling in love.

Screw it. Let's do this.

Drink still in hand, her eyes locked with his, Elora stood up and walked around the large desk. She stopped a few inches from Zaidan's side, and he swiveled his chair to face her. She downed the last of her drink and placed the glass on the desk in front of him.

"Did you want more to drink?" he asked, feigning innocence.

Elora slowly shook her head and slid the glass away. She then turned her back to the desk, placed both hands on the edge and popped herself up to a sitting position on the top in front of Zaidan. She leaned forward, gripped either side of his shirt below the collar, and pulled him toward her, spreading her legs to bring him in close until their faces were only an inch apart. She took a moment to search his eyes and expression in the faint light cast by the single lamp in the corner of the room. Satisfied nothing malicious was lurking beneath the surface and that he was just as willing and ready for this as she was, she reeled him in the rest of the way for a kiss. Zaidan slipped his fingers into Elora's hair and cradled her head, pulling her in tighter to deepen the kiss. Elora slid her hands down from his shirt collar, around to his lower back, and pulled him into her. Their torsos pressed together, and hardened against her as she wrapped her legs around his hips.

Severing their kiss, Zaidan brushed his lips down Elora's neck as he unbuttoned her blouse. She squirmed with anticipation while he took his time unhooking each one. Zaidan finally pulled her shirt open and pushed it down over her shoulders, revealing a simple black bra. Elora turned her attention to Zaidan's shirt and impatiently pulled it apart with enough force to make every button pop open in succession, but she was careful not to rip anything. It was obvious the shirt hadn't come from a random Baghdad street market and didn't look cheap.

Elora pushed the shirt down Zaidan's back, and he let it fall to the floor. He was even more beautiful than she imagined. Smooth olive skin covered his chest and solid abs, which transitioned into an irresistible "V" shaped underwear muscle that disappeared down into the waistband of his low-cut pants.

"Holy shit…you're gorgeous," Elora muttered; she hadn't meant to say it out loud, but it slipped out.

"And you are intoxicating," he whispered as he kissed the top of her breasts. He slipped a hand around her back and, with a simple flick of his wrist, had her bra unhooked in a split second. Obviously not his first rodeo. Elora tossed her bra over the side of the desk, then put her hands on either side of Zaidan's face and pulled him in for another kiss. The sensation of her bare nipples pressing against his warm chest sent jolts of ecstasy shooting down between her legs. In that moment, she wanted nothing more in the world than for him to be inside her. She instinctively reached down to unbutton his pants, but he intercepted her hands.

"Not yet," he said with an evil grin. He gripped her wrists and pinned her arms to her sides as he glided his lips and tongue across her nipples.

"Oh my God, you're killing me," Elora said in a breathless pant, throwing her head back.

"No," he whispered in her ear, "right now you are *very* alive."

His breath on her cheek sent shivers down her spine, and she let out a weak moan. Zaidan laid her back on the desk, then leaned over her so their bodies were flush. He braced the bulk of his weight on his forearms so as not to crush her and kissed her again, slipping his tongue between her lips. He then slid his body south, kissing her chest and stomach as his hands trailed down her sides. She used her feet to push her shoes off as he unbuttoned her pants and slid them down and off. Lying on her back in nothing but her underwear, Elora ran her fingers through Zaidan's thick black hair as he bent down to kiss above the bandage on her right knee. "Do these still hurt?" he asked in a gentle tone as he lightly brushed his fingers across the bandages on her legs.

"No—nothing hurts right now."

He placed his palms on her knees and spread her legs open.

Her panties dampened as he stood back up and positioned himself between her thighs. Elora's body was on fire, and she quivered with anticipation as Zaidan unbuttoned his pants and pulled down his zipper. His gaze remained fixated on her face, his jade eyes blazing with lust. He slipped a hand between her thighs, looped a finger around the crotch of her panties and pulled them to the side. He slid his other hand into the waistband of his boxer briefs and released what Elora had been desperately waiting for. He guided himself into her, and Elora let out a low moan, her every nerve ending from head to toe exploding as he pushed deeper. He brought his hands back up and intertwined his fingers with hers, pressing her arms down onto the desk above her head. He bent down over her until their noses almost touched, and locked her eyes with his. Motionless, he held her gaze for a few long seconds, allowing the tension to build. Finally, without breaking eye contact, he thrust his hips forward and plunged his full length deep inside her. Elora gasped in pleasure as electricity coursed through every vein in her body—she was sure she'd combust at any moment. She closed her eyes and cried out as a mind-blowing orgasm washed over her.

When the wave of ecstasy receded, Elora gasped for air and twitched as the small post-orgasm convulsions danced throughout her body. Zaidan applied a few more forceful thrusts and then flooded her with his release. She'd never physically felt a man come inside her before, but with Zaidan she felt everything, and she felt it on multiple levels that she never even knew existed. It was the most intense sexual experience she'd ever had in her life—well beyond earth-shattering.

Zaidan remained inside her and softly kissed her neck as

she struggled to steady her breathing and heart rate. After a couple of minutes, he carefully withdrew and re-buttoned his pants. Elora, still tingling with minor convulsions, slid off the desk and retrieved her clothes from the floor. She eyeballed the door as she threw her clothes back on, plotting a swift exit upstairs to her room, but before she could finish dressing, Zaidan was behind her. He looped a strong arm around her and pulled her close as he rotated her to face him. The motion reminded her of when he'd grabbed her during the attack and spun her away from the shooter with one arm, as if she were weightless. She shivered at the memory of the chilling ordeal and pushed it from her mind. Zaidan slid his hands into her hair and held her head as he kissed her. The fire inside her blazed once more, and she couldn't believe she was again feeling week in the knees already. His touch and kiss were like live voltage that incapacitated her upon impact.

Zaidan pulled back and looked at her, continuing to hold her head in his hands. "I would invite you to spend the night with me upstairs, but there are many eyes and ears amongst us tonight."

"Yeah, I get it," she replied, trying her best to sound nonchalant.

But he wasn't sure she did *get* it. "Please know there is nothing I want more right now than to have you naked in my bed tonight, but for both our sakes, this needs to stay quiet—at least for now."

Elora knew Zaidan was right. She also knew deep in her soul that what they'd just ignited was going to be much more than a passing fling.

Chapter 12

Elora looked at her watch for the dozenth time; it was almost five thirty in the morning, finally a reasonable enough hour to slip down to the kitchen for a cup of coffee. The jet lag combined with the replay of the previous evening's events over and over in her head had made it impossible for her to sleep. While lying awake for the past several hours, she'd convinced herself that giving in to her desires and having sex with Zaidan was merely a primal reaction—rationalizing it as quintessential Psychology 101. He'd saved her life during a traumatic event, which, in turn, triggered her psyche into developing a strong sexual attraction to him. She chalked the entire incident up to basic human emotion and hormonal surges that, now satisfied, she should be able to move beyond.

She rolled out of bed, slipped on her shoes and a hoodie over her sweatpants, then headed downstairs. The plan was to grab a quick cup of coffee and promptly return to her room, where she'd hole up for the day and bang out her first article, conveniently giving her a perfect excuse to avoid Zaidan all day. She'd managed to reconcile *why* she'd slept with him, but she was still struggling to sort out her emotions and allay her fears that she'd made the biggest mistake of her career—hell, of her life.

The main floor was dark and quiet: the cooks hadn't even risen yet to start breakfast, so Elora had the kitchen to herself. There was a coffee maker on one of the counters and, after some scavenging, she located a tin of ground coffee and a canister of sugar. While the coffee brewed, she perused the fridge and came up with milk to use as creamer along with small squares of processed cheese and Iraqi flatbread to make a light breakfast. As she stood in front of the coffee maker waiting for it to finish, she heard the kitchen door open behind her. She casually looked over her shoulder, and her cheeks immediately blazed from a combination of excitement and embarrassment. Zaidan stood frozen in the doorway, looking as surprised to see her as she was to see him. He was fully dressed for his day—blazer and all—with his hair perfectly tousled and gelled. Without a word, Elora jerked her head back around and refocused her attention on the coffee pot, mortified that Zaidan was about to get a full frontal of her in all her UNglory—messy hair, unbrushed teeth, sweatpants and all, while he looked ready to pose for the cover of *GQ* magazine.

"Good morning," he greeted cordially as he came up beside her and opened a cupboard next to her head. "You're up early."

"As are you," she said, keeping her eyes glued on the coffee maker. She was groggy but her heart rate increased with Zaidan so close. "I'm still jet-lagged. What's your excuse?"

"I'm always up this early," he replied, pulling a coffee mug and teabag from the cabinet.

She scrunched up her nose and was about to shoot off a sardonic comment when it dawned on her. "Oh right, you're probably up for morning prayers," she blurted, relieved that she'd allowed her brain to engage before her mouth.

Zaidan smiled at her embarrassment and shook his head. "No, I just like to get up early. I enjoy the quiet stillness of the early morning right before sunrise. It gives me time to think and plan in peace before the rest of the world awakes."

"Do you adhere to any of the prayer calls?" she asked, realizing she hadn't yet seen him stop for any of the prayers since she'd arrived. She'd seen Fareed and several of the others kneeled on their prayer rugs several times after the calls had rung out from the nearby Mosque throughout the day, but never Zaidan.

"I prefer to pray on my own schedule," he replied with a crooked smile, "and in private," he added, raising his eyebrows.

"Of course, sorry, I didn't mean to be nosy," she said as she poured the freshly brewed coffee into her cup.

"No apology necessary," he replied, smiling. "By the way, I'll be tied up with meetings for most of the day. Will you be okay on your own for a while?"

"Actually, that's perfect," Elora said, grasping her coffee in one hand and scooping her bread and cheese off the counter with the other. "I plan to camp out in my room to get the first article written. If I can get it to the editors by tonight, they should be able to have it ready for publishing by tomorrow or the next day."

"Perfect, if you need anything, please don't hesitate to ask any of the staff or feel free to stop by my office."

"Sounds good. Uh…have a great day," she added as she slinked out of the kitchen and back up the stairs to her room.

Zaidan stirred a couple teaspoonfuls of sugar into his cup of tea and headed to his office. His first meeting of the day was with Hakim, New Dawn's de facto CFO. Hakim met with Zaidan every couple of weeks to brief him on NDU's financial state and bring any issues to his attention that may need to be passed along to Samir. As soon as Hakim stepped into the office, Zaidan took one look at him and immediately knew there was a problem. The two exchanged brief pleasantries before Hakim took a seat and got right to the point.

"We have an issue."

"No shit, it's written all over your face," Zaidan replied, taking a sip of his tea.

"General Yunis is backing out of his weapons deal," Hakim said in a grim tone. "He says he was offered a better deal by the Egyptian, Sayed Kamil."

"Of course, Kamil can offer a better price. His shit is assembled by child-soldiers in the Sudan, using crap refurbished parts. Our gear is brand new, direct from the MBDA factory in Italy."

"I tried explaining all this to him—he wasn't swayed."

Zaidan swiveled his chair to face the window as he steepled his fingers beneath his chin and gazed out at the small garden.

General Masoud Yunis was the leader of the Libyan National Army (LNA) and was working to establish a military dictatorship in Libya. He'd played an instrumental role in the recent overthrow of Libyan President Muammar Gaddafi and was poised to assume control of the now leaderless country. He was receiving financial and political support from Israel, the UAE, Egypt and, though they did not publicly admit it, the U.S. So as not to draw the disapproving eye of the UN, much of the financial aid General Yunis was taking from foreign governments was earmarked for humanitarian purposes. To circumvent these restrictions, Yunis purchased the weapons he needed to build and arm his militia from the black market—enter Malik Khalid and NDU. New Dawn had carried out several arms deals with Yunis already, selling him small orders of military grade vehicles and light weaponry, and had proven themselves worthy suppliers. They kept everything discreet, and the quality of their products was top-notch. Satisfied with his purchases thus far, General Yunis had placed a massive multi-billion-dollar order with NDU that included everything from body armor to guided missile systems. Yunis put in his order only a week before the Delta Force raid on the NDU compound in March. After learning about the raid, Yunis panicked and wanted to pull out of the deal; Samir and Zaidan had been able to convince him that, despite the sudden death of NDU's architect and leader, Malik Khalid, his order would still be filled to the very bullet. To sweeten the deal, Samir agreed to lower Yunis's deposit from fifty percent to only five percent, with the remainder of the balance not due until the order was fully filled. To cover the cost of manufacturing the order, NDU had to deplete their entire cash reserves and borrow from multiple outside sources and investors.

General Yunis's shipment had recently arrived in UAE from the manufacturer in Italy and was being stored in Crown Prince Al-Rafid's private warehouses outside Abu Dhabi. Since the order was worth such a colossal amount and he still didn't fully trust NDU, Yunis had refused to send the remaining balance he owed before physically receiving the weapons, and NDU wasn't about to hand over the shipment without getting their money. Both sides finally agreed to let UAE—a mutual friend they both trusted—serve as middleman. NDU arranged to have the weapons delivered and stored in UAE until Yunis paid his balance, while Yunis agreed to pay his balance once he had official confirmation from the UAE government that his order was en route to him. And, of course, UAE didn't offer to help broker this deal out of the sheer goodness of their hearts; NDU compensated Prince Al-Rafid handsomely for storing and safeguarding the shipment.

In the several months it took to manufacture the order, General Yunis had been offered a better deal for the same items from Sayed Kamil—an Egyptian lingerie salesman recently turned illegal arms dealer. Zaidan was familiar with Kamil and had heard grumblings throughout the Middle East about the subpar quality of the weapons he pushed, but there was no denying he had the lowest prices on three continents; he was basically the neighborhood thrift store of illegal arms. For cash-strapped warlords or even legitimate world leaders needing to pinch pennies to meet their defense budgets, Kamil's bargain deals were perfect. Even though the weapons NDU provided were far superior in quality, Zaidan knew he'd have to convince General Yunis why the benefits would far outweigh their hefty price tag in the long run. He also knew this wasn't something he and Samir would be able to do over the phone; they needed to get Yunis in a room and speak to him face-to-face, preferably in UAE, where Yunis could see the quality of the NDU weapons with his own eyes.

"I have to meet with General Yunis – in person," Zaidan said after mulling it over for several long minutes.

"I take it this means we're going to Libya," Hakim said with a touch of dread in his voice, knowing that wherever this meeting occurred he'd likely have to attend as well.

"Hopefully not," Zaidan replied. "We need to get him to Abu Dhabi, where he can tour the warehouses and see the products for himself. He knows his shit; he'll be able to recognize and appreciate the superior level of quality in our products over Kamil's. I don't think he'll want to back out of our deal once he sees everything."

"You sure you can convince him to come to UAE to meet with us?" Hakim asked.

"Nope. But I am sure of one thing. If this deal goes south...well, you're our CFO. You know full well what will happen."

"It will cripple us financially."

"Beyond recovery," Zaidan added. "So, unless you want to go back to driving a taxi to feed your family, we better figure out a way to salvage this deal."

"I do have an idea—though it's a longshot," Hakim said. Zaidan raised his eyebrows with interest and gestured for Hakim to elaborate. "Yunis is receiving economic aid from UAE. Perhaps you can convince Prince Al-Rafid to invite him to Abu Dhabi under the guise of a joint friendly weekend getaway combined with a brief meeting to discuss his next aid package," Hakim suggested. "Yunis won't want to do anything to jeopardize the support he's getting from UAE, so he'll feel obligated to accept the invitation. Tell the prince not to even mention us or the NDU arms deal. We will just happen to 'bump into them.' Then you and Samir can corner Yunis and hopefully convince him to follow through on our original deal."

Zaidan considered Hakim's idea and decided it was the best option they had. "I'll call the prince; you go bring Samir up to speed on the situation and tell Fareed to make arrangements for our travel to UAE."

Hakim stood and turned to leave, then hesitated. "What about the American journalist?" he asked.

"We'll bring her with us. She may be of use. If things get ugly, we could at least threaten Yunis with an unflattering story about him in the *Washington Post*," Zaidan half joked.

Zaidan called Prince Al-Rafid and explained the situation. He asked the prince to invite Yunis to come to Abu Dhabi for a visit and chat about his next aid package. "Be sure to convey to the general that taking you up on your invitation is not optional," Zaidan clarified. An hour later, Zaidan received a call back from the prince's private secretary confirming General Yunis had accepted the invitation and would be arriving in UAE in two days.

With the UAE portion of his plan in motion, Zaidan now had to get Elora onboard with the impromptu diversion to Abu Dhabi. He hoped she'd agree to come along peacefully, as she could be useful, but he decided if she wished to remain behind in Baghdad and await their return, he wouldn't twist her arm; his greatest fear was that she'd refuse both options and elect to return to the U.S. This gave way to another thought lurking in the back of his mind—if Elora did say she wanted to go back to America, would he be upset because he'd be losing her as leverage or because he'd be losing *her*?

Zaidan pushed all these thoughts aside and focused on brainstorming a way to pitch the UAE side-trip to Elora in a way that would most appeal to her and convince her to come along. While hashing out different approaches in his head, he was struck with an idea—an idea that gave a whole new meaning to the word *longshot*, but one that—if successful—just might solve their General Yunis issue altogether.

Elora was putting the finishing touches on her article when she was interrupted by a knock on her door. Glancing at her watch, she was surprised to see it was already past seven o'clock in the evening. She knew a genuine *Washington Post* reporter could have likely banged out three thousand words in an hour or so, but Elora struggled with this aspect of her false identity. She considered herself a decent writer, but speed was not her forte.

Thankful she'd changed out of her sweatpants earlier and into a respectable outfit, Elora abandoned her laptop to answer the door. She was pleasantly surprised to find Zaidan on the other side, though just one look at his face told her something was bothering him. His mouth was turned up in a cordial smile, but his eyes told a different story.

"Good evening. I trust you had a productive day?"

"Hello. Yes, thank you. It was nice getting some quiet time to write. Plus, you know, it's always great to make it through the day without getting shot at," she joked.

"The day isn't over yet," he teased, arching an eyebrow.

"So not funny."

Zaidan shot her a wink, then got to the point of his visit. "Dinner should be ready in about half an hour or so. Will you be joining us in the dining room or, if you'd like to continue working, I can have a plate brought up to you."

"I should be wrapped up here soon. I'll come down."

"Wonderful. Should you finish within the next few minutes, would you care to join me for a pre-dinner drink?"

"Ah," Elora said, nodding her head knowingly. "Kind of like last night's *drink*?"

"Did you enjoy last night's *drink*?" he asked, perpetuating the not-so-subtle euphemism.

"I did," Elora admitted. "And you?"

"It was sublime."

Fire rushed into her cheeks and Elora looked down at her feet, struggling to suppress a large grin. "I could actually use a break; let me just slip some shoes on," she said and ducked back into her room. A minute later, she was trailing Zaidan down the stairs. When they reached the landing on the second level, Zaidan walked past the stairway and continued down the second-floor hallway. Confused, Elora halted near the top of the final descending flight of stairs, thinking Zaidan was going to lead her to his office downstairs.

Sensing Elora was no longer in-step behind him, Zaidan stopped and looked over his shoulder. "Hakim is using my office right now," he explained. "I figured we'd take our drinks in my room."

Elora took a deep breath and followed Zaidan down the hall and into his room. The room was only slightly larger than hers, with a small sitting area tucked in the back near a large window. Elora made herself comfortable on the small sofa while Zaidan prepared their drinks. "I'll have the first article to you for review later tonight or tomorrow morning," Elora said, desperate to cut through the silent tension in the room.

Zaidan handed Elora her drink and sat down in a chair across from her. "I assume yesterday's mishap in the marketplace is the feature in your article."

Elora swallowed hard, hoping he didn't expect her not to mention the incident. "Yes," she declared matter-of-factly. "I told you when I took this assignment that I would write the truth, and that's exactly what I did. I simply reported that the NDU candidates were conducting a peaceful campaign event in a public area when they were brutally attacked by masked militants…and that I'm only alive today because of you," she added.

"I'm not sure that last bit needs to be included," he said, narrowing his gaze as he took a sip of his scotch.

"Every story needs a hero; people like heroes. They can get behind heroes," Elora countered.

"All heroes are flawed. Our goal is for New Dawn to become its own living, breathing entity, not something based around one person or even a group of people. It's the idea itself and what New Dawn represents that we want people—and the world—to believe in and get behind. The leaders can and will change, but the leader of New Dawn must always remain subordinate to the primary goals and mission of the organization: to serve the best interests of the Iraqi people—*all* Iraqi people."

"So, is it safe to say New Dawn is a changed organization now that Malik Khalid is dead?" She surprised even herself with the word *dead*. She'd meant to say *out of the picture*, considering she still harbored a slight belief that Malik was alive somewhere. She had to admit, though, she didn't see his hand in anything she'd witnessed since arriving in Baghdad—or Zaidan and Samir were doing a helluva job of pulling the wool over her eyes.

"Not necessarily *changed*," Zaidan clarified. "We are merely continuing the work he started."

"Why do you and Samir continue to worship him?" Elora asked in a frustrated tone. "He was a monster. He committed atrocities against innocent people—against Iraqi civilians, against Americans. I don't understand your infatuation with him."

"Samir and I stepped into simple roles. By the time we came along, the organization was established and functioning," Zaidan explained. "To put it simply, Malik had done all the dirty work needed to build things from the ground up. Starting a movement from scratch, especially here in the Middle East, is not an easy undertaking. It takes sacrifice and, yes, sometimes unsavory deeds, but if we can ensure New Dawn is a catalyst for good and justice moving forward, then we honor those sacrifices and those who lost their lives in the struggle along the way."

"So, you feel Malik simply did what he *had* to do to get New Dawn where it is today," Elora said, narrowing her eyes.

"In a manner of speaking…yes."

"And if Samir decides violence against innocent people is necessary, you will go along with that? As long as the ends justify the means?" she added with a sarcastic shrug.

"Samir is not Malik," Zaidan countered.

"You're blind. You're a good person, Zaidan; I see it in your eyes. Don't lower yourself to their level."

"Your confidence in me is flattering," Zaidan replied with a soft smile, "and I hope this faith is strong enough to convince you to remain with us on this assignment after what I'm about to tell you."

"I knew it, something *is* wrong," Elora said with a touch of dread. "Don't ever play poker. You're extremely easy to read. As soon as I opened my door earlier, I could tell something was weighing on you."

"Well, I guess it's lucky for me that not everyone is as intuitive as you," he said, stroking her ego. He cleared his throat and made a show of struggling to find his next words.

Elora sensed an opportunity. "You know you can talk to me," she said as she leaned toward Zaidan, trying to sound as empathetic as possible. "Completely off the record, I promise," she added.

"We have to make an unexpected trip to UAE," Zaidan said. "It should only take a couple of days, but we have to leave the day after tomorrow."

Elora wasn't sure what she was expecting him to say, but this was not it. "Oh," she said, furrowing her brow and leaning back against the sofa. "So, what does this mean? Do we cut this short and I return to the U.S.?"

"No, I was hoping you'd accompany us. Like I said, it'll only be a few days, and we'll pick up right where we left off here when we return."

Elora bit her lip as she mulled it over. "May I ask why you have to suddenly go to UAE?"

Zaidan took a deep breath. "I'm going to be honest with you, off the record, of course," he added, and Elora nodded in agreement. "We have a large arms sale we are trying to finalize, but our buyer is getting cold feet and wants to back out of the deal. The buyer will be in UAE for a few days, so Samir and I need to go there to meet with him in person and hopefully persuade him to go through with our deal."

Elora knew chances were slim Zaidan would reveal the client's identity but figured she'd ask anyway. "Who is the buyer?"

"Ultimately, General Yunis," Zaidan replied without hesitation.

Elora was shocked Zaidan had actually answered but even more stunned at the mention of the buyer's name. "General Masoud Yunis—as in, likely the next ruler of Libya?" she asked, her eyes practically bulging from her skull. Zaidan nodded. "This guy is currently building a full-scale national army. I'm guessing his order isn't for a couple cases of AKs."

Zaidan let out a stiff chuckle. "No, it is one of the largest arms deals New Dawn has ever procured, and one we have invested a massive chunk of our capital into. If the deal goes south…well, frankly, it will likely be the end of us. The financial blow will be so substantial NDU won't be able to recover."

A small voice in the back of Elora's head questioned why Zaidan was being so forthcoming with all these sensitive details, but it was drowned out by Elora's sudden elation at hearing Zaidan mention the end of NDU. *This could be the silver bullet we've been waiting for!* "So why does General Yunis want to back out of the deal?" she asked, trying hard not to sound excited.

Zaidan shrugged. "That's what we are going to UAE to try and find out."

"Yunis is not officially recognized as the rightful leader of Libya yet; him purchasing a massive amount of military grade weapons thus falls into the realm of *illegal* arms deals," Elora said in an accusatory tone.

"Technically, not illegal," Zaidan countered. "More of

a…gray area, but not *illegal*. Plus, we aren't selling directly to Yunis. There is a third-party broker, an Egyptian businessman named Sayed Kamil, who we sell to, then he sells the items to Yunis. Yunis doesn't even know we are the supplier. It's just safer for everyone this way."

Elora was familiar with this *Egyptian businessman*. The CIA was well aware of the lingerie-salesman-recently-turned-arms-dealer, but she played dumb. "So, considering Yunis doesn't even know you're part of the deal, he's technically refusing to buy from this Kamil guy?"

"That's our guess, but all our communication goes through Kamil, so the Egyptian could just be trying to screw us over. Which is why we need to get to Abu Dhabi to sort it all out. General Yunis receives aid from UAE, and he will be there in a few days to meet with the prince to discuss his next aid package. The prince has graciously granted us a few moments to meet with General Yunis during his visit to try and convince him not to abandon our deal."

"Why don't you just sell to Yunis directly and cut out the middleman?"

"Because, although he gets aid from UAE, the bulk of the general's financial support comes from Israel, so they are technically the ones bankrolling him on our deal. However, the money he gets from Israel is specifically earmarked for humanitarian purposes. He can't legally use the money to buy weapons or he risks Israel cutting him off. Of course, Israel doesn't really give a shit what he uses the money for but, on paper, it can't be traced to weapons purchases or Israel will have to deal with serious blowback from the UN. Sayed Kamil owns legitimate businesses across Egypt and can disguise the arms sales as humanitarian supplies."

"He's the launderer," Elora said with a knowing nod.

"Precisely."

Of course, this was all total bullshit. Yunis was fully capable of laundering the money himself, which was why, in reality, he was in fact purchasing directly from NDU. Zaidan just hoped Elora wouldn't read too deeply into it and would take the bait, which, so far, she seemed to be swallowing.

While processing everything Zaidan had just relayed, Elora was struck with an idea, and her heart raced at the thought of how easy it might be to pull it off. It took everything in her to keep from racing up to her room to get a message out to Nick for him and the team to pull whatever strings they could to block the arms deal between General Yunis and Sayed Kamil. *Foil this deal, and we may be able to bring down NDU without even firing another shot.* Elora knew it was true the general was receiving financial support from Israel; it should be easy enough to get Langley to pressure Israel into threatening to cut off Yunis's aid if he purchases weapons specifically from Sayed Kamil. Without Kamil to act as their third-party seller, NDU's arms deal would fall through and, if NDU was in as deep as Zaidan indicated, the entire organization would go bankrupt and collapse, or so Elora thought. A twinge of remorse for what this would mean for Zaidan shot through her, but she knew she couldn't let that stop her. Sadly, he would be collateral damage, and she comforted herself with the thought that he'd be better off finding a way to accomplish his dreams for Iraq without using a corrupt vehicle like NDU.

"I'll need to send word tonight to Nathan that I'll be

making a deviation in my itinerary," Elora said, snapping back to reality. "How far out should I push my departure?"

"Three or four days at most," Zaidan replied. "It shouldn't even take that long—I'm confident Samir and I can get this little wrinkle ironed out."

"I'll push it out five days, to be safe." She downed the rest of her drink and made a dramatic show of checking her watch. "It's almost noon in D.C. I should go ahead and get that message out to Nathan."

"Yes, of course," Zaidan replied and stood up to see her out. "Come back down when you're done, we'll squeeze in another drink before dinner," he added with a wink.

"Sounds great, see you in a bit," Elora blurted as she slipped out the door and proceeded to all but sprint up the stairs to her room.

Zaidan stood in his doorway and watched Elora dash off and up the stairs. He sipped his drink and almost felt guilty for how easily he was able to manipulate her. Almost. He just hoped she had enough pull to set his plan in successful motion, and in time.

Elora slid into the desk chair in her room and ripped open her laptop. She wanted to jump on the satellite phone to transfer the info to Nick, but it wasn't secure enough. If NDU caught wind of this, they'd find a way to work around it, not to mention, it would put her in deep shit. She decided to send Nick an email, typing in plain text the news about her impromptu jaunt to UAE that would set her return to the U.S. back a few extra days. She also mentioned a few details about how her trip had gone so far and attached her article along with three photos to the email. However, she renamed the photos with long random-looking, alpha-numeric file names:

itRvr4igeMgv8rgYbt5gvyE1emgt.JPG
igDm7beGmt2mivMgmmo11Gbe.JPG
oEe6be2eegGtbmv1eBtt97egTT56Er3emGt.JPG

The photo file names were actually key phrase cipher text codes Nick had made Elora memorize before she left for the mission. When decoded the files read as:

block4Yunis8kamil5arms1deal.JPG
have7israel2threaten11aid.JPG
ndu6is2supplier1will97fall56wo(without)3deal.JPG

Of course, no encryption or code was unbreakable, but it was worth the risk. If her plan worked, she honestly didn't care if NDU found out and shot her in the head. She would die happy, knowing she'd destroyed NDU and achieved justice for Brendan.

Elora clicked *Send* and leaned back in her chair, breathing a hopeful sigh. The Task Force would likely be able to get the ball rolling on the plan before the end of the day in D.C. Nick had several close contacts at Mossad, who if he asked them to jump would ask how high and what color shoes he'd like them to wear. As early as tomorrow afternoon, NDU could essentially be bankrupt. Elora almost felt guilty about how easily she was able to manipulate Zaidan. Almost.

"Were you able to get in touch with Mr. Briggs?" Zaidan asked when Elora returned.

"Yes, well, I sent him a message," Elora replied, trying to sound as natural as possible as she resumed her seat on Zaidan's small sofa. "I'm sure he won't have any issues with me taking a quick side-trip to UAE."

"Perfect." Zaidan flashed his irresistible sideways smile and, once again, ensnared Elora in his hypnotic gaze. Elora's cheeks blushed and her stomach flip-flopped as Zaidan took a casual sip from his scotch without breaking eye contact. The gaze transformed into a lustful glare as Zaidan slowly approached her, placing his whiskey glass on the coffee table along the way. Her pulse steadily rose as he closed in on her; she was sure her heart would explode when he finally took a seat on the couch beside her.

"May I kiss you?" he whispered, leaning in until their faces were almost touching.

Unable to speak, Elora simply nodded.

Zaidan leaned in the remaining few inches and kissed her, slipping his tongue between her lips. Elora closed her eyes and melted into his chest as the kiss grew deeper. Encircling her in his arms, Zaidan pulled her in tight and effortlessly swept her up from the sofa as he stood up. Without breaking their kiss, he glided across the room with her in his arms and gently laid her on the bed. Within seconds he had her shirt and bra off and was running his tongue across her nipples until they stood on end. He unbuttoned his shirt and let it fall to the floor, revealing his chiseled upper body. Cradling the back of her head in one hand, he slipped his other hand down to unbutton her pants.

Elora ran her fingertips over his shoulders and down his back. His skin was smooth and flawless except for an odd patch of rough skin on his lower left side. She'd noticed it the night before too when her hand had brushed over it, but she hadn't gotten a good look at it. She had no intention of stopping to examine it now, either.

Her pants now unbuttoned, Zaidan slid his hand into Elora's underwear, and she moaned in pleasure. She arched into his touch and began gasping when the moment was abruptly derailed by an unexpected knock on the door. Elora's eyes popped open in terror. She found Zaidan staring directly back at her with an equal amount of surprise in his expression. They both stopped breathing and froze.

"Zaidan?" Samir called out from the other side of the door. "Were you going to come down for dinner? The food is getting cold."

Zaidan clamped a precautionary hand over Elora's mouth and pressed a finger to his lips in the universal gesture to be quiet. "Oh, sorry, I got sidetracked with some work," Zaidan called back, sounding incredibly relaxed and nonchalant. "Just have them wrap a plate up for me and put it on the kitchen counter. I'll be down later."

"Oh…uh…okay," Samir called back, a discernible tinge of disappointment in his tone. "Well, have a good evening, then."

"You too, Samir. See you tomorrow."

Although Zaidan had handled the unexpected interruption with great finesse, not even Daniel Day Lewis could have given a performance good enough to undo what Samir had already overheard. He'd been standing at Zaidan's door for several seconds before he knocked, having noticed curious sounds coming from the room. He'd pressed an ear to the door and heard the moans of a woman. His heart sank, and a dull pain followed by the bitter sting of jealousy penetrated the pit of his stomach. He knew who the moans belonged to and his jaw clenched in resentment.

As soon as he heard Samir's footsteps disappear back down the stairs, Zaidan removed his hand from Elora's mouth.

"Oh, shit!" Elora exclaimed in a panicked whisper. "Do you think he heard us?"

"Don't worry about it. Even if he did hear, I can handle him," Zaidan replied and slid his hand back down between her legs to finish what he'd started before the disruption.

When they were finished, Elora and Zaidan lay naked together in his bed. With one leg draped over him as he dozed on his stomach, she kissed the base of his neck and then moved south. She pushed the covers down to Zaidan's hips and sprinkled kisses down his spine. When she reached his lower back, her lips brushed over the scar she'd felt earlier. Pulling back, she examined it for the first time and saw it was quite significant. The scar stretched a good six to seven inches across his lower left side. Though Elora was no medical expert, she could tell it was not a surgical scar and was the result of an injury of some sort.

"What happened here?" she asked as she traced the length of the scar with the pad of her thumb.

Zaidan inhaled slowly. "Car accident," he replied as he rolled over to face her. Seeing she was going to ask a follow-up question, he decided to beat her to the punch. "It was about a year ago. The car rolled over and glass from the broken windshield sliced into my back."

"Shit, that's intense; you're lucky to be alive." The corner of her mouth turned up into a tantalizing smirk. "Well, actually, I guess *I'm* lucky you're alive," she added playfully as she leaned down to press her lips to his. As content as she was in that moment and in being naked in bed with Zaidan, a fearful chill ran down her spine. There was no denying it; she was falling fast—and she knew it.

Chapter 13

Forty-eight hours later, Elora and the NDU group arrived in UAE via private jet. The group checked into half a dozen suites at the Marriott Hotel in downtown Abu Dhabi and enjoyed a couple of hours to rest and freshen up. Prince Al-Rafid invited the NDU team for dinner to welcome them to Abu Dhabi and go over their strategy for handling General Yunis. The prince and General Yunis were scheduled to meet the following morning at the Abu Dhabi Presidential Palace to discuss the general's next aid package from UAE—or so the general thought. Samir and Zaidan would "happen" to show up unannounced to put Yunis on the spot and try and convince him not to back out of his arms deal with NDU. Zaidan had informed Elora of the plan during the flight from Baghdad but, of course, had told her Sayed Kamil would also be in attendance, to keep up the ruse that Kamil was still the key to the entire deal.

Elora sat in her hotel room, hoping her plan to foil the arms deal between General Yunis and who she though was NDU's middleman, Sayed Kamil, would work. Staring at her laptop screen, she bit her nails and nervously tapped her foot as she hit the refresh button on her email every eight seconds in anxious anticipation of a confirmation of some sort from Nick or the team that Israel had come through on forbidding Yunis to buy from Kamil. So much was riding on this one little ploy; thwarting this arms deal would solve everything. NDU would go bankrupt and soon collapse, the Task Force would be able to celebrate a successful mission accomplished, the American public would get justice for the deaths of Ambassador Casey and the other Americans killed in the NDU bombings, and, above all, Brendan's murder would be avenged. A small voice in the back of her mind also added that Zaidan would be free. He'd no longer be working for the enemy, and she might be able to divert him from the treacherous path NDU was taking him down and bring him toward the light.

Finally, Elora heard the familiar chime of an incoming email and practically jumped out of her skin in excitement when she saw Nick's alias *Nathan Briggs* in the "Sender" field. Popping open the email, she found a brief canned response to her email she'd sent the night before with her attached article and coded photos.

Hey Elora,
Got your article, will review it today. Photos look great. Please provide some captions. Stay safe!
~ Nate

The same photos she'd sent over the night before with the coded file names were still attached to the email, but the file names had been changed, and Elora feverishly began deciphering Nick's message. Once decoded, the message read:

Israel urged to forbid Yunis/Kamil deal
They will threaten to withhold aid
Israel to contact Yunis ASAP

Elora breathed a massive sigh of relief, but she knew it was still much too soon to celebrate. There were still numerous things that could go wrong and derail her plan. First and foremost, would Israel even be able to get in touch with General Yunis in time, *before* Samir and Zaidan were able to get in a room with him and convince him to go through with the original deal. Elora still didn't know why Yunis was backing out of the deal, but she did know all too well how persuasive Zaidan could be—she knew firsthand how extremely difficult he was to say no to.

In the suite next-door to Elora's, Zaidan too anxiously paced his room—also hoping that Elora's message to Langley was received and carried out. Removing Kamil from the playing field would solve all of NDU's issues by giving Yunis no option but to reinstate the original arms deal. New Dawn was relying on the deal to not only carry the organization to the next level but keep it alive. Since he still hadn't told Samir or Hakim about Elora's true identity, he was the only one on the NDU team who knew about the scheme he was trying to use Elora to accomplish.

On top of his arms deal issue, Zaidan was also struggling to come to terms with the additional info he'd recently learned about Elora. As promised, Bashir had compiled a more complete profile on her and dropped by Zaidan's office to give him the file just before the team took off for UAE. The thick packet contained all the basics: Elora's current and previous addresses, phone numbers, full printouts of her social media footprint, copies of everything from her birth certificate and driver's license to her military records and college transcripts, and more.

On the page summarizing Elora's basic information, one line in particular had jumped out at Zaidan.

Marital Status: Engaged *(fiancé **deceased**, see supplemental #4.)*

He recalled Elora mentioning their relationship hadn't "worked out," but she never indicated her fiancé had passed away. Zaidan quickly flipped to the supplemental section of the report for more details.

Supplemental #4: Engaged to U.S. Army Major Brendan Jacobs, KIA 12 March 2012, Delta Force special operation, northwestern Iraq.

Zaidan felt like someone had punched him in the gut. He knew exactly what Delta Force special op had occurred in northwestern Iraq on March 12th. *She's not here to simply gather intel. She's here for blood.* This made Elora significantly more dangerous and Zaidan knew he'd have to keep more than one eye on her.

He tried to shove all this to the back of his mind so he could focus on figuring out how to save the arms deal with General Yunis. If his plan to manipulate the CIA into having Israel kill Yunis's deal with Kamil failed to work out, he would have to convince Yunis on his own. He went over what he planned to say in the meeting to persuade Yunis to buy from NDU instead of Kamil, and he'd already made arrangements to have transportation standing by so he could take Yunis to see his order in person. Zaidan was confident if Yunis saw everything boxed and ready to ship to Libya he would be more inclined to go through with the deal.

Later that evening, Prince Al-Rafid dispatched two government SUVs to pick up the NDU group from their hotel and take them to the restaurant. The occupants of both vehicles rode to dinner in total silence. The gravity of the upcoming meeting weighed heavy on everyone's mind and created a palpable tension in the air.

The prince was already sitting inside the restaurant with his bodyguards when the NDU vehicles arrived. He had made special arrangements to have the restaurant closed to the public for the evening to ensure privacy. The prince welcomed Samir, Zaidan and Hakim with handshakes and the customary alternating kisses on each cheek. He then greeted Elora. "Ah, Miss Reid!" he said, his face lighting up with a wide grin. "How lovely to see you again. Welcome to Abu Dhabi! Our country's *other* crown jewel."

Elora forced a nervous smile and thanked the Prince as she shook his hand. Everyone took a seat at the large table situated in the center of the restaurant and then spent the next few minutes fidgeting or shifting their eyes, waiting for someone to speak; the uncomfortable atmosphere from inside the vehicles had carried into the restaurant. The prince glanced around the table at his unusually quiet guests and frowned. "Come on guys, you've got to relax. You all look like you're about to face the firing squad," he added with a chuckle, hoping to lighten the mood.

"Apologies, we don't mean to be rude," Samir spoke up in a sincere tone. "We are a little tired from the flight. That is all."

"Of course," the prince replied knowingly and snapped his fingers as he looked over at the maître d', signaling that he'd like to get the meal underway.

"So, let's get down to business." The prince threw an

uncertain glance in Elora's direction then looked back at Samir and Zaidan to ensure they were comfortable discussing the subject in her presence. Zaidan gave a quick tip of the head and the prince continued. "Yunis arrived here in Abu Dhabi this morning. Everything is set for our meeting tomorrow at the Presidential Palace—as planned, he is under the impression we will be discussing his next aid package from us. I will chat with him for a few minutes, then you can come in and join us," the prince explained, addressing Samir and Zaidan collectively. "If we are lucky, he will stay and hear what you have to say. Unfortunately, there is nothing more I can do beyond getting you all in a room together. I do not have the authority to threaten to withhold any support or aid from UAE in exchange for him going through with your deal. I apologize."

"No need to apologize," Samir replied. "We are sincerely grateful for all you have done to assist us—we are forever in your debt."

"For you, you know it is my pleasure," the prince replied to Samir, then shifted his gaze to Zaidan.

Throughout dinner, the prince tried to keep the conversation around the table upbeat, but he was playing to a tough crowd and eventually threw in the towel. The group finished their meal in relative silence, and Samir promptly excused himself and the NDU entourage. "Please forgive us for the brevity of this get-together, Your Highness, and our rather stale demeanor," Samir said to the prince. "Perhaps tomorrow evening we can reconvene and, hopefully, we will all be in much better spirits."

"I look forward to that," the prince said kindly. "I'm sure

everything will work out for the best."

Following a sleepless night, the weary NDU envoys arrived at the Abu Dhabi Presidential Palace sporting bloodshot eyes and stifling yawns. Elora figured Zaidan would ask her to remain behind at the hotel, so she was surprised when he informed her that she would be accompanying the group to the palace. She had made a final attempt the night before to reach out to Nick to find out if he knew for sure yet whether their plan to sink the Yunis/Kamil arms deal had been successful. To her disappointment, he messaged back that he still had no confirmation from his contacts in Mossad that they had been in contact yet with General Yunis.

The prince's private secretary greeted the NDU entourage as they entered the palace and escorted them to a conference room on the second floor. "Prince Al-Rafid and General Yunis are already inside," the secretary informed them. "The prince said you are welcome to go in any time."

Samir thanked the secretary, who disappeared back down the stairs while Zaidan approached Elora. "You will wait out here with Fareed and the others while Samir, Hakim, and I go in to speak with the general and Prince Al-Rafid," Zaidan instructed.

Desperate to hear how the conversation would go down, Elora wrinkled her forehead in confusion and irritation. "Then why am I even here if I'm supposed to sit outside during the meeting?" Elora asked, crossing her arms with a huff.

"I'm sorry. Please, just wait out here with Fareed and the others," he added, imploring her with his eyes not to make a scene.

Elora clenched her jaw but did not argue and plopped herself into a nearby chair. Samir stared at her with a smug look on his face—Elora had a feeling he was behind her sudden exclusion from the meeting. Over the last forty-eight hours, it had become more and more obvious to Elora that Samir was less than fond of her.

With Elora settled, Zaidan turned his attention back to Samir and Hakim. "You two ready?" he asked with a stony expression.

Samir's sadistic smirk faded. All three now looked as if they were about to storm the beaches of Normandy. Elora almost felt sorry for them, but she knew it was still too early to celebrate. She was hoping to have a front-row seat to the collapse of the arms deal; she desperately wanted to see the look on Samir's pompous little face when he realized NDU was finished. Samir nodded for Zaidan to open the door, and the NDU trio waltzed in, interrupting General Yunis midsentence. Startled by the sudden disruption of his private meeting with Prince Al-Rafid, Yunis stared wide-eyed at the unexpected guests, but his confusion quickly transformed into indignation as he realized who the men were. The general looked back at the prince whose culpable expression confirmed Yunis's suspicions—NDU was here with the prince's blessing.

"I had a feeling there was an ulterior motive when you shoved this last-minute invitation down my throat," Yunis said with an accusing glare.

"I told them they could have five minutes to kindly ask you

to reconsider their arms deal," the prince replied flatly. He flashed a stern look at the NDU group and gave a sharp nod indicating the clock on their five minutes was ticking.

"General Yunis," Samir jumped in, "please allow us to explain why purchasing from Sayed Kamil is not in your—"

"I'm going to stop you right there," Yunis interjected, putting his hand up to silence Samir.

Zaidan panicked. *Fuck, he's not even going to give us a chance to plead our case.*

"There is no need for you to say anything," Yunis continued. "Either you have powerful friends or Sayed Kamil has powerful enemies. Perhaps it's both; honestly, I don't care. Bottom line, I will no longer be purchasing from Kamil and will be reinstating our original deal. I planned to contact you as soon as I returned to Libya."

The three NDU men exchanged surprised looks and breathed a collective internal sigh of relief. "That is wonderful," Samir declared with a wide grin, looking back at General Yunis and the prince. "Please, allow us to take you on a tour of the warehouses so you can review your order first-hand and—"

"That won't be necessary." Yunis said, cutting Samir off again as he pushed his chair back from the conference table. "The balance will be wired to your account by five p.m. tomorrow. I need to return to Tripoli now"—he shifted his glare back to the prince— "I have a country to rule," he added firmly.

The conference room door suddenly flew open and Elora and Fareed practically sprang from their seats. Elora immediately recognized the stout older man in military uniform with a stern look on his face—General Masoud Yunis himself. He blew past

Elora and Fareed without so much as a glance in their direction as he and his entourage made a beeline for the large marble staircase that descended to the main lobby. Yunis didn't look happy, but Elora wasn't sure if that was a good sign or bad. She wanted to see Zaidan; one look at his face and she'd know the outcome of the meeting, but Yunis and his men were the only ones who emerged from the conference room and had closed the door behind them. Elora sat back down and anxiously tapped her foot as she impatiently waited for Zaidan and the others to come out.

"Well, he looked pissed," Fareed remarked with a sarcastic snort after the general and his men disappeared down the stairs. "You can relax, though. When they come out pissed off that typically means we got what we wanted."

"Yeah, I can see how Samir would have that effect on most people he does business with," Elora replied dejectedly. Fareed looked as if he was about to reply but then changed his mind.

Twenty minutes later, the conference room door opened again and Prince Al-Rafid exited with Samir, Zaidan and Hakim in tow. A stab of disappointment struck Elora in the chest—all three faces of the New Dawn men were awash with a combination of relief and elation. It was obvious they'd been able to salvage the arms deal. *Fuck.*

The jovial mood in the car during the ride back to the hotel was a complete one-eighty from the strained uneasiness that had permeated the atmosphere surrounding the

NDU group for the past few days.

"Tonight, we celebrate!" Samir hollered as their SUV sped down the dusty Abu Dhabi freeway. Whoops and cheers resounded throughout the vehicle, and Elora forced a smile to disguise her disappointment. She had so many questions for Zaidan, but she bit her tongue, knowing she needed to wait to get him alone before talking to him.

When they reached the hotel, Elora climbed out of the vehicle and tried to slip off to her room to sulk in privacy, but Zaidan called out for her to wait. She rolled her eyes and reapplied her fake smile before turning to face him as he jogged to catch up with her.

"So, I take it the meeting worked out in your favor?" she asked, making a concerted effort not to sound bitter.

"Yes, it did," Zaidan replied matter-of-factly, raising his eyebrows and smiling.

"I saw General Yunis. He didn't look too pleased, but I guess you were able to talk him down off the ledge and convince him to go through with your original deal?"

"Well, we made some modifications, but for all intents and purposes, yes, the deal is back on."

"Did you find out why he wanted to kick you guys to the curb in the first place?"

"Not exactly, but it seems his issue is with Sayed Kamil, so that was one of the modifications we made. As you suggested, we cut out the middle-man, and Yunis will buy directly from us instead of going through Kamil."

Elora wrinkled her forehead in confusion and crossed her arms. "I thought Yunis couldn't buy directly from you? Doesn't he need Kamil's business fronts to launder the money through?"

Zaidan shrugged. "I guess he figured out a way around it," he replied in a flippant tone.

"Ah, well *I guess* congratulations is in order, then." Elora was slightly comforted knowing her plan may have worked after all but Zaidan had simply managed to find a way around it.

"Thank you," Zaidan replied. "Tonight, eight o'clock—please join us in the hotel restaurant for a celebratory dinner." Elora wanted to decline the invitation but worried a flat-out refusal may arouse suspicion. She smiled and nodded, then planned to come up with an excuse to duck out early after making an appearance.

It was well after 8:00 p.m. when Elora arrived at the hotel restaurant to meet up with the NDU team, who were well into their pre-dinner drinks. The guys raised their glasses and boisterously toasted her arrival as she approached their table and took a seat across from Zaidan.

"Ah, our trusty American correspondent has decided to grace us with her presence," Samir proclaimed with a noticeable eyeroll and hint of a slur in his words.

The waitress returned to the table and offered the party another round of drinks; Elora asked for a coke and cup of soup. She planned to make short order of her meal, then feign feeling unwell so she could excuse herself to her room for the remainder of the evening.

When the food arrived, Elora quietly sipped her soup as the others celebrated around her. She listened to their animated conversations but did not actively participate. She did, however, notice she wasn't the only one at the table disengaged from the festivities. Zaidan was also silent and sat staring at her from across the table. She met his gaze several times and flashed a thin smile before shifting her eyes back down to her food, but Zaidan's suffocating stare was unrelenting. She felt like a lab rat. As usual, he wasn't just looking at her; he was studying her, analyzing her every breath. What she found most frustrating was that even when he made her uncomfortable, rumbling waves of desire still rolled deep within her core. The dichotomy of her feelings toward him drove her mad; she had the urge to pull away from him while simultaneously wishing to be closer. A part of her wanted to lunge across the table, punch him in the face, and scream at him to stop staring, while another part wanted to rip his clothes off and have him ravage her right there on the table in front of God and everyone. When they were together, alone and naked, she felt safe and at peace in his arms, but when he stared at her like this, she felt vulnerable and weak, which she despised.

Unable to take Zaidan's incessant staring any longer, Elora dropped her spoon into her nearly empty soup bowl, letting it clang loudly to make a point. "Please excuse me, everyone. I'm not feeling very well," she said as she stood and scooped up her bag. "Think I'll go ahead and call it a night; see you all in the morning. We leave at nine for the airport, correct?"

Zaidan nodded. "Actually, I'm ready to head up myself," he said as he stood up. "I'll walk with you."

"No!" Elora snapped more forcefully than she'd meant to. "I mean...that won't be necessary," she added, forcing a small smile.

"I insist," he replied, reflecting her smile back at her.

Elora grumbled to herself as she spun around and marched

out of the restaurant, leaving Zaidan to trail behind. She walked, cross-armed, to the hotel elevator and smashed the up button with her palm, ignoring Zaidan's presence as he came up and stood beside her. She held her breath and kept her eyes fixed on the closed elevator doors, willing them to open. Once they were on the elevator, Elora continued to stare at the doors from the inside while Zaidan focused his gaze on the side of her face. She felt his eyes on her skin, as noticeable as if he were touching her with his hand, but she refused to acknowledge him—remaining silent with eyes front.

"Do I make you nervous?" Zaidan finally asked.

Elora's jaw tightened and she swallowed hard. "You can be a bit…intimidating," she said but still did not turn to meet his eyes.

Zaidan studied her profile for a few more seconds, then relented and joined her in staring at the elevator doors for the remainder of their ascent. When they arrived on their floor, Elora jumped out and briskly made her way down the hall toward her room. She stopped in front of her door and fumbled around inside the small zipper pocket of her bag for her keycard.

"I don't intimidate you," Zaidan said, arriving behind her just as she found her keycard. Abandoning her resolve, she turned to confront him, but before she could say a word, he pushed in close to her. She retreated until her back was pressed against the hotel room door. Zaidan leaned down and whispered in her ear. "What scares you is yourself. You're terrified of what you feel." He reached down between her legs and slid a hand up the inside of her thigh, pushing her pencil skirt up as his hand crept north. "What you can't. Help. Wanting." Elora closed her eyes and her legs turn to jelly. Zaidan's cheek brushed across hers as he pulled back to find her lips with his mouth. He pressed his body against her, pushing her harder against the door as their kiss grew deeper and more intense.

Back downstairs in the restaurant, Samir couldn't stop thinking about the strange looks Elora and Zaidan had exchanged at dinner. Curiosity getting the better of him, he excused himself from the table a few minutes after Elora and Zaidan departed. Two of the NDU security guards rose to join him, but he ordered them to remain behind. Samir exited the elevator and turned the corner just in time to see Zaidan halfway down the hall, pressing Elora against her door, her skirt hiked halfway up her thighs and his hand buried between her legs. Samir quickly ducked back behind the wall and peeked around just enough to maintain a visual without being noticed. He watched as the couple engaged in a passionate kiss; what he already knew in his heart was now being confirmed by his eyes.

Elora broke free from Zaidan's kiss and swiped her keycard to open the door. She turned back, grabbed him by the collar, and pulled him inside her hotel room. Zaidan slammed the door and pushed her up against the wall just inside, resuming their erotic kiss. He pushed her skirt up to her waist, revealing a pair of blue lace panties. He knelt before her and gently pulled her underwear down and off, then trailed kisses up the front of her body as he stood back up. He helped her out of her shirt and removed her bra; her nipples were already standing on end, but he gave them each a few flicks with his tongue for good measure. Elora was already squirming when he slipped his hand back between her thighs and softly dipped his fingers inside her, sending her racing toward the edge. "So, I intimidate you?" he whispered in a teasing tone as he sprinkled kisses down her neck. Unable to speak, Elora responded with a whimper of pleasure. "Your body is anything but intimidated right now." He pulled his hand back, unzipped his pants, and then effortlessly lifted her off the ground. She wrapped her legs around his hips as he pulled her toward him, burying himself inside her. She gasped and cried out his name as he thrust deeper, bringing her, within seconds, to an earth-shattering climax.

Elora opened her eyes to sunlight pouring in through the hotel window. She was lying on her stomach, naked beneath the luxurious hotel sheets. Flashbacks from the night before flooded into her mind, and she rolled over to see if he was still there. She was pleasantly surprised to find him beside her, wide awake. The morning sun reflected off his eyes, they were sea green today. The shade shifted with his moods: deep emerald green when he was worried or intently concentrating on something, electric jade when he made love to her, and sea green when he was content and relaxed.

"Your eyes are beautiful," Zaidan said, plucking the words right out of Elora's head.

"*My* eyes are beautiful?" she asked incredulously. She'd always considered the color of her eyes to be dismal and bland. A weird grayish blue that reminded her of the color preschoolers end up with when they mix too many different-colored finger-paints together.

"They are like the sky in Baghdad when a storm is coming in."

"So, they remind you of shitty weather," she teased.

"A storm brings rain, which cleanses the earth and spawns new growth."

"Or brings destruction and chaos," she countered.

"Sometimes all the above," he conceded with a smile and kissed her on her forehead. She knew they were talking about much more than eye color; she just wasn't sure if she was the storm in his world, or if he was the one in hers—perhaps both.

"You stayed all night," Elora said with a contented sigh.

"I was going to leave after you fell asleep, but I wanted to watch you wake up."

Elora smiled self-consciously and buried her face in her pillow.

"I'll run downstairs and grab us some coffee," Zaidan said as he rolled off the bed. "You should go ahead and get ready—we need to leave for the airport in half an hour."

Zaidan went down to the coffee shop in the lobby and placed his order. While waiting for the baristas to prepare the drinks, Samir appeared at his side.

"What are you doing?" Samir asked in a scolding tone.

Zaidan knew what he was referring to but played coy. "And good morning to you too. What does it look like I'm doing? I'm getting coffee."

"Don't patronize me," Samir spat back. "You know *exactly* what I'm fucking talking about."

Zaidan pivoted to face Samir and stared him down with a razor-sharp glare. Samir nervously shifted his weight and crossed his arms, noticing the muscles in Zaidan's face contract as he clenched his jaw. Samir had seen that face many times, though rarely directed at him. Samir swallowed hard and looked down at the floor with an agitated huff.

"It's nothing you need to worry about," Zaidan finally said. "It's business."

"Business! Are you trying to convince me of that bullshit, or yourself?"

"Drop it, Samir."

"Can you honestly look me in the eye and tell me you're just fucking her? That it's nothing more? That you're *not* falling in love with her?" Samir searched Zaidan's face for an answer, but it remained silent and expressionless. "She's everything we hate in this world," Samir continued. "A spoiled, entitled American cunt who will only use you and then throw you away."

The barista called out Zaidan's order and set two coffees on the counter. "Be back down here ready to leave for the airport in ten minutes," Zaidan barked to Samir as he snatched the cups off the counter and blew out of the coffee shop.

Though Zaidan didn't want to admit it, Samir was right—Elora was the enemy, more so than Samir even knew. He tried to convince himself he was simply using her and would easily discard her—one way or another—without a second thought when the time came, but even as he said this to himself, he knew he was lying.

Chapter 14

Elora watched the open desert roll by outside the SUV window. The NDU caravan of six white Nissan Armadas was almost a hundred miles outside Baghdad traveling north at a steady pace of ninety miles per hour. They were passing through the area that, at the height of the Iraq War, was known world-wide as the Triangle of Death. During her deployment to Iraq six years earlier, it would have been unthinkable for an American to be driving through the area in anything less than an armored military vehicle wearing body armor from head to toe. It was hard for her to believe she was now passing through in a civilian vehicle, wearing jeans and a T-shirt, the sole American rolling along with three dozen Iraqis who oversaw one of the most powerful militant groups in Iraq. *I really am fucking crazy.* They did not, however, travel as if they were out on a leisurely Sunday drive. Though the area was not as volatile as it had once been when it earned its infamous nickname, it was still far from calm, and by no means safe for an NDU caravan. As head of security, Zaidan organized and directed the convoy with military precision. The vehicles stuck close together and moved swiftly. The group only stopped at predesignated safe-areas along the route, everyone was under strict orders to maintain radio silence, and nearly every occupant was armed with an AK-47 or pistol—or both. Additionally, an extra dozen NDU militiamen had been dispatched from the north the day before to come down and assist in escorting the group from Baghdad to the NDU -controlled territory of northern Iraq west of Mosul.

Elora turned her head to look out the front of the vehicle and caught Zaidan's eyes on her in the rearview mirror. She held his gaze for several seconds before he shifted his eyes back to the road ahead. With one hand on the wheel, he used his free right hand to pop open the SUV's center console compartment. He reached inside, pulled out a folded piece of dark-gray fabric, and held it up between the seats. "You'll need to wear this while we are up north," he said, looking at her again in the rearview mirror. Taking the fabric from Zaidan's hand, Elora realized it was a head scarf. "The area we will be in is a little more conservative than Baghdad," Zaidan explained. "You'll need to keep your hair covered while we are out and about up there."

"Of course," Elora replied understandingly. She wrapped the scarf around her head and carefully tucked any errant wisps of hair beneath the fabric.

The convoy had departed Baghdad before sunrise, so the sun was just now breaching the eastern horizon. Elora soaked in the magnificent view as the sunrise cast an eerie yet beautiful glow across the land, complete with angelic rays that reminded her of a biblical painting. Fitting, she thought, considering she was currently traversing the cradle of civilization. Sadly, it was a land whose people had been assaulted and battered by religious wars and theocratic struggles for millennia. Elora never considered herself a religious person. Her family called themselves Methodists, but they only prayed at holiday meals and never attended church—not even on Christmas. She was a firm believer in evolution and had a distinct distaste for religious zealots, but even she sensed a strange power and vibration in Iraq that seemed to resonate from the Earth itself and touch the soul. Iraq is not a beautiful land. It's sandy and barren in many areas, rocky and cavernous in others, neither pleasant to look at. But when she stood still and closed her eyes, a unique energy permeated her body from the ground beneath her feet. Subtle movement, as if the land were breathing beneath her—inhaling and exhaling ever so faintly. Though she far from understood it, she didn't rule out a mysterious power at work in Iraq, responsible for the region's thousands of years of unrest and bloodshed. She'd made the mistake of trying to explain the sensation to one of her intel unit colleagues she'd deployed with to Baghdad back in 2006. He all but laughed her out of the country. "The warmth you're feeling is the oil," he'd quipped. "And that 'tingly feeling' you're talking about is the transcendental energy of the massive boners Dick Cheney and the assholes at BP get every time they think about it."

It was almost noon when the convoy pulled through the gates of a compound with a large two-story building at the center. The building was traditional Mid-Eastern architecture with a flat roof, sand-colored concrete walls, and outdoor balconies off the second-story rooms. Surrounded in all directions by open land, there were no visible neighbors, but Elora had noted when they passed through a small town comprised of a few simple buildings a mile or so up the road. The convoy vehicles parked inside the compound walls and the occupants poured out, shaking and stretching their limbs after the long drive.

Elora slung her backpack over her shoulder and followed Zaidan toward the two-story main house. "I'll show you to your room," he said as he led her through the double front doors. The building was a lot rougher around the edges than the Baghdad Headquarters, but it was comfortable and had indoor plumbing, a convenience Elora never took for granted. She'd spent enough time bunking in military tents in Iraq (where your toilet is a port-o-john or hole in the ground and your shower is a package of baby wipes) to learn to appreciate the simple luxury of indoor plumbing. Zaidan led her up the stairs to a small room at the end of the second-floor hallway. "I know it's not much, but we're only here for a few days, and we'll be out and about for most of that time," Zaidan said apologetically. "Take an hour to settle in and freshen up, then come downstairs and we'll head into town to kick off the tour." Elora nodded and Zaidan turned to leave but stopped short. "Oh, and please go ahead and check in with your editor back in D.C. to let him know you arrived here safe and sound," Zaidan said with a wink. "I know Nathan is nervous about this leg of the trip, and the last thing I want is him sending the Navy SEALS here to retrieve you."

Elora couldn't help but laugh at the irony of Zaidan's wisecrack. "Roger that, I'll call him ASAP." Of course, Zaidan was being dead serious.

Zaidan left and Elora plopped her bags in a corner. After a quick look around the small room, she followed through on her promise to check in with Nick. As Zaidan had predicted, Nick was less than thrilled about Elora spending the next week in what he considered the belly of the beast. "I want a sit-rep from you every twenty-four hours at a *minimum* while you're out there," Nick ordered during Elora's check-in call. "If I do not hear from you after twenty-four hours and three minutes, I will send in the entire fucking U.S. Army to find you."

Elora couldn't help but smile at Nick's empty threat. "That's sweet, *Nate*, but you and I both know you don't have that kind of power."

"Don't fucking try me, Elora," Nick warned.

"I have to go now; I'll talk to you later."

"*Elora…*"

"In *less* than twenty-four hours," Elora quickly added. "I promise."

She shoved the sat-phone back inside her backpack and crossed to a pair of glass doors at the rear of the room that opened out to a small, private balcony. Stepping onto the balcony, Elora could see down into the rear yard of the compound and had a panoramic view of the massive field stretching out behind the complex clear to the horizon. It suddenly struck her that this compound was very similar to the one the Delta Force team had raided. Where Brendan was killed. She wasn't exactly sure where she was on the map, but she knew the compound that had been raided was located farther northeast from where she was now. She couldn't help but wonder if they would pass by the fateful location during their time touring the area. A part of her hoped they would; perhaps seeing the place where Brendan fell would bring some sort of closure. However, another part of her feared it would only bring more pain. All she knew for sure was that she honestly had no idea how she would react if she saw the rubble of the raided compound. She decided it was best to hope she wouldn't have to find out.

A few yards beyond the compound's rear wall, Elora saw two rows of single-story, flat-roofed huts with a dirt yard between them that contained military obstacle course-looking equipment.

To the far left of the huts was what appeared to be an outdoor weapons range with target markers and a few lean-tos for shade. Farther off in the distance she spotted a group of a dozen or so men jogging across the field holding AK-47 rifles high above their heads. After watching them for several seconds it dawned on her—the men were recruits and this was the New Dawn militia training compound.

After lunch, Elora and her hosts loaded back up into three of the SUVs and headed toward the small town they'd driven through on their way in from Baghdad. The plan for the afternoon was to visit a couple of the NDU social service projects in the area, including a school and small hospital. Zaidan drove the lead vehicle in the group with Elora in the passenger seat beside him. Samir rode in the vehicle behind them and was joined by a local Sheikh who served as the de facto foreman overseeing the school and hospital projects. Each of the three SUVs was also stocked with several armed security guards. It had been several weeks since any of the NDU leadership had visited the area, so the Sheikh was excited for the opportunity to bring Samir and the others up-to-speed on the projects and show off the progress.

The group's first stop was the primary school NDU had recently built and was funding. The school day had just ended when the line of SUVs pulled into the lot and parked. Elora hopped out of the vehicle and snapped a quick photo of smiling children pouring out the large double doors and down the main steps of the two-story building, crowned with a large Iraqi flag waving proudly from a rooftop pole. Once the children had cleared the front entrance, the Sheikh led the NDU group inside the school. They were greeted by the school's headmaster, a kind looking bespectacled man who appeared to be in his early forties. The principal took his special guests on a tour of the ten classrooms and briefed the group on the school's current activities and stats, mentioning along the way a few needs that he hoped would soon be met. He wanted to hire at least two additional teachers with suitable qualifications, the school library was woefully understocked, and the classrooms were still short a few dozen student desks. Zaidan and Samir both listened intently as the headmaster rattled off his wishlist, and Samir assured him that all his requests would be met as soon as possible.

Before they left, Elora asked if she could get a quick photo of the entire group for her article. Everyone except Zaidan lined up in front of a chalkboard in one of the classrooms. After Elora took a few photos, the principal walked the group out to the line of SUVs, thanking the Sheikh and Samir profusely as they climbed back into the vehicles. Elora had to admit the new school and happy children were an inspiring sight, but Saddam Hussein had also built schools; there were plenty of photos of him being greeted by cheerful children and smiling teachers, so she remained skeptical regarding the genuineness of New Dawn's benevolence and whether it would spur long-term prosperity for the local populace.

Continuing their tour, the small convoy made its way from the school toward the NDU hospital a couple kilometers away. Along the way they passed two road crews, a small team repaving a stretch of road, and a large crew with heavy machinery rebuilding a collapsed bridge. Elora lifted her camera and got several photos of the bridge crew as Zaidan slowed the vehicle down to help keep her pictures in focus. "I'm guessing these workers and their equipment aren't being funded by the Iraqi government," Elora commented.

Zaidan smiled. "The central government couldn't care less if this part of the country remained in ruins; any construction going on within a fifty-kilometer radius of here is financed by NDU. The prime minister and two dozen of his cousins went from driving taxis to becoming billionaires in the last two years yet, for some strange reason, the government doesn't have enough money to fix a single fucking pothole in this province."

A few minutes later, the NDU convoy pulled up and parked in front of a white, three-story building; a sign written in Arabic above the main entrance read *Al-Zahra Private Hospital.* A couple dozen members of the staff were lined up outside on the sidewalk, waiting to greet the visitors. Once everyone was out of the vehicles, the Sheikh guided Samir down the receiving line, introducing him to the staff. Zaidan and Elora fell in behind Samir and the Sheikh, shaking hands with the medical personnel as well. Elora realized Zaidan already knew a couple of the doctors and nurses, greeting them by name before introducing them to her. Most of the nurses blushed and giggled as Zaidan shook their hands, and Elora couldn't help smiling at their blatant flirtation. She couldn't blame them, though; she was all too familiar with the potency of Zaidan's charm. It oozed out of him and ensnared any unsuspecting female who wandered too close.

As they neared the end of the line, Elora's attention was

caught by an attractive Iraqi woman whose gaze was conspicuously fixed on Zaidan. Her arms were crossed over her chest, and she wore a long white medical coat, indicating she was one of the physicians at the hospital. When Elora and Zaidan arrived before her, she did not offer her hand to Zaidan to shake and kept her arms crossed.

"Welcome back...*Zaidan*," the doctor said through semi-narrowed eyes with a hint of bitterness in her tone.

"It's good to see you again, Layla," Zaidan replied with a smile, but there was a noticeable stiffness in his voice. "Elora, please meet Dr. Layla Shaheen, head of surgery here at Al-Zahra Hospital."

Dr. Shaheen briefly tore her eyes from Zaidan to exchange pleasantries with Elora and shake her hand, then turned her gaze back to Zaidan. It was obvious Zaidan and Dr. Shaheen were more than *acquainted*, and their relationship had at some point been an intimate one. Zaidan directed Elora on down the line but she made a mental note to ask him later what the story was between him and the beautiful doctor.

Elora stood on the narrow balcony off her room, sipping sweet Iraqi chai from a small glass as she watched the sun set across the vast field stretching out behind the compound. Just as the sun began to dip behind the distant hills, she heard the Imam's poetic call to prayer echo across the wind from the mosque in town, alerting the locals it was time to observe the twilight *Salat*

Al Maghrib prayers. Elora watched as the militia recruits ambled out of their hut-barracks, prayer rugs in hand, and lined up facing the direction of the holy city of Mecca, which lay two thousand kilometers to the southeast. The recruits were joined by several staff and security guards who emerged from the first floor of the compound building below Elora. She observed as the groups converged, laid out their rugs, and then stood with their hands crossed in front of them, reciting the prayers before kneeling onto their rugs. Though the light was dim, Elora scanned the crowd and soon recognized one of the figures; Zaidan's profile was unmistakable. Elora watched as he rocked forward from his kneeling position to touch his forehead to the ground as he proffered the incantation, "*Allahu Akbar.*" In the two weeks since she'd arrived in Iraq, this was the first time Elora had seen Zaidan pray.

When the prayers ended, Elora continued to watch Zaidan as he carefully rolled up his prayer rug and began the walk back toward the compound. After passing through the gate in the yard wall, he paused and looked up, trapping Elora in his hawk-like sights. She instantly froze, knowing she'd been caught. Though she was not violating any rules or customs by watching, she still held her breath and searched Zaidan's face to gauge his reaction to her observance of his prayers. His expression remained empty for several seconds as he gazed up at her. Finally, a hint of his signature sideways smile played across his lips, and Elora exhaled in relief. She returned his smile, and he continued inside the compound building, falling from her sight as he passed below the balcony.

Later that night, Elora lounged on the bed in her room,

balancing her laptop on her thighs. She'd just finished writing her second article chronicling her visits to NDU's humanitarian sites and sent it off to Nick. Within minutes, she received a reply from *Nate* confirming receipt of her email and informing her that her first article had been published the day before and was garnering quite a bit of legitimate attention. Elora immediately pulled her article up on the *Washington Post* website and began scanning the comments section; much to her surprise, most of the reviews were positive. She chuckled at the thought that if things ever went south with her CIA career, she could fall back on journalism; she was honestly starting to enjoy her fake profession. She wondered if Zaidan had seen the published article yet and was in the process of emailing the link to him when there was a knock on her door. She answered it and found Zaidan standing in the hallway.

"I just wanted to check in on you and make sure you have everything you need for the evening."

"I think I'm good, thanks," Elora said, glancing around her room. "Oh, the first article dropped yesterday. Did you get a chance to check it out online yet?" she asked excitedly.

"I did," he replied with a smile.

"Of course, you did," Elora said, rolling her eyes, "you're like the all-seeing Eye of Sauron."

"The what?" he asked in genuine confusion.

"Never mind."

"Well, I don't want to keep you from your work. Have a good night and I'll see you in the morning; we'll be heading out at ten to visit some of the other NDU humanitarian projects in the area," he added.

"Why don't you come in for a few minutes?" she invited,

not wanting him to leave. "I was about to drink some chai. Would you like some?"

"No offense, but your room is a little cramped," he teased. "Why don't you come to over to mine? I at least have a couple chairs...and a larger bed," he added with a sly smile.

Ten minutes later, Elora was sitting in Zaidan's room, blowing on her steaming cup of tea. She still hadn't asked him about the beautiful doctor they'd seen at the hospital whom he obviously had a complicated history with and figured now was as good a time as any to broach the subject. "So, what's the story between you and *Doctor* Shaheen?" Elora asked, diving right in head-first.

Zaidan let out an embarrassed sigh and smiled sheepishly. "Not much gets past you does it?"

"Well, razor blades were shooting out of her eyes when she saw us, so it was kind of hard to miss."

"The razor blades weren't directed at you, if it makes you feel any better."

"Oh, I know," Elora said, taking a sip of her chai, "they had your name written *all* over them."

Zaidan cleared his throat. "Layla was the one who stitched me up, after... my accident." He looked down and gestured at the scar on his back.

Elora cocked her head and furrowed her brow. "I have a feeling there's a lot more to your story with Layla than that she simply gave you a few stitches."

"The story between Layla and me is...complicated."

Elora waited for him to elaborate but when he remained silent, she refused to relent.

"Complicated in what way?" she prodded.

Zaidan shot her a tight-lipped smile. "What's that saying? I don't *kiss and tell*?"

Elora narrowed her eyes but saluted his honorable intention not to gossip about a former lover. "Fair enough," she said, dropping the judgmental tone. "I respect that. I won't pry anymore."

"Thank you. I do enjoy talking to you, but watching your lips move when you speak drives me completely fucking crazy," he said, pulling her close and kissing her.

"Crazy in a good way, I hope," she teased.

"Crazy in the best way," he whispered, taking her hand and guiding it south to feel what she had awakened below his waistline. Elora's skin turned to fire, and the world around them evaporated. Before she knew it, her clothes were on the floor and her body was entangled with Zaidan's in his bed. She ran her hands over his shoulders and down his back as he kissed her. The fingertips on her right hand brushed across the scar on his lower left side, and he flinched, catching Elora off-guard. He took her hand and pulled it around in front of him, clutching it firmly near his chest as he continued to kiss her. Elora was surprised by his curious reaction; it had never seemed to bother him before when she'd happened to brush over his scar. She shrugged the incident off and merely made a conscious effort to keep her hands well above his waist. She was more than happy to occupy her fingers by running them through his thick hair and across his perfect bronze shoulders.

Afterward, they lay exhausted in each other's arms, sweat glistening off their skin in the moonlight that streamed into the room. Elora had just begun to doze when Zaidan pulled her close and kissed her forehead. "Be back in a few minutes," he whispered. "Gonna grab a quick shower."

"I should actually head back to my room," Elora said, sitting up as Zaidan slid out of the bed.

"No, please stay. I want you right here when I get back," he added with a wink and leaned across the bed to kiss her again.

He disappeared into the adjoining bathroom—another upgrade his room had over hers—and Elora soon heard the shower running. Now wide awake, she sat on the edge of the bed and surveyed the room. It was quite different from his room back at the NDU compound in Baghdad, much homier and *lived in*. From the disheveled stacks of books sitting on various shelves and tables, to the bed sheets permeated with his scent, the room had *Zaidan* written all over it, while his room at the NDU headquarters in Baghdad was sterile and hotel-like. It was obvious he'd spent a lot more time in this one.

Elora scooped Zaidan's button-down shirt off the floor and slipped it on, fastening only enough buttons to secure the shirt around her. She shuffled over to a small shelf near the door and scanned the books, picking up and flipping through a couple, but it was too dark to make out much of the text. Not wanting to turn on any lights, she abandoned the bookshelf and crossed back to the other side of the room. Along the way she stumbled on a pile of clothes containing the pants, blazer, and few other articles Zaidan had been wearing earlier. Her foot fell on top of the blazer and she felt a small solid object beneath her heel. Realizing it was likely something in the pocket of the blazer, she picked the jacket up and squeezed around the pocket areas until she felt the object through the material with her fingers. She slipped her hand into the left inside breast pocket of the blazer and clutched what felt like a necklace. She pulled it out and held it up to the moonlight, narrowing her eyes at the charm dangling from the chain. "What the hell?" Elora said, pulling the charm closer. It was an intricate gold crucifix.

"We all pray to the same God," a voice behind her declared.

Elora shrieked at Zaidan's unexpected arrival and dropped the necklace to the floor. Spinning around, she saw he was shirtless and wearing only a pair of jeans, his hair wet and disheveled from the shower. She dropped to her hands and knees to retrieve the necklace from the floor. "Shit, I'm sorry," she sputtered. "I accidentally stepped on your jacket…and I felt something…so I just—"

Zaidan cut her off. "Elora, it's fine."

She popped back up and pressed the necklace into the palm of his hand, her heart still racing. He laid the crucifix on his desk and turned back to Elora, ready for the next question he knew was coming.

"Wait, is that *yours*?" she asked in total confusion.

"Yes, it is," he replied plainly.

Elora narrowed her eyes and looked as if she was about to ask a follow-up question but stopped short. Zaidan could see the wheels turning in her head and decided to jump in.

"I am Christian."

"I'm sorry, I'm confused," Elora said, wrinkling her forehead.

"I was born and raised Catholic."

"But…but I just saw you, earlier this evening, praying with

the others?" she stammered. "I'm no Catholic, but I'm pretty sure that's *not* how they do it," she added in a sarcastic tone.

Zaidan smiled and dropped his head. "No, what you saw earlier was traditional Islamic prayer. Most of the New Dawn staff don't know I'm Christian. It just makes things…simpler if I keep that information to myself," he explained. "For the most part, it's *don't ask don't tell*, but up here—especially around the militia recruits—I try to make more of an effort to blend in."

"Who all knows the truth? Samir? Hakim?"

"Of course," Zaidan replied. "As does Fareed. Essentially, everyone in the upper echelon of the organization knows I am a Christian. It's not that big of a secret. I simply don't blatantly advertise it, and when I'm up here, I sometimes take it a step further by participating in the Muslim prayers. An act of solidarity, if you will."

"Doesn't that feel…wrong? Don't you feel like a fraud?"

"Not at all…and it's not technically fraud. Like I said, we all pray to the same God. Muslims, Jews, and Christians all believe in the God of Abraham. We simply don't agree on who the one true prophet is. Plus, I don't recite the full Islamic prayers when I participate with the others. I say my own prayers. I may not adhere to strict Catholic format, but I doubt it'll offend Jesus, or Mohammad, for that matter."

Elora looked at the ceiling and shook her head. "Every fucking day, it becomes more and more mystifying as to why you're here," she lamented in frustration. "How are you mixed up with NDU? A radical militant *Islamic* organization. You're not even fucking Muslim!"

"Are you angry?"

"No, I'm not angry." She let out a sharp exhale and rubbed her temples. "It's just…a lot to process."

"Welcome to Iraq," he said with a crooked smirk. "Nothing here is ever simply black or white."

Chapter 15

It was just before dawn when Elora and Zaidan were awoken by a knock on Zaidan's door. Fearing it was Samir again, Elora considered dashing into the bathroom to conceal herself.

"Relax, it's okay," Zaidan said, noticing her panicked look. "Just wait here. I'll be right back." He pulled on his jeans and answered the door but didn't open it enough for whomever was outside to see Elora in the bed. Elora's anxiety subsided a bit when she heard Fareed's voice floating in from the hallway.

"We just got word, more fields were scorched outside Tal Afar last night," Fareed reported in a loud whisper.

Zaidan let out a low, grumbling sigh. "Goddamn it. Are they still burning?"

"The fires are out, or at least under control," Fareed answered.

"What's the damage?"

"Three farms. Fifty hectares or more."

"Fuck," Zaidan said, shaking his head. He leaned on his arm against the door frame and looked at the floor for several seconds. "All right, rearrange today's itinerary," he instructed, looking back to Fareed. "I want to go see the fields, and we'll need to visit at least one of the farmers' homes."

"Roger that," Fareed replied obediently. "You still want to roll out at ten?"

"Yes, that should be fine; any earlier and we'll never hear the end of it from *Princess* Samir," Zaidan added with an eye roll.

Fareed smiled and nodded.

Seconds later, Elora heard Fareed's footsteps disappear back down the hall as Zaidan closed the door.

"Is everything okay?" she asked after Zaidan slipped back between the sheets.

"It will be," he said. "Go back to sleep; I'll explain in the morning," he added, rolling over and kissing her.

From what Elora could feel through his jeans, though, she had a good idea *sleep* wasn't what they'd be doing until morning.

A few hours later, an eight-vehicle-strong NDU convoy sped east down the dusty highway toward Tal Afar. For security reasons and as a show of support, Zaidan had rallied as many people as possible to join the group in visiting the farmers who'd lost their wheat fields to arsonists the night before. After Zaidan explained to Elora that the fields had been purposely torched and that it was a common issue in the area, her natural question was why.

"Iraq is one of the largest importers of grain and flour in the Middle East," Zaidan explained to her from behind the wheel of their SUV. "Iraqi wheat farmers can currently supply about half of the country's demand under good conditions. *Good Conditions* meaning a decent rainy season and American planes not bombing the shit out of our crops—no offense," he added looking over at

Elora from beneath his brow.

"None taken," she replied.

"The rest is subsidized with imports. Bottom line, the less wheat, and subsequently flour, we produce ourselves, the more we must import from other countries. Our grain industry is still essentially nationalized, a remnant left over from the *Oil for Food Program* implemented by Saddam while we were under sanctions, so private importation of wheat is banned and only the government is authorized to import wheat. The government then passes the wheat out to the mills across Iraq—all are supposed to get an equal share, but you can guess what happens. Then, the mills must sell the flour they produce back to the government, who then distributes the flour to the people. The Iraqi mills are not allowed to sell any flour on the private market. If the people want more flour—or a higher quality flour—than what the government provides them each month, they can go to their local markets and buy imported flour from Turkey or Syria or whatever countries the Iraqi central government has approved flour imports from. However, since Tehran's ass-puppets have taken control in Baghdad, I'll bet you can guess from whom the Iraqi government has greatly increased wheat and flour imports."

"Iran," Elora chimed in.

"Bingo. And they've started limiting imports from other countries to help Iran corner the market."

"So, Iran is sabotaging Iraqi wheat fields so they can sell you more wheat and flour?" Elora asked skeptically. Zaidan nodded. "Seems like a lot of effort for a cheap commodity and little gain."

"On the surface it doesn't seem like a very lucrative scheme but, again, this is Iraq; there's always much more going on beneath the surface. Since we're talking about massive government contracts here, you can simply skew a few numbers here and there, and you've got a couple extra million dollars you can skim off the top. The politicians in Baghdad and Iran split the excess profits amongst themselves and no one is the wiser. There is zero oversight; no one is holding a magnifying glass over the system to point out the discrepancies, and the politicians along with their cronies walk away with millions."

"Wow, that's unbelievable," Elora commented, shaking her head in disbelief.

"Not when you think about it," Zaidan replied. "Wheat has been at the center of economic warfare and government corruption in this area of the world since the dawn of civilization. Turns out it's just as effective today as it was three thousand years ago."

"Why reinvent the wheel?"

"Precisely. The suspicious burning of the fields started a couple of years ago," Zaidan continued. "We've been doing our best to provide security and patrol the farms in this region, but it's too massive of an area for us to secure. And it's not as if the Iranians march in dressed in uniforms, carrying torches and set fire to the fields. Often, they pay a local to carry out their dirty work. They hand a poor farmer more money than he makes in a year to flick a match into a field—you can't expect him to turn that down."

"So, what do you do now? Help the farmers replant?"

Zaidan shook his head. "It's too late in the season. Hakim and his team will assess the farmers' losses and compensate them enough so they can survive and feed their families until next season. That's the short-term solution. Long-term solution is for us to become more autonomous in the area of wheat imports and flour production, so the people in our area aren't forced to buy their flour from Iran. To solve the issue of the corrupt government middleman, NDU went rogue. We have a decent-sized flour mill in the area that is essentially operating off the government grid. We supply the mill with wheat, and they supply the NDU-controlled region with flour to circumvent the entire corrupt system."

"Let me guess," Elora jumped in, "the fields that got scorched last night were the ones providing wheat to your illegal mill."

Zaidan shot her a wink.

"Then what makes you so sure it was the Iranians and not your own government who torched your fields? You're running illegal milling operations. Plus, from what you explained earlier, you're cutting into the profits they are lining their pockets with. Sounds like the Iraqi government has as much motive to torch these fields as the Iranian government—if not more."

"They are one and the same, Elora."

"What does NDU get out of all this?" she asked, narrowing her eyes in suspicion. "It sounds like a simple free-market system you've set up, yet you're providing security to the fields and keeping the government off the mill's back. I assume you're getting paid for these services?"

"Let's just say, we are partners in all these businesses. We get a percentage of their profits."

"You realize what you're describing is a mafia system? Ever

heard of a little movie called *The Godfather*?"

Zaidan smiled. "I've read the book."

"Well, now that a massive chunk of your wheat is gone, will this put your mill out of business?"

"It definitely puts a kink in our system, which is why we have been developing phase two of our long-term plan: privately importing our own wheat."

"Which is illegal."

"Yes, so I'd appreciate it if you didn't mention any of this in your next article," he said, lowering his voice. "NDU recently struck a deal with Russia to purchase wheat from them under-the-table and smuggle it in through Syria. We already operate smuggling routes from the Syrian border, so getting the wheat across and to our mill won't be too difficult. Of course, Russia can't sell wheat directly to us; as you pointed out, that would be a violation of Iraq's trade laws. Even Russia doesn't want to be caught with its hand in mid-eastern black-market wheat dealings. So, Russia adds a few thousand extra tons of wheat to Syria's usual order, Syria 'misplaces' those extra tons (wheat bandits, mold, fucking fairies, whatever excuse Russia tells them to use), and the wheat ends up in our mill."

"How can you expect, or even hope, that NDU will ever be acknowledged as a legitimate organization while spinning this massive web of illicit operations?" Elora asked, truly baffled by Zaidan's unbelievable naiveté.

"If a law is unjust, a man is not only right to disobey it, he is obligated to do so."

Elora rolled her eyes. "Thanks, George Washington."

"Thomas Jefferson, actually," Zaidan corrected with a

cheeky smile.

The convoy turned off the main highway onto a narrow dirt road and bumped along for about a mile before pulling over and parking along the shoulder in front of a modest home. The wheat and barley fields that had once lined either side of the dirt road were now barren patches of black stretching to the horizon in both directions. Elora began snapping pictures of the scorched fields while more than a dozen NDU security guards dismounted from the convoy and established a perimeter around the flat-roofed cinderblock home that was barely more than a hut. Samir and his personal security team made their way toward the home with Hakim, Zaidan, and Elora following. An older Iraqi man wearing a traditional, long, tan-colored *dishdasha* exited the home and approached the group with a wide, ear-to-ear grin. The farmer invited the group inside his home, where his wife and three adult children were waiting with fresh chai and sweets to offer their guests.

Once everyone was seated with a small cup of tea, the farmer launched into the tale of the previous night's harrowing blaze. According to his story, he'd awoken around midnight to the smell of smoke and looked out his window to see flames shooting out of his wheat crop. He rushed to wake his family, and they all ran outside with wet towels and blankets to do what they could to put down the flames. They were soon joined by several neighbors whose crops were also at risk. Together, they worked long into the night fighting to squelch the blaze. When the sun rose, the farmers surveyed the damage and estimated more than fifty hectares, nearly one hundred and fifty acres, had been destroyed. Elora learned that each hectare was worth approximately three hundred and twenty-five U.S. dollars, which equated to a total loss of nearly seventy-five thousand dollars. Even dividing the loss up among the three farmers affected by the fire, each share was an entire year's worth of income.

One of the farmer's sons stepped forward and showed the group a grainy video he'd captured on his cell phone from the night before. Though the video was dark and shaky, several shadowy figures could be seen sprinting from the burning field. The quality was too poor to identify any of the people in the video, but it was enough evidence to convince the farmers that the fires had not been an act of God and were intentionally set. They'd also found remnants of a mobile phone and plastic bottle, which they believed were an explosive device detonated to ignite the fire.

When the farmer finished his story, tears were streaming down the faces of his wife and daughter while his two sons hung their heads, ashamed that they were unable to help their father protect the family's livelihood. Elora's heart broke for the family and their loss. Zaidan put a comforting hand on the old man's shoulder while Samir assured the farmer his family would be compensated for their loss. Samir also promised that the New Dawn militia would provide more security patrols of the area to help safeguard against future attacks.

Elora asked if the farmer and his family would be willing to let her take their picture, explaining she wanted to show the people of America the hardships rural Iraqi's were facing due to the economic shadow war raging in the country. The old man and his two sons obliged and stepped outside where Elora could snap a few photos of the men with the charred remains of their wheat field stretching out behind them.

Twenty minutes later, the NDU convoy was back on the main highway, making the return trip to the militia training compound. The line of vehicles was traveling at a steady eighty-mph clip when Elora noticed their SUV suddenly began to slow and fall back from the two vehicles ahead of them. She glanced over at Zaidan, and the expression on his face told her something was very wrong. With lightning-fast reflexes, Zaidan snatched his two-way radio from the center console and tried to alert the others, but it was too late.

As if it were happening in slow motion, Elora saw the distinct trail of smoke from a rocket-propelled grenade streak across her line of vision. *Fuck, not again*. The RPG slammed into the front passenger tire of the second vehicle in the convoy—the SUV Samir and his security detail were in—and exploded into a ball of flames. Zaidan slammed on the brakes and their Nissan Armada came to a screeching halt in the middle of the highway. The NDU security guards riding with Elora and Zaidan swung the backseat doors open and began firing their AKs toward the field, aiming in the direction from which the RPG was launched.

"*Get your head down*!" Zaidan screamed to Elora and pushed her upper body down until her head was between her knees. Zaidan inched their vehicle forward to close in on the disabled SUV in front of them, smoke now billowing high into the air from the front of the vehicle. Elora hoped the incident had been a one-off fire-and-dash attack, but her hopes were soon crushed. Within seconds, she heard the distinct *Clack! Clack!* of AK-47 fire coming from the opposite side of the road. It was officially an ambush. Elora heard several rounds ding off their vehicle and whizz past the windshield. She dropped down to the floorboard and squeezed herself between the glove compartment and seat, sinking as low as possible for cover. The guards in the backseat now directed their fire off both sides of the road, and Zaidan too joined in, pulling one of his browning pistols from the waistband of his pants and firing out his window. An enemy bullet breached the interior of the SUV; entering through Zaidan's open window, it streaked across the front seat area and exploded into Elora's closed passenger side window. She shrieked as shattered glass rained down on her but was quickly distracted by the sickening sound of bullet connecting with flesh. Blood spattered across her seat and door as one of the men cried out in pain. *Zaidan!* Without a second thought, Elora sprang from her crouched position on the floorboard to check on Zaidan and saw his shirt was ripped and bloodied near his upper left arm, but the wound was not serious. "Get back down!" he commanded as he reloaded his pistol and continued to return fire. Ignoring him, Elora reached down and yanked Zaidan's second pistol from the thigh holster on his right leg. Positioning herself atop the center console, she jammed a knee into Zaidan's back to brace herself, then slid the 9mm Browning past the side of his head and joined him in firing out his window. She assumed Zaidan would already have a round chambered and she was correct. She pulled the trigger and fired into the field where she counted at least four combatants firing back on the convoy's position.

Minutes later, as quickly as it had all begun, the enemy fire ceased and the insurgents fell back, disappearing deep into the fields. Several NDU security guards leapt from their vehicles to give chase, but Zaidan radioed for them to fall back to the convoy. His priority was to assess injuries and for the entire group to get the hell out of the area. Elora slid off the console and dropped back down into the passenger seat. She laid the pistol in her lap and clasped her hands together to quell their shaking as the adrenaline subsided. Zaidan swiveled around to face her and grabbed her by the shoulders. "Are you injured at all!" he shouted, his eyes wide as he scanned her body. She shook her head but was unable to speak. He frantically ran his hands down her torso and across her back checking for injuries.

"I'm fine," Elora managed to get out, but Zaidan either didn't hear or ignored her and continued to feel around for damage. "Zaidan, stop! I said I'm fine!" she yelled and pushed him away. He finally relented and sat back in his seat. Elora saw his ripped shirtsleeve was now completely saturated with blood, though the bleeding appeared to have slowed. "Let me take a look at your shoulder," she said as she reached for his injured arm.

"It's only a graze," he replied impatiently and slid out of the vehicle before she could get a good look at the wound. His full attention was now on getting Samir and the others out of the RPG-damaged SUV in front of them. Zaidan and a couple of the other NDU security guards jogged up to the crippled Armada and ripped open the back doors. Zaidan pulled Samir from the smoke-filled interior and assessed his condition. He was shaken and suffering from minor smoke inhalation but otherwise unscathed. Out the other side of the vehicle, Fareed and another NDU guard emerged, supporting a third guard between them who was unconscious and covered in blood. Zaidan directed Samir to his and Elora's vehicle, while Fareed and the others distributed themselves amongst several other vehicles. They abandoned the crippled SUV and evacuated the area; it was still ablaze in the middle of the road as the rest of the convoy roared past and continued down the highway, speeding toward the security of the NDU compound.

Chapter 16

Several days after the Delta Force raid on the NDU compound outside Mosul, young New Dawn security guard Ahmed Assad returned to Baghdad. With the future of the organization on shaky ground following the American assault, his uncle and NDU head accountant, Hakim, had urged his nephew to resume his studies at Baghdad University. Ahmed had taken a semester off from college to train with the NDU militia and was subsequently assigned to work security at the compound. After the raid, his uncle recommended he finish his degree so he'd have a fallback should NDU fail to recover and ultimately collapse in the wake of the American attack.

Though he rarely spoke with his uncle, Ahmed had heard about the recent deadly ambush on the NDU convoy in northern Iraq outside Tal Afar. When he learned three NDU guards had perished in the attack, he was struck by survivor's guilt. He knew he could have easily been one of the fallen men, that he *should* have been one of them. No details had been confirmed, of course, but rumor was that NDU had been attacked by Shiite militia goons dispatched from Baghdad under direct orders from Iranian Republican Guard General Ali Ansari. Like many Sunni Muslims, Ahmed was resentful of the strong Iranian influence currently sweeping across Iraq.

A few evenings after learning of the ambush, Ahmed met up with some of his college buddies at an outdoor café in one of

Baghdad's predominantly Sunni neighborhoods. The friends were hanging out, drinking chai, and smoking hookah, when a procession of vehicles began to slowly roll down the street in front of the café. Horns blared while armed passengers stood in the beds of pickup trucks or hung out the windows, whooping and shouting as they fired AK-47s into the air. The ruckus captured the attention of the patrons in the café as well as everyone in the general vicinity. Ahmed and his friends went over to the curb where they joined a crowd of curious onlookers trying to figure out what the hell was going on. After pushing his way through a wall of spectators to get a view of the impromptu parade, Ahmed's blood turned cold. The procession was made up of Iraqi Police vehicles, but it was difficult to tell they were even Iraqi. Iranian flags were draped across hoods, flying from vehicle rooftops, and clutched in the hands of many of the passengers. The occupants, some in police uniforms others in civilian clothing, yelled out pro-Iranian or Shiite chants and cheerfully waved the flags in the faces of the bystanders lining the street as the obnoxious parade rolled by. It was clear the intent of the spectacle was to taunt the local residents of the Sunni neighborhood.

In a matter of seconds, Ahmed's blood turned from cold to a raging boil, and he began pushing his way back through the crowd toward the café. "Ahmed? Ahmed! Where are you going!" one of his friends called out after him, but Ahmed ignored his friend's beckons and made a beeline for his car, which was parked in the lot behind the café. Reaching his car, he tore open the trunk and pulled out an AK-47 rifle. "Ahmed don't!" his friends pleaded, but he ignored them and held the AK tight to his chest as strode back toward the roadway. The final vehicle in the procession had just passed when Ahmed stepped off the curb, took several steps out into the street, and aimed his weapon at the back of the rear vehicle. He pumped the trigger and popped off several bursts of rounds, hitting the rear vehicle multiple times and shattering its back window. The crowds on the street hardly reacted when Ahmed opened fire, but they scattered in a shrieking panic when they saw the convoy come to a screeching halt and the armed men pour out of the vehicles.

"Ahmed! *Yalla! Yalla!*" his friends screamed. "Let's go, they're coming! We've got to get out of here!"

Ahmed and his two friends sprinted back to his car and jumped inside. Ahmed passed the AK to his friend in the backseat who quickly began to disassemble the rifle while Ahmed fumbled to ram the key into the ignition. "Hurry up!" his other friend screamed from the front passenger seat. The engine finally roared to life, and Ahmed ripped the gearshift into the reverse position. He stomped on the gas pedal and glanced in the rearview mirror just in time to see the blinding headlights of a large truck racing up behind him. A military Humvee smashed into the back of Ahmed's car, ramming it forward and pinning it between the bumper of the Humvee and the rear wall of the café. Reeling from whiplash, Ahmed and his friends struggled to regain their senses and attempted to bail out of the car, but they were unable to escape before the vehicle was surrounded by armed men shouting and pointing rifles at them. Ahmed was dragged from the vehicle, slammed to the ground, and the barrel of a rifle was shoved in his face. He froze in terror when he realized the rifle was not an AK-47, but an American M-4 with a U.S. Marine standing at the other end of it. *Oh fuck.*

Within minutes, Ahmed and his friends were thrown into the back of the Humvee with their arms zip-tied behind their backs and hoods over their heads. After a thirty-minute drive and a blind walk from the vehicle into a building, Ahmed was shoved down into a metal folding chair. The hood was yanked off his head, and he saw that he was in a tiny room with makeshift plywood walls. Standing before him holding the hood was a tall American man dressed in a black polo shirt tucked into khaki-colored cargo pants. Ahmed's jaw clenched in fear; he knew if you ended up in a small room with an American wearing civilian clothes, you were in deep shit.

In the corner of the room sat a young man in a U.S. Army uniform, though Ahmed immediately knew he was actually an Iraqi, most likely a local interpreter hired by the Americans. Ahmed stared in disgust at the man in the corner who looked to be about the same age as him. "You fucking traitor," Ahmed spat in venom-laced Arabic directed at the uniformed man. "Do you enjoy being the Americans' little bitch-boy? You fucking pussy!"

"Excuse me," the American man interjected in English, "I will be asking the questions here, if you don't mind."

The interpreter ignored Ahmed's insults and translated the American's statement.

"So, Ahmed... Your name is Ahmed, right? That's the name we found on your national ID in your wallet, at least." The interpreter translated and Ahmed gave a quick nod. "Nice to meet you, Ahmed. My name is Mike, and my question for you is simple. Why in the hell did you shoot at our Marines?"

Ahmed was confused. "What Marines?"

"The United States Marines parked in the Humvee down

the street from where you opened fire with your AK-47," Mike replied in an exasperated tone.

"I didn't shoot at any Americans," Ahmed proclaimed. "I was shooting at the Iranian dogs!"

"So, you admit you were the one shooting in the street?" Mike reiterated.

Ahmed wanted to defend himself but clenched his jaw and bit his tongue, knowing he'd already said too much.

"Look, kid, you can cooperate with me or I can hand you over to the Iraqi police," Mike threatened. "They're *dying* to get in a room with you to find out why you turned two of their cars into Swiss cheese and seriously wounded an officer."

"If you give me to them, you know what will happen. They will drill holes into me until I am dead and then dump my body in the street. That's what they do, these *police* you handed our country over to."

"Well, I don't know about all that," Mike said skeptically, "but I do know that unless I have a reason to keep you in U.S. custody, I won't have a choice but to release you to them. That's simply the law, which we follow here in Iraq now that your buddy Saddam is dead."

"He wasn't my *buddy*," Ahmed said in a disgusted tone and then shifted back to the main subject. "I didn't see any American vehicles on the street when I pulled the trigger; if I hit a U.S. Humvee it was an accident."

"An accident?" Mike asked suspiciously. "Yeah, we hear that a lot." Ahmed stared at him in defiance but did not add any more to his statement. "Okay fine, if it was in fact an *accident*, then I guess we're done here; I'll go draw up the paperwork to get you transferred over to the Iraqi Police."

"No!" Ahmed shrieked. "They will kill me!"

"Then you better give me a reason to hang onto you," Mike said. "Tell me something that'll make it worth my while to keep you out of an IP cell. I'm going to need more than this bullshit '*it was an accident*' story."

"But this is the truth! I don't know what else to tell you about it!" Ahmed lamented.

"Then give me something *else*. It could be completely unrelated to tonight's events," Mike explained. "If you want me to protect your ass, I need something valuable in return. I have a feeling you have information in your head that I may find interesting. There's a reason you have such a bitter distaste for the Iraqi Police. Your visceral reaction to them is quite telling. Why, Ahmed? Why do you hate them so much? Who taught you to hate them like this? The resistance? Al-Qaeda?"

Ahmed laughed.

"What's so fucking funny?"

"You fucking Americans," Ahmed said, a faint smile still playing across his lips. "You think everyone is an Islamic extremist working for Al-Qaeda. For such a large powerful country, you sure do have small simple minds."

"Are you done insulting me now? Because, from where I'm sitting, it appears my *small mind* has you cornered like a fucking rat. And if you don't play your goddamn cards right, I will drop you into the fucking snake pit. And yes, I know exactly what they would do to you, but guess what—I don't *even* fucking care. No matter what, I'll still sleep like a baby tonight. So, what's it gonna be, Ahmed? Do you have anything to give me or not? 'Cause I'm done sitting here playing grab-ass with you."

Ahmed closed his eyes and dropped his chin to his chest. "Yes," he said in little more than a whisper.

"Yes, what?"

"Yes, I have information I can give you."

"Out-fucking-standing, Ahmed," Mike said in a condescending tone, spreading his arms. "So, let's hear it; I'm all ears."

"No way, I want a promise—*in writing*—that once I give you information, you won't hand me over to the Iraqi Police anyway."

"Unfortunately, Ahmed, I don't have that kind of power. Whatever information you provide will have to go up the chain of command to be evaluated, and if you want to convince the people above me to make any deals with you, you better make damn sure it's information they'll deem highly valuable."

Ahmed lifted his head and looked Mike directly in the eye. "Get something to write with."

A manila folder in hand, Derek excitedly rapped his knuckles on the door of Nick's office. As soon as Nick gave the go-ahead for him to enter, Derek practically burst into the room and alighted in the chair across from Nick's desk.

"Well, hello, Derek, won't you please sit down," Nick said sarcastically after Derek was already perched on the edge of the seat.

"I think you want to see this," Derek exclaimed and waved the folder in front of Nick.

"I was about to head out, so why don't you go ahead and give me the CliffsNotes version, and I'll read the full report later—maybe."

"It's a summary of an interrogation Task Force one-twenty-two conducted with a twenty-year-old detainee at Taji Air Base last night. His name is Ahmed Assad. He was picked up yesterday after stepping into the middle of a Baghdad street and firing his AK-47 at an Iraqi Police convoy. What the kid didn't realize was there was a U.S. Marine Humvee also downrange that absorbed several rounds from his little temper tantrum."

"Okay, so they hauled his ass in. I'm still waiting for why this matters to us," Nick said in a bored tone.

"The kid claims to be a member of NDU, or at least, he was. He's now a full-time student at Baghdad University but says he was trained at NDU's militia compound in northwestern Iraq and served as a security guard..."

"Derek, NDU has over two thousand foot soldiers in their militia," Nick interrupted dismissively. "We catch and release these assholes on petty shit like this all the time."

"This kid wasn't just a member of the militia," Derek countered. "He says he was one of the security guards on duty at the New Dawn HQ compound the night of the Delta Force raid."

This sparked Nick's interest. "I'm listening," he said as he leaned forward in his chair.

"Of course, everyone throughout NDU—from the very top to the fucking janitors—knows about the raid," Derek conceded. "However, this kid gave a precise description of the entire event.

He knew details we haven't released yet, shit that only a few people with access to the classified report know. The kid was either there that night or he knows someone who was."

"And he somehow survived," Nick added in a speculative tone.

"The kid claims they *all* survived...including Malik Khalid."

"Fuck." Nick dropped his head. "Well, we know not *everyone* survived. Bodies were recovered from the tunnel."

"According to this kid, they were already dead. They were bodies exhumed from a local cemetery and planted down there when the tunnel was built...to throw off an investigation in case of this very scenario."

"So, the kid saw Malik escape? How does he know for sure Malik is alive?"

"We don't know yet—he stopped talking. He refuses to say anything else until we offer him a deal."

"Of course," Nick snorted with a chuckle. "What are his demands? A mansion in Beverly Hills and Kim Kardashian to give him hourly blow jobs?"

"Essentially. He wants full immunity, a ticket to the U.S., and a Green Card."

Nick rolled his eyes. "We could just beat the info out of him," he said, only half-joking.

"Yes, well, you and I both know how the optics inevitably play out on that. Though, we could rendition him to Amman and let our friends in Jordanian intel work him over. See if they can get anything else out of him while we keep our hands clean."

"No, that'll take too long. If this kid has info on Malik's

whereabouts, we need to act fast, *before* Malik finds out we have him, but I highly doubt this kid knows Malik's current location."

"It's likely he at least knows what he looks like, which is a lot more than we have at this point," Derek said with a shrug. "He did also offer another interesting tidbit, though I wasn't able to connect it with anything in our report from the raid, so I'm not sure it's even relevant. Before he clammed up, he mentioned Malik suffered a moderately severe stab wound to the lower left side of his back. He said Malik got into a fight with one of the American soldiers during the raid who managed to slice him with a large knife."

Nick furrowed his brow in confusion. "Well, if one of the Delta Force guys was in a hand-to-hand scuffle during the raid and stabbed anyone it would be in the mission debrief report."

"That's the problem, this is the one detail in the kid's story that doesn't match up with anything in our records. I went through the entire debrief summary three times. None of the Delta Force members mentioned anything about stabbing anyone."

"At least none of the guys that gave a post-mission statement," Nick said ominously. "There was one who never went through the debriefing."

"Brendan," Derek answered grimly.

"And he was found with his field knife in hand," Nick added. "He held onto it until after he was...gone. They didn't pry it from his fingers until they were prepping his body for the flight home."

Derek's eyes widened. "Brendan may have been killed by Malik himself."

Nick reached for his phone. "But not before Brendan was

able to ram his knife into the asshole," Nick said as he dialed a number. "Which means Brendan's knife may have Malik Khalid's DNA on it."

"Holy shit!"

Brendan's knife was still in evidence lock-up pending the completion of the Department of Defense investigation into the raid, which was still ongoing. Nick called to find out if the knife had been submitted for DNA analysis. Considering how old the evidence was, nearly a year now, and how much of Brendan's own blood contaminated the knife, Nick had doubts they'd be able to recover any of Malik's DNA, but it was worth a shot. He submitted a request for the analysis to be expedited and results sent ASAP to the NDU Task Force.

"Should we pass any of this to Elora?" Derek asked after Nick hung up the phone.

Nick took a deep breath and thought for a moment. "No, let's wait until we have something more tangible than this kid's story. I'm afraid this may only fuck with her head and possibly cause more harm than good at this point."

"Good point, in the meantime, what do you want to do about the NDU kid in custody? Task Force one-twenty-two is waiting for word from us on how to proceed with him."

"Make the deal," Nick said. "If we can't pull any DNA off Brendan's knife, we're going to need the kid to provide us with a detailed description of him, in addition to everything else he knows, and hopefully it'll help us hunt that fucker down once and for all."

Three days later, Nick was intercepted by Derek as soon as he walked into work. "DNA analysis on Brendan's knife came back," Derek blurted with a wide grin before Nick could even get his key in the door of his office.

"From the look on your face, I'm guessing they were able to pull something," Nick said as he entered his office with Derek on his heels.

"Sure did, and I already ran it through the databases." He passed Nick a single piece of paper. "We got a match."

"Malik Khalid is in our database?" Nick scanned the paper, wide-eyed.

"Well, not him personally," Derek clarified, the excitement waning in his tone. "But a parental and sibling match."

"Nadia Ibrahim: 98.7 percent Parental Match," Nick read from the sheet. "Farah Khalid: 67.3 percent Sibling Match."

"It's much easier to establish child-parent relationships via DNA than sibling relations," Derek explained. "But 67.3 percent is still a pretty solid match, considering the sample they got from Brendan's knife was heavily degraded due to the elements. Plus, it was confirmed via other sources that Nadia and Farah are, in fact, mother and daughter. I'm fairly certain these are Malik Khalid's mother and sister."

"Let's not celebrate yet," Nick warned. "We still aren't positive the DNA from Brendan's knife belongs to Malik Khalid in the first place."

"Keep reading," Derek urged.

Nick continued reading aloud from the sheet. "Nadia Ibrahim, age forty-three and Farah Khalid, age fourteen, killed 18 May 2003 during U.S. Marine raid on residential home in southeast Mosul. Full investigation into operation conducted by NCIS… No charges filed." Nick shot Derek a knowing look.

"I was re-reading the transcript from Elora's interview with Samir Al-Bakr in Dubai. He mentioned in that interview that Malik Khalid's mother and sister were killed in a U.S. airstrike," Derek said.

"Well these women weren't killed in an airstrike," Nick said, shaking his head. "According to this, these women were victims of small arms crossfire that broke out during a raid."

Derek shrugged. "Maybe Samir fudged the details a bit to throw off anyone who might sniff out the trail?"

"Or these women aren't Malik's mother and sister," Nick said skeptically, then reversed his tone. "Or they are and perhaps Elora was right all along—Samir Al-Bakr may just be Malik Khalid," Nick declared, raising his eyebrows. "Where are we at with Ahmed Assad's deal? Did you get authorization from the State Department to approve his Visa yet? We need that fucker talking. I want to know what else he knows."

"Nothing yet," Derek said, shaking his head. "Jason is still working on it."

"Jesus fucking Christ," Nick said, rolling his eyes in frustration, "no wonder our immigration system is such a fucking mess. *We* can't even get the goddamn State Department off their asses to get anything done in a decent amount of time. Well…pack your bags, Derek," Nick said, giving him a playful slap on the shoulder. "You and I are going to Mosul to see where the mother and sister lead us."

Derek twisted his lip up in confusion, "But they're dead?"

"Ah Derek-son," Nick said in a Mr. Myagi accent, "the dead

still have stories to tell and much information to offer."

Chapter 17

Nick and Derek touched down at Erbil International Airport in Iraq's Kurdistan region and headed to the nearby CIA station. The next morning, they drove into Mosul and began searching burial records to locate the bodies of Nadia Ibrahim and Farah Khalid—Malik Khalid's supposed mother and sister. Once they found the women's bodies, they planned to work backward to try to track down any living family and friends to speak with, hoping someone along the way could lead them to Malik.

They kicked off their search at a Mosque located a few blocks from where the pair were killed. With Derek translating, Nick spoke with the Imam's personal secretary and explained they were American aid workers searching for the family of a fallen coworker. Their cover story was that their fellow aid worker, an Iraqi national, had recently passed away from a heart attack while the trio were working together at a village in southern Iraq. Their friend was from Mosul and had expressed his desire to be buried alongside his predeceased mother and sister. Nick informed the secretary they didn't know where in Mosul the women were buried, but they knew their names, dates of birth, and date of death. The secretary bought the story and happily offered his assistance. He searched the mosque's funeral and burial records using the information Nick provided but came up empty-handed. There were no records of any funerals for females matching either name taking place within the two weeks following their date of death.

Disappointed but not deterred, Nick and Derek moved on to the next Mosque on their list but hit another brick wall. Nothing matched Nadia or Farah's names in their funeral or burial records, nor had anyone at the Mosque ever heard of them.

They visited two more Mosques but were still no closer to finding Nadia and Farah when Nick decided to call off their search for the day. It was getting late, and he wanted to make it back to Erbil before dark. Nick was weaving their car out of the city when he came to a halt at an intersection where a group of schoolchildren were crossing the street. Nick and Derek gazed impatiently out the windshield as the children dawdled in the crosswalk. Several long shadows of the surrounding buildings cast by the setting sun fell across the hood of the car and stretched down the road ahead. One shadow in particular caught Nick's attention. As his eyes traced the familiar shape of a cross on the ground, a theory suddenly took shape in Nick's head. He turned to look out his window and was greeted by the stone façade of a Catholic church; a tall steeple crowned with a massive golden cross reached high into the sky above the ancient building.

"What if their funeral wasn't in a mosque?" Nick muttered half to himself, then turned back to look at Derek. "What if they aren't even Muslim?"

Derek wrinkled his forehead in confusion, and Nick pressed his finger to the window, pointing toward the church.

Derek looked at the church, then back at Nick. "That wouldn't make any sense," he said, shaking his head. "If they're Christian, then our entire theory is shot to hell. It means these women aren't Malik Khalid's mother and sister, the blood on Brendan's knife isn't Malik's, and the detainee we're about to give asylum to is lying to us."

Nick looked back at the church, rubbing his chin in thought for several long seconds. "Or, the Islamic Jihadist we're chasing is actually a Christian."

Derek snorted at the notion. "Well that would definitely be a new one."

Nick and Derek decided to return to the Catholic church the next day to follow up on Nick's outrageous theory. They employed the same story about their deceased friend wishing to be buried with his mother and sister, and the priest along with his assistant obligingly searched the church's records but found no trace of Nadia or Farah. Discouraged, Nick and Derek thanked the priest and his assistant for their efforts and concluded it was time to rethink their strategy. On their way out, the priest recommended they search the records at the Al Tahria Catholic Church, as it was one of the largest churches in Mosul. Not yet ready to completely abandon his hunch that the women were Christian, Nick decided to follow up on the priest's suggestion.

At the Al Tahria Church, Nick and Derek once again asked if the priest could do a quick search of the church's funeral records. Neither held out much hope of finding the women and began discussing their next move after the priest disappeared into the church's archives room. Both were surprised, however, when the priest returned a mere ten minutes later and handed Derek a small sheet of paper with a few handwritten lines in Arabic. Derek glanced down at the paper and his eyes bulged from his skull.

Seeing Derek's reaction, Nick quickly leaned in over his

shoulder. "What is it?"

Derek read from the paper, translating the text into English for Nick. "Nineteen May 2003, joint funeral service held for Nadia Ibrahim (mother) & Farah Khalid (daughter). Place of Burial: Syriac Catholic Church of the Virgin Mary cemetery, Bakhdida, Iraq." Derek looked up from the paper. "Holy shit, Nick, you were right—they were Christians."

Nick and Derek's joy was short-lived as they both realized the chances these women were related to Malik Khalid were now unlikely. Even Nick admitted his theory that Malik Khalid could possibly be a Christian was far-fetched at best. Either way, they'd come this far, so Nick planned to keep following Nadia and Farah's trail.

Although the women's joint funeral had been held there at the Al Tahria church in Mosul, they'd been buried at a cemetery in Bakhdida, a small Christian village about fifteen miles southeast of the city. Nick had Derek ask the priest if he had personally known the women or if the church had any other information or records on them, but the priest shook his head. He recommended they pay a visit to the small church in the village where the women were buried and provided Derek with directions to Bakhdida.

Half an hour later, Nick and Derek parked in front of Bakhdida's small Syriac Catholic Church. Although they were both certain these were the women they were searching for, Nick still needed a DNA sample for official cross-confirmation should anything they find out need to be presented in a court trial. Nick was excited to be closing in on his target but dreaded his next task. Convincing an Iraqi Catholic priest to grant a couple of Americans permission to exhume bodies from his church's cemetery to collect

DNA would not be easy. They entered the church and were soon warmly yet cautiously greeted by an old priest who walked with a cane. The church was empty, and the priest appeared to be minding the building alone, likely preparing to close up for the day as it was nearly sunset. Derek explained to the priest in Arabic that they had come looking for information on two women buried in his cemetery and gave him Nadia and Farah's full names. The priest nodded in recognition and asked Nick and Derek to follow him to his office. Inside his small dimly lit office, the priest ambled over to an ancient-looking file cabinet in the back corner, opened a middle drawer, and thumbed through the files. He finally plucked a tattered manila folder from the cabinet and plopped it on the desktop in front of Nick. Nick opened the folder and began shuffling through the papers inside. Since everything was in Arabic, he handed the top couple documents to Derek to start translating. While Derek scanned the pages, Nick randomly shuffled through the remainder of the contents in the file—copies of birth certificates, death certificates, baptismal certificates, communion certificates, etc. As he neared the bottom of the stack of papers, he noticed the corner of a color photograph sticking out from beneath the documents. Nick pulled the picture out and held it beneath the single lamp on the priest's desk. Looking at him from the photo was an attractive young Iraqi woman holding a toddler girl on her right hip. To the woman's left stood a boy Nick estimated to be eleven or twelve years old. The boy was wearing a long white robe and held his palms pressed together in prayer with a rosary dangling from his hands—a communion photo. When Nick looked into the eyes of the boy staring back at him from the photo, he was simultaneously struck with relief and fear—relief because he would no longer have to ask the priest for permission to exhume Farah and Nadia's bodies, and fear because Elora was in serious danger. Nick had looked into those same green eyes before, during his trip to Dubai with Elora. Though the face had matured and thinned into one with more angular features, the resemblance was uncanny. The boy in the communion photo was Zaidan Al-Sadiq, NDU leader Samir Al-Bakr's chief of staff and head of security.

"Ah, you've found young Malik," the priest commented with a smile when he noticed Nick with the photo. At the mention of Malik's name, Derek dropped the documents in his hands and shifted his attention to the photo Nick held; however, Derek did not recognize the boy. "Poor child went through such tragedy," the priest continued in a somber tone, "like so many of the children in Iraq."

"Do you happen to know what became of *young Malik*?" Nick asked, struggling to keep his tone even.

"Afraid I do not," the priest answered after Derek translated the question. "I believe he returned home to Baghdad after his mother and sister's funeral. That was the last time I saw him; hard to believe it's been ten years already."

The priest hooked his cane over the back of the chair behind his desk and took a seat. Nick stared at him, silently begging him with his eyes for more information without saying a word. The priest obliged.

"Malik's parents, Nadia and Yousif, were both born and raised here in Bakhdida, but Malik and his sister, Farah, were both born in Baghdad and grew up there. The family only came up here to the village on holidays and special occasions to visit with extended family. Malik's father, Yousif, left the village after high school to attend the University of Baghdad's College of Pharmacy. After earning his degree, he worked as a Pharmacist in one of the large hospitals in Baghdad. Shortly after landing that job, he returned here to the village to marry his childhood sweetheart, Malik's mother, Nadia. They married right here in this very church," the priest recalled with a sad smile.

"Both Malik and Farah were baptized and celebrated their First Communions here, but aside from those occasions, Christmas Eve masses, and a few weddings, we rarely saw the family. Also, as you can see, Yousif is not in Malik's First Communion photo. Tragically, he died when Malik was ten years old; he perished in an American air raid during the First Gulf War—he was one of the victims of the infamous 1991 Amiriyah Shelter Bombing in Baghdad. Nadia struggled to raise the children on her own after that. I know her parents tried to convince her to move back up here to the village so they could help her more, but she refused. Baghdad was her children's home, and she didn't want to uproot them from their lives.

"Then, of course, Nadia and Farah were killed shortly after the Americans arrived in Mosul following the fall of Baghdad in 2003. The family had come up here to avoid the chaos of the invasion in Baghdad and got caught up in a clash between a U.S. Marine unit and some resistance fighters. Malik was in college at the time, and I heard he returned to his studies at Baghdad University after the funeral. He too was studying to become a pharmacist, like his father.

"Over the next few years most of Malik's extended family left Iraq through the UN refugee program and are now scattered across the globe—Australia, New Zealand, the UK, Sweden, the Netherlands, and more. I'm not sure he even has any family left around here; he himself may have left Iraq. I hope wherever he is, he is doing well and has found peace; life dealt him a crummy hand but he was a sharp young man. If anyone could overcome adversity, it's Malik Khalid," the Priest added with a fond smile. "He was highly intelligent but also kindhearted."

The priest's final remark about Malik being kindhearted caught Nick by surprise, but he made an effort not to allow his face to betray his sentiments.

Though they never came out and said it, the priest knew Nick and Derek were hunting Malik Khalid. The priest was an old man far removed from current affairs, but he'd heard whispers on the wind and rumors throughout the village about a young man from a local family being linked to the origins of the popular New Dawn Underground militant group. He also immediately knew Nick and Derek's story about being aid workers was complete bullshit. "Was there anything else I could help you gentlemen with?" the priest asked, eager to have the Americans move on. "Sunset will be here soon, and I need to make my rounds to secure the church grounds."

Nick shook his head and stood up. "Thank you for your time and assistance, Father. You've been extremely helpful. May I snap a photo of this picture with my phone?" he asked pointing at Malik's Communion photo.

"Take it with you," the priest answered with a wave of his hand. "With everyone in the family now gone or passed on, we will just keep the main records and dump everything else from the file soon. If you should happen to *bump* into Malik, please pass the photo along to him," he added in a slightly cryptic tone. "He may like to have it."

"I sure will, Father." A part of Nick wanted to stick around and pump the priest for more info, but his first priority was getting back to the car and calling Elora from the satellite phone to warn her of Zaidan's true identity.

Nick swiftly shook hands with the priest, then spun on his heels and made a beeline for the exit.

"Why are you in such a hurry?" Derek asked as he jogged to keep up with Nick's speed-walk pace. "I think this priest knows more than what he's said. Shouldn't we stay and find out what else he can tell us about Malik?"

"No, we have what we need," Nick said curtly, "I need to call and warn Elora."

"Warn her of what?" Derek asked confused. "That Malik Khalid is a closeted Christian?"

Nick stopped abruptly and spun around to face Derek, who nearly plowed into him.

"Warn her that Malik is alive and well and *not* hiding in some obscure cave," Nick spat in hushed voice. "He's been right under our noses." Derek shot him a confused expression. "The boy in this picture," Nick said, shoving the communion photo in front of Derek's face, "is Zaidan Al-Sadiq."

"Samir Al-Bakr's chief of staff?" Derek stared at the photo until a wave of recognition flooded over his face. "Zaidan Al-Sadiq is Malik Khalid?"

Nick nodded. "Malik Khalid has been posing as the right-hand man of his own fucking replacement. As Samir Al-Bakr's chief of staff and head of security he's been able to continue to keep his fingers in everything, while diverting the spotlight to Samir. He is controlling NDU's every move under the guise of acting on orders from Samir, but Samir is merely a figurehead—a stand-in. The fucker has been playing us for months, and right now, he has Elora." Reaching the car, Nick ripped the door open and dove inside to retrieve the satellite phone.

"Wait, wait!" Derek shouted, grabbing Nick before he could get a hand on the phone. "Let's think this through. If we call her now and drop this bomb on her, she may slip up and cost herself her cover. Or Zaidan…or Malik, whoever the fuck he is, will be able to tell that she knows the truth, and this will put her in even more danger. Hell, for all we know, she may have already figured it out herself."

"Or Zaidan may have already figured *her* out," Nick added. "He's one of the most intelligent targets I've ever tracked, Derek; Elora is no match for him. I'm sure he already knows who she is. She needs to know the truth. It'll give her the best chance of coming out of this alive, and once she knows, we've got to figure out a way to get her out of there."

Nick dialed the number to Elora's sat-phone and impatiently waited as it rang on the other end. "Fuck! She's not picking up," he barked in frustration. He ended the call and immediately dialed her number again. Still no answer. "Shit," Nick huffed and tossed the phone back into the car. "Get in, we've got to head back to Erbil. It'll be dark soon." Nick dialed Elora's sat-phone every three minutes as they sped back toward the Kurdish border but still couldn't get a hold of her.

Derek was still reeling from the revelation that Malik Khalid was a closeted Christian. "There are a ton of Christians in

Iraq who've been through Hell, but I've never heard of any of them converting into Islamic Jihadists. You think he suffered a mental breakdown or something?"

Nick shook his head. "I doubt he truly converted. Zaidan is no zealot; he's simply wielding Islamic Jihad as a means to gain power. The fact he was born a Christian is something he likely views as a minor inconvenience. He possesses all the traits of the perfect extremist leader—ambition, tragic motivation, charisma, business savvy, calculated ruthlessness... Yet, even with all this, he knew he'd still never get anywhere as a hillbilly Catholic from a rural Christian village. He transformed himself into what he needed to be to build a successful militant organization and gain power. He simply uses Islamic extremism to control his foot soldiers and manipulate his followers. In his heart, he is still Christian. For people like him, religion is just a tool. So, to answer your question, no, Zaidan did not have a mental breakdown. Every move he's made has been carefully calculated and executed. He knows *exactly* what he's doing."

An hour after they arrived back at the CIA station in Erbil, Nick's sat-phone rang and he immediately answered it. "Elora!" he blurted into the phone but, to his disappointment, it wasn't her on the other end; it was Jason calling from the Task Force office back at Langley. He informed Nick that the State Department had approved Ahmed Assad's travel, and Assad was currently on a diplomatic flight bound for D.C. A sketch artist had accompanied him aboard the flight and would soon be emailing over a rendering of Malik Khalid based on Assad's description. As if on cue, Nick heard his laptop chime, indicating an incoming email. Nick opened the email and clicked on the attachment, but he already knew what he was going to see. Staring back at him was the pencil-sketched face of Zaidan Al-Sadiq—complete with a special notation at the bottom of the drawing. *Note*: *Subject has unique, "Cat-like" green eyes.*

Chapter 18

"It was a fucking set up!" Samir yelled as he banged his fist on the large table in the militia compound dining room. Joining Samir around the table were Zaidan, Fareed, Hakim, and Bashir, NDU's Intelligence Director. It had been several days since the NDU convoy had been ambushed on the highway after visiting the burned-out farms. NDU had lost three men in the ambush and a dozen more sustained injuries ranging from minor to serious, including Zaidan whose upper arm graze wound required sixteen stitches. The guard who Fareed had helped carry out of Samir's SUV succumbed to his injuries and died several hours after the attack. He'd been in the front passenger seat when the RPG hit the vehicle. Two other NDU guards also died on the scene, one suffered a head shot and died instantly, while another was killed by arms fire that severed an artery in his arm. He bled out before they could get him rushed to medical attention.

In the days following the ambush, Bashir and his team worked round-the-clock shaking every source they had across Baghdad and beyond to find out who was behind the attack. According to what little intel they'd been able to dig up, there was evidence to support the group that ambushed the NDU convoy were directly linked to General Ali Ansari's Badr Brigade, which was no surprise to anyone. Ansari had dispatched the squad from Baghdad soon after learning the NDU leadership had traveled north. Bashir suspected the same group who'd ambushed the convoy had also set fire to the wheat crops the night before the attack. His theory was that the fires were not only set to destroy the fields but to draw out the NDU leadership.

"They were counting on you traveling out from the security of the compound to go survey the damage and visit the farmers," Bashir explained. "They likely had scouts along the highway between here and the farms outside Tal Afar. Your visit to the farmer gave them ample time to set up an ambush to attack you on your return trip. It also enabled a scout to identify the vehicle Samir was traveling in, which is likely why his SUV was the one struck by the RPG."

"Fucking Ansari," Zaidan grumbled between clenched teeth. "I swear to God, I will rip his fucking guts out and strangle him to death with them. Where are we at with Karim and the militia? Anybody from General Ansari's camp try to make contact or reach out to Karim yet?"

Bashir pursed his lips and shook his head in disappointment. "Nothing yet, but we haven't given them an opportunity to carry out anything significant enough to establish themselves as more than a street gang."

"An extremely *well-funded* street gang," Samir interjected with a huff. "Those assholes are costing us a fortune and getting us nowhere."

"And, unfortunately, the money is creating a problem in itself," Bashir chimed in. "It's attracting the wrong attention. The Americans have grown suspicious and are poking around trying to figure out who is bankrolling Karim. If the Americans get curious enough and follow the money trail back to us, no doubt they will share this info with the central government."

"And by proxy, the general," Zaidan added with a frustrated sigh. "And it'll all have been for nothing."

It was just after two o'clock in the morning when Elora suddenly awoke to Zaidan thrashing in his sleep and grumbling indecipherably. She pushed herself up on one arm to see what was going on and immediately recognized the symptoms—he was having a stress nightmare, common in those suffering from PTSD. Brendan had suffered bouts of them here and there, and Elora had learned the hard way not to try to wake up someone having a PTSD nightmare. She'd once tried to shake Brendan awake while he wrestled in his sleep with an imaginary attacker, and she'd ended up with his hand around her throat. Luckily, he'd quickly snapped back to his senses, and Elora was relatively unharmed, but she was shaken enough to never touch Brendan again when he slipped into a nightmare. If he showed any signs of one at all, she would simply slip out of bed and watch him from a safe distance until he came out of it on his own.

Once Elora realized what was happening, her first instinct was to roll out of bed and wait it out, but a sudden impulse overruled her. She scooted closer to Zaidan, wrapped her arm around his torso in a bear hug and whispered in his ear. "Zaidan… Zaidan, it's okay, you're safe," she said in a soothing tone as she squeezed him tighter. "Wake up, Zaidan," she continued, laying her head on his shoulder. "Wake up."

Zaidan's eyes flung open, wild with panic from battling the demons of his subconscious. Breathless and sweating, he lay silent and still with his head turned away from Elora. She maintained her hold on him until his heart rate slowed to a normal pace. "Are you okay?" she finally asked once she felt his body relax.

"Yes," he replied flatly, continuing to stare at the wall.

"Is there anything I can do?"

Pulling out of Elora's embrace, he rolled up to a sitting position on the edge of the bed. "No, I'm fine," he said, running a hand through his damp hair. "Go back to sleep."

Elora laid her head back on her pillow but continued to stare at Zaidan's back. He was shirtless and the scar on his lower back seemed to glow in the moonlight. The more she looked at it, the surer she was the scar wasn't the result of a car accident. She was curious to know what had really happened, but it wasn't worth hounding him over. She had a feeling he'd tell her the truth in time, when he was ready.

Zaidan went into the bathroom, and Elora heard the water in the sink turn on. He returned to bed a few minutes later but continued to lay turned away from her, seemingly as far away from her as possible. They lay in silence for several minutes, both knowing the other was wide awake, until Elora finally spoke. "What if I can get you out of here?"

"What are you talking about?" he replied in an agitated tone.

"You don't belong here," she continued. "You're a good person, you have so much potential, and this country is a crumbling shithole. You're going to die here. And for what? For NDU? To break yourself against a wall of corruption?" She sat up and reached over, rolling him onto his back so she could see his face. "I can get you to the U.S. You could have a life there, away from all this…shit. I think you'd be happy."

"If you think I'd be happy in America, then you don't know me at all," he replied in a callous tone. "What would I do in the U.S., huh?" His emerald eyes flamed with contempt, cutting to her soul. "Work at Starbucks, making coffee for entitled yuppies? Drive a taxi?" he continued, his voice growing in volume and anger. "Stock shelves at Walmart! You know full well I would be nothing there, no matter how much *potential* I have."

"You'd be alive!"

"Some things are worse than death," he replied, his tone resuming its usual softness. "Iraq is my country, my home. As I was born here, so too shall I die here, whenever God wills it."

"If you stay here, that won't be long," she said, shaking her head. "You're going to get yourself killed sooner rather than later."

"You're probably right," he said, placing a tender hand on her face, "but at least I'll have died fighting for something. My death will have meaning…purpose." He gently swiped a single tear from her cheek with his thumb.

"What about me?" she said, her voice cracking with emotion. "If something happens to you… I mean… I can't…" She struggled to find the words she wanted but gave up. "Fuck!"

She was sure it was the universe's sick twisted joke. Zaidan was the last person on Earth she should fall for, the last person she ever *thought* she would fall for, but here she was. Zaidan looked into her eyes and she knew that he knew.

"I think I'm in love with you," she whispered in defeat, dropping her head into her hands.

"That's not good," he said grimly.

"No shit, you have no fucking idea how *not good* this is."

Zaidan swallowed hard. He knew what he was about to do meant only one thing, that he was in love with her too, which was unacceptable. He had to let her go. "You should leave."

"I know," she said, closing her eyes as tears streamed down her cheeks. She rolled out of the bed and threw her clothes on. Elora knew he didn't mean she should simply return to her room; he meant she should leave Iraq.

"We return to Baghdad the day after tomorrow," Zaidan said as Elora reached for the door to leave. "I'll arrange a flight for you back to D.C. that evening."

Unable to speak, Elora simply nodded and opened the door.

"Elora," Zaidan called out, halting her once more. She looked over her shoulder at him again, waiting for him to speak. He stared at her for several long seconds, a million things he wanted to say, but all he offered her were three words. "In another life."

Elora closed her eyes and inhaled sharply. Choking back sobs, she managed a nod, then slipped out into the hallway, pulling the door shut behind her. Tears stung Elora's eyes as she crept down the dark hallway to her room. Zaidan's words reverberated in her head. *In another life*. Elora sensed a pattern—it seemed her happiness was always *in another life*; this life held only pain, loss, and disappointment.

She entered her room and closed the door as quietly as possible. There was enough moonlight coming in that she didn't need to turn on the light, and she began to shuffle toward the bed.

Halfway across the room, a voice suddenly sliced through the darkness, and Elora gasped as her heart leapt into her throat.

"I take it you're done fucking him for the night," Samir announced in a drunken slur, his voice dripping with bitter resentment.

"Samir?" Elora called out in a hushed whisper. She peered through the darkness and made out a shadowy figure seated in a small chair near the foot of her bed. "What are you doing in here?"

"I came to see you." The pungent aroma of alcohol enveloped the room. Samir's left arm dangled over the side of the chair, clutching a bottle of liquor, and Elora watched as he brought the nearly empty bottle to his lips to take a swig. His right hand rested palm-down on his thigh, a metallic object pressed beneath it. Elora fought the urge to hyperventilate when she realized the object was a pistol. Slipping into fight-or-flight mode, she contemplated making a run for the door but feared he'd shoot her before she could get out the door. "I actually came a few hours ago," he continued. "When you weren't in, I decided to wait until you returned. I didn't realize it would take nearly all night before you came back, but here we are."

"What do you want, Samir?" she asked as calmly as possible.

"I want you to leave him alone."

"I will… I am," Elora stuttered. "As soon as we get back to Baghdad, I'll be on the first flight to D.C., I promise."

Samir smirked and shook his head. "You fucking American bitch. You bomb the shit out of us and then roll in and find other ways to fuck us over." Samir stood up and leveled the gun at her, his hand shaking from intoxication. She threw her hands up instinctively and backed against the wall as he approached her.

"Samir, I said I was leaving, I swear. I won't touch him again," she said through fearful gasps as she eyeballed the gun pointed at her. "I won't talk to him or even look at him. I swear. I'm sorry."

Samir continued toward her until their chests were nearly touching. Elora froze in fear as he pressed the barrel of the gun to her left cheek. "I could solve everything right now, blow your pretty little face off and splatter it across that wall over there."

Elora squeezed her eyes shut and racked her brain to figure out a way to survive the ordeal. "I know you love him," she said, thinking her best option for the moment was to keep him talking. "I understand that now and I'm ready to walk away. Ask Zaidan yourself. I leave for the U.S. the day after tomorrow; you'll never see me again."

"It's not that simple." His voice was now devoid of emotion, and Elora knew she was fighting a losing battle. "He's in love with you. No matter where you are, as long as you're in this world, he will never be free of you. You will destroy *everything* he and I have built together."

Elora opened her eyes and looked directly into Samir's; she saw absolutely nothing, utter emptiness. She knew she had to make her move before he pulled the trigger. Summoning her limited hand-to-hand combat and self-defense training, Elora swiftly jerked her right leg up, aiming for Samir's crotch with her knee. She hit her mark and he crumpled in agony. Unfortunately for Elora, he collapsed forward into her, pinning her to the wall with his weight. She flailed and scratched at his arm that held the gun, trying to wrestle it from his grip as he struggled to catch his breath in the wake of the blow to his groin. He pulled back from her a few inches, giving her enough room to throw a twisting elbow strike to his neck. She aimed for the carotid artery, hoping to render him unconscious or at least stun him long enough for her to flee the room. The strike to his neck didn't knock him out, but it was forceful enough to cause him to drop the gun. The pistol clattered to the floor, and Elora dove down on top of it. She wrapped her hand around the grip and rolled over to take aim at Samir. As she raised her arms, he lunged toward her, and she pulled the trigger three times in rapid succession, aiming at his chest. Samir stumbled backward and collapsed to the floor with a sickening thud. Elora scrambled to her feet, continuing to aim the gun at him until she was sure the threat had been fully neutralized.

Satisfied Samir would not be getting back up, Elora stuffed the gun into the rear waistband of her pants and sprang to her door to lock it. She knew someone had to have heard the shots and would eventually come to her room to investigate. Unsure what to do next, she dug her sat-phone out of her backpack and called Nick, who answered within a split second.

"Elora?" Nick blurted excitedly as he answered, but Elora was too flustered to notice Nick's tone. In shock and shaking uncontrollably, she struggled to form words. "Elora? What's wrong?"

"I killed him," Elora sputtered. "Nick, he's dead… There's blood everywhere… They're going to be coming soon… What do I do? You've gotta get me out of here!"

"Elora, take a deep breath. You have to calm down and we'll work through this together."

"Okay...okay," she said, trying to calm her breathing.

"First of all, are you sure he's dead?"

"Yes," she replied, her voice cracking.

"It's good you killed him; Derek and I just connected the dots on this end. Elora, he was Malik Khalid." Nick assumed the person Elora had just killed was Zaidan. While Elora, too flustered to realize she never said Samir's name, thought Nick was telling her Samir was Malik Khalid.

"I fucking knew it!" she exclaimed in a high-pitched whisper.

"We only found out today; we're in Erbil right now," Nick said. "I've been trying to get a hold of you. I've called a hundred times. Where have you been?"

Realizing she'd left the sat-phone behind in her backpack while she was in Zaidan's room, Elora dodged the question. "Nick, how do I get the fuck out of here? I'm in the middle of nowhere—a good sixty miles west of Mosul."

"Don't worry, we will get you out, but first, I need you to collect a DNA sample so we can positively confirm his death and close the book on this bullshit once and for all. Do you have the DNA collection kit handy?"

"Yes."

"Get it and your digital camera."

Elora dashed to her backpack and retrieved the DNA kit and camera. "Okay, got 'em."

"Is the body on the floor?" Nick asked.

"Yes."

"Face down or on his back?"

"Face down." A pool of blood, deep purple in color, was steadily expanding around Samir's body.

"Okay good. First, I need you to lift his shirt to expose the lower left side of his back," Nick instructed. "There should be a large scar, approximately five to seven inches long, visible across that area of his back. I need you to take two photos: a close-up of the scar and a full-body shot with his head to the side, exposing his profile."

Elora froze as soon as Nick mentioned the scar. "What?" she asked, feeling a knot instantly form in her stomach. "A scar?"

"We have new intel that Malik Khalid has a distinct scar from a stab wound he received during the Delta Force raid," Nick explained. "Elora...the scar is from Brendan," he added in a somber tone. "He stabbed him during a scuffle and, we believe, Malik was then the one who shot Brendan."

Elora felt like someone had punched her in the stomach; all the air was instantly sucked out of her lungs. Images of running her fingers across Zaidan's scar flashed through her mind and she was suddenly nauseous.

"I thought you should know," Nick continued. "Hopefully, it'll make this easier to deal with." Nick waited for a response, but Elora was dead silent on the other end of the line.

Elora reached down and yanked up Samir's shirt to reveal his bare back, but she already knew there would be no scar. Just as she'd feared, his back was pristine. *No, no, no*. Her heart sank to the floor and smashed into a million pieces.

"Elora?" Nick asked with concern. "Elora, you there?"

Elora forced herself to composure. "I'm here, Nick. I got it. I'll get the photos and the blood sample, then I'll call you back." Without letting Nick answer, she disconnected the call and tossed the phone onto the bed. Just as the phone made a soft plop on the mattress, Elora caught movement out the corner of her eye. She snapped her head to the side and saw Zaidan standing in the doorway. He'd managed to quietly unlock the door from the outside and slip into the room. He stared down at Samir's body on the floor, but his face remained expressionless. Finally, he shifted his gaze to Elora. He immediately saw in her eyes that she knew the truth.

Elora took several swift steps back from Zaidan, dropping the camera and DNA kit as she retreated. She pulled the pistol from her waistband and leveled it at him.

"Don't fucking move!" Elora commanded.

"Okay," Zaidan replied calmly. "I'll stay right here, but at least let me close the door before someone sees him." Zaidan shifted his eyes to Samir's body, then back to Elora.

Elora gave a quick nod and Zaidan quietly shut the door. The two stared at each other in silence for several heavy seconds. Elora continued to point the gun directly at Zaidan's chest. She struggled to speak around the massive lump in her throat. "You killed him?" she half stated, half asked in a voice barely louder than a whisper. Zaidan knew Elora was referring to Brendan, but he remained silent. "Fucking tell me the truth!"

Zaidan took a deep breath but still no emotion passed across his face. "Yes."

Elora squeezed her eyes shut and struggled to fight back sobs. When she reopened her eyes, Zaidan had closed the distance between them by half. "Back the fuck up!" she demanded, but he continued to move toward her. "I will shoot you in the fucking face!" Zaidan still did not stop and walked right up to the end of the pistol until it was pressed against his chest, directly over his heart.

"Pull the trigger," he whispered.

Elora looked at him in disbelief. "You're a fucking psycho," she said, curling her brows in torment and confusion.

"This is what you came for, isn't it? Your *mission*," he stated in an accusatory tone through narrowed eyes. Elora realized he knew who she was and had known for some time. "Do it. I want you to do it," he continued calmly. "I don't want to be alive in a world where you hate me."

Elora considered how easy it would be to pull the trigger, but she knew it wouldn't be that simple. "Yeah? I kill you right now and what happens to me? Your men will put a bullet in my head before I can even get out of this room."

"No. You will be free to go. Fareed has instructions that if anything happens to me—*anything*—he is to return you to the U.S. unharmed."

She'd been fantasizing of killing Malik Khalid for so long—this was her chance. With renewed resolve, she rammed the barrel of the pistol hard into his chest. But she couldn't pull the trigger. The person standing in front of her wasn't Malik Khalid; it was Zaidan, and she was hopelessly in love with him. She let out a howling scream of frustration and leaned forward in defeat, her forehead coming to rest on Zaidan's chest. She lowered her arm, and the barrel of the gun slid down the front of his body until the pistol hung loosely in her hand at her side.

Zaidan wrapped his arms around her and held her tightly to his chest as she shook and cried. He glanced over her shoulder at the lifeless body of his best friend lying on the floor in a pool of blood. The once scrawny boy with a stutter whom he'd rescued from schoolyard bullies when they were fourteen. The loyal friend who'd risked his life to play a dangerous role to help Zaidan keep his dream alive. Much more than a friend, a brother. A brother who loved him on more levels than he'd ever be able to reciprocate. Zaidan knew what Samir had longed for more than anything in the world, and it had broken his heart knowing he'd never be able to give it to him. He closed his eyes and squeezed back tears, but as much as Samir's death broke his heart, Zaidan knew that if he'd had to choose between Samir's life and Elora's, he would choose her. Even though he knew he was about to lose her too, anyway.

Elora pulled back and twisted herself from Zaidan's arms, then retrieved the camera and DNA kit from the floor where she'd dropped them, hoping nothing had broken. She breathed a sigh of relief when she pushed the power button on the camera and heard the familiar beeping noise as the shutter opened. "Turn around and lift your shirt," Elora ordered Zaidan in a monotone voice.

Zaidan knew what she was about to do. "Don't do this. It will cost you everything. Just go."

"Don't tell me what to fucking do," she snapped.

"Elora, it's too risky," Zaidan continued to protest. "I can't let you do this."

"They will never stop hunting you. This asinine notion you have that you can change their minds and convince them you and NDU aren't the monsters they think you are is beyond a fucking fantasy. Even if you manage to sway a few in Washington and the media, Langley will never let you live. So shut the fuck up and turn around."

Zaidan reluctantly acquiesced and slowly turned his back

to her. He pulled his black T-shirt halfway up his back and held it there as he stared blankly at the wall in front of him. Elora flipped on the small lamp beside the bed and studied the jagged scar, seeing it now in a whole new light. The scar she'd brushed her lips and fingertips across so many times now told an entire story of pain and betrayal. The scar that Brendan made, his final mark on the world before he left it, and her, far behind. No, she corrected her thoughts, before Malik Khalid *took* him from this world, stealing her future and happiness. She closed her eyes and shook her head in disbelief.

Elora walked over to Samir's body and pushed it several feet across the floor, moving him away from the pool of blood. "Over here," she said abruptly and motioned for Zaidan to come to her. "I need you face down in your friend's blood, cheek to the ground," she instructed in a harsh tone. Zaidan followed her instructions and laid himself in Samir's blood. Elora pushed his shirt up again to expose the scar, then raised her camera and took a couple full-length photos of Zaidan's body, prone on the blood-stained floor. She zoomed in on the scar and took a few more pictures. "I need a close up of your face, so I'm going to turn the light off for a minute to get your pupils to dilate as much as possible." She flipped the lamp off, counted to sixty in her head, then turned it back on and quickly snapped a couple photos of his profile and face with his eyes half open. She shoved the camera in her backpack and grabbed the DNA collection kit. She opened it and pulled out a butterfly needle attached to a small tube that fed into a blood collection vial. "Sit up," she commanded as she knelt beside him. She extended his arm out and felt for a vein in the soft crook opposite his elbow. She jabbed the needle in with more force than required, but Zaidan didn't so much as flinch. He stared at her while she focused on the vial, watching it slowly fill with blood. His eyes burned into her, but she refused to meet his gaze.

When the vial was full, she yanked the needle out of his arm. "You're dead," she declared matter-of-factly. "I shot you three times in the chest," she added as she secured the lid on the blood vial and slipped it into the thigh pocket of her cargo pants. She dashed around the room, snatching her belongings, and shoving them into her duffel bag and backpack. Zaidan returned to his feet and slipped his T-shirt, now covered in Samir's blood, the rest of the way off over his head. He turned away from Elora and used the partially dry side of his shirt as a makeshift towel to wipe as much of the blood from his body as possible. Once the shirt was soaked, he dropped it to the floor with a sickening *plop*.

"Elora, I just want you to know—" he began as he turned to face her, but Elora flung up her hand to stop him mid-sentence.

"Please don't," she interrupted. "I just want to get out of here."

Zaidan nodded. "I'll have Fareed take you wherever you want to go."

The closest international airport was Erbil, but Nick had mentioned he and Derek were there right now, and Elora wasn't ready to face them yet. She needed time to wrap her head around what had just happened and the serious crime she was about to commit, which could land her in prison for the rest of her life, or worse. "I need to go to Baghdad."

Nine hours later, Elora sat in a business-class seat aboard a Royal Jordanian Airlines 787 jetliner bound for D.C. She'd called Nick during the drive to Baghdad to inform him that she'd be able to get herself out of Iraq. After arriving at the airport, she caught the first available flight to Amman and then booked a flight to D.C. from there. Nick had tried to pump her for more details, but she cut the call short, saying her sat-phone battery was nearly dead. Nick told her he and Derek would be on the next flight out of Erbil, and they all planned to meet up at the NDU Task Force offices first thing the next morning to start the mission debrief, and for Elora to turn over the DNA and photographic evidence confirming Malik Khalid's death.

Elora slid her hand into the thigh pocket of her cargo pants and wrapped her fingers around the vial of blood. It was now cold, as cold and dead to her as Zaidan. *No, his name is Malik*, she corrected herself, scoldingly. She closed her eyes and her face grew hot as she recalled the intense fire that would ignite between them when their bodies touched. That fire had now been reduced to a small glass tube of cold blood. She pulled the vial out of her pocket and held it up to the light streaming in through her airplane window. She slowly tipped the vial back and forth, mesmerized as she watched the thick blood slosh from one end of the vial to the other. Even his blood was beautiful. The blood she would use to fake his death. The blood that would likely end her career, her freedom, possibly even her life. She tightened her fist around the vial and brought her hand to her mouth. She closed her eyes and gave her hand a long kiss. Her heart was shattered, and the farther the plane pulled away from Iraq, the more her soul died.

Chapter 19

Six Months Later

Elora sat alone at a small table in the main cafeteria at Langley, aimlessly stirring a cup of coffee that had long gone cold as she gazed out the window in a trance-like stare. In the six months since she'd return from Iraq, her life appeared to have resumed a semblance of normalcy on the surface; beneath the surface, though, she was far from okay. She was drowning, slipping further and further below the raging water with each passing day. She'd tried to throw herself back into her work. Tried to forget what she'd done. Tried desperately to forget *him*. But it was useless. The depression was swallowing her, and she was nearing her breaking point.

On a positive note, much to Elora's relief, the NDU mission debrief had gone smoothly. She'd submitted Zaidan's DNA sample along with the photos and, within a couple of weeks, analysis confirmed a positive match to the DNA from Brendan's knife. Between that, the evidence Nick and Derek discovered in Mosul, and Ahmed Assad's interrogation testimony, the CIA officially declared Malik Khalid deceased. His funeral was held outside Tel Afar the day after Elora arrived back in the U.S. Reports from the Erbil CIA station indicated thousands had lined the streets to pay their respects as his funeral procession left Tel Afar. His body was driven to Bakhdida where he was buried next to his mother and sister in the small Syriac Catholic Church cemetery. The NDU task force remained up and running for a few weeks following Elora's return to monitor for any resurgence of the group or a new leader, but NDU stayed quiet and, once again, went underground. The Task Force was eventually disbanded, but Elora, Nick, and the others continued to work closely together on a new target. The remnants of Al-Qaeda in Iraq had recently resurfaced and joined forces with Islamic extremists in Syria; the group called themselves the Islamic State of Iraq and Syria (ISIS). They were rapidly becoming a huge problem, threatening to further destabilize the region.

Elora was abruptly ripped from her daydream when she felt a hand on her shoulder. She jerked in surprise and spun her head up to see who was behind her. "Hey, you," Nick said, looking down on her with a kind smile. "Mind if I sit?" he asked, gesturing at the empty chair across the table from her.

"Of course," she replied, forcing a smile and pushing the chair out for him with her foot.

"How's the coffee?"

"It's shit," she replied, glancing down at her cup, "but at least it's caffeinated shit."

"I'm worried about you," Nick said, his tone turning serious. "We're all worried about you."

Elora wrinkled her brow and shook her head dismissively. "Nick, I'm fine," she replied, but she knew Nick saw right through her lie.

"You're *not* fine, you're a fucking mess. You're distant, completely withdrawn. You haven't left your townhouse in six months except to come to work or visit Brendan. You barely speak and, frankly, your work has been shit since you got back."

Elora rolled her eyes in indifference as he ran down the list of her distressing behaviors, until he mentioned her work performance, that one got her attention. Her work was all she had left. Realizing her career may be at risk quickly brought her to her senses.

"It's to the point where others are noticing," Nick continued, "people outside the team. I won't be able to contain this if it persists much longer. Have you spoken to any of the counselors?"

"I don't need a counselor, Nick."

"You need *something*, Elora," he countered. "You never came back from Iraq. The Elora I knew is not the Elora that returned from Baghdad six months ago. I should have never let you go. It was too soon after Brendan—," he stopped short and dropped his chin to his chest. "You weren't ready or properly trained for that assignment, and that's my fault. I take full responsibility, which is why it's my responsibility now to help you, whether you want me to or not."

"Please don't blame yourself," she said. "What I'm going through has nothing to do with you or anything you did."

"What happened over there, Elora?" he asked, trying to search her eyes, but Elora looked away. "You know you can talk to me. Please, talk to me."

"You know everything that happened over there. It's all in my report."

Nick sighed in defeat. He knew she was hiding something, but he still didn't know what, or why she was shutting him out.

Elora tried to play it cool and act like she wasn't fazed by Nick's sudden intervention, but she was terrified. She knew she'd have to make a visible effort to pull herself out of her depression and convince those around her she was improving, or deal with the catastrophic fallout.

"And I do leave my house, thank you very much," she declared, slipping into a more upbeat tone. She knew there was one thing that would divert Nick from his current inquisition. "In fact, I'm going out tomorrow night to see that new movie, *Wolf of Wall Street*. My girlfriend who lives next-door was supposed to go with me, but she bailed this morning. Would you want to come with me? Perhaps grab some dinner before?"

Nick was genuinely surprised by Elora's sudden invite and mood swing, but he wasn't about to look a gift horse in the mouth. "I'd love to."

"Pick me up at six?"

"You got it."

"Great, I gotta run." She stood up and swiped her coffee cup off the table. "My lunch break was over ten minutes ago."

Elora immediately dreaded her upcoming *date* with Nick but knew she had to do something to throw him off her trail. The story about her friend bailing on her was total bullshit, of course; she didn't even know who the hell lived next-door to her, much less were they friends.

Over the next couple of months, Elora made a concerted effort to socialize, appear more outgoing, and put on a happy face, especially at work. She allowed Nick to take her on weekly dates and made sure their "relationship" was as public as possible. However, things between them had not physically progressed beyond anything more than brief goodnight kisses at the end of their dates. Nick, God bless him, remained as patient as Job with her, never pushing for anything more than she was willing to give and allowing her full control over the forward momentum of the relationship.

She continued to visit Brendan's gravesite in Arlington at least weekly and found solace in talking to him; he was the only one she could be completely honest with, and she prayed wherever he was, that he forgave her. When she wasn't out with Nick or visiting Brendan, Elora sat alone in her house feeling like a shameful fraud. She was leading him on and felt awful knowing she'd eventually have to break his heart, and she wasn't sure how much longer she could maintain the ruse. She considered quitting her job and moving to the west coast to start over and escape the pressures of masking her depression while simultaneously keeping her dark secret locked away from the world, but she couldn't fathom leaving her work. She loved her job and was scared that without it, she wouldn't last long. It was the last line tethering her to the Earth. She was also well aware that she should just be happy that her little stunt hadn't landed her in prison, at least not yet. Between submitting fraudulent evidence, making multiple false official statements, and aiding and abetting an international terrorist, she knew she could face multiple life sentences or even the death penalty if they prosecuted her under the espionage act. She already was in prison, though, a prison of her own making, and the walls were closing in fast.

She tried desperately not to think about *him*, but she failed miserably. Her feelings vacillated evenly from longing and regret to bitterness and hatred. Because of *him*, she had compromised her honor and integrity, she was having to lie to everyone she knew and cared about, and she was miserable every day; above all, he had brutally murdered Brendan. Aside from Zaidan, she hated someone else—herself, because even after everything, she was still completely in love with him, and it made her sick.

Unable to take it any longer, Elora decided she had to get away, at least for a while. She was suffocating emotionally, and it was physically draining her. She recalled fond memories of spending her childhood summers at her grandparents' vacation house in North Carolina's Maggie Valley; it would be the perfect place to escape and recharge. She hoped a couple of weeks in the quiet serenity of the remote cabin nestled in the Smokey Mountains would help her clear her head and find her center. She wanted to lose herself and try to find the "reset" button on her life and soul.

Elora submitted her request at work for two weeks of vacation and told Nick where she'd be. He offered to join her, but she politely declined, saying she wanted to spend some time visiting with her grandparents, which was a lie—her grandparents wouldn't even be there this time of year. A secondary goal of her trip was to figure out how to break things off with Nick in the simplest and most painless way possible, which would be tough to do with him around. She'd done everything in her power to force herself to love him, but she had nothing left to give. She tried to reason with herself that Nick was the type of guy she was supposed to be with, that there was no reason she shouldn't love him. He worshipped her and she knew he would be there for her for the rest of his life. On paper they were a perfect match, but she couldn't convince her heart. With Brendan there had been fire, with Zaidan it was a raging inferno, with Nick there wasn't even a spark, and she could no longer pretend.

Settled by the fireplace with a mug of hot chocolate, Elora was enjoying her second evening in her Smokey Mountain retreat when her laptop dinged with an incoming instant message. Her first impulse was to ignore it, but she knew she'd just sit there wondering if it was important, so she grudgingly set her cup down and plodded across the living room to the small desk holding her computer. She flipped the lid up on her laptop and double-clicked the instant messenger icon. A window popped open near the bottom right-hand side of the screen with a single line of text.

W. Wallace: *Every day since you left, I've woken up dead.*

Elora stopped breathing and her heart dropped into her stomach. She immediately knew who'd sent the message; she recalled Zaidan mentioning *Braveheart* was his favorite movie. *Motherfucker*. A part of her was enraged, but she couldn't deny that another part of her was elated. She wished she had the willpower to ignore the message and simply return to her hot chocolate by the fire, but she couldn't make herself do it. Everything in her head screamed for her to slam the laptop shut, but her heart wouldn't allow her to obey. She sank into the desk chair and her hands slid up to the keyboard.

> **E. Monro:** *You are dead. Do not contact me again.*

She tried to get up from the desk, but an invisible force held her where she sat. She stared at the screen and bit her fingernails. Deep down, she knew her harsh words were an invitation and she anxiously awaited Zaidan's reply. Several long minutes passed, and her words remained the last inside the small chat window. She sat back in her chair with a sigh of disappointment. *Maybe he came to his senses.* She'd nearly given up on receiving a response when the familiar *ding* rang out again.

> **W. Wallace:** *Death didn't scare me, until I met you. It would have been a welcome relief from the nightmare I was living. When I met you, I realized life could be worth something again. For the first time in a long time, I saw the beauty in the world around me.*

Elora was furious, furious that she *didn't* hate him. He was everything in the world she was programmed to despise. An international criminal, the leader of an Islamic militant group responsible for taking American lives, and, of course, the reason Brendan never came home from Iraq. H*ow could you allow yourself to fall for him? You've been manipulated and played.* She felt stupid and weak, two things she swore she'd never be in her life, and Zaidan had made her both.

E. Monro: *I fucking HATE you! You took everything from me. If I ever see you again, I* ***will*** *kill you.*

W. Wallace: *I would welcome such a fate. I'd happily die by your hand right now if it meant seeing you again. It would be more than worth dying for.*

E. Monro: *Why are you doing this? What do you want from me?*

W. Wallace: *I want you to be happy and safe. Right now, I fear you are neither. You've been sinking and now you're all alone in a cabin in the woods, and I'm worried of what may happen. What you may try to do—to yourself.*

The hairs prickled on the back of her neck; he knew where she was. She instinctively scanned the room, then dashed to every window and door to ensure everything was locked and all curtains were closed. He was watching her. She realized he'd probably been watching her for some time. Weeks? Months? Also, he apparently thought she was suicidal.

E. Monro: *You need to tell whoever you have watching me to fuck off, and I'm not going to kill myself—you're not that hard to get over. I just want you to leave me alone. I want you out of my fucking head, and I sure as hell want you out of my computer. I came to the middle of nowhere to escape you. To get away from thinking about you every second of every goddamn day. It's fucking TORTURE. I hate it. I hate myself. And I*

HATE YOU! Leave. Me. Alone!!

Hot tears were now streaming down her cheeks. The more she screamed that she didn't want him, the more she wanted him. She was sure she was suffering from some demented form of Stockholm syndrome. She slammed the lid on her laptop, snatched it off the desk and walked out onto the balcony. With every ounce of her strength, she flung the laptop over the railing and sent it spinning like a metal Frisbee down into the deep ravine descending below. She let out a howling scream as she watched the computer bounce from the top of a tree and smash into several branches as it plummeted downward, eventually disappearing beneath the canopy of pine trees and brush below. She went back inside, slammed the glass door behind her, and collapsed onto the sofa, sobbing uncontrollably until she slipped into a restless sleep.

The next morning, Elora sat at the kitchen island sipping a cup of coffee when she was startled by a loud knock on the front door. A twinge of panic shot through her body. Random visitors to the remote cabin were rare, and she sure as hell wasn't expecting anyone; even the mailman didn't come this far up the mountain. She plunked her coffee down and reached for her purse, pulling out her 9mm Beretta pistol. Gun in hand, Elora slid off the barstool and tiptoed to the front door. Before she reached the door, another knock, more forceful than the first, came pounding from the other side.

"Who is it?" Elora called out, keeping her voice as steady as possible.

"DHL delivery," a man's voice answered in a bored tone.

Fucking DHL. Nothing deters those guys. They routinely

deliver to caves in the middle of Taliban-occupied regions of Afghanistan.

Elora pulled the curtain back just an inch and peeked out the window to scan the front porch and yard. A familiar canary colored DHL delivery van was parked in the driveway, and the delivery man standing on the porch was in full uniform. She unlocked the door and opened it halfway, concealing her hand holding the gun behind the door. The delivery man shoved a bright yellow *DHL EXPRESS* envelope in Elora's face. She grabbed the envelope and muttered a thanks as she began closing the door.

"Wait! I need a signature, ma'am." The DHL man wedged his foot against the door to stop it from closing and waved a clipboard in the air. Elora tucked her gun into the back of her waistband, scrawled her signature on the clipboard, and handed it back to the delivery guy. "Thank you kindly," he replied in the familiar Appalachian drawl common to the area and Elora relaxed. *Yup, he's legit.*

Back inside with the door closed and locked, Elora tore open the package and turned it upside down over the kitchen counter. Out slid an Air Emirates ticket envelope and a short, typed note:

> *Elora,*
> *Meet me in Dubai.*
> *Please give me a chance to look in your eyes and apologize.*
> *Just a few days, that's all I ask.*
> *~ Zaidan*

"Your name isn't even Zaidan!" Elora yelled to no one as

she crumbled up the letter and tossed it across the kitchen. She opened the airline envelope and found a roundtrip ticket from Ashville, NC to Dubai, UAE, with a layover at JFK airport in New York. The departure was for 10:00 a.m. the next morning with the return flight landing exactly forty-eight hours before she had to return to work from her two-week vacation. In addition to knowing where she was currently staying, he knew how long her vacation was as well.

He is insane. Elora scooped the crumpled letter up off the kitchen floor and, together with the plane tickets, tossed them in the trash can. She then grabbed the keys to her Ford Ranger pickup truck and headed into town to buy a new laptop. She also made a mental note to wipe out all her current email and social media accounts—she'd start fresh with a new online identity.

Elora and Nick trudged along beneath the blazing Iraqi sun; she felt like they'd been walking for days. The endless desert stretched out clear to the horizon in every direction. She saw no roads, no buildings, nothing but sand. Utterly exhausted and unable to take another step, Elora stopped and closed her eyes. When she opened them again, she had teleported to a cold, dark room. She realized she was standing in a hospital morgue. She spun around and saw Zaidan's lifeless body splayed out on a metal table, naked except for a thin sheet draped over his lower half. His skin was a faded ashy blue color. A single bullet hole was visible near the temple of his head. She stared in shock for several seconds and then crumpled onto his chest in hysterical grief. She could physically feel her heart transforming into sand as she repeated over and over, *I'm so sorry, I'm so sorry…* She placed a hand on his ice-cold cheek, then bent down and kissed his purple lips, taut and lifeless like old rubber. She gazed upon his face, willing him to open his beautiful eyes so she could look into them one last time. Her whispers echoed in the hollow morgue. *Please open your eyes…please.* She needed to tell him what she still refused to admit to herself—that she was madly in love with him—but there was nothing of him left; he was gone, and she was struck with an indescribable emptiness that left her completely destroyed. No matter what she did, her soul was tied to his, and with his death, she was dying too.

She was still sobbing and stroking Zaidan's icy cheek when she was finally ripped from the nightmare and flung back to consciousness. She shot up in bed, gasping for air and shaking in a swampy pool of bedsheets soaked with sweat. Swiftly, she wiped the tears from her soggy face to clear her vision, then glanced down at her watch and saw it was 7:32 a.m. *I can make it.* She sprang out of the bed, threw on some clothes, and shoved everything she'd brought with her into her small duffle bag. Throwing her duffle bag over her shoulder and grabbing her backpack, she ran out the front door of the cabin. As soon as she closed the door, it dawned on her. *Fuck.* She dropped her bags on the front porch, spun around and ran back inside to the kitchen. She grabbed the garbage can and flipped it upside-down, scattering the contents across the shiny wooden floor. She picked out the airline ticket envelope and grabbed Zaidan's crumpled note with the other hand. Then, like a track and field Olympian, she leapt up from the floor and bolted to the front door. After locking up, she jumped in her truck and tore off down the steep, twisting driveway. At the bottom of the mountain, she made a sharp right turn that sent her small pickup fishtailing out onto the main highway heading east out of the valley. She floored the accelerator and stole a glance at the clock on her dashboard: 7:56 a.m. It was a good hour-long drive to the airport; she calculated that by the time she got parked and into the terminal, she'd have less than an hour before her flight took off.

Twenty minutes into her drive, her heart rate returned to a normal pace as her adrenaline subsided. Her mind cleared and she began to have second thoughts. *What the fuck am I doing?* A voice inside her head told her she was beyond crazy. What did she expect to happen? She'd go meet Zaidan in Dubai and then what? They'd spend a few days having mind-blowing sex and then she'd fly home to D.C., return to her desk job at Langley, and they'd never speak again? What was the alternative? Would she stay with him? Where? In Baghdad? Become the wife of a twice dead weapons trafficking militant? She laughed aloud at that last one. She was within seconds of slamming on the breaks and flipping a U-turn when a quote she'd lived by since high school echoed in her head. *Twenty years from now, you'll regret the things you didn't do in life much more than the things you did do.* She knew in her heart if she didn't go, she'd regret it for the rest of her life. She'd be forever plagued by the *what ifs.* What she needed was closure; what she wanted was to be near him again. She wanted to touch him, to feel his breath on her neck, to have his arms around her. She closed her eyes and shuddered at the thought of lying beneath him one more time and looking up into his beautiful face. *Eyes on the road, Elora!*

She made good time on her drive to the airport, arriving at the check-in counter just before 9 a.m. She was thankful she was in the habit of always taking her passport wherever she went. Once she reached her gate, she still had a few minutes to spare before boarding began. She pulled out her cell phone and called Nick. Technically, she wasn't supposed to travel internationally without reporting it to the agency and getting approval. Considering her limited timeframe, the best she could do was tell Nick where she was going and hope he could run it up the chain for approval, but whether permission for her to travel to UAE was granted or not, she'd be over international waters by the time the answer came back from above.

Nick answered just as the boarding announcement for Elora's flight bellowed out over the loudspeakers. "Nick!" Elora shouted into the phone, shoving her finger in her other ear to drown out the echoing loudspeaker voice. "Hey, Nick, it's Elora."

"Hey, you!" Nick said, happy to hear from her, considering she hadn't so much as texted him since leaving for North Carolina. "How's vacation going?"

"It's great," Elora blurted. "I've, uh, actually decided to take an impromptu trip to Dubai. Can you please just let the travel approval department know so I'm not in violation."

"Dubai?" Nick asked, confused. "I thought you were spending your vacation at your grandparent's cabin in North Carolina?"

"Yeah, change of plans," she said as casually as possible. "I'll still be back Monday after next, though. I've gotta run—thanks a million, Nick."

"Elora? Elora, you there?" She was gone. True to his nature,

Nick typed up Elora's travel request and submitted it on her behalf.

Elora spent her three-hour layover at JFK airport in New York trying to talk herself out of boarding the flight to UAE. *You can still turn back; you can catch the next flight back to Asheville and forget you ever considered this insane idea.* She said this to herself at least a hundred times in her head, but her heart piped in with the same retort each time. *No, you won't. We're doing this.* When the boarding announcement rang out over the loudspeaker, she grabbed her bags, got on the plane without a second thought, and settled in for another twelve-hour journey to the opposite side of the world.

Chapter 20

Elora's stomach instantly filled with butterflies as her flight touched down in Dubai. She still hadn't done anything to give Zaidan any indication that she was coming; she wanted to give herself until the last possible minute to abort her plan if she decided. Though, considering how much Zaidan already knew about her life and whereabouts, she was certain he knew she was on that plane. Even so, she wasn't going to give him the satisfaction of confirming it until she was good and ready. Elora disembarked and shuffled to customs with the other two hundred plus passengers aboard her flight. Standing in line at customs, she wondered if Zaidan was there at the airport awaiting her arrival. If not, she planned to hail a cab outside and head to one of the hotels near downtown. But she already knew in her gut she would not be needing a taxi. Zaidan was there. She could feel him. It was beyond explanation; she just knew he was close by. It was a feeling that made her excited and anxious at the same time.

After clearing customs, Elora made her way to the passenger greeting area—no sign of Zaidan. Once in the open area of the airport's main sector, she stopped for a moment and scanned the massive room. Still no Zaidan. She was half relieved and half disappointed. She spotted signs directing passengers to the ground transportation exit and headed that direction. A few paces into her walk across the terminal, an unknown force suddenly stopped her dead in her tracks. She slowly looked to her left, and her heart caught in her throat. There he was. Leaning against a wall, arms folded across his chest. He was wearing a pair of snug dark blue jeans that accentuated his perfectly defined lower body. Elora slid her sight up his body to the black T-shirt that was stretched tight across his chest and hugged the biceps of his smooth olive arms. The arms Elora had desperately longed to have wrapped around her for the last eight months. A slight smile played across his lips while his signature gaze burned a hole directly into her. He had spotted her long before she'd noticed him; but even once he knew she had seen him, he didn't make any attempt to approach her. She realized he was giving her a last-minute out. She could go to him or she could pretend he wasn't there and keep walking. For several seconds, she considered doing just that. Her heart raced as she glanced several times between Zaidan and the terminal corridor extending ahead of her. She took a deep breath and stepped off the invisible cliff, knowing what she was about to do would forever alter the course of her life. *God help me*.

She veered across the main thoroughfare and advanced toward him, stopping directly in front him with her jaw set and shoulders squared. They stared each other down in motionless silence—taking one another in like it was a high noon standoff. After several tense seconds, Elora broke the silence. She shrugged and raised her eyebrows in cautious agitation. "Well? I'm here. Now what?"

"I'm glad you came," Zaidan said.

"Well, I'm not sure yet if *I'm* glad I came," she shot back.

"I understand; we have a lot we need to talk about."

"You bet your ass," Elora snapped, her eyes wide.

Zaidan pushed himself off the wall and closed the distance between them to mere inches. He wrapped her in his arms and pulled her gently into his chest. Elora closed her eyes and surrendered herself to him. She heard his heart beating through his chest and the familiar rush of electricity shot through her body. It was as if she'd been unconscious for the last eight months and had just been jolted back to life by a bolt of lightning. Feeling her body soften and lean into his, Zaidan tightened his embrace and placed a lingering kiss on her head. "I missed you," he whispered into her hair.

"I missed you too…so fucking much."

"Come on, let's get out of here," he said, pulling her duffle bag off her shoulder and hoisting it up onto his own.

"Where are we going?" she asked, though she really didn't care.

"I reserved us a suite at the Waldorf Astoria hotel out on Palm Island. *Two* suites to be exact, just in case," he added to ensure she wouldn't think he'd been overly presumptuous when he'd made the reservations. Elora smiled at his cautious planning. Her smile grew even bigger at the thought of spending the next week alone with Zaidan in a luxurious hotel suite out on Dubai's infamous Palm Island.

Elora stood before a wall of glass and gazed out at the incredible sight. Zaidan's seventh floor suite at the Waldorf Astoria offered a panoramic view stretching from Dubai's downtown cityscape and out across the Persian Gulf to the horizon, now glittering in the afternoon sun. She'd accompanied him to his room but had also checked into her own separate suite under her *Washington Post* alias, Elora Reid—just in case. She closed her eyes and focused on re-centering herself. Jet lag and the emotional jolt from being with Zaidan again were both taking their toll.

"Are you okay?" Zaidan asked, stepping up behind her and putting his arms around her waist. He nuzzled his face into the side of her neck, breathing in the sweet smell of her hair.

"Yes," she replied, opening her eyes. "This is beautiful," she added with a contented sigh, referring to both the scenery and her current mood; just being with Zaidan felt beautiful.

"*You're* beautiful," he whispered back, his breath hot on her cheek. Elora swiveled around to face him, then popped up on her toes and gave him a quick kiss on the lips. "I'm sure you're worn out from the flight," he said as he delicately brushed a wisp of hair from her eyes. "Did you want to rest? Or shower? Are you hungry? We can order some food. Or did you want to sit down and *talk* now?" he rattled off nervously.

"No, I don't want to do any of that," she said, shaking her head. "All I want right now is to be here with you and not think about anything else…at least for a little while. For this brief moment in time, we have no past and no future. It's just you and me here together, completely stripped down, emotionally, politically…" she trailed off as she reached down and began pulling up his black t-shirt, "and physically," she concluded with a devilish smirk.

"As you wish," he replied, helping her slip his t-shirt off

over his head.

For the first time in nearly a year, the fire that Elora feared had been forever extinguished once again ignited in her core as she soaked in the sculpted perfection of Zaidan's upper body. She reached up and delicately placed her hands on the tops of his shoulders, as if she half expected him to disappear into a cloud of dust upon contact. Once convinced he was not an apparition, she slowly slid the palms of her hands down his chest, continued south over his defined abs and halted at the top of his jeans. "I've missed this," she said with a breathless sigh. She slipped her hands partially around his waist and her fingertips brushed across the scar on his lower back. Elora's breath caught in her throat. The dam exploded and everything came rushing back, washing over her in a raging flood. The room started to spin as she jerked her hands away from his body and froze.

"It will forever remind you of him—of what I did—won't it?" Zaidan said, his voice laced with regret.

Fighting her emotions, Elora shook her head. "I'll be fine," she tried to lie as convincingly as possible.

He put a finger beneath her chin and lifted her head; her eyes met his and she came clean.

"Yes," she whispered, a twinge of guilt in her voice.

"A part of you will hate me forever."

"I hate what you did to each other," Elora corrected. "I hate what this world has made us *all* do to each other."

He took her right hand, guided it around his side, and gently pressed her palm over the scar. She held her breath and closed her eyes as he held it there for several intense seconds. To her surprise, her anxiety dissipated, and a relaxing calm took its place. Zaidan moved his hands up to cup her face and kissed her. The kiss grew deeper, and he began backing up toward the king-size bed in the middle of the room, pulling her with him as he moved. He lay on the bed and pulled her down on top of him, her long auburn hair cascaded over her shoulder and onto the mattress beside his head. He removed her shirt and kissed her breasts through her bra. After a few seconds, he paused and looked up at her to ensure she hadn't slipped back toward apprehension.

Elora's gaze locked with Zaidan's electric green eyes, and she a wave of warmth rushed down her body. She knew in her soul there was nowhere else on Earth she belonged more than right where she was—lost in Zaidan's arms. She leaned down and pressed her forehead to his. Putting a hand on his cheek, she whispered his name, his *real* name, "Malik." Zaidan tensed up at hearing his given name. He pulled back to look at Elora's face and study her expression. His forehead wrinkled with confusion and a tinge of fear. Elora smiled at his sudden rush of anxiety. "Malik," she repeated more forcefully. Zaidan continued searching her eyes, afraid to speak and preparing himself for the worst. "I love you, Malik. The *real* you," Elora said tenderly. "I may have fallen in love with Zaidan, but I no longer want there to be any deception between us. No aliases. No lies. Nothing. All that goes away now and forever."

"I love you too," he replied, relaxing but not completely. "I've loved you since the night we met," he whispered. "But Malik Khalid is gone," he added plainly, looking her in the eyes. "Do you understand? You killed him, and I'm glad you did. He was not a good person, he was lost and broken, and this world is better off without him." Elora nodded and Zaidan gently rolled her over onto her back. He relieved her of her bra, then pulled off her jeans and panties. The late afternoon sun cast a warm orange glow into the room through the wall of glass. The light fell across Elora's naked body, draping it in a robe of translucent silk. Zaidan stood over her for a moment, drinking her in with his eyes.

"What are you doing?" Elora asked, pushing herself up on her elbows.

"I'm admiring the most beautiful thing I've ever seen," he replied. Elora blushed and rolled her eyes. Zaidan removed his jeans, then leaned down on top of her and sank his hips between her thighs. Elora's heartrate doubled as she wrapped her legs around Zaidan's body. He held her suspended in euphoric anticipation for several long seconds before finally slipping inside and immediately sending her into panting gasps of delirious pleasure.

"God, I've missed being inside you," Zaidan professed. It was the one place on Earth he felt truly at peace.

Elora wanted to tell him how much she missed having him inside her, but she was too overcome by exhilarating bliss to even speak. She closed her eyes and, once again, allowed Zaidan to sweep her over the edge of the world and across the universe.

Afterward, they lay silently, arms and legs intertwined, taking in the magnificent view. The sun was now a blazing orange globe hovering just above the sea. It cast its final rays of the day across the sparkling water before dipping beneath the waves and thrusting Dubai into darkness.

Elora opened her eyes and found the hotel room bathed in moonlight. Glancing at her watch, she saw it was 3:37 a.m. Her stomach let out a low cavernous grumble. The last time she'd eaten had been on the plane, but even more than food, she desperately wanted a shower. She rolled over and looked at Zaidan. He was lying on his back sound asleep, his rugged face relaxed in tranquil slumber. No nightmares tonight. The moonlight cast a silvery glow across his body. Her eyes drifted from his face down his torso. The bed sheet came up just high enough to cover him, halting at his hips. She knew it was irrational, but she also knew the only thing she truly needed in her life was to be close to him. She'd never known the kind of happiness she felt when she was near him, and she was ready to do anything, sacrifice anything, to be with him forever.

Elora gingerly rolled out of the bed, taking care not to wake Zaidan. She grabbed her duffle bag and padded into the spa-like bathroom, closing the door behind her. She tilted her head back beneath the rainfall shower and let the refreshing water run across her face and down her body. She tried not to let her mind run wild, but it was difficult to keep it corralled. *What the fuck am I going to do now? Where do we go from here? What happens next? What even* can *happen? There's no way this turns into anything but a twisted shit-show.*

She heard the bathroom door open and shut again. A few seconds later, the glass door of the shower opened and Zaidan stepped in behind her. Elora didn't move from her position beneath the falling water. Zaidan wrapped his arms around her and moved himself under the water too, pressing his body into her back. She'd never felt more at home anywhere in the world than she did in his arms. They stood there in silence for a few minutes, enjoying the calm before the storm they both knew was ahead of them. They had more than a few matters to discuss, but neither was anxious to launch into the much-needed conversation.

Elora turned to face him, her wet breasts pressing against his chest. She stretched up to kiss him while simultaneously sliding a hand down below his waist. He groaned in pleasure and instantly hardened as she massaged him in her moist palm. She kissed her way down his chest and stomach until she was resting on her knees. She took him into her mouth and swirled her tongue as she rhythmically slid her lips up and down his length.

Zaidan's breathing sped up as he laced his fingers through her hair. "You're killing me," he said in a whispered pant.

Been there, done that. Elora sarcastically thought to herself. She pushed him deeper into her mouth. A few seconds later, she felt the gentle pulsation between her lips as his body went rigidly tense. When he'd finished, he half collapsed forward and braced himself with an outstretched arm on the tiled shower wall.

Elora returned to her feet and Zaidan pulled her in for a kiss.

"That was beyond amazing," he said, still trying to catch his breath.

"Well, as delicious as you are," she said, seductively wiping the corner of her mouth, "I am starving right now." She gave him another quick kiss on the lips, then opened the shower door and stepped out. "I'm going to order some room service. You want anything?"

"Just get me whatever you're having."

When their breakfast arrived, they settled at the small table on their balcony overlooking the gulf. The sun hadn't yet breached the horizon, but the predawn light provided plenty of illumination for their meal. Halfway into her scrambled eggs and toast, Elora decided to rip off the Band-Aid.

"How did you find out?" she asked, without looking up from her plate as she stabbed a forkful of eggs. "And please be completely honest with me."

Zaidan swallowed the food in his mouth and exhaled slowly. Though she hadn't come right out and said it, he knew she was asking how he'd discovered she was CIA. "It wasn't too difficult. I'd just been targeted by an American Delta Force raid and I'd survived. I knew the CIA would eventually figure out I wasn't dead and come back to finish the job, one way or another. It was only a matter of time before they popped up, that much I expected. What I didn't expect, was you," he said, looking her in the eye. "*You* were most un*expected*. By the night of the gala in Dubai, it was obvious you weren't a professional journalist," Zaidan continued. "At least not a top *Washington Post* correspondent."

Elora balked at his criticism. "You think I acted unprofessionally in UAE?"

"No, you weren't unprofessional. Your personality was just…*off*, I guess. I'm not exactly sure how to explain it. I'm familiar with journalists, and they all have the same methods and idiosyncrasies. They rapid fire questions and talk, *a lot*; they're only quiet long enough to get the quotes they need and then their mouth is moving again. You, on the other hand, were reserved and observant. You watch, you study, and you analyze. That was my first indication that you likely weren't who you said you were.

Once I realized that, I was determined to use any and every resource available to me to figure out exactly *who* you were. Though I had a fairly good idea, which turned out to be correct."

"When did you know for sure, and how?" she asked.

"I found out from Bashir that you were CIA the night of the attack in the marketplace. He told me just before we left for dinner at the Al-Rasheed hotel."

Elora glanced up in thought, recalling the day of the campaign stop. "I guess that explains why you were in such a shitty mood during dinner that night." She looked back at him and tilted her head with a sudden thought. "And then you took me down to the river for a 'walk'. Were you going to shoot me in the head and dump my body in the Tigris?" she asked, half-jokingly.

"It crossed my mind," he said coolly. Elora swallowed hard; she'd asked him to be honest.

"So why didn't you?"

"Because I was already in love with you. When you bought that painting from the young boy in the street market outside the Al-Rasheed Hotel…"

"Malik," Elora cut in with a nostalgic smile. "Who had also lost a little sister."

"Yes, a bizarre coincidence," Zaidan said, raising an eyebrow. "When I observed your interaction with him, I saw who you truly were. The way you treated that boy wasn't an act… It wasn't part of a scheme to manipulate or play any games. It was genuine."

"I did honestly love that painting," she said with a touch of sadness.

"I have it hanging in my office in Baghdad. I considered

sending it to you, but I was afraid it may raise suspicion and cause you trouble. Plus, to be honest, I didn't want to part with it. I look at it every day—it makes me feel close to you."

"Aside from the fact that I was CIA, what else did you know about me and my past that night by the river?"

Zaidan knew what she was trying to get at. She wanted to know when he figured out she was the fiancée of the man he'd killed during the raid. "After first learning who you were, bits and pieces of additional information about your past trickled in from Bashir. I didn't find out about your connection to"—Zaidan paused and inhaled—"*him*, until the day we flew to Abu Dhabi to deal with General Yunis and the arms deal issue."

"Brendan," Elora whispered, putting a name to Zaidan's *him*. She closed her eyes as a pang of guilt etched with sorrow shot through her body.

"Yes," Zaidan confirmed solemnly. "When I found out the American I'd killed that night was your fiancé...it really got to me." He lowered his eyes. "Not because I'd killed him, but because my killing him hurt you. And I felt guilty knowing that if I had it all to do over again, I'd still pull the trigger, because if I hadn't killed him, we'd have never met."

Elora closed her eyes and squeezed back tears. "Tell me what happened that night," she said decisively. "I want to know everything."

Zaidan lifted his eyes and searched her face. "No, you don't."

Elora clenched her jaw. "You tell me every detail, or I leave right now."

Zaidan exhaled in defeat, then proceeded to recount the

night of the Delta Force raid. Reaching the part where he shot Brendan in the stomach, he paused and closed his eyes. "I didn't want to kill him," he said, shaking his head. He opened his eyes and looked back at Elora. His heart broke seeing the tears streaming down her face. "I think he would have survived the first gunshot wound, but he was still conscious, and if he'd seen me go into the pantry, he'd have been able to tell the others and they would have found the tunnel."

"So, you shot him in the throat," Elora said, struggling through a tight sob.

"No. First I tried to knock him unconscious with a chokehold, but he was very strong and there wasn't enough time. I heard the others coming and…I did what I had to do."

They sat quietly for a few moments, both staring out at the sea. Finally, Zaidan broke the silence. "Were you in love with him?" What he really wanted to know was if she was *still* in love with him, but he was too afraid to ask.

Elora took a deep breath. "I was." Zaidan's expression fell in disappointment but he remained silent. "But then I fell in love with you," she continued, "and I realized I didn't know what real love was. I loved Brendan, and I missed him—I *still* miss him—but I never felt for him what I feel for you. When he was killed, I was sad and angry that he'd been taken from me, like he was a treasured childhood toy someone had stolen. When you and I were apart, though, I felt like my very soul had been ripped from my body. I thought I was in Hell after Brendan died, but it didn't burn nearly as much as the excruciating Hell I was in when I thought I'd never see you again."

"It was the same for me," Zaidan said, slipping his hand

over hers.

"By the way, I truly am sorry about Samir." She tried to sound sincere but, like the way Zaidan felt about Brendan, she was really only sorry that Samir's death had hurt Zaidan. "I know you loved him. I also know he was *in love* with you," she added, lowering her tone.

Zaidan inhaled sharply. "Samir was like a brother to me. He was my best friend and, after my mother and sister died, he was the last person left in this world that I trusted completely. During your interview with him here in Dubai, the story he told you about how we met in middle school was true."

Elora recalled the story of Samir being bullied at school and Malik coming to his rescue. "He had a stutter and the other kids made fun of him," Elora recapped. "Until you swooped in and beat the shit out of them."

Zaidan smiled at the memory. "From that day forward, Samir and I were pretty much inseparable."

"When did you realize his feelings for you went *beyond* friendship?"

Zaidan narrowed his eyes in thought. "Oh, I don't know, I guess I knew within a few weeks after meeting him. I always just tried to ignore it, for both our sakes. It wasn't something we ever sat down and talked about; you don't discuss that sort of thing in Iraq, not even in private. After high school, Samir's family had arranged for him to marry the daughter of a close family friend. Of course, Samir was adamantly opposed to the whole thing, but Samir's father was not the kind of man who put up with being deified by his children. He beat the shit out of Samir one night during another argument about the wedding, after which Samir locked himself in his room and opened up both his wrists with a razor blade. Of course, they got him to a hospital in time, but he'd shamed the family with the suicide attempt and they disowned him. It did solve his main issue, though, needless to say, the girl's family called off the marriage when they found out. I was off at the military academy when all this happened, but I managed to get a few days of leave to go visit him in the hospital, and then I arranged for him to stay with my mom and sister at our house in Baghdad when he was released."

"So, you did actually attend the Iraqi Military Academy?" Zaidan nodded. "The Task Force looked into that story and found records in the archives under *Zaidan Al-Sadiq*," Elora continued. "Of course, once we learned you were actually Malik Khalid, we figured you'd simply stolen someone else's identity."

"No, the name is simply a fabrication. Most everything your team found under Zaidan Al-Sadiq are my legitimate records. I just had my name changed from Malik Khalid to Zaidan Al-Sadiq on as many of them as possible."

"How in the Hell did you manage that?"

"It's Iraq," he said with a snort. "Throw some money at a few employees with access to records, and you can become Mickey Mouse if you want. I had Bashir and his guys ensure my name was changed in as many records as possible—in case *someone* went snooping around in my past," he added with a wink. "My college records, however, were forged. I don't have a Political Science degree from Baghdad University. I actually don't have a degree at all. I was a year shy of earning my Pharmaceutical Degree when the war started."

"Like your dad," Elora added somberly. "And like a

Political Science degree, a major that requires you to learn English."

"Bingo."

"I'm sorry about your family too. When I got back to Langley, I learned about what happened to them. I understand why you hate the U.S. so deeply. It still isn't a valid excuse to murder innocent people, but I acknowledge it's a reason. I am still curious to know how you launched NDU."

Zaidan took a moment to collect his thoughts. "After my mom and sister were killed, I joined the resistance in Mosul. I was pissed off and wanted to kill Americans, so they took me in. A lot of them were former special forces guys in Saddam's Republican Guard. They taught me how to build and plant IEDs and, I guess you could say, that was the beginning of my 'outlaw' career. But I soon realized that indiscriminately blowing up random American Humvees wasn't going to achieve anything or solve Iraq's issues. So, I decided to break off and go a different direction—that's when I started building NDU."

"And you just naturally progressed to international weapons trafficking?" Elora asked in a skeptical tone.

"Something like that," he replied with a smirk but didn't elaborate.

"Let's talk about what happened in UAE, the whole arms deal with General Yunis," Elora said, hoping to drill down a bit more. "If you knew who I was at that point, why would you give me all that info about the deal and your middle-man Sayed Kamil? You had to know I was going to feed it back to Langley and that they'd find a way to use it against you."

Zaidan shot Elora a cat-that-swallowed-the-canary grin.

"About that... Kamil wasn't our middleman."

Elora closed her eyes and tilted her head back as it dawned on her. "Motherfucker. He was your fucking competition. And we eliminated him for you!" Elora dropped her forehead into her hands in disbelief.

"If it's any consolation, I was incredibly impressed by how quickly you and *Nick* were able to get that accomplished."

Elora lifted her head back up and shot him an icy glare. "Fuck you."

"I love you," Zaidan replied, capping it with his signature sideways smile that he knew Elora was incapable of resisting. He pulled her out of her chair and into his lap. Placing his hands on either side of her face, he looked her directly in the eyes. "I will *never* lie to you again," he said in a serious tone. "I swear on everything I am, everything I have, and everything I ever will have, I will never deceive you, for as long as I live."

Elora had no reason to believe him, but she did.

Chapter 21

It had been three days since Elora had called Nick to tell him she was taking an impromptu trip to Dubai, in the middle of what was supposed to be her two-week vacation to the Smokey Mountains. Since then, he'd left her dozens of voicemails and even more text messages, but she hadn't responded to any of them. A million dark thoughts ran through his head until he couldn't take it anymore and decided to go to Dubai to track her down. Perhaps something bad had happened; she could be in trouble and needing his help.

After landing in UAE, Nick headed for the Dubai Police Force Headquarters in downtown. He walked in and asked to speak with Commander Omar Al-Abaidy. Nick had worked with Al-Abaidy a couple of years before, back when the NDU task force was following leads on Malik Khalid's weapons trafficking activities in UAE. They'd gotten along well during the two-week joint investigation and Al-Abaidy had proven to be capable and trustworthy. Nick hoped their previous relationship would play into his favor now.

"Ah, Mr. Nick!" The commander greeted Nick with a jovial smile as he entered the lobby.

"Great to see you again, Omar," Nick replied, shaking his hand.

"Come, let's speak in my office," Al-Abaidy said and gestured for Nick to follow him down the hall. He knew that whatever the reason Nick was there, it likely wasn't something they should be discussing in the very public lobby of the station. "So, my friend, what brings you to Dubai?" Al-Abaidy asked once he and Nick were behind closed doors.

"One of my agents is here in Dubai, and I haven't heard from her in over seventy-two hours," Nick explained.

Al-Abaidy wrinkled his head in concern. "Is she here in an *official* capacity?"

"No, no, she's here on holiday," Nick said casually to allay the chief's worry that there was possibly a larger issue afoot. "It's just that she's never gone this long without communicating—at least without contacting me," Nick said in a hinting tone. "This is more of a *personal* matter."

"Ah, I understand," Al-Abaidy replied, relaxing back in his chair.

"I'm just worried and want to make sure she's okay."

"Say no more," Al-Abaidy said with a wave of his hand. "Let's find her for you." He leaned forward in his chair and pulled his computer keyboard closer to him. "I assume she is staying in one of the hotels here in the city?"

"Yes, I believe so, and thank you," Nick said gratefully.

"It is my pleasure, my friend. I'll run a name search through the hotel registries. Our system is linked with most of the large hotels in Dubai. If she's not registered in any of those, we may have to resort to the old-fashioned method and visit the smaller hotels in person, but let's start here."

"Perfect. Her name is Elora Monro: M-O-N-R-O," he said, spelling her name out for the chief.

Al-Abaidy typed Elora's name into the computer and ran

the search. After a few seconds he shook his head in defeat. "I'm sorry, nothing,"

Nick thought for a few seconds. "Try Elora Reid: R-E-I-D," he suggested.

Al-Abaidy typed in the new name and ran the search. Within a few seconds, his face lit up.

"As you say in America—Bingo!" he said with a wriggle of his brows. "She's at the new Waldorf Astoria Hotel out on Palm Island, Room number three oh six," he said triumphantly and spun his computer monitor around for Nick to see. "She's got good taste," Al-Abaidy added with a wink.

"Thank you so much!" Nick said as he practically sprang out of his chair. "I really appreciate it."

"Happy I could help," Al-Abaidy replied modestly. "One of my men will give you a ride out to the hotel, and please let me know when you have confirmation that all is well with the young lady."

"Will do chief, thank you again for all your help."

"Go now, find your girl," Al-Abaidy said with a wink and shooed Nick out of his office.

The young Dubai police officer guided his cruiser into the valet area at the front of the Waldorf Astoria Hotel. "Would you like me to wait?" he asked as Nick opened the passenger door.

"No, that won't be necessary," Nick said, climbing out of

the car. "Thanks for the ride."

Entering the hotel, Nick took one of the main lobby elevators up to the third floor and found room 306. He lightly rapped on the door and waited a few seconds. Silence. He knocked again a little louder. "Elora?" he called out. "Elora are you in there?" Nothing. Figuring she'd simply stepped out, Nick went back downstairs. He took a strategic seat at the hotel bar that gave him a panoramic view of the massive lobby. He could see the front entrance, the main check-in desk, and clear over to the hallway leading to the bank of guest elevators. He ordered a beer from the bartender and waited.

Nick was halfway through his second Carlsberg beer when he saw her. Elora walked in the main door of the hotel, wearing a pair of dark sunglasses, a light green T-shirt half tucked into a pair of skinny light-blue jeans, and a pair of suede ankle boots. Her long auburn hair was in a high ponytail that swung as she walked. His heart swelled with joy and relief. She was healthy and smiling; everything was okay.

He took a final swig of his beer, slid off his barstool, and walked around the bar to settle his tab at the register. He no longer had a visual on Elora but noted she was heading in the direction of the elevators and figured she was going up to her room. Once his tab was settled, Nick exited the bar and made a beeline for the elevators, shoving his wallet into his back pocket.

As he neared the bank of elevators, he saw Elora standing ahead with her back to him. He wanted to run to her, but there was a light crowd of other guests moving toward the elevators ahead of him, blocking the way. Just a few yards from Elora, Nick saw one of the men who'd been walking ahead of him approach her from behind and intimately slip his arms around her waist. Nick halted in stunned shock and stood frozen as he watched Elora turn into the stranger's embrace with a wide smile.

The elevator doors opened behind Elora and she and the mystery man boarded. When the doors closed, Nick hustled up so he could watch the floor counter above the elevator. The counter slowly rose until it stopped at number seven and held steady. Nick jumped into the open elevator across the hall and punched the number seven button on the keypad.

Arriving on the seventh floor, Nick waited a few seconds before stepping out, listening to make sure the coast was clear. He heard faint voices coming from a distance, so he stepped out into the elevator alcove and peeked his head around the corner to see down the hall. Elora and the man were halfway down the hall, standing in front of one of the rooms. Nick had a clear view of the man's profile, but the dim lighting in the hall made it impossible to see his face clearly. Elora swiped a keycard and opened the room door. As the door opened, the bright afternoon light flooding in through the room's panoramic wall of windows poured out into the hallway, illuminating Elora and her companion.

Nick's heart dropped into his stomach. *Holy fucking shit.* It was like someone kicked him in the chest and everything slipped into slow motion. The mystery man was Zaidan Al-Sadiq, A.K.A. Malik Khalid, the supposedly dead militant leader, international criminal, and asshole who had murdered Brendan.

Elora and Zaidan disappeared into the hotel room while Nick worked on suppressing an overwhelming urge to vomit. His feet felt as if they were planted in cement but, once he heard the door close, he managed to wrest them free and headed down the hallway toward their room.

He casually strolled past the room, taking note of the number as he went by, 713. He was half tempted to stop, knock on the door and confront them. He desperately wanted to know what the fuck was going on; he wanted even more to smash Zaidan..Malik... whoever-the-fuck-he-was in the face with his fists. For the time being, though, he knew he had to swallow his anger and pain and come up with a plan. He decided to return to the bar downstairs to clear his head and think. He took a seat on the same barstool he'd vacated earlier and ordered a scotch on the rocks.

"Upping our game, I see," the bartender joked as he poured Nick's drink.

"Yeah, a beer isn't going to cut it right now," Nick replied with a stony glare. He downed his drink and glanced at his watch; it was almost 6:00 a.m. back in D.C. He pulled his agency-issued cell phone out of his backpack, activated the phone's encryption software, and called Derek.

"Derek, it's Nick," he said in a monotone voice after Derek answered. "I have visual confirmation on Malik Khalid—he's alive and currently in Dubai, staying at the Waldorf Astoria Hotel out on Palm Island."

"Come again?" Derek asked in confusion. "Wait, when did you go to Dubai?"

"I'll explain later," Nick said with a touch of agitation in his voice. "Right now, I need you to get the ball rolling on having Langley issue an official arrest and extradition request for Malik Khalid to the UAE authorities."

"I'll get right on it, but it's going to be at least a few hours before we hear anything back."

"Just get it done ASAP," Nick spat. "Call me when you have an update."

Nick downed another scotch, then went to the reservations desk and checked into a room for the night. He requested the seventh floor to keep tabs on Elora and Zaidan until he could approach them with some leverage.

On the way to his room, he passed their door and heard muffled voices from within; they were still inside. His room was a few doors down and, once inside, he propped his door open so he could hear if anyone in the general vicinity entered or exited their room. After settling in—which included plugging in his phone charger and plopping his backpack with a single change of clothes in a corner—Nick sat on the edge of the bed with his head in his hands. His mind raced to make sense of the situation, grasping for a scenario that gave Elora the benefit of the doubt. *Maybe she's using him for something? Or perhaps he is holding her against her will, and she's playing along to gain his trust? But how is he even still alive? Maybe she only thought he was dead and, after she made her getaway, they were able to revive him? Please, God, don't tell me she's willingly fucking this son of a bitch.* His nausea suddenly came rushing back and this time he wasn't able to keep it down. He sprang off the bed and burst into the bathroom, spewing vomit consisting mostly of scotch, beer, and bile across the marble tile floor and toilet. He cleaned himself up and gave the bathroom a quick wipe down before returning to his seat at the foot of his bed, a keen ear aimed in the direction of the open door. He just hoped they hadn't slipped out while he was in the bathroom.

Fifteen minutes later, Nick heard a door click shut down the hall in the direction of Elora's room. The sound was the proper distance away for it to be his targets on the move. He shot to his doorway and peeked around the doorframe. It was them. Elora had changed out of her jeans and was now wearing cut-off shorts, sandals, and a red tank top. Nick could also see the teal strings of a swimsuit top tied up around the back of her neck. He figured the pair was either headed to the hotel's pool area or out to the private beach.

When Elora and Zaidan disappeared into the elevator alcove, Nick slipped out of his room and headed the opposite direction down the hall to the stairwell. It was too risky to take the elevator—should they linger too long near the elevators in the lobby or decide to double-back for any reason, he could find himself face-to-face with them. He flew down the several flights of stairs and then cracked open the door leading from the stairwell into the lobby. No sign of them. Nick made his way into the main part of the lobby, scanning his surroundings in every direction. Satisfied they were no longer in the lobby, Nick looked out onto the pool deck from behind the relative concealment of the lobby's tinted glass windows. After a couple of passes, he caught sight of Elora's red tank top. They were making their way to the far-side of the pool area and appeared to be headed for the beach.

He went outside to the pool deck and followed at a safe distance as they continued out onto the sandy beach area. They finally settled at a cabana bed in a semi-private location, and Nick took a seat on a lounge chair a few yards behind, his position partially shielded by the flowing curtains that hung from the top of their cabana. Zaidan lay down on the bed while Elora stripped down to her bikini. A primal rage brewed in Nick's gut as he watched Zaidan watching Elora. He visibly cringed when Zaidan pulled her down on top of him and engaged her in a passionate kiss. Concluding their kiss, Elora rolled over and lay beside Zaidan with one leg draped across his body. The flames of Nick's fury were stoked every time Zaidan reached over to stroke Elora's face or hair as she dozed.

An hour later, the couple began to stir and rose from the cabana bed. Nick straightened up in his chair to resume his concentrated surveillance after the break in action. They walked down to the water and slowly waded into the warm waters of the Gulf. When they were chest-deep, Zaidan pulled Elora close to him, and she twined her arms around his neck. Nick fantasized of storming into the water and shoving Zaidan's head beneath the surface until he stopped flailing. Just the thought of Malik and what he'd put them through made Nick's stomach churn. Seeing him like this with Elora was a knife to the heart.

Retreating from the water, Zaidan and Elora walked directly toward Nick, so he lowered his head and pretended to fidget with his cell phone to obstruct his face from their view. They collected their belongings from their cabana bed and headed up to the hotel. Nick followed the pair back upstairs and watched them return to their room. His patience running thin, he glanced at his watch and noted it was nearly 10:00 a.m. in D.C. He hoped Derek had some news for him by now. He pulled out his cell phone and dialed Derek's number. "Where are we at, Derek?" Nick barked impatiently into the phone as soon as Derek answered. "Have Dubai police been notified yet of Malik's presence?"

"I'm trying, boss, but the suits upstairs aren't convinced this is something worth cashing in a favor from UAE over," Derek replied dejectedly into the phone. "The last update I got was that they are 'mulling it over.' Considering we just announced to the world several months ago that we positively confirmed Malik's death, they're a tad nervous about the optics of turning around and telling UAE that he isn't dead after all and is currently in their fucking backyard. Couple this with the fact that UAE never considered him a high value target to begin with, we're fighting a pretty steep uphill battle. They never officially recognized him as a terrorist, and the government considers most of his arms trafficking activities in the country legitimate business transactions. We know he had, well I guess has, powerful friends in the top tiers of the government over there, so I'm sure you can understand the hesitation here."

"Derek, he has Elora!" Nick screamed into the phone.

Derek was silent for several long seconds as he processed Nick's words. "What do you mean? He snatched her? Why didn't you mention this before? It gives us a lot more leverage for our request. Do you know if she's okay?" he asked anxiously.

"Derek, right now I just need you to get the assholes upstairs on board so they can get the ambassador to issue the arrest and extradition request," Nick replied with irritation. "I'll see what I can do on my end to speed things up." Nick hung up on Derek, immediately dialed the number for the Dubai Police Force Central Command, and asked to speak with Commander Al-Abaidy.

"Ah, Nick, did you find your girl?" Al-Abaidy asked in a cheery tone as he came on the line.

"Omar, we've got an issue," Nick replied in a sullen voice. Nick explained the situation but left Elora out of the story and simply implored the commander to dispatch a team to the hotel to arrest wanted terrorist Malik Khalid. When Al-Abaidy expressed his need for Nick to submit the request via the proper channels, Nick decided to engage his leverage. "Omar, he's got one of my agents."

"The agent you were looking for," Al-Abaidy replied knowingly, "your *girl*."

"Yes. Langley is working on the official order now. It'll be waiting for you by the time we return to central command with him, I promise. I'm fearful for her safety and don't feel comfortable waiting."

The commander went silent for several seconds as he considered Nick's request, then decided to grant his friend the favor. "Give us half an hour."

"Thank you, Omar. I owe you one."

Twenty-eight minutes later, Al-Abaidy and four of his officers, dressed in full swat gear, met up with Nick at the Waldorf Astoria. To avoid causing an unnecessary scene that may startle the hotel guests, as well as mitigate the risks of tipping off the target, the police commander and his team entered via the loading dock at the rear of the hotel. Al-Abaidy met with the hotel manager and briefed him on the situation. The manager expressed his desire to fully cooperate and provided the police commander with a key card for Zaidan and Elora's room. Before raiding the room with just five men, Al-Abaidy wanted to ensure Malik Khalid didn't have any security personnel staying with him at the hotel. The manager told Al-Abaidy the couple appeared to be alone at the hotel, and Nick confirmed he hadn't seen them interacting with anyone outside hotel staff since he'd started surveilling them earlier that afternoon. The team planned to conduct a 'no-knock-raid' on the room to maintain the element of surprise and prevent Malik from having a chance to hurt Elora or use her as a bargaining chip. Nick agreed this was the best course of action. He then asked Al-Abaidy to allow him to accompany the team during the raid. "It won't hurt to have an extra man, and I'm the one most capable of positively IDing the target," Nick contended.

Against his better judgment, Al-Abaidy acquiesced to Nick's request and handed him a SIG Sauer 9mm handgun. "Just in case," he said with a smile as Nick took the pistol, "but you must remain behind my men," he ordered.

"Of course," Nick replied with a dutiful nod.

The swat team, with Nick in tow, rode a service elevator up to the seventh floor, then made their way down the hallway to Zaidan and Elora's suite. Al-Abaidy swiped the keycard on the door, and the team rushed into the semi-dark suite.

"Dubai Police!" Al-Abaidy shouted as the team stormed into the room. "Hands up where we can see them!"

Elora and Zaidan were seated on the sofa and immediately did as they were instructed. Nick had hung back in the hallway just outside the suite door, but he had a direct line of sight into the room and could see both Elora and Zaidan. She was back in her jeans and T-shirt, and Zaidan was also wearing jeans but was shirtless. Elora remained calm but looked worried, while Zaidan appeared confused and agitated. *We've got you now, fucker*, Nick thought to himself.

"What the hell is going on?" Zaidan asked as he lifted his

hands into the air and stood up from the couch.

"Malik Khalid, A.K.A. Zaidan Al-Sadiq. You are under arrest by order of Dubai Police Force Commander Omar Al-Abaidy, pending extradition to U.S. custody."

Zaidan said nothing in response to the police commander's proclamation and turned to Elora, who was also standing with her hands raised. "Don't worry," he said calmly. "Stay here, I'll be back soon."

Elora was worried but hoped Zaidan would be able to talk his way out of whatever was going on. However, if he was being extradited to the U.S., someone on her side knew he was still alive, which meant they also knew she'd forged his DNA evidence. *Fuck.* Zaidan leaned in to kiss her on the cheek, but before his lips made contact, Nick dashed into the room and shoved his way through the line of UAE police. "Don't you fucking *touch* her," Nick demanded and leveled his pistol at Zaidan.

"Nick?" Elora blurted, both surprised and confused.

"Move away from him, Elora." Nick ordered.

"Nick, put the gun down. You don't understand."

Zaidan protectively stepped between Elora and Nick's raised weapon but kept his hands up. "I will go with you peacefully," Zaidan said, specifically addressing Al-Abaidy. "There is no need for anyone to point weapons," he added, casting a judgmental expression in Nick's direction.

"Nick, my friend," Al-Abaidy said in a gentle tone. "We have this under control." Nick lowered his gun but refused to back away.

Zaidan turned his attention to Elora and lowered his hands. "I'll be back before dawn," he promised and leaned in to kiss her goodbye. As Zaidan rotated his body toward Elora, Nick was presented with a clear view of the jagged six-inch scar etched across the lower left side of Zaidan's back. Seeing the scar instantly triggered images of Brendan's cold lifeless body in Nick's mind. He recalled the face of his friend, splattered with his own blood, robbed of life by the monster standing ten feet away from him, who was about to kiss the woman Nick was madly in love with. It was too much. Just after Zaidan and Elora's lips touched, two gunshots exploded in the room, causing a deafening reverberation in the confined space. Elora felt the air rush out of Zaidan's lungs and pass from his lips. The light in his eyes dimmed as his body collapsed forward into her. She tried to catch him, but his weight pushed her down onto the couch, and he landed half in her lap and half on the floor.

Elora let out a panicked scream. "Zaidan! Oh, my God." She maneuvered him off her lap and laid him flat on his back on the floor. Blood was seeping from a wound in Zaidan's upper right arm near the shoulder, but Elora quickly assessed that it was not life-threatening. The wound that terrified her was the hole in the side of his torso just below his armpit. From his labored breathing and the faint gurgling sound she heard each time Zaidan tried to inhale, she knew the bullet had likely punctured his lung.

"Somebody call an ambulance!" Elora screamed as she applied pressure to Zaidan's wounds. He was barely conscious, looking up at Elora. Al-Abaidy radioed for help as Nick stepped in and pulled Elora away from Zaidan. She howled in protest, but Nick easily overpowered her and dragged her to the far side of the room.

"Are you hurt?" Nick asked, yelling over Elora's wailing,

and attempted to check her for injuries. Her entire front was covered in blood, but Nick realized it was all Zaidan's.

"What the fuck did you do!" Elora screamed as she managed to break away from Nick's grasp. She tried to return to Zaidan, but Nick grabbed hold of her wrist and yanked her back again.

"I'm saving you!"

"Did I look like I needed saving!"

"Perhaps I'm saving you from yourself," Nick replied, lowering his voice a few levels.

Elora shot Nick a disgusted look as she tried again to pull away from him.

"What are you doing!" Nick screamed, refusing to let her break free. "Have you lost your fucking mind?"

"He's dying," Elora whimpered as she watched the UAE police officers try to keep Zaidan from bleeding out before the paramedics arrived. "Zaidan!" she called out as she dropped to her knees. "I'm right here—just hang on. Please, hang on."

"What the fuck, Elora? That asshole murdered Brendan!" Nick yelled, as he dropped down in front of her. "He killed my friend, *your* fiancé! Have you forgotten who he is?"

"Nick, you don't understand," Elora said through labored sobs.

"How is he even alive? Did you fucking *lie* for him?" Nick paused to search her eyes for clues, but he didn't have to look hard. The truth was written all over her face. "How could you do this? I trusted you! We *all* trusted you! Jesus Christ, I fucking *loved* you. You've ruined your life. Your career is over and likely mine too."

Elora heard Nick in her peripheral, but she was fully

focused on Zaidan, who was now surrounded by paramedics. She allowed herself a small prick of hope when one of the paramedics reported a pulse, weak but existent. "We need to decompress his chest," the lead paramedic announced as he reached into one of the medical bags and produced a large tube-like needle. He then leaned over Zaidan's body and pushed the needle into his chest. Within seconds the paramedic monitoring Zaidan's vital signs reported his numbers had stabilized a bit. "Okay, let's move him." The medical team lifted Zaidan onto a gurney, then rushed him out of the room and down the hallway to the service elevator. Elora sprang to her feet to follow but Nick grabbed her arm. "Nick, let me go!" Elora demanded through gritted teeth.

"Think, Elora, think," Nick pleaded. "You're not seeing clearly right now."

Once Zaidan was out of the room, Al-Abaidy turned his attention to Nick and Elora. "We're going to need you to come back to central command with us to provide a statement for our report," he said to Nick in a grim tone.

"I won't provide anything for any reports," Nick said coldly. "A U.S. intel officer was being held *against her will* by a registered terrorist group leader that *this* country was harboring. I took action to ensure her safety. If you need any more information, you can contact the U.S. Ambassador if you like."

The commander sighed and looked to Elora for help. "I'll be at the hospital if you need me," Elora said to Al-Abaidy. She then looked back at Nick with razors in her eyes, yanked her arm free from his grip, and bolted out of the room to catch up with Zaidan and the paramedics.

"Elora!" Nick hollered after her. "You're going to regret

this for the rest of your life!"

But Elora was sure this was one decision she wouldn't regret.

Chapter 22

Elora held Zaidan's hand while he lay unconscious in the hospital bed, jumbles of tubes and wires protruding from his body at every angle. The room was silent aside from the rhythmic beeping of the machines currently keeping him alive. It had been nine days since thoracic surgeons opened his chest to extract a bullet and repair one of his lungs. He'd been in a medically induced coma ever since. At first, the surgeons informed Elora he'd likely lose his right lung, but they were able to save it. They placed him in a coma to give the lung time to heal and regenerate. Elora hadn't spent more than fifteen minutes away from his bedside since he came out of surgery, and she'd spoken to no one outside of the hospital staff and a detective from the Dubai Police Force who'd come to the hospital to get her statement regarding the shooting.

Her cell phone had rung incessantly the first twenty-four hours after she'd arrived at the hospital with Zaidan. She'd finally shut it off and hadn't looked at it since. Knowing she could avoid it no longer, she now pulled it out of her backpack and powered it on. As anticipated, her voicemail inbox was full. She took a deep breath and began listening to the barrage of messages. According to the first few voicemails from Nick, he'd managed to cover for her the first week past her scheduled return date from vacation. HR at Langley had given her a one-week extension but said they'd need to speak with her personally after that if she hadn't returned by then. He left her several messages during that timeframe, begging her to come to her senses and fly home. When her extra week was up, his messages turned threatening. Since he'd been covering for her, his ass was now on the line too.

"Elora, it's me again," Nick's final voicemail began, "this is your last chance. I can't cover for you any longer. I'm *begging* you, come back. It's now Friday afternoon. If you're not here by Monday morning, I will have no choice but to report you to the agency as AWOL. You know I'll have to tell them everything. They will label you a defector, Elora. They will indict you for treason and God knows what other charges, likely aiding the enemy along with falsifying evidence and official statements, to name a few. You'll never be able to set foot in this country again—or most of the world for that matter—without standing trial. You will spend the rest of your life in prison…if you're lucky. If they push for full espionage charges, they can seek the death penalty. Are you *hearing* what I'm saying, Elora?"

Elora hung up; she couldn't bear to listen to anymore. She was about to flush everything she'd worked for since she was eighteen years old down the toilet. What scared her most was that she didn't even care. All that mattered to her, the only thing she wanted in the world, was to see Zaidan open his eyes again. She was more than happy to sacrifice it all if it meant getting him back. At that point, though, it was highly possible she could lose everything, including Zaidan. He was far from out of the woods and her career, her freedom, even her life, would all soon be on the line. She tried to shove everything to the back of her mind and focus on Zaidan. She knew she needed to stay positive and strong for him, and that was where she focused her energy. She returned to his side, slipped her hand back into his, and resumed her vigil.

A few hours later, Elora heard the hospital room door open behind her, but assuming it was a nurse coming in to check Zaidan's vitals again, she didn't so much as glance up. She flinched when someone placed a hand on her shoulder. Twisting her head around to see who it was, Elora half froze in surprise when she saw the hand on her shoulder belonged to Prince Al-Rafid.

"How is he doing?" the prince asked in a gentle tone as he surveyed Zaidan and the cluster of medical equipment surrounding his bed.

Elora shrugged. "He's holding on," she answered in little more than a whisper. "They are going to try and bring him out of the coma tomorrow. Once he's awake, they'll be able to better assess where he stands…*if* he wakes up," she added solemnly.

The prince gave Elora's shoulder a comforting squeeze. "He will, he's strong—and *extremely* stubborn," he said with an encouraging smile. "Plus, he has you to wake up to. Nobody would pass that up." A nurse brought a second chair into the room and placed it next to Elora. Thanking her, the prince took a seat. "I didn't even know he was in Dubai until this morning. I'd heard about the shooting at the hotel last week, but I had no idea it was Mal—" The Prince stopped short and attempted to correct his blunder. "Uhh, *Zaidan*, who'd been shot."

"It's okay, I know who he is."

Visibly relieved, the prince continued. "I assume he knows you're *not* a reporter for the *Washington Post*."

Elora gave a quick nod.

"We received an official extradition request from the U.S. Ambassador today."

Elora's heart rate jumped, and she shot the prince a panicked look.

"Don't worry," he said reassuringly, seeing the fear in her eyes. "I squelched it, at least for now. If we had to hand over everyone who passed through our country that the U.S. thought was a terrorist, we'd have to add on an entire express extradition terminal onto our airport," he added with a sly smirk, but the joke fell flat with Elora.

"Think you'll also be able to suppress the extradition request that will likely be coming for me soon?" she asked dejectedly.

The prince's smile faded. "That would be a lot more…difficult," he said, assuming a more serious tone. "Rejecting an extradition request for a random Iraqi businessman is one thing; providing safe harbor to a rogue American intel officer is...another. Once he is stable enough to make the trip, I suggest you both return to Iraq as soon as possible. Should it come to us receiving an extradition request for you, we will likely only be able to suppress it for a week or two," the prince warned. "Have you talked to any of Zaidan's people back in Iraq? Do they know the situation?"

Elora shook her head. "His cell phone has been ringing like crazy over the past couple of days, but I've been ignoring the calls. I even shut it off," she admitted. "I'm not sure what all he's told them, or who knows what about me, so I figured it was best to ignore them for now and just hope he wakes up soon."

"I'll call Hakim and fill him in on the situation," the prince offered. "We can trust him."

"I don't know," Elora said skeptically. "It was his asshole

nephew that fed Langley a ton of intel on Zaidan—well, Malik—in exchange for a ticket to the U.S."

"Don't worry, Hakim is not his nephew."

Elora was still doubtful but was too tired to argue.

The next morning, Zaidan's medical team came in to bring him out of the coma. The nurses halted the sedatives and gave him a mild stimulant to bring him back to consciousness. Then they waited. Elora leaned close to Zaidan's face. "Wake up, Zaidan," she whispered. "Open your eyes." The head physician in charge of monitoring Zaidan's condition sat on the other side of the bed from Elora. He too was leaning close to observe Zaidan. Whether or not he awoke in the next few minutes would set the tone for the remainder of his recovery—or lack thereof. "Come on, babe," Elora said more forcefully, lifting his hand to her lips and kissing his fingers. "Come back." She bounced her eyes back and forth a couple of times between Zaidan and the doctor, her forehead wrinkled with worry. A few seconds later, Elora picked up on a faint flutter of Zaidan's eyelids. The movement was so minuscule she wasn't sure if she'd really seen anything or simply imagined it, but the doctor had noticed it too.

"Here he comes," the doctor announced confidently.

Elora's heart rate jumped, and she tightened her grip on Zaidan's hand. Zaidan slowly opened his eyes and looked directly at her. Elora's face lit up as tears of joyous relief streamed down her cheeks. Zaidan tried to speak but only managed a grunt due to the intubation tube.

"Don't try to speak yet," the doctor said, leaning over Zaidan's face. "You have a breathing tube in your throat right now, but we'll take you down to the O.R. in a couple of minutes to remove it. Try to relax," the doctor added with a warm smile. "We're all glad to have you back."

Over the next two weeks, Zaidan's condition improved and, though he still needed a lot of rest, the doctors were confident he'd make a full recovery. Elora was beyond relieved as they were quickly approaching a point where they needed to leave UAE. A couple of days after Zaidan woke up, she'd received an anonymous email with a single page attachment—her official indictment:

United States of America v. Elora R. Monro
Offense Description
1. 18 USC 2381 – TREASON
2. 18 USC 2384 – SEDITIOUS CONSPIRACY
3. 18 USC 2383 – REBELLION OR INSURRECTION
4. 18 USC 1038 – FALSE OFFICIAL STATEMENTS
5. 18 USC 1519 – ALTERATION OR FALSIFICATION OF EVIDENCE

She was officially a traitor and, as she'd feared, an extradition request soon followed. The day after she learned of her indictment, the prince returned to the hospital to check in on his friend's recovery, and to also warn Elora that his government would only be able to sit on her extradition request for a maximum of two weeks. If Zaidan was unable to travel in the next few days, he advised her to go to Iraq on her own and wait for him to follow later. Elora's heart sank at the thought of leaving Zaidan behind, but the prince had already gone far above and beyond to protect them, and she didn't want to put him in any more of a precarious position.

Zaidan contacted Fareed and Hakim and filled them both in on the situation and prepared them to receive Elora. The plan was for her to stay at the New Dawn political headquarters in Baghdad until Zaidan was well enough to travel to Iraq. However, much to Elora's elation, Zaidan's doctors cleared him for travel the day before she was scheduled to leave. They reworked the plan and decided to depart together on a private jet to ensure the journey was as smooth and comfortable as possible for Zaidan. Fareed warned that civil unrest in Baghdad was currently approaching a boiling point, so he suggested the couple fly into Erbil and that Zaidan complete his convalescence at the NDU militia compound outside Tel Afar. Though the issue with ISIS just across the border in Syria was also growing more dangerous, everyone agreed it would still be the safest place for Elora and Zaidan to lay low for a few months, considering the bulk of the NDU militia was stationed in northwestern Iraq. Elora wasn't thrilled about returning to the militia training compound—where she'd killed Samir and held a gun on Zaidan—but she knew she was in no position to be picky about her accommodations.

Once Elora and Zaidan were settled in at the NDU militia training compound, Hakim arranged for a doctor from the nearby Al-Zahra hospital to stop in daily to examine Zaidan and monitor his recovery. Elora was less than thrilled when the doctor turned out to be Zaidan's old flame, Dr. Layla Shaheen. However, Elora and Layla's awkward relationship soon blossomed into a respected friendship. Layla proved to be an incredible support and confidante to Elora as she struggled to adjust to her new life as an international fugitive hiding out in the rural hills of Iraq.

Several weeks after arriving in Iraq, Zaidan was still confined to either his bed or, for short stints, the sofa in the main living area, and Elora soon found herself struggling with a severe case of cabin fever. Layla stopped in one morning to conduct her routine check-up on Zaidan and found Elora motionless on the couch, staring blankly out the window with her knees curled up beneath her chin. Elora didn't even notice Layla had entered the room until she felt the sofa move as Layla took a seat beside her. Elora jerked her head around and forced a smile when she saw it was Layla. "How is he today?" Elora asked, referring to Zaidan.

"I haven't gone up yet to examine him," Layla replied. "How are *you* doing today?" she asked, turning Elora's question back on her.

Elora shrugged. "I'm fine…I guess."

"No offense, but you make a shitty housewife," Layla joked as she glanced around the disheveled living room area.

"Yeah, I know," Elora admitted with a guilty sulk and jumped up to clear the dirty dishes from the coffee table. As she reached for a used coffee mug, Layla grabbed her wrist to stop her.

"Sit," Layla commanded gently. "You cannot remain holed up in this compound forever. You're not built for this kind of life."

"No shit," Elora snapped, "but it's not like I have much of a fucking choice right now, is it?" Layla remained silent and Elora sat back against the couch with a heavy sigh. "I'm sorry," Elora put a hand over her face. "I don't mean to take it out on you. You've been an amazing friend. I just feel so…useless," she explained in frustration. "All I've known since I was eighteen is a seventy-hour-a-week grind. Having absolutely no *purpose* in my life anymore is fucking torture."

"Just because you can no longer serve the purpose you used to serve doesn't mean you'll never find purpose again in your life. You have so much to offer this world, Elora. You just have to figure out how to leverage your gifts in a new way. Though I am certain those talents do not lie in the realm of domestic service," Layla added with a smirk, prompting Elora to nudge her with an elbow. "I have an idea," Layla continued. "Why don't you come down to the hospital tomorrow morning? We're always in need of an extra pair of hands to help out with random tasks. I think it'll be good for you, and you may actually enjoy it."

Elora rolled her eyes. "Layla, I have exactly *zero* medical experience."

Layla cocked her head in defiance. "It's not like I'm going to ask you to assist me with an open-heart surgery," she replied as she stood up. "I'll see you tomorrow at nine a.m.," she added and promptly left the room before Elora had a chance to object.

"ISIS is becoming a huge problem," Fareed said, addressing the group gathered around the large conference table in the NDU militia compound. Zaidan, Hakim, Bashir, Fareed, and two of NDU's top militia commanders had come together to discuss NDU's current state of affairs, and officially address the major threat looming just across the border in Syria—ISIS. "They are attacking our wheat imports and other shipments that we're moving along our smuggling routes between here and Syria. Plus, they are pushing closer to the border every day."

"I fucking hate those assholes," Hakim commented, shaking his head, but Zaidan remained silent. Elora sat at the far end of the table, not officially part of the meeting but happy to observe. Her primary motivation for attending the meeting was to keep an eye on Zaidan. He still wasn't back to one hundred percent, and this was his first major sit-down with the NDU leadership. She wanted to make sure he didn't overdo it.

"Double the security patrols along our smuggling routes from Syria and assign more armed men to escort the shipments," Zaidan instructed. "We can't afford a major stall in the flow of goods or our people don't eat, and the militia doesn't get paid. Also, I want more checkpoints around our entire perimeter. I don't want anyone coming in or out of our controlled area without us knowing their fucking shoe size," he said, directing his last order at the two militia commanders. "What's the situation in Baghdad?" he asked, shifting his attention now to Bashir.

"It's a powder keg about to explode any minute," Bashir answered. "Major protests haven't broken out yet, but they aren't far off. There's a ton of chatter across social media, especially among the university students. They've begun organizing demonstrations. It won't be long until crowds of students start marching on Baghdad."

"What about General Ansari?" Zaidan inquired of his chief nemesis. "What's he been up to? I'm sure he knows what's brewing amongst the students."

"He's aware, but he also knows he may soon be fighting a war on two fronts," Bashir said. "The Americans are asking for his help in bringing down ISIS, plus he knows things are about to go sour between the people and central government in Baghdad. He's preparing his men to contain and suppress protests in the capital, but his main focus right now is ISIS. No one knows how much of a fight the protesters will put up, if any at all, but ISIS has already proven a lethal threat. However, Ansari's dream of uniting all the significant Shiite militias has come to fruition, and rumor has it he plans to bring in more Iranian Revolutionary Guard soldiers from Tehran. He'll soon be commanding a force here in Iraq larger and more powerful than the Iraqi Army."

"Has Ansari approached Karim yet to bring him and his militia under the umbrella of his newly united militia corps?" Bashir shook his head. "What the fuck?" Zaidan shrieked. "We're spending a fortune paying those assholes to build a fucking Shiite militia, yet they're the only group that Ansari hasn't asked to join his little club?"

Bashir shrugged. "Karim said it's been difficult to grow his ranks over the last few months. He's only sitting at about sixteen hundred armed members at this point. We were hoping to be at two thousand plus by now. Ansari has shown little interest in groups commanding less than two thousand viable fighters."

"We don't have any more time or money to dump into them," Zaidan said, frustrated. "We need to come up with something else to grab Ansari's attention and it needs to be fast. We need Karim and his guys on the *inside* before any major government protests break out. If the civil uprisings are powerful enough, we can ride the wave of that momentum to push in from the outside, while Karim can be our Trojan Horse and attack from within. If we execute these two maneuvers in tandem, we just may be able to sweep the legs out from under the central government and push them out."

"It's a good plan, in theory," Bashir said, "but it all still hinges on figuring out how to get General Ansari to absorb Karim and his militia into his ranks. Anyone have any bright ideas?" Bashir asked, looking around the table. Everyone dodged his gaze and remained silent.

"Bomb NDU headquarters." The words flew out of her mouth before Elora even realized she'd spoken. All eyes in the room were instantly trained on Elora. Funnily enough, this was a situation Elora was quite comfortable with; she'd often dealt with being the only woman in the room throughout the course of her time in the military and then at Langley. She confidently stood up, cleared her throat, and proceeded to elaborate on her comment. "Have Karim organize a massive attack on NDU headquarters and bomb it to the fucking ground. I know sacrificing that building will be a lot cheaper than paying the salaries of four hundred more militiamen for God knows how long. Plus, it'll be a damn sight quicker. If an act like that still doesn't snag Ansari's attention, then he's likely already suspicious of Karim or privy to your scheme and knows you're the one bankrolling his militia, in which case you may as well cut your losses now." Elora scanned the faces in the room, searching for any kind of reaction to her suggestion, but no one revealed anything in their expression. She looked back to Zaidan and was relieved to see he had on his *contemplation* face.

"It's not an awful idea." Elora was floored that it was

Hakim who first spoke up in support of her plan.

"Thanks, Hakim, I guess 'not awful' is at least a start," she said facetiously.

"Honestly, I think it's a pretty good idea," Fareed chimed in.

"It *could* work," Bashir added.

Elora exhaled a sigh of relief; she was starting to worry they all thought she was insane. She looked back at Zaidan, who continued to remain silent, but she could see a faint smile playing across his lips. She knew there was no way he could speak up in support of her plan before the others reached the decision to support it on their own. Her idea was more than good; it was perfect, and Zaidan knew it the moment she'd said it.

Three days later, Zaidan and Bashir traveled to Baghdad to meet with Karim and set Elora's plan in motion. Zaidan wanted the staged attack on the NDU building in Baghdad to be carried out within the next couple of weeks, so they had to work fast. To ensure the strike looked as legitimate as possible, Zaidan employed a scheme he'd used in the past. He planned to exhume a dozen recently deceased bodies and plant them inside the Baghdad compound for emergency personnel to *recover* following the explosion. Sadly, ISIS was leaving plenty of fresh bodies to choose from in the wake of their rampage.

Zaidan and Elora both agreed it would be best for her to remain up north while he went to Baghdad. She wouldn't be able to do much to assist, and she was happy to stay behind and tend to her duties at the hospital. To her surprise, in the three months since she'd started assisting at the hospital, she had grown quite fond of her new role and was grateful Layla had strong-armed her into giving it a shot. Elora had started out by assisting with random administrative tasks and menial duties, but soon progressed into taking a more active role in the hospital's operational management. Layla was part of a talented team of doctors and medical staff, but Elora realized early-on that the organization in general lacked competent logistical oversight. She immediately recognized this as the area where she could make the most significant impact and threw herself head-first into improving the overall efficiency and operational inner workings of the hospital's daily activities.

Zaidan was thrilled Elora had found an outlet for her energy and skills, and he admired her passion—it was one of the things he loved most about her. Though he did sometimes worry that she was working too hard. She spent more time at the hospital than most of the staff, aside from Layla, and was utterly exhausted. It seemed she only returned home to shower and eat, and even when she was home, her mind was still preoccupied with whatever project she currently had going on at the hospital. She was wholly consumed by her new mission, achieving any semblance of a work-life balance was *not* one of her many talents. He was, however, smart enough to know to keep his concerns and opinions regarding this subject to himself.

A couple of days after Zaidan left for Baghdad, Elora was working late one night at the hospital when Fareed burst into her office. It was rare for Fareed to come to the hospital looking for her, so Elora was immediately concerned. "What's wrong?" she asked in a worried tone. "Is it Zaidan?"

Fareed shook his head and Elora relaxed. "We have a situation at one of the checkpoints," he told her. Elora shot him a puzzled look. Fareed and Hakim were jointly in charge while Zaidan was away, and Elora did not fall anywhere on the NDU chain of command. She was confused as to why he was coming to her about a *situation* at an NDU militia checkpoint. "The guards at one of our checkpoints detained two men driving a box truck loaded with weapons. They were trying to cross through NDU territory and were headed for the Syrian border." Elora continued to stare at him blankly. "We're fairly sure they're Americans but, of course, they're not talking to us. We brought in a translator but still no luck. I thought…perhaps maybe…they'd talk to you?" he asked, sounding unsure of his own words.

Elora let out an incredulous snort and squeezed her lips together to stifle a laugh. "No way," she said, shaking her head. "Even if they *are* American, I highly doubt they'll talk to me, anyway." Elora saw the flood of disappointment wash across Fareed's face, and she decided to humor him. "Fine," she said with a huff. "I'll ride out there with you, but don't get your hopes up." A small part of her did want to see if the captives were, in fact, Americans. The militia boys could be rough around the edges, and if they did have a couple of Americans, she felt obligated to ensure they were treated properly.

Twenty minutes later, Fareed and Elora pulled up to the checkpoint situated in the middle of a desolate stretch of highway. Fareed parked the SUV along the shoulder of the road, then he and Elora hopped out and walked in the nearly pitch-black darkness toward a couple of NDU pickup trucks parked ahead. A box truck as large as a mid-sized U-Haul was parked on the opposite side of the highway, facing in the direction of the Syrian border. In the center of the road was a makeshift roadblock with two NDU militiamen armed with AK-47s manning the checkpoint. Elora heard voices coming from in front of the pickup trucks as she and Fareed closed in. Before she stepped around the front of the lead pickup truck, she heard the two detainees talking to each other in English. No doubt, they were Americans.

"They're going to sell us to fucking ISIS!" one of the men lamented in a whispered screech.

"Shut up, Sergeant," the other reprimanded in a husky voice with a distinct midwestern drawl.

"We are so fucking dead!"

"You need to get ahold of your shit and keep it together. You're fucking losing it, man."

Elora decided to put the guys out of their misery. "No one's going to sell you to ISIS," she announced in English as she popped around the front of the pickup truck. The two Americans fell silent and stared at her in bewilderment. They were on their knees in the dirt in front of the NDU pickup truck with their hands zip tied behind their backs. Two more armed NDU militiamen were standing guard over them. Fareed handed Elora a flashlight, and she squatted down in front of the detainees, shining the light in their faces. She noticed they both had bloodied lips and swollen cheeks. Elora looked at Fareed disapprovingly. She tapped a finger to her own lip while simultaneously shooting him a *What the fuck?* expression.

Fareed shrugged. "What? We needed them to talk."

Elora cut her eyes at him but didn't say anything and shifted her attention back to the detainees. She tilted the flashlight to illuminate the rest of their bodies as she scanned them from head to toe. They were not wearing uniforms. Both were dressed in khaki cargo pants, T-shirts, and light jackets, though they were wearing military-style boots. One looked to be in his mid-twenties, while the other was about ten years older. Since she'd overheard one address the other as *Sergeant,* she was confident they were active duty military, likely special ops guys with JSOC.

"Who are you boys running weapons for?" Elora asked, but as she expected, both remained silent. Elora looked over at the box truck and stared at it in contemplation for a few seconds before shifting her eyes back to the Americans. "You boys are with JSOC, aren't you?" Even though neither spoke, Elora got her answer when the younger one darted his eyes to his buddy as soon as she mentioned JSOC. Elora switched back into Arabic. "What kind of weapons are in the truck?" she asked, addressing Fareed but continuing to look at the detainees.

"Rifles, ammo, RPGs, a few cases of mortars and launchers, some other random supplies," Fareed rattled off.

From the list, Elora had a good idea what the JSOC guys were up to. "Have the Kurds pushed into Syria yet to go after ISIS?" she asked Fareed as she stood back up.

"A few Peshmerga units moved in a couple of weeks ago," Fareed replied.

Elora nodded knowingly. "My hunch is these guys are trying to get that truck across the border to the Kurds," Elora said. "CIA likely bought all those weapons, and these boys are the delivery team. Washington knows the Kurds are their best ally in eliminating ISIS, but I know D.C. isn't ready to go public with the fact they're arming another stateless military in the Middle East, which the Kurds technically are." Elora bit her lip as she contemplated an idea. "It'll be good for NDU if the Kurds can keep the ISIS fight in Syria and out of our backyard, even better if they can eliminate ISIS entirely. I say we just let these guys continue on their way to deliver the shipment to the Peshmerga."

Fareed shook his head. "If we were able to nab these guys this easily, there's no way they'll make it through to the Kurds. ISIS is patrolling the area between here and the Peshmerga Units. If they get ahold of these weapons, that's no good for anyone, not to mention, a couple of bloody lips will be the least of these guys' problems."

"How far off the regular NDU smuggling routes are the Peshmerga troops camped right now?" Elora asked.

"We're not exactly sure where they are, but I don't think they are too far from where our routes pass through," Fareed answered.

"Can we send a couple of the NDU militia guys who know the area to escort these boys safely past ISIS and through to the Kurds?"

"In theory, but I'm not sure it's worth the risk."

"It's either this or escort them back to Baghdad, in which case JSOC will just send two more assholes in a truck to try and get through tomorrow."

Fareed grumbled under his breath, knowing Elora was right. "Okay, I'll have the guys take them across and through to the Kurds."

Elora squatted back down in front of the Americans. "All

right guys, here's what's going to happen. A few of our militia boys are going to escort you on across the border to where the Peshmerga units are currently camped. Bands of ISIS fighters are roaming the areas between here and there so go exactly where our guys tell you to go. Once you make your delivery, don't try to come back this way. Stay with the Kurds until you can hitch a ride with them back out through Kurdistan. Once you're out, tell JSOC *not* to attempt to run any more weapons up through here from Baghdad—it's too risky. You got it?" Elora waited for a response, but both maintained their silence. "Fine, don't speak," she said in a frustrated tone. "Just nod if you're on board with this plan?" The men exchanged glances, then both looked back at Elora and gave terse nods.

Chapter 23

Zaidan lifted the sheet and slipped into bed as gently as possible, trying not to wake Elora, but his efforts were futile, she had woken as soon as he'd entered the room. As he gingerly scooted close to her body, she rolled over and gave him a 'welcome back' kiss. "I'm sorry," he whispered, "I didn't mean to wake you."

"It's okay. I'm glad you're back. I missed you."

"I missed you too," he said, laying his head on her chest.

"What time is it?" she asked.

"Almost three a.m."

"Did everything go okay?"

"For the most part," he replied. "We'll know for sure the day after tomorrow."

Elora figured that was the day the *attack* would take place on the NDU compound in Baghdad. Since she hadn't spoken to Zaidan in several days, she hadn't had a chance to tell him about the incident at the checkpoint with the JSOC guys. She hoped her executive decision to have the NDU militiamen escort them across the border to the Kurdish position in Syria didn't rub Zaidan the wrong way and piss him off. She thought of telling him now but reconsidered and decided it could wait until morning. She rolled back over and started drifting back to sleep when Zaidan's voice pulled her back to consciousness.

"Elora, I need to ask you something," he said in a semi-serious tone.

Elora's eyes popped back open. *Oh, fuck.* Her brain raced to formulate a defense for her decision regarding the JSOC incident as Zaidan gently rolled her over to face him. Elora held her breath and her jaw tensed. "Will you marry me?" Zaidan finally said.

His words caught her off-guard, and she exhaled sharply in surprise. Rendered speechless, she struggled to voice a response. "Uhh…"

"You don't have to answer now," Zaidan added. "I didn't mean to spring it on you like that. Or feel free to say no. I would understand."

"No… I mean, *not* no… It's not that..." she stammered. "It's just, I thought you were going to ask me about…something else," she said, shaking her head. Zaidan wrinkled his forehead in confusion, and Elora decided now was as good a time as any to come clean. "The other night, the guards at one of the checkpoints detained a couple of Americans, and they asked me to…"

"The JSOC guys?" Zaidan asked, cutting her off.

"Yes," Elora replied, narrowing her eyes. "Fareed already told you, didn't he?"

"What? Were you worried I wouldn't approve of you ordering my men to escort a secret American arms shipment into Syria to meet up with the Kurds?" he asked with a smirk.

"It *may* have crossed my mind that you might not be totally on board, yes."

"You did the right thing," he said in an encouraging tone.

"No shit. *I know* it was the right thing. I just wasn't so sure *you'd* see it that way," she said, raising her eyebrows at him.

"Can we get back to my original question now?"

"Oh, right, sorry." Elora took a deep breath and sat up in the bed. Zaidan watched her, anxiously anticipating her response. "Zaidan, I love you…"

"I'm sensing there's a *but* coming."

"I'm not *Iraqi* wife material. I'm not sure I can be what you want."

"Elora, you're *exactly* what I want. You, as you are, right now. I wouldn't want you to change a thing. And you're right; you're not *Iraqi wife* material. If I wanted an Iraqi wife, I would be married to one of the thousands of available candidates within a five-mile radius of here."

"I can't cook—I fuck-up toast, for God's sake, I'm messy, I don't do housework… Honestly, I have zero domestic skills."

"We'll get a maid and a cook," Zaidan assured.

"And…" she started but stopped short.

"And what?"

"And I'm not sure I ever want children."

"Elora, I can live with all of these—actually, these are a part of why I love you. What I can't live without is you. You're the only person in this world I could ever, *will ever*, want to spend the rest of my life with. I love you, all of you, exactly as you are. Messy house, fucked-up toast and all! And as far as kids, I have plenty of immature juveniles to manage right now, anyway," he added jokingly. "But I don't want to pressure you. We can wait…or never get married at all. I know that's 'a thing' in the U.S. Though, here…well…"

"I get it, people will think I'm a whore," she said plainly.

"I honestly don't give a shit what people think. Fuck 'em. I'm happy to continue with things the way they are. As long as we're together, that's all I care about. I just don't want you to have to deal with the bullshit that will inevitably come along with us not being married. Or we could simply tell people we're married. It's not like I haven't faked documents before," he added with a sly wink.

Elora rolled her eyes. "Can I sleep on it?"

"Of course."

The next morning, Zaidan rolled over and reached for Elora, but her side of the bed was empty. Lying on her pillow was a small paper, folded in half. Zaidan stared apprehensively at the note until he finally picked it up and opened it. Inside she'd written a single word in Arabic:

Na'am—Yes

Zaidan closed his eyes in blissful relief. Then, for the first time in a long time, he allowed himself to feel genuine happiness.

Less than seventy-two hours later, Zaidan and Elora stood facing each other in front of the ancient altar at the small Syriac Catholic Church in Bakhdida. The church where Zaidan and his late sister were baptized and took their First Communion, where his parents were married, where generations of his ancestors dating back to the twelfth century had prayed and celebrated life's milestones. Aside from the priest (the same priest Nick and Derek had interviewed a year ago) and two Altar boys, only three others attended the ceremony. Fareed stood beside Zaidan, and Layla flanked Elora. Hakim had graciously offered to bring Elora down the aisle and then stood behind the couple as they exchanged their vows. Elora wore a simple white lace dress with matching veil, which Layla had helped her procure from a dress shop in Mosul. With their limited timeframe, they'd had to convince the reluctant elderly shop owner to sell them a pre-made dress hanging from an antique mannequin in the store window.

In the moment Elora and Zaidan exchanged their first kiss as husband and wife, two hundred fifty miles to the south, a massive explosion erupted in a quiet Baghdad neighborhood. When the smoke cleared, curious onlookers saw the main building at the center of the NDU political headquarters compound had been completely razed to the ground.

Karim and his Shiite militia publicly claimed responsibility for the attack on the NDU political headquarters compound in Baghdad. New Dawn officially condemned the attack as a "treacherous act of cowardice, costing the lives of two dozen New Dawn political staffers," and vowed revenge against the "Shia thugs" responsible, and their leader, Karim Sadat. As hoped, General Ansari took the bait. A few days after the attack, he dispatched one of his aides to extend an invitation to Karim for a meeting to discuss the future of Karim's militia in "serving a larger purpose for Iraq." Whether Ansari approached Karim because he was truly impressed by the group's bold attack against NDU, or if he simply didn't want a rogue militia running around blowing up random sites in Baghdad didn't particularly matter to Zaidan. All he cared about was Ansari effectively absorbing Karim's militia into his newly united force, which was now known as Iraq's Popular Mobilization Units (PMU). To ensure Karim didn't blow his cover or do anything to incite General Ansari's suspicion, Zaidan and Bashir went down to Baghdad and coached Karim to prep him for the meeting.

"Do not act too eager," Zaidan instructed Karim in the crowded café where the trio agreed to meet. "If and when he does offer to merge your militia with the PMU, he's going to expect you to ask him what's in it for you, so go ahead and play right into this. Most likely he'll have a canned response ready to go. It'll be utter bullshit, but since he thinks you're likely only a couple steps above an ignorant thug, he'll expect you to buy it, so just smile and nod."

"However, do tell him you have a couple of conditions," Bashir added. "Tell him you'll agree to defer to his general command, but you want to remain the de facto commander of your men, and you require your militia remain together as a unit. Tell him they trust you and will follow you, and likely won't agree to fight under anyone else in the PMU."

"If he breaks up the militia and scatters you all to various corners of the PMU, it does us no good, and this will all have been for nothing," Zaidan said. "Now, the tricky part."

Karim rolled his eyes. "We haven't gotten to the *tricky* part yet?"

"Shut up and pay attention," Bashir barked.

"He's going to ask you where you're getting your money," Zaidan continued. "No doubt he knows by now that you're not being supported by any factions within Tehran or the Iraqi central government. You tell him you're being funded by the Americans. If he digs deeper, keep it vague. Tell him you don't even know for sure what agency they're with, but you suspect they are CIA. You meet with two American men every couple of months who pay you in cash and give you random tasks for your group to carry out—they are the ones who asked you to bomb the NDU headquarters, and they paid you extra for it. Ansari knows the Americans don't tell him or the central government everything they're doing, so he'll consider this a plausible scenario and hopefully drop it from there."

"If everything goes well and he asks you to merge your forces with his PMU, simply agree and do whatever he tells you," Bashir instructed. "Most importantly, *do not* contact us. We can't risk you being linked to us once you're on the inside. The three of us meeting now is extremely risky but necessary; we had to make sure you're properly prepared, so you don't fuck this up. No offense."

Karim grunted in frustration but kept his mouth shut.

"We will get in touch with you once we're ready to execute the next stage of the plan," Zaidan jumped in. "If things don't work out during the meeting and Ansari doesn't ask you to merge with the PMU or he threatens you, go to the Nahrain Internet Café on the westside of town and tell whomever is behind the counter that you need to leave a message for Bashir. Then, I highly recommend you don't return home. Head north to the NDU militia training compound."

"What if he already knows and decides to put a bullet in my head at the meeting?" Karim asked in a sullen tone.

"If Ansari knew you were in our pocket, you'd already be dead," Zaidan said, though this was little consolation to Karim. "Look, you've done an incredible job bringing your militia this far. We all appreciate you and everything you've risked for the cause.

Now it's time to bring this over the finish-line and push that fat Iranian fuck and his trolls out of our country."

Derek was in his new office at the CIA outpost in Erbil, reading through a JSOC report that had caught his attention. He'd been promoted and reassigned from Langley to Erbil to serve as deputy chief of station a little over a month prior. The report he was reviewing was a mission summary detailing a covert arms shipment JSOC had transported from Baghdad to a Kurdish Peshmerga unit in a remote area of Syria just across the Iraqi border. The part that specifically piqued his interest was the debriefing statement from the two JSOC members who carried out the mission. They described being held captive for several hours by an unidentified militant group right before crossing the border. The men went on to report being "scared shitless" that they'd been nabbed by ISIS. However, one of the militants spoke broken English and emphatically informed the Americans they were not affiliated with the "ISIS pigs." The militants then tried questioning the JSOC members regarding their identity. When they refused to talk, their captors proceeded to assault them, resulting in minor injuries. Once they realized their captors likely weren't ISIS, the JSOC members still feared they may be sold to ISIS, until an *American woman* arrived and questioned them. She never identified herself by name, and the only physical description the JSOC members gave was that she was Caucasian and looked to be in her late twenties or early thirties. They reported that she had knowledge of U.S. covert operations, and she correctly identified them as JSOC, though they never confirmed this to her. She also deduced on her own that they were trying to run weapons across the border to the Kurds. Much to their surprised relief, the woman not only arranged for the militants to release them, but they also provided escort for the remainder of their journey into Syria and assisted the JSOC members in rendezvousing with the Peshmerga unit.

Once he finished reading the report, Derek immediately reached for his secure phone and called his contact at JSOC. He wanted to interview those two operators ASAP and requested they be flown up to Erbil so he could meet with them. Less than twenty-four hours later, Derek had the two JSOC guys in his office. As soon as the men sat down, Derek dove right in. "The American woman who assisted you on the road when you got caught up with those armed militants a couple of weeks ago—what did she look like?"

The two exchanged glances and shrugged. "It was pretty dark, sir," the senior JSOC member, U.S. Marine Corps Captain Kevin Whitmore, answered shaking his head. "Other than what we said in our statement, we don't know how else to describe her."

Derek flipped open his laptop and pulled it toward him. "I need you to step out into the hallway for a few moments please, Sergeant," he instructed the younger JSOC member, U.S. Army Sergeant Shawn Maddox. "And please close the door behind you."

The sergeant immediately obeyed and vacated the room. As soon as he closed the door, Derek pressed a few keys on his laptop and spun it around to face Captain Whitmore. The screen now displayed a large photo of Elora. "Is this the woman who helped you, Captain?" Derek asked.

Captain Whitmore studied the photo for only a few seconds before his face lit up in recognition. "Yes, sir, I'm fairly confident that's her."

"Thank you, Captain. Now please go tell Sergeant Maddox to come back in."

Derek showed the same photo to the sergeant; he was even more confident than Whitmore that the woman in the photo was the one who'd helped them.

"That's her!" the sergeant exclaimed. "Do you *know* her? Who is she?"

"Her name is Elora Monro," Derek replied. "She's former CIA."

"Wait, is she the chick they indicted a few months ago?" Captain Whitmore chimed in, "the defector, right?"

"Oh man, no way, she's the fucking traitor that's been all over the news?" Sergeant Maddox blurted.

"Watch your mouth, Sergeant," Derek barked scoldingly. "That *fucking traitor* saved your ass out there."

Derek pulled up a map of the northwest section of Iraq and asked the JSOC guys to identify where they had been detained. Just as he'd suspected, the area was in the heart of NDU territory. "Get some rest boys. We're going on a fieldtrip tonight," Derek announced. "You think you can find the same location where they stopped you?"

"I'm sure we could, but I doubt they'll still be there," Captain Whitmore replied skeptically. "It was just a makeshift roadblock they'd thrown up for the night to serve as a random checkpoint. Even if they set up another checkpoint in that area tonight, I'm sure it'll be in a different location."

"Well, we'll just drive up and down that entire corridor until we find them," Derek said.

"Or until they find us," Sergeant Maddox added nervously.

About an hour after sunset, Derek and the two JSOC guys loaded up in a white pickup truck and headed west out of Kurdish territory toward the Syrian border. Once they reached the stretch of highway in the area where the JSOC guys had their run-in with the NDU militia, Derek reduced his speed, and the men scanned the area as they trolled along toward the border. There was little moonlight, making it difficult to see more than a few feet beyond their vehicle in the blackness of the remote Iraqi landscape. Derek was only a few seconds from doubling back when Captain Whitmore picked up on faint shadows in the road ahead. Derek slowed the truck to a crawl, and the shadows slowly developed into figures of two pickup trucks and several people as they closed in. Suddenly, multiple bright spotlights flipped on and shined directly at the small pickup truck. Derek immediately slammed on the breaks, and all three men threw their hands up in surrender.

"God, I hope these are the guys we're looking for and not fucking ISIS," Captain Whitmore commented.

"ISIS hasn't breached the border yet," Derek answered. "I'm pretty sure these are NDU militia."

They heard several AK-47 shots ring out from behind the spotlights, and the men jumped.

"Just warning shots," Derek said reassuringly. He reached into his pocket and pulled out a printed copy of Elora's photo. "Everybody out, *slowly*," he instructed.

Before they were able to get their doors open, several

masked militants armed with AK-47s rushed the vehicle, shouting in Arabic as they shoved their rifles in the Americans' faces.

"Aww fuck," the sergeant lamented. "Here we go again."

The militants lined the trio up on the side of the road and ordered them in Arabic to get down on their knees, to which Derek and the other two complied. Derek calmly explained in Arabic that they were searching for the American woman, *Elora*. He flapped the photo in his hand, and the head militant stomped over to his position. The masked gunmen snatched the photo from Derek's hand and shined his flashlight on it.

"Why are you looking for her?" the militant demanded in Arabic. "Who are you!"

"A couple of weeks ago, she and your men helped us," Derek said. "I need to speak with her. Please, if you can contact her, tell her *Derek* needs to speak with her. She will know who I am."

The militant considered Derek's request for a few seconds, then barked an order to one of his men. "Call Fareed."

One of the masked men took off in a jog toward the militia vehicles.

"Thank you," Derek said, addressing the leader.

"Shut the fuck up," the militia commander spat back.

Back at the NDU compound, Fareed, Hakim, Elora, and Zaidan were all having dinner together when Fareed's satellite phone rang. "Somebody probably got freaked out by their own damn shadow again," he grumbled to the group as he stepped away from the table to take the call. A couple minutes later, Fareed returned to the table with a sober expression. "They detained three Americans at one of the checkpoints," he informed Zaidan. "Two of them are the same guys they caught a couple of weeks ago that we escorted through to meet up with the Kurds."

"Fuck," Elora said, closing her eyes. "I fucking *told* them not to try and bring weapons through here again," she said through clenched teeth.

"They aren't trying to get through with anything," Fareed explained. "They're in an empty pickup truck this time. It seems they specifically came looking for you," he said, eyeballing Elora. "They have a picture of you and asked for you by name."

The color drained from Elora's face. "You mentioned there were three this time. Who is the third guy that's with them?"

"He says his name is Derek…and he wants to talk to you," Fareed said, holding the sat-phone up and giving it a small shake.

Elora looked wide-eyed at Zaidan, who shrugged. She turned back to Fareed, stared at the phone for a few seconds, then slowly took it from him.

"Put him on," Elora said into the phone as she put it up to her ear.

A few seconds later, Derek came on the line. "Elora?"

"Derek," she replied in a stone-cold tone.

"It's good to hear your voice," he said through a genuine smile. "I wanted to personally thank you for what you did for the JSOC guys the other—"

Elora cut him off. "Did you seriously come all the way out here to get an AK shoved in your face just so you could have a chance to call me and say *thanks*?"

"No. I do have something important to discuss with you, but we can't talk about it over the phone. Is there any way we can meet somewhere?"

"Not going to happen, Derek," she said, suppressing a snort. "The three of you need to get back in your truck and return to Baghdad. I warned those JSOC clowns you're with not to come through here anymore."

"Elora, please, I honestly think you'll be interested in what I have to say," Derek blurted. "Both you *and* Zaidan," he added. "You and I both know ISIS is breathing down your necks right now. We can all help each other, Elora. Please, all I'm asking for is five minutes."

Elora went silent for several long seconds. "Fine," she finally said to Derek, then handed the phone back to Fareed. "Can you take me out there again?" she asked.

"I *can*," he replied hesitantly, looking at Zaidan.

"Wait," Zaidan jumped in, "something doesn't feel right, Elora. This could be a ploy of some sort, to draw you out."

"Are we sure these three are alone?" Elora asked Fareed.

Fareed nodded. "I'm fairly certain. Plus, our guys currently have them on their knees at gunpoint on the side of the highway. Unless this Derek guy is David fucking Copperfield, I doubt it's a trap."

"There's no way I'm letting you go out there alone. I'm coming with you," Zaidan said to Elora. "And I want a truck full of armed men to follow us," he added to Fareed.

Half an hour later, Elora and the entourage arrived at the checkpoint where Derek and the others were being held. Before she exited the vehicle, she reached down and slid her new wedding ring off her finger. She was about to slip it into her pocket when she stopped and reconsidered. *I'm not ashamed,* she chided herself. So what if the CIA finds out she'd married Zaidan; she was already wanted for treason. How much worse could it get? She pushed the ring back onto her finger and climbed out of the SUV.

With Zaidan and Fareed closely flanking her on either side, Elora walked up and stood in front of Derek. He was still kneeling on the shoulder of the highway with the two JSOC guys. Derek smiled when he saw Elora, but her expression remained blank. "Your five minutes starts now," she said firmly.

"We still have a lot of weapons we need to move up from Baghdad and funnel across the border to the Kurds," Derek said, getting right to the point. "Moving them along NDU's established smuggling routes is the most efficient and secure method. I'm authorized to offer NDU substantial compensation if they will help us transfer the weapons through to the Peshmerga."

"We aren't fucking UPS, Derek," Elora quipped.

"Plus, we don't need your money," Zaidan chimed in, "and we sure as hell don't want it."

"Look, without these weapons and supplies, the Peshmerga don't stand a chance in stopping ISIS," Derek warned. "So, unless you and your militia want to deal with ISIS yourselves—who will be in your backyard within the next month—I recommend you reconsider this deal."

"Get back in your truck and go back to Baghdad, or wherever the hell you came from," Zaidan demanded. "Let's go," he said to Elora and Fareed.

"Elora wait," Derek called out. "Ask me for it," he said cryptically.

Elora stopped and looked back at him. "Ask you for what?"

"You know I can't offer it to you, but you can ask for it. You can make it a *required condition* of this deal."

She suddenly realized what *it* was—withdrawal of her indictment. Zaidan caught on too.

"The indictment *fully* withdrawn?" Zaidan interjected, stepping back toward Derek with renewed interest. "All five charges and her record completely expunged?"

"I can't promise anything, but it's possible," Derek replied.

"If you assholes want us to do this for you, those are our terms," Zaidan said decisively. "Elora better not have so much as a fucking parking ticket on her record, and she will be allowed to travel freely in and out of the U.S. whenever she pleases."

"I'll present it to Langley," Derek said. "I think they'll go for it."

"We want everything in writing and submitted to our legal staff in Baghdad to review, then notarized and witnessed at the U.S. Embassy," Zaidan ordered. "We don't move a single bullet until her record is spotless."

Derek nodded. His eyes drifted down to Elora's hand, where he spotted the simple gold band around her left ring finger. "Congratulations," he said sincerely.

Elora swallowed hard and slipped her hands into her pockets.

"A couple of our guys will escort you back to Baghdad," Zaidan said.

"Actually, we came from Erbil. I'm deputy chief of station

there now," Derek added, looking at Elora.

"Congratulations. Is Nick in Erbil too?" she asked sharply.

"No, early retirement," Derek said, but his tone said much more. "Last I heard he was living off the grid in a cabin somewhere in Wyoming."

"If you happen to run into him again, can you tell him—" But she stopped short. She was going to ask Derek to tell Nick that she was sorry, but she reconsidered. She wasn't sorry.

"Yes?" Derek prodded.

"Never mind," she said, shaking her head. "Take care of yourself Derek." Elora shot him a thin-lipped smile, then turned and disappeared with Zaidan into the black shadows of the Iraqi night.

Epilogue

Langley held up their end of the deal and facilitated the eradication of Elora's indictment in exchange for New Dawn's assistance. NDU spent several months transporting arms and supply shipments along their smuggling routes from Baghdad to the Kurds and other allies fighting ISIS just across the Syrian border. Unfortunately, even with New Dawn's help running hundreds of supply shipments, the Kurdish and Iraqi forces were unable to thwart ISIS, and the extremists pushed through into Iraq. The NDU militia managed to hold their perimeter and, for the most part, deflected ISIS around NDU territory, but the truth was they got lucky. ISIS simply wasn't interested in the NDU area and had their sights set on a bigger prize—Mosul. Had ISIS ever launched a full-frontal assault, the NDU militia would have likely been decimated.

As a precaution, Zaidan sent (or rather, forced) Elora to go south to the relative safety of Baghdad while ISIS ravaged the north. At first, Elora adamantly refused to leave Zaidan, Layla, and the others behind, but Zaidan was able to reason with her, explaining there was no way he'd be able to focus on leading NDU against ISIS if he was constantly worried about her safety. In the end, Elora acquiesced as she knew her staying would unnecessarily jeopardize the safety of others. Her decision was soon solidified by another factor—the week before she left for Baghdad, she discovered she was pregnant. Elora watched from Baghdad in helpless horror as ISIS decimated Yazidi and Christian villages across northern Iraq, including Zaidan's family village of Bakhdida, where she learned ISIS burned the Syriac Catholic Church to the ground almost exactly one year to the day that she and Zaidan were married. Just as the ISIS crisis reached a crescendo, Elora reached the final weeks in her pregnancy. Now that she was authorized to travel to and from the U.S. as she pleased, Zaidan demanded she return to give birth to their son in the safety of a U.S. hospital.

Over the next year, NDU did what they could to provide shelter to fleeing refugees who came their direction. Layla and the staff at Al-Zahra Hospital spent the entire year living in the hospital and working round-the-clock to provide medical care to thousands of victims injured during the ISIS invasion and subsequent occupation. For a brief moment in time, Zaidan and General Ali Ansari found themselves on the same side of the battlefield. NDU fought as part of a massive coalition of factions who put their differences aside temporarily to unite in the face of a larger evil—the *largest* evil. Such is the nature of politics in Iraq, though; one day you were fighting a common enemy on the same side of the battlefield, the next you were on opposite sides squaring off against each other.

Several months after the defeat of ISIS, civil unrest in Baghdad once again reached a boiling point as the economy and conditions throughout Iraq deteriorated even further. The central government now blamed the poor conditions and lack of resources on ISIS, trying to convince the people the country's coffers were drained by the war with the Islamic State. To the credit of the Iraqi public, they saw right through the government's bullshit lies and decided enough was enough. Sparked by social media campaigns organized by Baghdad's university students, small demonstrations erupted across the city. They soon evolved into full-scale mass anti-government protests that pushed closer and closer toward the heart of Iraq's central government in Baghdad's fortified Green Zone.

The Iraqi central government vested General Ansari with full discretion and power to contain and control the protests in Baghdad and safeguard the Green Zone in any manner he saw fit. Much to Zaidan and Bashir's delight, Ansari assigned Karim's militia unit to secure and defend the northeast section of the Green Zone's perimeter. While Zaidan and the NDU leadership brainstormed the best way to leverage Karim's current position to launch a sneak attack on General Ansari and the central government itself, they caught a lucky break. Some of Ansari's PMU factions committed a string of overly brazen attacks directly targeting U.S. troop positions and bases in Iraq. Whether or not these attacks were personally ordered or even sanctioned by Ansari is still unclear, but as the official commander of the PMU, the U.S. held Ansari responsible and shoved a hellfire missile up his ass. With the press of a button, NDU's primary nemesis and a dozen of his right-hand aides were snuffed out in a ball of flames and twisted metal when two missiles launched from a U.S. Air Force drone struck their vehicle convoy in the middle of a Baghdad street.

The momentum from the ongoing protests combined with the U.S. killing of General Ansari created a perfect opportunity for NDU to make their move. Leaving only a small contingent up north to maintain security of NDU territory, Zaidan moved the bulk of the NDU militia south to Baghdad where they mobilized in front of the northwest gate of the Green Zone. What unsuspecting bystanders feared would soon erupt into a bloody clash between the NDU militia and Karim Sadat's Shiite unit of the PMU poised to defend that section of the Green Zone's perimeter, fizzled into an amicable meeting of the two sides, who met up, shook hands, and joined forces as stunned onlookers gawked in bewilderment. Karim's unit essentially greeted the NDU forces with open arms and graciously welcomed them inside the Green Zone.

With Zaidan and Fareed at the center of the mass, the newly united forces marched toward the Iraqi Parliament building. They discovered the Prime Minister cowering beneath his desk as NDU forces seized control of the most vital offices and agencies of Iraq's central government. Fareed personally dragged the Prime Minister out from under his desk and into the hallway outside his office, where Zaidan proceeded to forcefully shove the barrel of one of his signature Browning 9mm pistols beneath the Prime Minister's chin.

"You have exactly three seconds to resign," Zaidan declared calmly.

It was two seconds more than the Prime Minister needed. He relinquished his office and proceeded to piss himself. As Zaidan and Fareed emerged from the Parliament building dragging the Prime Minister out to face the angry protestors now gathered on the steps, the crowd chanted in unison, *"A new dawn has come! A new dawn has come!"*

Zaidan formed a small interim governing council to temporarily lead the country until Iraq's official system of government and the Constitution could be reworked to better serve the people. Citing "too many cooks in the kitchen," the Iraqi Parliament was dissolved and the Parliamentary system itself was abandoned in favor of a Presidential system more reflective of the U.S. form of government, complete with a separation of powers between the legislative and executive branches. Over the weeks it took to reorganize the central government and rewrite the Constitution, the country, as well as the world, were ablaze with gossip and rumors over who would ultimately assume control of Iraq.

Though Zaidan tried to keep a low profile (he had no ambitions of becoming Iraq's next president) the people soon learned the identity of the green-eyed architect and mastermind behind the New Dawn movement who'd "made the Prime Minister piss himself on the steps of Parliament." Greatly embellished tales of Zaidan's prowess and courage circulated throughout Baghdad and across Iraq, resulting in massive public rallies calling for Zaidan to assume the presidency. Zaidan laughed it off at first, sure that as soon as word got out that he was a Christian married to an American ex-CIA officer, public sentiment would swiftly change direction. However, he underestimated just how pissed off and desperate for change the Iraqi people truly were. Even as these details about his personal life emerged, though support for him waned slightly, popular opinion remained predominantly steadfast in its desire for Zaidan Al-Sadiq to be Iraq's president.

The U.S., of course, was elated. Not only were they heartened by NDU's relatively balanced and secularist interim rule of Iraq, they fully supported the Iraqi people's desire for Zaidan to become president; his wife and son, after all, were both American citizens, and the CIA had proved how easily they could use Elora to control and manipulate her husband. Yes, they had cleared her indictment and criminal record, but it is well known that what the CIA giveth, the CIA can also taketh away. Elora was rock-solid leverage for the Americans. As far as Washington was concerned, they couldn't have picked a better first lady for Iraq.

Though the people would have been happy for Zaidan to declare himself president and be done with it, Zaidan refused and required the country to host a free election. To ensure a legitimate and transparent election process, NDU facilitated the elections to be organized, executed, and monitored by an impartial third-party election oversight committee based in Switzerland. The elections resulted in Zaidan capturing sixty-three percent of the popular vote to edge out two other candidates who essentially split the difference between them.

As soon as he assumed office, Zaidan immediately set out to put Iraq's oil wealth to work for the people. Just as he'd facilitated years prior in the NDU territory of northern Iraq, he initially focused attention on infrastructure projects as well as providing the people with basic utilities and social services. He also focused on building a robust military and made a deal with all foreign powers, including the U.S., for a full withdrawal of foreign troops from Iraq within five years. Washington initially balked at this, but Zaidan put his foot down and the Americans eventually agreed, albeit reluctantly.

Five years into Zaidan's presidency, he and Elora traveled to the U.S. with their son. They arrived in D.C. for an official state visit to celebrate half a decade of relative peace and prosperity in Iraq. They also attended a media ceremony to conduct a symbolic signing of the agreement calling for the American troop withdrawal from Iraq. Zaidan and Elora arranged for two days of free time in D.C. following the completion of their official engagements. Elora wanted a chance to take both her husband and their eight-year-old son on a tour of the city—her former hometown.

Though Arlington National Cemetery was on their list of sites to explore, Elora did not plan to visit Brendan. She was not worried about making Zaidan uncomfortable; she was unsure how she herself would feel about it once physically there. However, as soon as she stepped into Arlington, an incredible calm washed over her, and she was immediately drawn to Brendan. Zaidan and their son followed as she weaved her way through the rows of headstones until she came to a halt in front of a single granite marker. Elora had not mentioned where she was leading them, but as soon as she stopped, Zaidan knew. Elora knelt in front of Brendan's grave while Zaidan remained back with their son to give her a few moments of privacy. After a couple of minutes, Elora turned to Zaidan and motioned for them to come join her.

"I'd like you to meet someone," Elora said to her son as she took his hand and pulled him gently to her side. "This is Brendan. He was a very brave soldier."

"Brendan?" her son asked, looking up at her. "Like me?"

Elora smiled. "Yes."

"Brendan, I'd like you to meet my son," Elora said,

addressing Brendan's headstone. "*Zain Brendan Al-Sadiq*."

"Was he a hero?" Zain asked his mother.

"Yes, he was," Zaidan answered, taking Elora by surprise as he stepped up behind her and placed a comforting hand on her shoulder. "He was an incredibly brave hero," Zaidan added.

Elora returned to her feet and turned to walk away with Zain, but Zaidan remained behind, staring at Brendan's grave. Elora paused to look back, but Zaidan still did not budge, so she decided to proceed without him.

Once Elora and Zain had gone, Zaidan slowly reached into his pocket and pulled out a small tattered piece of cloth. It was the embroidered reverse American Flag patch that Zaidan had ripped off the arm of Brendan's uniform during the raid. "This belongs to you," Zaidan whispered as he reached down and placed the patch on top of the granite headstone. "Rest in peace, soldier. May you and God both forgive me."

The End